PATHS OF FIRE

Christopher Mitchell is the author of the epic fantasy series The Magelands. He studied in Edinburgh before living for several years in the Middle East and Greece, where he taught English. He returned to study classics and Greek tragedy and lives in Fife, Scotland with his wife and their four children.

By Christopher Mitchell

The Magelands Origins

Retreat of the Kell
The Trials of Daphne Holdfast
From the Ashes

The Magelands Epic

The Queen's Executioner
The Severed City
Needs of the Empire
Sacrifice
Fragile Empire
Storm Mage
Soulwitch Rises
Renegade Gods

The Magelands Eternal Siege

The Mortal Blade
The Dragon's Blade
The Prince's Blade
Falls of Iron
Paths of Fire
Gates of Ruin

Brigdomin Books Ltd
First Edition, March 2021
ISBN 978-1-912879-53-3

For James

ACKNOWLEDGEMENTS

I would like to thank the following for all their support during the writing of the Magelands Eternal Siege - my wife, Lisa Mitchell, who read every chapter as soon as it was drafted and kept me going in the right direction; my parents for their unstinting support; Vicky Williams for reading the books in their early stages; James Aitken for his encouragement; and Grant and Gordon of the Film Club for their support.

Thanks also to my Advance Reader team, for all your help during the last few weeks before publication.

DRAMATIS PERSONAE

Falls of Iron

    Corthie Holdfast, Champion

    Kelsey Holdfast, Blocker of Powers

    Aila, Demigod & Shape-shifter

    Naxor, Demigod

    Belinda, The Third Ascendant

    Irno, Count of the Falls of Iron

    Vana, Sister of Irno and Aila; cousin of Naxor

    Silva, Former Courtier of Belinda

    Van Logos, Captured Banner Captain

    Sohul, Captured Banner Lieutenant

    Gadena, Trainer of Mercenaries

Alea Tanton

    Felice, God; Governor of Lostwell

    Latude, God; Former Governor of Lostwell

Catacombs

    Blackrose, Dragon

    Maddie Jackdaw, Dragon Rider

    Sanguino, Former Bloodflies Dragon

    Millen, Torduan Fugitive

    Deathfang, Leader of the Catacombs

    Burntskull, Deathfang's Advisor

    Darksky, Deathfang's Mate

    Frostback, Deathfang's Daughter

    Halfclaw, Green Dragon

    Grimsleep, Sanguino's Father

Implacatus
> **Leksandr,** The Sixth Ascendant
> **Arete,** The Seventh Ascendant

Fordians
> **Gurbrath,** Leader of Fordians in Ruined City
> **Gellith,** Demigod; Leader of Fordians in Yoneath

Others
> **Sable Holdfast,** Fugitive Dream Mage
> **Bartov,** Demigod in Capston
> **Amalia**, Former God-Queen of the City
> **Gloag,** Count of the Glebe

CHAPTER 1
BELINDA

Plateau City, Imperial Plateau – 25th Day, First Third Autumn 524

The three kittens were playing on the floor of the attic, stalking each other, then springing and wrestling, their backs arched, and their sharp but tiny claws pulling up threads from the soft rug. Belinda sat cross-legged, watching them, her eyes shining. She reached out with a hand, and one of the kittens attacked, rolling onto its back with its paws in the air, the front ones clinging on to Belinda's fingers, while the rear legs kicked.

'Ow,' she cried, withdrawing her hand as thin fresh lines of red appeared on her skin.

Corthie laughed. 'I told you,' he said; 'they'll claw you if you do that.'

Belinda gazed at the blood on her wounded hand for a moment, then turned back to watching the kittens. 'They're the best present in the whole world, Corthie,' she said, her eyes welling from joy. 'I love them.'

'I thought you needed someone to play with,' he said, beaming from the edge of the rug. 'You know, for when you're all alone up here.'

She smiled at the twelve-year-old boy, then blushed. 'I made you something.'

'Aye?' said the boy.

Belinda reached back across the floor to where an untidy pile of books and jotters sat. She picked up a notebook and opened it. Her cheeks flushed again, then she clutched a piece of paper that had been tucked into the pages of the notebook. It was the colour of lavender, and had been cut into the shape of a heart. She stared at it, nervous about showing him, then held it out.

Corthie took it, his smile broadening. He was always smiling, she thought.

'You're getting good with the scissors,' he said.

He read the words she had written, the script clumsy and childlike.

To Corthie

I love you

From Belinda

'Thank you,' he said; 'your writing's great! I'm going to put this up onto my bedroom wall with the other cards you've made for me.'

'I'm going to make cards for the kittens,' she said, 'to welcome them into the house. Do you think they'll like them?'

'Of course they will,' he said.

'But what if they don't?'

'They will.'

The door to the attic room opened and Karalyn walked through, her arm guiding blind old Laodoc in. She led him to a chair and helped him sit, then glanced at the three kittens, a slight air of bemusement in her eyes.

'Don't let them poop on the rug,' she said, 'and look at what they've done to your hand already, Belinda. Corthie, I wish you'd spoken to me about this first.'

Corthie grinned as he picked up one of the kittens and placed it onto his lap. 'If I'd done that, sis, you would have said no.'

'Aye, and with good reason.'

Belinda gazed up at Karalyn, her dark eyes sad. 'You don't like them?'

Karalyn frowned, but said nothing.

'I think it's a wonderful idea,' said Laodoc from his chair, his hands resting on his walking stick. 'They'll keep you company, Belinda, for when we can't be up here with you, and pets are excellent for instilling a sense of responsibility in someone. You did a commendable thing, Corthie, my boy.'

Belinda smiled, though she didn't understand some of the words her teacher had used.

Karalyn sat and picked up a book on spelling. 'Fine. You win; the cats can stay, but I'm not cleaning up any poop, and I don't want them going downstairs.' She opened the book. 'Shall we begin today's lesson?'

'But I want to play with the kittens,' said Belinda. 'I love them. Can we play with them instead?'

Karalyn rolled her eyes.

'Please?'

Belinda watched as Karalyn's expression began to soften. She sighed and closed the book.

'Alright,' she said. 'Ten minutes.'

'Thanks, sis!' said Corthie. He passed the kitten on his lap to Belinda, who took it and held it up to her face.

It was so beautiful, she thought; a little bundle of fur, bright eyes and claws, and it was hers. She hugged it to her chest, but it squealed and wriggled in her grasp.

'Not so tight,' said Karalyn. 'They're fragile.'

Belinda nodded, and relaxed her grip. The kitten launched itself onto her arm, and scrabbled up to her shoulder, where it started to play with her long, dark hair.

She smiled; she had never been so happy.

Falls of Iron, Western Khatanax – 1st Abrinch 5252

Belinda awoke, and opened her eyes. The morning sun was already straining to get through the shutters, and the air in her chamber was warm and humid. She pulled back the thin sheet and sat up, then selected some clothes from the neatly folded piles sitting by her bedside table. She washed, dressed, then sat back down on the bed again, her eyes scanning the mattress.

Where was Naxor? She felt the familiar ache in her chest re-appear, the same ache that she had felt ever since the demigod had left the Falls of Iron to find and help Sable. For nineteen days she had waited, and each morning when she awoke in the large bed, she hoped that it would be the day he would return; then, each night, she would cry, alone in the dark room, her hopes dashed again.

There were only two alternatives, she reasoned. Either he was dead, or he had run off with Sable Holdfast. What troubled Belinda was that she didn't know which was worse. If he had died, then at least she wouldn't have to imagine him in Sable's arms, but maybe she had manipulated him; maybe she had used her dream powers to seduce him, in which case he would be innocent. Tainted, but innocent.

Either way, he wasn't where he was supposed to be; with Belinda; sharing her life and her bed.

She raised her left hand and gazed at it. She was desperate to show Naxor her new power, especially as he had doubted that Karalyn had been telling the truth. Belinda had been starting to doubt it too, though she would have never told anyone, and as the days had passed, her doubts had grown. She smiled, concentrated, then watched as small sparks appeared at her fingertips; little arcs of lightning that jumped from finger to finger. She glanced at a candle on the table that she had been practising with the previous evening, and the sparks shot out, lighting the wick.

It was a small start, she knew, but the joy it gave her helped balance the loss of Naxor's absence. Karalyn had not been lying; her powers were returning, and the ability to spark was only the beginning. She closed her eyes and slowed her breathing, focussing on feeling out her mind. She felt her vision powers – battle, line and range. No inner-vision yet, which was possibly the power she was most looking forward to having restored. The intricacies of speech still tripped her up, and there were times when she failed to understand the true meaning of what people said to her. She had stopped assuming that everything was to be taken literally, and had ceased asking for clarification, conscious that it made others look at her in a strange way, so instead, if someone said something cryptic or shrouded in irony, she would often remain silent rather than reveal her incomprehension. Inner-vision would allow her to read the genuine intent hidden behind the words spoken by others, and she would finally be able to know what Naxor really thought of her, without having to rely on the things he said.

Her healing powers were also unchanged. She focussed on her body, trying to feel out every inch, from her toes to her fingers, and sensed the energy buzzing through her; the same energy that meant she was destined to live forever.

Nothing had changed elsewhere in her mind, though she was unsure how death, stone and flow powers would feel. Presumably she would know when they had arrived. Her nascent fire powers, on the other hand, were budding. The ability to spark had come first, but she felt it was only a matter of time before she would be able to control fire as well. She opened her eyes and glanced at the candle burning on the bedside table. She smiled. She could feel the flame, sense it within her, even without the power to move it. She extinguished it with her fingers, her self-healing immediately soothing the singed skin, then stood.

There was a scratch at the window shutters, and she opened them, letting in the stray castle cat that had taken to coming into her room every day. He was a silver-grey tom, thin but strong-limbed, and his head butted her hand as she stroked him. He meowed in expectation, and she opened the cupboard under the table and withdrew the little bowl of tidbits that she had saved for him the night before. The tom jumped to the floor, his head soon buried in the bowl. Belinda crouched by him on one knee, stroking his back as he ate.

If Naxor returned, he would no doubt object to the presence of Belinda's new friend, but she didn't care. She could deal with that if it happened.

'Good boy,' she murmured, rubbing behind his ears and feeling his head push up against her hand.

She closed the cupboard door and got to her feet. The Weathervane was lying on a chair, and she reached out and took it, then buckled it to her belt. She glanced in the small mirror on the wall, then pulled her hair into a ponytail, a short black ribbon tying it in place. Others may call her beautiful, but she hated her reflection. It felt like a stranger was staring at her every time she looked in a mirror; a person with a past who refused to reveal her secrets. She frowned, watching the woman glare back at her, then went to her door and opened it.

Silva was sitting in a chair outside in the hallway. She might have been sleeping, but her eyes opened the moment Belinda walked through.

'Your Majesty,' she said, rising and bowing. 'Did you sleep well?'

'Yes,' said Belinda as she kept walking.

Silva hurried to keep up with her as she walked towards the kitchens. It was a longer walk than it had been previously, but Belinda had felt it better to move her room to a location within the castle that was out of range of Kelsey's ability to block powers. Belinda's mind was unreadable by anyone except Karalyn, but she had known that Silva would follow her to her new quarters, and if Naxor was trying to contact the Falls of Iron, then someone needed to be available.

'Have any of your powers been restored, your Majesty?' Silva said.

'No.' said Belinda. She hadn't told Silva about her sparking ability, though she wasn't entirely sure why. It was probably because she found the woman annoying.

She walked down a flight of steps and entered the dining area close to the castle kitchens. Many people ate outside on the terraces, or up in their rooms, but a few of the staff chose to eat in the small dining room. That morning however, the chamber was full of people. Corthie and Aila were there, getting ready for their departure, while Irno was close by, chatting to a militia officer.

'Morning, Belinda,' said Corthie.

'Good morning,' she said. 'When are you leaving?'

'Any moment. The wagons are loaded by the gatehouse; we were just filling up on some breakfast.'

'We should be back in ten days or so,' said Aila, 'hopefully with some good news.'

'I judge your chances to be slim,' said Belinda. 'I don't think the other three Counties will want to get involved in our problems.'

'Yeah, I know,' said Aila, 'but we have to try.'

'I think you'll do very well,' said Irno, striding over. 'The other Counties depend on us for iron and steel; they won't want to see us attacked again, that is, if the gods of Implacatus decide to come back for more.'

Belinda nodded, though she doubted Irno's assumption was correct.

'And you two make fine ambassadors,' Irno went on; 'my sister, and the renowned warrior who destroyed the invading task force.'

Corthie raised an eyebrow. 'Belinda might have helped too, you know.'

'Of course,' he said, 'which is why I feel it prudent that she remain here. I can't have both of my champions away at the same time.'

'The Queen is not your champion,' said Silva, echoing Belinda's unspoken thoughts.

Irno smiled. 'It was merely a figure of speech, Lady Silva. Come; let us walk to the gatehouse before it gets too hot.' He gestured to the militia, and they began filing out of the dining area.

Belinda strode alongside Aila as they walked along the cool, stone passageways.

Aila glanced at her. 'I take it there was no sign of...?'

Belinda shook her head, hoping that Aila would leave the subject of Naxor alone. She mentioned his absence most days, and every time she did it, Belinda wanted to crawl into a dark corner and hide.

'He'll be fine,' Aila went on; 'he's very resourceful. I'm sure he'll be back soon.'

Belinda said nothing, her stomach clenching.

'If he does get back,' Aila said, 'please ask him to contact me. I do worry about him.'

'If he was willing or able to contact you,' Belinda said, 'he would have done it by now.'

Aila narrowed her eyes. 'The same goes for you.'

Belinda nodded. 'I know.' She kept her face expressionless, despite the emotions churning through her. It had taken a lot of patience and training, but she was good at keeping her feelings hidden from others. For a long time she had been an open book, her raw emotions on display for all to perceive, but she had learned that such people were easily taken advantage of. It was better that people thought her cold rather than weak.

Aila and Belinda continued on in silence, and they left the keep and entered a large courtyard. Kelsey was standing there, waiting for them.

'Try not to kill anyone, brother,' she said to Corthie, a crooked smile on her lips. She glanced at Belinda. 'Hey, god-face, why didn't you tell me you could spark?'

Belinda frowned at the Holdfast woman, as Silva's mouth fell open.

'I sensed you use it yesterday evening,' Kelsey went on, 'and again this morning.'

'Is that right?' said Corthie, grinning. 'That's great news.'

'Your Majesty,' said Silva, 'are you able to spark?'

Belinda suppressed her anger. 'Yes.'

'You don't look very pleased about it,' said Aila.

'I knew Karalyn was telling the truth,' she said. 'It was just a matter of time.'

'Still,' said Aila; 'I thought you'd be excited.'

'I am.'

The demigod raised an eyebrow as they resumed walking towards the gatehouse. Silva trailed along behind them, her eyes lowered, and Belinda guessed that she was upset about being lied to. A small wave of guilt passed through Belinda, but she shook it off. Her powers were her business, no one else's. She eyed Kelsey.

'Don't tell people what I can do,' she said.

Kelsey looked surprised, and Belinda wondered if it was feigned. 'Eh?'

'If you sense me doing something,' Belinda said, 'then don't tell people. I want to tell them myself.'

Kelsey snorted. 'Forget it. Folk have a right to know just what you're capable of doing.'

Silva strode between them. 'How dare you speak to her Majesty in that manner?'

'Get lost, weird person,' said Kelsey.

'You're not going to squabble like this when I'm gone, are you?' said Corthie.

'We squabble while you're here, brother,' Kelsey said, 'so I don't know why you and Aila's departure would change anything.'

They reached the gatehouse, where three covered wagons had been hitched to horses. Along with a handful of militia, Corthie and Aila were taking a large quantity of supplies, not only for their journey, but to be distributed as gifts to the rulers of the other Counties.

Irno raised his hand, his sister Vana appearing by his side. 'Farewell!' he cried. 'Malik's blessings upon you, and may Amalia watch over your journey.'

'I bloody hope not,' muttered Aila as she climbed up into the lead wagon.

'Aye,' said Corthie; 'that would be a little disconcerting.'

Irno laughed. 'You know what I mean. Good luck.'

The wagons began to move, and the clip clop of the horses' hooves echoed across the forecourt. Belinda watched them leave through the gate, then turned back to the kitchen, her stomach rumbling.

Belinda watched the cat on the bed next to her. It was padding its front paws into the soft pillow, while a loud purr was coming from its sleek body. Belinda leant down, placing her face close to the cat, and he responded by butting his head against her nose and cheeks. His claws were digging holes into the cotton fabric of the pillow, but Belinda didn't care; he had chosen her room to visit, and that meant that she wasn't completely without merit. The cat wouldn't judge her for what she had done, nor would he look at her as if she were strange, the way Aila and Kelsey did.

She kissed the cat and smiled, wishing all of her relationships could be as simple.

She moved on the bed, propping her back against the wall, and picked up the book she had been reading. Irno had been very generous, allowing her full access to the hundreds of volumes stored on the shelves of his study, and she had selected several. She opened the book at the page she had stopped reading the previous evening. It was a work of fiction, set hundreds of years before, and many of the scenes took place in the city of Dun Khatar as it had been before its destruction. While the story might have been made up, there were plenty of references to daily life in the enormous city, and she had smiled at a few fleeting mentions of the "wise old queen" that ruled alongside Nathaniel.

The cat meowed for her attention, and she half-smiled, half-frowned as she lay the book aside to stroke him.

'Shush,' she whispered to him, as her fingers trailed through his soft fur; 'I'm supposed to be sleeping, remember?'

She cocked her ear, listening for any signs of movement outside her door. It was silent, but she knew Silva would be there, sitting in the chair in the hallway. She sighed. Would the woman ever leave her alone? How had it got to the point where she had to lie to her, tell her that she was going for a nap, just to get some peace? All day long, Silva would follow her around like a faithful dog, telling her how wonderful she was, while at the same time lamenting the fact that Belinda showed no sign of wishing to resume her old life. And now she was hurt by Belinda's lie concerning her spark powers. She hadn't mentioned it, of course, but Belinda could tell she was upset from the exaggerated sighs and sideways glances.

She picked up the book again, and the cat butted his way onto her lap, pushing the book aside until he had her full attention. Then he circled, and settled down, his front claws digging into her knee.

Voices echoed from outside the door.

'No,' Silva was telling someone; 'her Majesty is sleeping; you can't go in.'

Another voice mumbled something, and the door handle began to turn.

'I cannot allow it,' Silva said, her voice rising.

'It's important, you idiot,' came the other voice.

Belinda frowned. Kelsey.

The door opened. Through the entrance, Silva was standing, her face enraged, while Kelsey pushed past her. The Holdfast woman came into the room and closed the door behind her. She glanced at Belinda, then her eyes fell on the cat.

'Scram, moggie,' Kelsey cried, her arms waving.

The cat dug its claws into Belinda, then sprang for the open window, and disappeared over the ledge. Belinda narrowed her eyes.

'I have news,' Kelsey said.

'Go away.'

Kelsey smirked. 'Charming.' She sat on a low stool and lit a cigarette.

'Don't smoke in here.'

'What?'

'I said...'

'I heard you. You really are a miserable cow, aren't you? I trek all this way, to the arse-end of the castle, to bring you good news, and all you can do is scowl at me? And that's once I got past your doorkeeper. When are you going to send her away? Silva's a maniac; deluded, and she does my head in.'

Belinda glanced away, suppressing an urge to slap Kelsey. She would enjoy it, but didn't want to have to deal with the aftermath. She controlled her breathing, and kept her face still.

'What is your news?'

'Oh, so you *do* want to know?'

'Yes.'

'Then say please.'

'Please.'

Kelsey cackled, her laughter filling Belinda with anger. 'Alright.

Guess who I just sensed approaching the Falls of Iron? Your idiot boyfriend.'

Her eyes widened. 'Naxor?'

'Aye. He was using his range vision to check out the town.'

Belinda shuffled forwards on the bed, and starting pulling on her boots. 'Where?'

'About a mile away, on the road from the port, but that was fifteen minutes ago. It took me that long to walk all the way to your room.'

'You came up here just to tell me?'

'Aye.'

Belinda glanced at her. 'Thank you.'

'I figured you'd want to know.' She glanced at the book and picked it up, raising an eyebrow. 'I would never have guessed that you read this sort of crap. I had you down as a reader of academia; politics, history, that sort of thing.'

'I read that too,' Belinda said as she laced up her boots.

'Aye, but romance? Yuck.' She flicked through a few pages. 'Are there any sex scenes?'

'A few.'

'Ahh, now I get it. You're missing a bit of carnal action, eh?'

'None of your business.'

'Don't get me wrong,' Kesley said; 'I respect you more after discovering this. It makes you seem like you might actually be human.'

Belinda stood. She glanced in the mirror, and frowned at her reflection.

'Pyre's arse,' Kelsey said; 'I don't know what you have to frown about. I'd wrestle a dragon to have hair like that.'

Belinda glanced away. 'Sable's prettier.'

Kelsey laughed. 'Debateable. Give it a few decades, though, and then I imagine there will be a clear winner. When we're all old and haggard, you'll look the same.'

Belinda gestured to the door. 'Out. I don't want you poking through my things when I'm not here.'

Kelsey stood. 'Fine. Judging by that book, you have nothing I'd want anyway.'

They left the room. Silva was standing outside in the hallway, her eyes lowered.

'I'm sorry, your Majesty. This rude girl shoved me out of the way.'

Kelsey stuck her tongue out at the demigod.

Belinda ignored them both, and hurried for the stairs.

'Praise Malik,' Naxor said as he saw her approach. He was looking worn and tired, his clothes fraying and filthy. Several days' worth of stubble was on his face, and his hair was unkempt and tangled.

Belinda rushed towards him, her heart racing and her stomach in knots, and they embraced on the narrow lane, halfway between the town and the castle.

'I had almost given up hope,' she said, her eyes filling with tears as he held her close.

'You're all I've thought about,' he said; 'all that's kept me going.'

'What happened?'

He pulled back from her and spat on the cobbles. 'Sable Holdfast,' he said, his eyes fierce. 'The bitch betrayed me.'

Belinda's anger swelled within her. 'What did she do?'

'Come on,' he said, taking her hand, 'let's get up to the castle; I'm choking on a drink and a smoke.'

They walked up the steep steps to the castle forecourt, and then passed through the gates, the militia saluting Belinda and Naxor as they passed. Silva was waiting there for them, her head bowed, along with Kelsey, who was eyeing Naxor with a half smile. They went into the keep and entered the ale room.

'Wine,' Naxor cried. He turned to Kelsey. 'And a cigarette? I've been out for days.'

The Holdfast woman passed him one and they sat. Belinda's nose wrinkled as the acrid smell of smoke arose from Naxor, but she said nothing. She was pleased to see him, and relieved, but already her rage at Sable was clouding her thoughts.

'How's my aunt?' said Kelsey as the wine arrived.

Naxor's face fell, and he shook his head. 'I saved her. She was in chains inside a cell within the Governor's residence in Alea Tanton. I risked everything to rescue her, and then I patched her up with salve. She had a broken leg.' He shook his head again.

'And then?' said Kelsey.

'Then I stole a Quadrant,' he said; 'snatched it right out of the hand of a god.'

Belinda frowned, dreading what was to come next.

'I was so stupid,' Naxor went on. 'I let my guard down, despite everything people had said to me about Sable. I wanted to give her a chance, so I trusted her.'

Kelsey lit her own cigarette. 'And?'

'She betrayed me. She stole the Quadrant, and left me unconscious in the middle of the Governor's residence. I was awoken by soldiers and arrested. It took me a dozen days to escape from the dungeons, and then I ran down to the harbour, but Irno's boat had gone. Sable took it. I spent a day at the port evading capture, before I managed to get passage here, working my way as a common sailor on a merchant galley.'

Belinda's fury coiled within her, and she slammed her fist down onto the table, making everyone jump.

'That bitch,' she cried. 'You saved her life, and she stabbed you in the back.'

Naxor nodded, his face grave. 'You were right about her, my darling. I should have listened.'

Kelsey narrowed her eyes. 'It's a pity we only have your side of the story.'

'What's that supposed to mean?' said Belinda.

The Holdfast woman shrugged. 'Well, if Sable were here, then maybe her version might have a different... slant to it.'

Belinda got to her feet, her fists clenched. 'Are you calling Naxor a liar?'

'Settle down,' Kelsey said. 'If Naxor's telling us the truth, then why didn't he try to send us a message?'

'I knew *you* were here,' he said. 'I knew you would block my powers.' He took a draw on his cigarette. 'I also knew that some would doubt my story. I've had plenty of time to think it over, both while I was stuck in prison, and on the journey back here.' He glanced at Belinda. 'I don't care if other people disbelieve me; the only thing that matters is that you believe me, my darling Belinda.'

She gazed into his eyes as she retook her seat. She hated the way that the others mistrusted him. He had done a few things in his past that were dishonest, but who hadn't? She, for example, had lied to Silva that very morning about her spark powers. What was important was the fact that he was trying to change; he was trying to be better. From the way he was looking at her, she knew that he loved her, and she loved him in return. They belonged together, their hearts entwined forever; why would he lie to her?

She took his hand. 'Of course I believe you, Naxor.'

He smiled. 'Thank you, my beautiful darling. I knew I could count on you.'

CHAPTER 2

A HIGHER PURPOSE

The Glebe, Western Khatanax – 3rd Abrinch 5252

Corthie wiped the sweat from his brow. Within the darkness of the forest, the air was still and humid, and the heat oppressive. On either side of the paved track, tall trees spread for miles, the ground covered in thick layers of brown pine needles. Every so often, they had passed clearings, where chunks of the forest had been cut down, but just as numerous were areas where young saplings were striving upwards, aching to reach the sun. Wagons pulled by gaien, their chassis loaded with stacks of timber, would head down from the mountains, passing them regularly. Each time, the wagons carrying the party from the Falls of Iron would pull over to the side of the track, their horses restless and fearful until the huge, lumbering reptilian beasts had disappeared into the gloom of the forest behind them.

'We're gaining altitude with every hour that passes,' Aila said, waving a fan in her face. 'Hopefully, it'll start to get cooler soon.'

Corthie glanced at her sitting next to him on the wagon bench. His clothes were sticking to his skin with sweat, and he longed for rain. He lifted a waterskin and drank a mouthful, but the liquid was tepid and failed to satisfy him.

'It's the middle of summer,' said their driver, a soldier from Irno's militia, 'so it won't get much cooler, ma'am. There's a mountain stream that runs through the centre of the Glebe that dampens the heat in the town a bit.'

'How much longer until we get there?' said Corthie.

'About an hour, I reckon, sir,' he said. He pointed up at a high ridge just visible through the trees. 'The Glebe is nestled in that valley.'

Corthie nodded. He had been glad to get away from the Falls of Iron, and the memories he associated with the place; and had enjoyed spending time with Aila. They had stopped over twice on the journey, at comfortable hostelries where they had been treated as dignitaries. Word had spread throughout the Four Counties about what he had done to the Banner of the Golden Fist's battalion, and he had attracted crowds, just as he had back in the City of Pella. He had smiled and waved, but part of him was still torn about having killed the unarmed soldiers in the castle.

'You alright?' said Aila.

'Aye.'

'You seemed lost in thought.'

'I was thinking about the soldiers in the castle.'

'Again?'

'Aye.'

She took his hand.

'Killing greenhides was fine,' he went on; 'it was fun, if I'm being honest, but killing unarmed people? It weighs on me.'

'You didn't notice them throwing down their weapons,' she said. 'You didn't intend to do it.'

He nodded. Inside, however, his stomach was twisting. He had sworn over and over that he hadn't noticed what the soldiers were doing, but it wasn't completely true. He remembered every second of his battle frenzy outside the keep. Part of his mind had been perfectly aware that the soldiers had surrendered, but his battle-vision-powered fury hadn't cared. Only the sight of his sister running out in front of him had been enough to stop him, and even then, he had been close to cleaving her in two. Down in the town the following morning had been much the same. He had entered the same frenzy as before, and had ploughed his way along the narrow alleyways until blood was flowing down every street. His armour had taken a battering from the swords of the Banner, but he had carried on regardless, ignoring the countless injuries on his body, ignoring everything but his lust for blood.

Irno had proclaimed him the greatest mortal warrior to have set foot in Khatanax, but Corthie understood the truth; he was the greatest mortal warrior who had ever lived on any world – he had proved that fighting the greenhides. He knew it with a certainty, but what was he supposed to do with such knowledge? Seek out noble causes, and topple tyrants, or try to live a normal life and use his skills only in the defence of his family? Did he have a responsibility to others?

He glanced at Aila, wondering how she was interpreting his silence. He needed her more than ever, her love for him confirming that he remained someone worthy of love. When others saw her by his side, they would think that he couldn't be that bad, that he must have some redeeming features. He lowered his eyes; how had his self-worth fallen so much? He had walked around the City with his head high and his confidence intact, but somewhere along the way it had dissipated into a tangled mess of contradictions – his strength against his vulnerability, his lust for blood against the empathy he felt for people, his optimism against the dimming view of a future filled with bloodshed.

The driver broke him out of his thoughts by lifting a hand and pointing. Corthie glanced up, and saw the land open up a little in front of them, the sides of the dense forest parting. Wooden houses and farms dotted a flat shelf of land at the foot of the high ridge they had seen earlier. The road joined the banks of a wide, shallow river, the water rushing down over weirs and foaming around jagged rocks that rose from its stony bed. Directly ahead of them, there was a great cleft in the ridge, and sitting on a rocky platform was a small town. A tall, wooden palisade wall rose up to surround it, and the high spires and towers that lay within. Beyond, the sky was a deep blue, and a breeze was floating down from the mountains.

'There it is,' said the driver; 'the Glebe. Our scouts will have arrived yesterday evening, so they should be expecting us.'

The three wagons rolled along the paved road, the drivers holding their hands up to shield their eyes from the sun glaring down at them. As they got closer, soldiers became visible up on the tower overlooking the open gates. The walls to either side were a solid face of wood that ran for half a mile across the edge of the rocky platform, but there were no battlements other than on the tower. A troop of soldiers emerged from the gates, each armed with a spear and a longbow, with armour of hardened leather. They filed up the road in a double column, then parted to line the side of the paved way, while a woman on horseback approached between them.

She raised her hand and the three wagons came to a halt.

'I see from your insignia that you are the party from the Falls of Iron,' she said. 'I bear greetings from Count Gloag, and offer you a welcome to the Glebe.'

Aila stood up by the driver's bench of the lead wagon. 'I am Aila, sister of Count Irno, who also sends his greetings. May we enter the Glebe and talk with the noble Count Gloag?'

The woman on the horse said nothing. She kept her eyes on the lead wagon for a long moment, taking in Aila and Corthie, then glanced at the two rear wagons. After what seemed an age, she inclined her head slightly.

'Come this way.'

She turned the horse around, and set off towards the gates. Aila frowned, then nodded to the driver, and the wagon got underway. They passed between the lines of soldiers, and Corthie noticed several trying to get a good look at him. He, in turn, cast his eyes at their longbows. Each measured five feet from end to end, and were unlike anything he had seen since he had visited Kellach Brigdomin years before. A well-aimed arrow from one of them would pierce his steel armour; maybe not the thickened breastplate, but probably anywhere else. He wondered if he had the patience to learn how to use one properly.

'Here we go,' said Aila as they passed under the large wooden arch that formed the gateway. Beyond, there was a large, clear marshalling yard, and then rows of tall, wooden houses and other buildings spread out into a maze of streets. The woman on horseback led the way through the town, and the wagons followed. Locals watched from the sides of houses, or out of open windows as they passed, and none looked too pleased to see the standard of the Falls of Iron flying from each wagon.

Corthie prepared himself. Despite how he was feeling on the inside, he knew he had to display a calm confidence on the outside. He had trained for this, he thought to himself; as a member of an aristocratic family in the Holdings, his mother had long instilled in him the need to preserve ones outer appearance. It was like wearing a mask, she had often told him.

Aila's expression matched his, he noticed, though no doubt she was calm due to her long experience over centuries of dealing with gods and demigods.

'I'll let you do the talking,' he said. 'You know how to speak to people like this.'

They approached the only stone building in the town – a round, high-walled bastion that rose above the surrounding streets like a rock in a river. Wooden balconies and battlements ringed the tower, and people were gazing down at the three wagons. The woman on horseback stopped before a deep, narrow moat next to a slim bridge that crossed over to a gate in the wall of the bastion. She dismounted, and a soldier led her horse away.

Aila nodded to their driver, and the three wagons slowed to a halt. Corthie gripped the side of the railing and jumped to the ground, then he lifted his hand and helped Aila climb down.

The woman regarded them both. 'Lady Aila,' she said, 'only you and your companion may enter. No weapons are allowed within the Tower of the Glebe.'

'We're not carrying any,' said Aila. 'May I ask, what will happen to our escort and our wagons while we remain inside?'

'Your militia will be housed, and your possessions will be guarded,' the woman said. 'The ties of hospitality that bind the Four Counties together will see that no harm comes to you while you reside within the walls of the Glebe.' She turned, and walked across the bridge.

Aila glanced up at their driver. 'You're in charge now. We're guests here, so keep out of trouble, and we'll see you soon.'

'Yes, ma'am,' he said.

Aila and Corthie stepped onto the bridge. Below them, the surface of the moat was reflecting the sun's rays, and they were dazzled for a moment by the blinding light. They crossed to the other side and entered a dark hallway. Corthie picked out the dim silhouette of the woman as she set off down a narrow passageway, and they followed, coming into a large, circular hall in the centre of the tower. The roof was open to the sky, though wide canvas sheets hung above them, suspended on wooden rails. In the shade beneath, a hearth sat in the middle of the floor, with benches and tables gathered before a high seat, where an old man was sitting. Soldiers were posted along the length of the wall, guarding the various entrances, while windows dotted the sides as they rose to a level of ten storeys or more.

The woman led them past benches crowded with men and women until they stood by the dark hearth in front of the high wooden seat. It had been placed upon a wide platform made from the trunk of a single tree, and the seat rose up out of it as if it were a living extension of the platform.

The woman bowed. 'Father, I have brought you Lady Aila of the Falls of Iron, sister to the Count; and her companion, the Banner-Slayer.'

The man gazed down at them from behind a long beard. His eyes tightened slightly, but other than that, his expression remained tranquil. Corthie kept his glance on the old man, ignoring the dozens of Glebe folk around them. Unarmed and without armour, Aila and he wouldn't stand a chance if they were attacked.

'I am Count Gloag of the Glebe,' the old man said. 'I trust my daughter bid you welcome?'

'She did, my lord,' said Aila, 'and I thank you for your hospitality. I am new to these lands, but my brother has been allied with the Glebe for many centuries. He wishes to know if you would be open to a deepening of our alliance.'

The old man smiled, but his eyes remained cold. 'Straight to business, Lady Aila? It would have pleased me to have gone through a few more pleasantries first, but so be it. A "deepening of our alliance", you say? By which Count Irno means that he wishes to place the people of the Glebe into a position of great danger.'

'With all respect,' Aila said, 'the Four Counties are facing a threat from the gods of Implacatus; a threat we would be better able to resist if united.'

'And why are we facing such a threat, Lady Aila? Could it be because the man standing by your side slaughtered hundreds of their mercenary soldiers?'

'They were besieging the Falls of Iron, my lord. We acted in self defence.'

'Yes. Unfortunately, the reasons for the siege that you mention are also known to us. You wrongfully imprisoned one of the gods, a certain Lady Joaz, and executed her without a trial or hearing. It seems to me that you have needlessly provoked the wrath of Implacatus, and if they choose to retaliate, you wish that we die by your side. It has also come to my attention that the gods believe that the secret of the salve trade can be found within the Falls of Iron. If this is true, then you have imperilled the whole of Khatanax, and as your closest neighbour, it would be in our interests to disown you utterly, in the hope that we might be spared when the storm comes.'

Corthie frowned. 'Sometimes you have to fight for what is right.'

The old man slowly turned his gaze to Corthie. 'That is what the Fordians believed two and a half centuries ago. Tell me, where did their defiance get them? Their land was ruined, and their people slaughtered, the survivors scattered as refugees, homeless and destitute. You are a young man, and perhaps ignorant in the ways of politics, so I will forgive your foolish outburst. But let me say this, Corthie Holdfast, one should only fight when there is a chance of success, but against the might of Implacatus, there is no such chance; only death.'

Corthie glanced at Aila. 'We're wasting our time here. We should move on to Cape Armour.'

'You will get the same response from them,' said Count Gloag; 'and from Kaulsnaughton, if you choose to speak to them. Did you think that we would not discuss the folly of the Falls of Iron among ourselves? But come, you are our guests, and I insist that you remain for the night. A feast has been arranged in your honour, and I have gifts for you to take back to Count Irno.'

Aila bowed. 'As we have gifts for you from my brother, my lord. We would be honoured to stay here tonight, thank you.'

The old man nodded. 'Daughter, show our guests to their rooms; this audience is over.'

The woman bowed to her father, then gestured to Aila and Corthie. Aila bowed again, then the woman led them back through the crowded benches towards one of the arched doorways. The gathered men and woman of the Glebe remained silent as they passed, and, to Corthie, it seemed as if every face was staring at him, their eyes narrow with fear and anger.

Corthie lay back on the bed, his hands clasped behind his head. The narrow window of their room faced inwards, and had a view of the circular meeting area in the centre of the tower below them, though much of it was blocked by awnings. The interior space of the tower was shrouded in shadow as evening approached, and a few lamps had been lit.

He glanced at Aila. She was crouching by a luggage trunk, looking through the clothes she had brought on the journey, trying to pick something to wear to the feast.

'It's almost exactly a year since we first met,' he said.

She glanced up at him. 'It seems longer.'

'If we were in the City, it would be Izran, your father's month; and that's when we met.'

She held up a dress. 'What do you think of this one?'

'I think I now know my purpose,' he said.

She frowned. 'What?'

'I can't be here by chance alone, just as it couldn't have been chance that I was sent to the City to fight the greenhides. I must be here for a reason, and I think I know what that is – I need to fight the gods of Implacatus. Only I can defeat them.'

Aila said nothing for a moment, then she put down the dress and sat on the bed.

'Why must you be here for a reason? I don't believe in fate, and I didn't think you did either.'

'I didn't before now, but if I'm the greatest mortal warrior in history, then I must have a destiny. I can't be fated to live out my life on a remote farm, ploughing the soil year after year until I drop down dead. My life has to have meaning.'

She got back up and began to change into the dress she had selected.

'You don't believe me?' he said.

'No. I don't believe in destiny. Life is a mixture of chance and will; sometimes the two are aligned, sometimes they're not.'

He shook his head. 'There's got to be more to it than that.'

She finished dressing in silence as he watched her.

'Lady Aila?' came a voice from behind the door while she was strapping on her sandals.

'Yes?'

'I'm here to escort you and your companion to dinner.'

'Sure. Just give us a moment.'

She turned to Corthie. 'You ready?'

He slid his feet off the bed and pushed them down into his boots. 'Aye. Let's get this over with.'

Aila checked her reflection in the small silvered mirror on the wooden table, then opened the door. A man bowed to her, and Corthie recognised him as one of the courtiers that had been standing by Count Gloag's throne.

'This way, please,' he said.

He led them down tight and narrow staircases, through the ring of rooms and chambers that circled the open meeting space in the centre. They emerged on the ground floor, and Corthie saw that the area had been transformed. The throne remained where it had been before, but the tables and benches had been arranged in rows, and the hearth was burning. A metal frame had been assembled over the flames, and skewers and large pots were suspended there. The area was even more crowded than earlier, with almost every seat taken. Count Gloag was sitting by a raised table near the hearth, and Aila and Corthie were led past the crowds to his side, where two seats lay empty.

'You and your companion have the places of honour tonight, my lady,' said the courtier, gesturing to the seats.

Aila bowed to Count Gloag. 'My thanks.'

Gloag nodded, while all around, every eye was on them. 'Sit, please.'

Aila and Corthie took their places, and music began to float up through the air, from string and wood instruments, a soft melody to accompany the background noise of talking. The food began to arrive, and Corthie ate, but his mind wasn't on it. A serving boy offered him a large tankard of mead, and he took it, but after a sip, left it lying. Anything could happen, and he didn't want to be drunk if it did.

'How do you find the food?' said the count.

'Excellent, thank you,' said Aila.

'And your accommodation?'

'Perfect, my lord.'

Corthie eyed the crowds around them. Many were eating and drinking, or listening to the music, but his nerves were on edge.

'I'm glad you like it, Lady Aila,' Gloag said, 'especially as it will be your home for the foreseeable future.'

'Excuse me, my lord?'

Count Gloag turned to them, a smile on his lips. He had a letter in his hand, and he opened it in front of them.

'This arrived a few days ago,' he said, 'all the way from Alea Tanton. Governor Felice has made one or two requests, which I feel obliged to honour. It was a difficult decision, but I have to think of my people. You understand, I'm sure.'

He lifted a hand, and the open hall fell into silence, the music cutting off abruptly. The count's daughter approached. She gestured to a soldier carrying a large sack, and he emptied it out in front of the table, spilling half a dozen heads onto the paved ground.

'You murdered our militia?' cried Corthie. He reached for a knife on the table, but a group of soldiers behind them raised their longbows, each with an arrow nocked and aimed at him.

Aila's eyes widened. 'We're here as ambassadors,' she cried. 'The Four Counties have a tradition of hospitality stretching back centuries.'

'Indeed,' said Gloag, 'which is why you will not be harmed, Lady Aila. Your companion, on the other hand? Governor Felice has set her conditions for peace, and the price is the head of Corthie Holdfast. You, however, will be held here as a hostage, until your brother comes to his senses.'

Corthie remained still, half an eye on the archers behind them, his battle-vision thrumming. Aila glanced at him for a fraction of a second.

She calmed her expression. 'May I see the letter, my lord?'

'Of course, my lady.' Gloag held it out for Aila, and Corthie struck. He flung the contents of the tankard at the archers as he sprang backwards over the surface of the table, spraying them with mead. He dived towards the hearth as an arrow ripped across his raised forearm, and threw a huge blazing log into the crowd, his battle-vision dulling the pain in his arm, and his burnt hand. Sparks showered over the tables amid a cacophony of screams and cries. Corthie slammed back into the table, upending it and sending plates and bowls crashing around them; then he leaped at Gloag's daughter, grasping her by the throat and lifting her off her feet.

'Get back,' he cried, 'or I'll break her neck.'

The count's daughter writhed in his grip, her feet dangling.

'Don't hurt her!' shouted Gloag, backing off as archers and soldiers surrounded him, forming a shield between Corthie and their lord.

Corthie picked up a knife from the scattered detritus of dinner, and pulled the count's daughter towards him. He released his grip on her neck and raised the knife to her throat. She gasped for breath and staggered, but Corthie's arm kept her upright, the wound from the arrow leaking blood down the front of her dress.

'You can try to take my head, Gloag,' he said, 'but it'll cost you your daughter's life.' He glanced at Aila. 'Time to go.'

She climbed over the table and ran to his side as the crowd seethed around them. Corthie began to pull the count's daughter backwards, stepping by the side of the hearth. Aila edged along with him, her glance darting around. She pulled a long knife from the carcass of a roasting pig by the fire, and brandished it at the crowd as they made their way step by step towards the arched entrance that led to the bridge. The crowd parted, but stayed close on either side, the soldiers watching them as Corthie dragged the count's daughter along. The woman was struggling, and she scratched Corthie's cheek, but the pain hardly registered. They made it to the entrance, then through the passageway and out onto the bridge as the crowd followed, keeping a yard from them.

Corthie edged along the bridge, his eyes taking in the wagons and carts on the other side. Next to them was a large grey gelding, a saddle strapped to its back.

At the far end of the bridge, Corthie halted. He lifted the count's daughter off her feet and hurled her into the crowd of militia who were standing halfway along the bridge, then grabbed Aila by the arm and pulled her to the horse. He leaped up onto its back, and it reared and bucked under him. He grabbed the reins, then scooped up Aila, setting her down onto the saddle in front of him as a roar of voices closed in. An arrow sped by his face as he kicked his heels into the sides of the gelding. The horse took off, bolting down the street, its hooves clattering over the paving stones. Another arrow nicked Corthie's right shoulder, ripping through the cloth of his tunic and spattering Aila with blood. Corthie ignored it, and kept his head down as the gelding raced through the streets. They reached the open gateway, where soldiers were posted up on the tower, and the horse galloped through. More arrows came after them, striking the track to either side as Corthie urged the horse on. He aimed the gelding at the wide river, and it bounded down into the shallows, then across the stream and into the woods on the other side. He kept the horse at its quickest pace as the sounds and light of the Glebe started to fade into the distance, his eyes picking out the way through the trees, until, at last, the forest was still and silent around them.

Several hours passed before Corthie allowed the gelding to rest. He dismounted in the darkness of the woods, then helped Aila down. She had said nothing for the entire journey, and looked up at him, her expression shrouded in the thick shadows.

'It was a trap,' she said. 'They'd already decided to kneel before the gods before we showed up. Thank Malik you know how to ride a horse.'

'I was taught as a boy,' he said; 'though it's been a while.'

'Are you hurt?'

'Only a bit.'

He took a look at his injuries. The battle-vision had dulled the pain during the escape, but it had started to flare the further from the Glebe they had travelled. He gazed at the wound on his forearm. It was ugly and deep, and he bound it with a strip of cloth torn from his tunic, the fingers on his other hand aching from the burns on his skin. The cut on his shoulder was light in comparison, and he stuffed more cloth down onto it to stop the bleeding.

'We'd better go,' he said, 'we need to keep moving. They'll be tracking us.'

'But I can't see a thing.'

'I can. You ride, and I'll lead.'

He guided her to the gelding and helped her climb up onto the saddle. Around them, the forest was in utter silence. He powered his battle-vision, heightening his eyesight and hearing, then took the reins in one hand and started to walk, leading Aila and the gelding into the endless gloom.

CHAPTER 3

AN ELBOW IN THE EYE

Falls of Iron, Western Khatanax – 4th Abrinch 5252

Van flicked the ash from his cigarette into a saucer and glanced at Sohul. The lieutenant was sitting in a chair, reading a book about Queen Belinda, the Third Ascendant, a mug of water balanced in his hand.

'About that thousand in gold,' Van said.

Sohul looked up over the top of the book. 'Captain?'

'The thousand I owe you,' Van said, his arm resting on the narrow window ledge; 'I'm not altogether sure when I'll be in a position to pay you back.'

The lieutenant raised an eyebrow. 'Right now, I'd be happy if we get back to Implacatus in one piece, Captain.'

Van shook his head. 'How many times do I have to tell you, Sohul? You don't need to keep calling me that while we're stuck in this cell.'

Sohul glanced around at the comfortable chamber where they had been placed. There were two single beds, one against each wall, and a table with jugs of fresh water for drinking and cleaning, and even a small toilet chamber in the corner by the outside wall of the keep.

'I can't help it, Captain,' he said, 'not while we're still officially under contract. As for the thousand in gold, I gave up on ever seeing that again after watching the Banner get ripped to shreds.' His face paled, as it always did when he discussed what had happened. 'I can pinpoint it to the moment when Major Ahito was sliced in two by that Holdfast beast.'

'But I'd already been captured by then.'

'I know, but even so, I still had faith that you'd escape or be rescued. None of the officers were told by Lord Renko what had happened to Lord Baldwin's mission to save you, and I didn't even know that Lady Joaz had been killed until you told me. My faith didn't falter until I'd seen five hundred dead Banner soldiers lying on the streets.' He put the book down. 'What do you think will happen to us, Captain?'

Van glanced out of the window. It was too narrow to squeeze through, and was without bars. Outside, the sun was high in the cloudless sky, and the chamber had been warm since an hour after dawn.

'We'll see,' he said.

Sohul took a cigarette out of his silver case and lit it, and Van frowned, feeling the loss of his own case to the dragon rider. 'You must have some inkling, Captain. You were privy to the thinking of Lord Renko and the others. How will they react to their defeat?'

'That's a different question altogether. The gods of Implacatus know only one way to react – with overwhelming force. I imagine that, right now, fresh contracts are being signed with other Banners, and a new, bigger, task force is being assembled. How that will affect us, however, is unclear. Our rescue is probably rather low on their list of priorities.'

Sohul sighed. 'I wish I'd never given you that gold.'

'And I wish I'd spent it all on wine, women and weed, despite the fact that this place is much nicer than my dingy old quarters in Serene. Do you miss home?'

'Yes. I did expect to be away for some time, but I've never been a prisoner before. I guess you know how it feels.'

'Captivity on Dragon Eyre was a completely different experience; the worst time of my life, without a doubt. This...' He gestured around the room, 'is luxury in comparison.'

There was a heavy thump on the chamber door. The upper half of it consisted of horizontal iron shutters that slid open and closed to allow food and supplies into the room, and the grating sound of them opening reached their ears. Van got to his feet and watched as the figures of two men became visible on the other side. One was a militia soldier, while the other stood back a little.

'You have a visitor,' said the guard, stepping away from the door.

'Lord Gadena,' said Van.

Sohul glanced up. 'That's Gadena?'

Van nodded as the man approached the other side of the door.

'I thought I'd pay you a visit,' Gadena said. 'I'm leaving the Falls of Iron today, and I wanted to ask you something.'

'Yes?' said Van.

'Yes. You were there when Baldwin slaughtered my trainees.'

'I was.'

'Why did he do it?'

'The truth? Because he liked killing, and Lord Renko gave him permission. That was it; there was no strategic reason, and it wasn't to teach you a lesson.'

Gadena nodded. 'I'm glad he's dead; I only wish I'd seen it, but I was still in that farmhouse we went to after my camp.'

'Is that how you survived?'

'Yes. Baldwin and Felice went off into the town to set up a portal, and I was left behind with the two soldiers that were guarding me. It took three days before anyone noticed us.'

'And my two men?'

'Both are in jail somewhere in the town with the other survivors of your Banner.'

'Have you seen them?' said Sohul, rising and walking to the door. 'Our men, are they alright?'

Gadena nodded. 'As far as I know. There are around one hundred and fifty altogether, or so I'm told, mostly those who were positioned by the far gates of the town, and some who were out on foraging expeditions.'

'And are there other officers among the captured?'

'A few more lieutenants,' he said. He nodded at Van. 'This one here is the most senior alive. Some presumably escaped when Renko activated the Quadrant.'

'Do you know what they plan to do to us?'

Gadena shrugged. 'None of my business. Having said that, I'm an old friend of Count Irno, and he's not someone who would readily kill prisoners without cause.'

Sohul frowned. 'You're a friend of the ruler of the Falls of Iron? Then you are our enemy.'

Gadena laughed and shook his head. 'We're all mercenaries, son. The only difference between us is that I wouldn't have chosen to work for the same scum that you signed up to serve.'

'How dare you,' said Sohul. 'You're nothing but a renegade.'

'Lieutenant, please,' said Van. 'Lord Gadena is right; we're all mercenaries, and this is a business discussion; keep your personal feelings out of it.' He turned to Gadena. 'Pay no heed; he's a good officer, if a little inexperienced.'

Sohul narrowed his eyes and strode back to his seat.

'I also have a couple of questions,' Van went on, 'if you're in a mood to talk.'

Gadena nodded. 'Go on.'

'Corthie Holdfast,' he said. 'What do you know of him?'

The mercenary chief laughed again. 'Someone tell you, did they?'

'Tell me what?'

'I trained Corthie Holdfast.'

Van smiled. 'I didn't know that; I was just guessing that you must have seen him in the castle these last few days. You trained him, eh?' He shook his head and lit a cigarette. 'I hope for the sake of every other mercenary outfit that not all of the warriors you train turn out like him.'

'That lad is unique,' said Gadena; 'I've never seen anything like it. Four years I had him, but he was already better than most when he first arrived as a fourteen-year-old. And the best part was, I got him for free. The god who had him was in a hurry, and she was trying to show off about the quality of her recruits, and she let me have him as a sample.'

'Is he a demigod without self-healing powers?'

'He told me that both of his parents were mortal, so I guess not. If I had to put money on it, I'd say that he's a freak of nature.'

'If you call him that again I will punch you in the face,' came a voice from down the hallway. Van and Gadena both turned, and watched as Kelsey Holdfast approached.

'Miss Holdfast,' said Gadena, inclining his head a little, 'I meant no offence; I was merely stating that your brother is one of a kind.'

Kelsey frowned up at him. 'I hold you partly responsible for turning my brother into what he's become.' She lowered her glance, her eyes wide. 'To think that I used to bully him as a child.'

Van raised an eyebrow. 'You bullied him?'

'Aye. Me and my other brother Keir made his life a misery. I could be a bit of a cow back then. Karalyn used to stick up for him, but she was hardly around because, well, she was a danger to the rest of the family.'

'Then I'd say that you and Lord Gadena are probably equally responsible for creating Corthie Holdfast.'

She glared, her fierce eyes boring into him, then looked puzzled for a moment. 'Maybe you're right. You got a cigarette?'

Van offered her one, passing it between the iron slats.

'Ta. Give me a light, Gadena.'

The mercenary chief struck a match and lit it for her.

'Ta.'

Van gave a wry smile. 'Did you come here for a reason?'

'What?' She frowned at him, then looked away as if distracted.

Van and Gadena shared a glance.

'Right. Bye,' Kelsey said, then turned and walked away.

Gadena waited until she had disappeared round the corner of the passageway, then turned back to Van. 'She's a strange one.'

'What do you know about the Holdfasts? How many are there?'

'Just the two of them here in the Falls of Iron,' Gadena said. 'I have no idea how many others might exist.' He paused for a moment. 'Logos, as much as I disagree with your choice of employer, I can see that you're a decent officer and a professional. If you are ever released, and are looking for a job, then come and see me. I'm going to rebuild my business from scratch, and could do with a few trainers of your calibre.'

Van nodded. 'Thanks for the offer; I'll bear it in mind.'

Gadena nodded, then strode off down the passageway. Van turned.

'Gone, has he?' said Sohul.

'Yes.'

'Good.'

'What's your problem?' said Van. 'He was coming to see us as a professional courtesy. And considering what the Banner of the Golden Fist did to his livelihood, that was pretty open-minded of him.'

'Thinking of taking him up on his offer?'

Van shrugged. 'Maybe. We'd have to get out of here first.'

'And who was the girl?'

'Kelsey Holdfast.'

'What? The one you told me about? The one that saved your life?'

'Yes.'

'She's the sister of that monster?'

Van nodded.

'What did she want?'

'Who knows? I suspect she might be a little crazy.' He took a draw of his cigarette, wondering if he should tell Sohul about the young woman's ability to block the powers of the gods. He decided against it. He didn't like her, but she *had* saved his life. Crazy or not, he owed her for that.

The afternoon passed. Van smoked and paced the floor of the chamber, while Sohul read his book in silence. When the sun got close to the horizon in the west, guards brought them dinner, along with fresh jugs of water and their cigarette allowance. The food was pushed through the iron slats on trays, and the two prisoners sat by their table to eat.

'How's the book?' Van asked.

'Alright, but it's not telling me anything about the Third Ascendant that I didn't already know. If I hadn't heard Lord Renko say that it was her, I wouldn't believe it.'

'And he was sure?'

Sohul pushed his empty plate to the side. 'He was. The moment he saw her approaching, fighting alongside the Holdfast beast, his eyes… changed. He actually looked scared. She's the real reason he fled with the Quadrant, I think. He gave up as soon as he saw her.'

'Joaz also believed it.'

'It seems too incredible to be true. Why would the Third Ascendant reappear after so long? And if this woman really is her, then why didn't she just lift her hand and destroy the entire Banner; why would she lower herself by actually fighting with a sword? It doesn't make any sense.'

'I wonder what the gods of Implacatus will make of it. Do you think old Edmond will be scared?'

Sohul frowned at him.

'Sorry. I meant, do you think the Blessed Second Ascendant might be a tad concerned at her return?'

The lieutenant opened his mouth to reply, then stopped and nodded to the door of the chamber. Outside, Lord Irno was standing, watching them.

Van glanced at the demigod. 'Can we help you?'

'Good evening,' Irno said.

'Finding our conversation interesting, were you?'

Irno nodded. 'Yes. I too wonder what the response of the Ascendants will be, just as I doubted that Belinda really is who she says she is. I doubt no longer, but I also doubted Corthie's story that he had battle-vision until I saw him in action. My sister seems to have attracted the strangest allies to my castle.'

'If you're here for information,' said Sohul, 'then you'll be disappointed.'

Irno laughed. 'Do you recall that man who came to visit you yesterday evening? He's my cousin, and he has vision powers. He read everything out of your heads that I might need.'

Van frowned.

'I see that you think I'm lying. I'm not. His name is Naxor, and I asked him to delve into your minds to look for any indications of what you think the gods of Implacatus might choose to do next. Based upon what he told me, I am here to make you an offer.'

'What kind of offer?' said Van.

'You are the most senior Banner officer in custody, Captain Logos. Only you have the authority to command the rank and file currently filling every prison cell in the Falls of Iron. I would like to offer you a contract, to work for me.'

Sohul snorted.

'The Banner soldiers are well-trained and disciplined,' Irno went on, 'and I am in need of good soldiers. I would pay double what you were earning under your old contract, and you would be released as soon as I had your agreement, your oaths, and your signatures.'

Van shook his head. 'Not possible, I'm afraid.'

Irno frowned. 'Why not?'

'Because our current contracts are still valid. Officially, we remain employees of Her Highness Arete, the Seventh Ascendant.'

'Even though you are prisoners?'

'Yes. Our contracts have a clause that relates to capture.'

'And what does this clause entail?'

'If any member of the Banner is imprisoned by hostile forces, then we remain under contract for a further fifty days, pending release, escape or execution. I was captured on the eleventh day of Tradinch, which still leaves another twenty-odd days to go.'

'I see. What if I were to triple your wages?'

Van shrugged. 'Then I estimate that you might attract twenty volunteers out of the hundred and fifty or so you have in your prisons, but the other soldiers would refuse. After all, as mercenaries, we are only useful if we are reliable, and that means we don't break our contracts.'

'And once you are out of contract?'

Van shrugged. 'Come back and talk to us then, but don't get any hopes up. Working for you would involve the creation of a new Banner, since the Golden Fist would disown us, and many of the soldiers would baulk at that. You might get fifty or sixty volunteers; maybe.'

Irno glared at him. 'But what about you, Captain? If you were to agree, then wouldn't you be able to persuade the other soldiers?'

'I've been with the Golden Fist since I was fifteen, so it's unlikely that I'd agree.'

'What if the alternative was execution?'

'Then I'd sign up, but it would be under duress, and according to the foundational laws of the Banners, I would be free to abscond at the first opportunity. In fact, it would be my duty to do so.'

Irno said nothing, his face red with anger. He turned his back on them, and strode away.

Sohul chuckled. 'Well said, Captain.'

'Just playing hard to get,' Van said. 'If he's really willing to pay treble, then I imagine that most of the lads would take his offer. We'll see if he comes back in a month or so.'

Van opened his eyes, the sound of the door being unlocked awakening him. He glanced around the darkness of the chamber and saw Sohul asleep in his bed, his body outlined by the dim flickering of a lamp in the passageway outside. He turned towards the door, and saw it open. A soldier had the keys in his hand, and he moved to the side to allow a hooded woman to enter, a bag over her shoulder.

'Thanks,' she muttered.

'No problem, ma'am,' he said. 'I'll be right here if you need me.'

The door swung shut, and the woman walked to the table as Van sat up.

'Oh, you're awake,' she said, pulling back the hood.

'What do you want, Miss Holdfast?'

'Don't call me that,' she said, taking a seat. 'My name's Kelsey.'

'Fine. What do you want, Kelsey?'

'A little chat.' She placed the bag onto the table. 'Come and sit.'

'Are you not worried about your safety?'

She snorted. 'No.'

He swung his legs out of bed and pulled on some clothes. He didn't like to admit it, but he was intrigued by her presence, and her brazen confidence. He grabbed a pack of cigarettes from a drawer and went over to the table.

'What time is it?' he said as he sat.

'I don't know. Night-time.'

He raised an eyebrow.

She groaned. 'This isn't going to work. You're an idiot.'

'Excuse me?'

'I said, you're an idiot.'

He let out a low laugh. 'I didn't think you could read minds.'

'I can't. No one can when I'm around.'

'Irno told me that someone called Naxor read my mind a couple of evenings back. Was he lying?'

She frowned at him. 'Oh, so that's why I was asked to go up to the roof for a while? I guessed it was for something along those lines. Naxor read you, eh? He didn't tell me. I should have spoken to him before coming here.'

'Why have you come here?'

'I need to know.'

'Know what?'

She shrugged, and opened the bag. She withdrew a bottle, followed by two glasses and a bundle of weedsticks.

He frowned. 'Is that dreamweed?'

'Mixed with keenweed,' she said. 'I don't want us falling asleep while we get drunk.'

'And what makes you think I want to get drunk with you?'

'I don't care what you want.'

She opened the bottle and filled the two glasses, then offered him one of the weedsticks. He stared at her for a moment, trying to fathom the reason for her visit.

'Did Irno send you?' he said. 'Are you here to try to persuade me to work for him?'

She squinted at him. 'No. Irno doesn't know I'm here. No one does, except for the soldier standing outside the cell, and I had to bribe him to keep quiet. Drink up.'

He picked up the glass and took a sip, feeling the spirits warm his throat. 'What's this?'

'Whisky,' she said. 'It's from my own world. I brought several bottles, and this is the last one. I was saving it.'

'It's good.'

'"Good?" You're joking, right? It's better than good, you fool; it's eighteen-year-old Severton, a gift from the Empress's personal stash.'

'And you thought you'd share it with me? Why?'

She lit a weedstick. 'How old are you?'

'Twenty-eight.'

She nodded. 'Parents alive?'

'My father is. My mother died on an operation a few years ago.'

'An operation?'

'Yes. She was a mercenary, like me.'

'Then why are there no other women in your Banner?'

'Most regiments of the Golden Fist are men-only.'

'Why?'

'I don't know. Tradition, I think. There are some mixed Banners, and some that only admit males.'

Kelsey took a draw and exhaled, the smoke spiralling up into the shadows of the ceiling.

'Is this the only job you've had?'

'Yes.'

'Do you like it?'

He shrugged. 'Sometimes.'

Her glance caught sight of the pile of books by Sohul's bed. 'Do you read?'

'I *can* read.'

'Obviously, but that's not what I asked.'

'Not particularly.'

'A pity. I think you should start.'

He took another sip of whisky. 'I'll bear that in mind.'

'Have you ever been married?'

'No.'

'Children?'

'None that I'm aware of.'

She shook her head. 'What a stupid response.'

He raised an eyebrow. 'Why do you care? I feel like I'm being interviewed for a job.'

'Maybe you are.'

'Yes? What job?'

'When you're at home,' she said, ignoring him, 'what do you do to pass the time?'

'Umm... I don't think I want to answer that.'

'Why not?'

'Because it's none of your business.'

'That's funny. You were happy to answer personal questions about marriage and children, but not this? What are you hiding?' She nodded towards Sohul. 'Should I wake him up and ask him?'

Van said nothing for a moment. He glanced at the bottle of whisky and the weedsticks, part of him not wishing to share them with Sohul.

'You'll judge me for it,' he said.

'I'm judging you with every word that comes out of your mouth.'

'Fine. I'm... uh... I don't cope well with civilian life. I tend to go off the rails, sometimes. My more notorious hobbies include drinking until I fall over, over-indulging in narcotics and spending time with prostitutes.'

She glared at him.

'See?' he said. 'I knew you'd judge me.'

'Prostitutes? You sad freak. Can you not get a woman without paying for one?'

He shrugged. 'I never bother to try. I like women, but relationships just complicate things. Life in the Banner means that I could be sent to any world with only a few days' notice. I'm not exactly marriage material.'

Kelsey lowered her head, and for a moment Van thought he saw a tear slide down her cheek.

'Why do you care?' he said. 'It's clear that you don't like me. Believe me, the feeling's mutual.'

She slapped him across the face.

Van refilled his glass, his cheek smarting. 'I'm having more whisky for that.' He took a drink then lit a weedstick as she watched him. 'I'm not wrong, am I?' he said. 'You don't like me.'

'You're not wrong,' she said.

'Then what's the problem? Look, I'm grateful that you saved my life. What you did took courage, and I feel like I owe you for it, but this is all a bit... weird.'

'Folk have been calling me that since I was little,' she said. 'I should have known that you'd do the same.'

'I'm sorry I disappoint you. Maybe if you told me why you were here, then I'd understand a bit better.'

'There's no point,' she mumbled.

They sat in silence for a while, sipping whisky and smoking, as Van tried to go through the possible reasons for Kelsey's presence in his cell, and her generosity. She kept her eyes lowered the entire time, and he wondered if she would notice if he took a few weedsticks for later.

'Have you ever been married?' he said.

'What? Why are you asking me that?'

'I don't know; just being polite, I guess. You asked me the same question.'

'Of course I haven't been married; I'm twenty-one.'

He shrugged. 'Some girls get married younger than that.'

'Don't call me a girl.'

'Fine. Some young women get married younger than twenty-one.'

'Aye, stupid ones.'

'And I'm guessing you have no children?'

'Why are you trying to be friendly, all of a sudden? I preferred it when you were being honest. You don't like me; you've made that clear; don't pretend you do.'

'Alright.'

She stood. 'I made a mistake coming here. I thought that... well, never mind what I thought; I was wrong.' She picked up the whisky, jammed in the stopper, and put the bottle back into the bag. She glanced at the weedsticks. 'You can keep those. I only brought them to Lostwell because I didn't know you could get weed here.'

'Thanks.'

She glared at him. 'Screw you, Van. I hope you choke on them; except I know you won't. Oh, and watch out for Sohul's arm. An elbow in the eye can be quite painful.'

Kelsey picked up the bag and walked to the door. She knocked, and the soldier on the other side opened it for her. She gave a last glance over her shoulder at Van, then left, and the door was closed and locked behind her. Van finished the last of the whisky that remained in his glass, then sat in silence for a moment, trying to work out what Kelsey had wanted. He felt like he had sat some kind of test, and failed. When she had first arrived, a tiny part of him had wondered if she liked him in a romantic way, but that seemed ridiculous; she hated him, it was clear, and that was fine with him. The last thing he wanted was for a crazy Holdfast to have a crush on him. But if not that, then what?

He picked up the bundle of weedsticks. The selfish part of him wanted to hide their existence from Sohul, but it would be impossible to smoke them without him finding out. He glanced at the lieutenant.

'Hey, Sohul,' he cried.

No response.

Van sighed and got up. He walked to the side of the lieutenant's bed, leaned over him, and shook his shoulder.

'Sohul, wake up; I've got a surprise.'

The lieutenant opened his eyes, then jumped, no doubt from finding a shadowy figure lurking over him. He lashed out, and an elbow struck Van in the eye.

'Ow!' Van yelled. 'What the...?'

Sohul sat up and stared around the room. 'What's going on?'

'You whacked me in the face, that's what.'

'Sorry, Captain.'

Van sat down on his own bed, a hand over his painful eye. He remembered Kelsey's last words to him, and he shivered. That's not possible, he thought. How could she have known?

He glanced at Sohul. 'Fancy a smoke?'

CHAPTER 4
AMONG THE DEAD

T orduan Mountains, Western Khatanax – 5th Abrinch 5252
Maddie pulled off her boots and ran into the water, her feet splashing through the shallows by the side of the vast mountain reservoir. The midday sun was roasting hot, and the feel of the cool water was wonderful on her toes.

She turned. 'Get in here, Millen; it's lovely.'

The young man frowned from the rocky bank. 'No.'

She kicked a great gout of water at him, spraying his clothes.

'Quit that!' he cried.

'Don't be such a misery guts,' she laughed. 'It's cool, clean water.'

'It won't be clean any more, not with your feet in it.'

She shook her head at him, then leaped into the deeper water a few feet from the bank, her travel-worn clothes bobbing up with air pockets. She submerged her head, and a swarm of bubbles rose to the surface, then she pushed herself up, grinning. She kicked out, and waded back to the edge.

'You're crazy,' he said.

'Come in, and we can be crazy together,' she yelled, her arms splashing him as she sat down in a foot of water.

'Stop it, that's really annoying.'

'Malik's ass, what's the matter with you? We've seen nothing but barren mountains for days, and before that nothing but ocean. Do you not want to cool off from the sun?'

'I'm fine here, thank you very much.'

Sanguino turned his thick scaly neck towards them. His vast bulk was stretched out along the bank, half in, and half out of the water.

'The boy obviously cannot swim,' said the dragon.

Maddie raised an eyebrow. 'But he lived right next to an ocean. Is that true, Millen; can't you swim?'

'No, as a matter of fact.'

Maddie shrugged. 'Neither can I.' She leaned backwards and fell into the water. Her hands reached for the stony bed of the reservoir, and she pushed herself along, her head facing the sky, the water lapping about her ears. When it got too deep, she brought her legs down and stood, the water coming up to her thighs. She pushed the wet hair from her face and glanced around. The reservoir was set into a natural bowl in the mountains that had been dammed at its western end. With no wind, its surface was reflecting the deep blue of the sky, and the dazzling rays of the sun. To the north, east and south bulked the huge mountains they had been flying over. They were the highest she had ever seen, much taller than the range near the City where they had found the salve mine, and they seemed to go on forever. She brought her glance down and saw Millen sitting on the bank a few yards from where Sanguino was resting his head. The dark red dragon looked magnificent. The wounds he had received in the Central Pits had faded, and his strength and health had seemed to improve with every day that had passed since his escape.

He wasn't Blackrose, she thought, but he was a fine looking dragon all the same.

She waded back to the bank and climbed out, dripping water onto Millen. He shuffled to the side, and she dripped some more on him.

'I'm going to keep annoying you,' she said, 'and not because I enjoy it. I mean, I do enjoy it, but not just for that reason.' She shook her hair, and he raised his hands as water flew at him. 'As your friend,' she went on, 'it's my duty to distract you, so that you're not thinking about Sable all the time.'

'I wasn't thinking about Sable.'

'Yeah, right. Go on, then; what were you thinking about?'

He glanced at her. 'Food.'

The dragon opened an eye. 'Are you hungry?'

Millen nodded.

'Then you should have said so.' Sanguino raised himself up on his great limbs. He stretched out his wings and shook them, showering Maddie and Millen with water. 'I shall hunt for you, and for myself. I glimpsed deer on the lower slopes, due west of here. Remain where you are; I shall be back soon and you shall feast.'

He beat his enormous wings and lifted into the sky.

Maddie sat down and watched him go, a frown on her face. 'And what am I supposed to eat? Weeds?'

'He can't hear you,' said Millen.

She glared at him. 'I know that. It's alright for you; you can gorge yourself on scorched deer flesh until you throw up, whereas I get nothing. Again. Maybe I should ask Sanguino to hunt some wheat or berries for me.'

'There are probably fish in the reservoir,' Millen said. 'What about them?'

'What? Are fish not alive? In what way does fish not count as meat?'

'Vegetables are also alive, in case you hadn't noticed.'

'Shut up.'

He laughed. 'A minute ago, you were accusing me of being the miserable one; now look at you.'

'It's your fault. Why did you have to bring up the topic of food?'

'Because I'm hungry.'

'So am I! Malik's ear trumpet, what I would do for an apple or some warm, fresh bread and a slab of cheese.' Her stomach rumbled. 'Did you hear that? I need a town, with a marketplace; I can't survive like this.' She lay down on the ground, one hand on her empty belly. She gazed up at the sky, squinting her eyes to avoid the sun. 'Nothing but blue.'

'I was lying before,' Millen said after a while; 'I was thinking about Sable.'

She eyed him. 'I knew it.'

'I can't help it; I worry about her. Why hasn't she been in contact?'

'She has no idea where we are; no one does.'

'Then we should have stayed closer to Alea Tanton for longer. She could be in trouble, and trying to speak to us, and she can't find us...' He groaned. 'Maybe I should go back.'

'Feel free to start walking,' she said.

'We've been searching these mountains for days, Maddie. I know he denies it, but Sanguino doesn't know where the wild dragons live. It's been forty years since he was last there, and he's forgotten how to find it.' He paused for a moment. 'What if we never find Blackrose?'

Maddie said nothing. Part of her, the hungry part, was starting to think that maybe Millen had a point, but she couldn't give up. It had only been two days without food; surely she could last a little longer? It was either that, or she went back to eating meat temporarily, but the thought made her feel sick.

'On the bright side,' Millen said, 'at least you've lost some weight.'

She glared at him, her fists clenching. 'Asshole.'

He lifted his palms. 'Only joking.'

'Hilarious,' she said. 'My brother used to make "jokes" like that; well, he did until I beat him to a pulp.'

'You have a brother?'

'Yeah, and a little sister.'

'In Kinell?'

'Where?'

'Kinell. You know, the place where you and Sable are supposed to be from?'

'Oh yeah. Kinell.'

'I'd love to see the capital of Kinell. What's it called again?'

'Umm, Kinell City?'

He laughed. 'Isn't it about time you told me where you're really from? I mean, we're in this together, like it or not. I can never return to

Alea Tanton, not after we were seen helping Sanguino escape. Once we find your dragon, are we going to travel to where you live?'

'That will be a "no".'

'Why not? Are you exiles? On the run? How do you know Sable?'

'Let me see. Exiles isn't the right word for it, but we're not on the run. And the truth is, I don't really know Sable – I've only spoken to her once in my head, when she helped free me from the fortress. I know her nephew, though.'

'Is he the guy you said could rip me in half?'

'Yeah, but don't feel bad, he could rip a greenhide in half. He's killed thousands of them.'

Millen laughed. 'Now I know you're exaggerating. Alright, if your home's not in Kinell, then where is it?'

Maddie sighed, trying to conjure reasons why she shouldn't tell Millen the truth. He had seemed trustworthy enough on their journey around the northern coastline of Khatanax, and during their search through the mountains, but she didn't know how he'd react if she told him she was from another world. She glanced at him. His gaze was on the surface of the reservoir, while twenty days' of growth was on his chin and upper lip. He was slight, but handsome, and the half-grown beard made him seem a little older.

'What do you want, Millen?' she said. 'Out of the two of us, you're the exile. You said it yourself; you can't go home. What if it doesn't work out between you and Sable? Because, let's face it, it's not looking likely at the moment. It doesn't really matter where I'm from; what's important is where I'm going; and you can't come with me. And I don't mean finding Blackrose, I mean after that.'

Millen remained still, sitting on the rocky shore with his hands clasped by his knees, his eyes on the horizon.

After a while, Maddie turned onto her side, her left arm propping her up. 'Say something.'

He shrugged. 'You've just told me that you're going to abandon me, presumably in a nest of wild dragons. What is there to say?'

'We could drop you off somewhere first. Maybe Kinell?'

'No,' he said. 'You have your destination; you know what you have to do, and I do too. I have to find Sable. Once we get to your dragon, then you can help me find her before you go.'

'I can't promise that. I'll need to ask Blackrose first; see what she thinks. You helped free Sanguino, so you might have a good chance. But I'd give up on Sable, if I were you.'

'Yeah, yeah, I know; I'm not in her league, I...' His voice tailed off. 'Look, Sanguino's back already.'

Maddie glanced up, and saw a tiny black speck in the sky above them. 'That was quick. He must be getting better at hunting.'

She sat up, and they both watched the speck circle lower. Maddie frowned. There was something strange about the way the speck was moving. Her eyes widened.

'Get into the water,' she said.

'Forget it,' Millen said. 'I've already told you...'

'Shut up,' she cried. 'That's not Sanguino.'

She grabbed his arm as he gazed open-mouthed into the sky. Above them, the black speck separated into two; a pair of dragons circling each other, and getting lower. Millen sprang up, and they ran into the water of the reservoir, splashing and wading until it was waist-deep. Maddie hunkered down, leaving just the top of her head above the surface, and she pulled Millen down to the same level.

'What if he's found a friend?' he said.

'Then we can get back out again. Now, stay as still as you can.'

The two dragons were swooping through the sky above them; black silhouettes against the harsh light of the afternoon sun. Maddie squinted, but it was impossible to tell if either of them was Sanguino. The larger of the pair wheeled away, and the other chased, and they soared lower, heading straight for the reservoir. The lead dragon pulled up just before striking the surface of the water, and extended its limbs, sending up funnels of spray to either side. The other dragon cried out, calling, then banked and landed by the shore.

Maddie gasped. The dragon by the shore was a silvery-grey female, her scales shining in the sunlight, while the dragon still swooping over the water was a dark green male, with streaks of blue on his wings. The silver dragon leaned her long neck forwards, and began to drink from the reservoir, while the other splashed and soared over the surface.

'What do we do now?' whispered Millen.

'Shut up,' Maddie hissed. 'And don't move.'

The green dragon swooped upwards, a large fish clutched in each forelimb. He banked, then turned for the shore, dropping one of the fish in front of the silver dragon, before landing next to her. The two dragons ate, then drank, their slender necks dipping into the water. The green dragon shoved the silver one, and they wrestled for a moment, each raising their forelimbs to push and grapple, then the silver dragon took off and settled down again a few yards away. She turned from the green dragon and began to preen herself, her head inspecting every corner of her great wings.

'We need to get out of here,' said Millen, his voice wavering.

'Shush; stay still.'

Millen started to edge backward, then his foot slipped on the bottom, and a small series of ripples eddied across the surface of the reservoir. The head of the silver dragon darted out, her eyes on the dark water, her entire body frozen as she scanned the surface. Her red eyes glowed, and she called to her green companion.

'Insects,' she cried. 'Insects, in our pool.'

The green dragon stopped drinking and swung his long neck round, then they both stared in the direction of Maddie and Millen.

'Soldiers?' said the green dragon.

'No,' said the silver. 'Dinner.'

The silver dragon beat her wings and took off. She shot forward in a burst of speed, then hovered directly over Maddie and Millen, her head gazing down at them.

'This is our pool, insects,' she cried, her rows of jagged teeth bared, 'and you will pay for trespassing.'

'Wait!' cried Maddie. 'We didn't know the pool belonged to you. We'll leave; we're sorry.'

'Too late for that,' she cried, as coils of lightning sparked and crackled over her jaws.

'Don't burn them,' said the green dragon, watching. 'I prefer my meat fresh.'

'How did you get here?' said the silver dragon, ignoring her companion.

Millen yelled in terror, and began to wade away as fast as he could, making for the shore. The silver dragon laughed, the cruel noise echoing off the steep mountain sides, then she lunged down, and grasped Millen with her right forelimb, plucking him out of the water. He shrieked and writhed, but the dragon held him fast. She rose up, her nose sniffing her captured prey, then she dropped Millen onto the rocky shore. He plunged fifty feet, screaming, then hit the ground and lay still.

'I'll take this one,' said the silver dragon. 'You can do as you wish with the other.'

She landed by the body of Millen, and nudged his motionless body with a claw.

'Leave him alone!' cried Maddie from the water, her body shivering despite the heat. She felt a shadow pass overhead, and glanced up to see the green dragon above her, his pale blue eyes regarding her with amusement.

'Run,' he said to her; 'I like the chase.'

Maddie stood up in the water, her eyes on Millen.

'I said run,' cried the green dragon.

'No,' she said, folding her arms. 'You killed my friend; I'm not running for your enjoyment.'

The silver dragon laughed. 'This insect isn't dead yet,' she said, pawing at Millen's body, 'but he will be, as soon as I bite his head off.'

Another shadow swooped overhead, and a dark red blur soared down, slamming into the flank of the silver dragon and knocking her off balance. The green dragon cried out, his head turning.

'Don't touch my humans!' roared Sanguino, his claws raised towards the silver dragon.

Maddie stared. She hadn't noticed how massive Sanguino truly was until that moment. The green and silver dragons were large, but Sanguino's bulk far out-weighed theirs. He towered over the silver dragon, his front limbs shielding Millen's body from her.

'You will pay for that!' cried the silver dragon as she regained her poise, her jaws open.

Above Maddie, the green dragon beat his wings and rose into the sky, as if fleeing. Sanguino kept his gaze on the silver dragon, his claws out, and the two of them froze for a moment, each waiting for the other to strike.

Without warning, a great burst of fire exploded down from the sky, engulfing Sanguino's head and neck. The green dragon dived, and his rear limbs raked their claws across Sanguino's red-scaled back. At the same time, the silver dragon's head shot forward, her jaws clasping round Sanguino's neck as he cried out. Despite his size, he floundered around, swiping at the two smaller dragons uselessly. The green dragon swooped again, his claws ripping through Sanguino's right flank, spraying blood over the rocky shore. The silver dragon's teeth were still clinging onto his neck, and he shrieked in pain and alarm, his cry reverberating across the valley.

Maddie waded to the shore as fast as she could, then ran to where Millen was lying unconscious on the ground, his right leg twisted beneath him. The three dragons were embroiled in one mass, as the green slashed out, his rear limbs digging into Sanguino's back, as the silver held his neck tightly in her jaws. Maddie started to drag Millen away, then stopped as a dozen more specks appeared in the sky, attracted by the fierce roars and cries. Maddie crouched down. They were trapped.

Three huge dragons swooped down and landed fifty yards along the shore, their eyes watching dispassionately as the silver and green mauled and tore at Sanguino. Others circled overhead, then came down on the far side of the fight, but none of them showed any interest in intervening. One of them, a sleek, small yellow-golden dragon, spied Maddie. Its eyes widened, and it began to stalk forwards, its wings low, its teeth glistening.

The ground shook as a black dragon landed in front of Maddie. It raised a forelimb at the yellow-golden dragon, who hissed and backed away, its orange eyes shimmering with hate.

'Blackrose!' Maddie cried.

She half turned her head towards her. 'Stay back, and stay low. Do you have a Quadrant?'

'Eh, no.'

Her dark eyes narrowed, but she said nothing, and turned to face the others.

'Blackrose,' Maddie said, 'you have to help Sanguino; they're going to kill him.'

'Who?' she said.

'The dark red dragon,' Maddie cried; 'they're tearing him to pieces. Please, Blackrose. He's a friend.'

Blackrose glared, her expression furious, but remained still.

'Please, Blackrose! Those two dragons were going to kill us. I owe him my life.'

'You bring me no Quadrant, and now you ask this of me? You try my patience, rider.'

The silver dragon released her grip on Sanguino's neck, and his head fell, the light in his lime green eyes fading. The silver dragon swept a clawed limb across his face, ripping through the scales and spraying the ground in blood, as the green dragon moved closer, ready to make the kill.

Blackrose beat her wings and surged forward. With a single blow, she batted the green dragon away, then she bared her teeth at the silver, her jaws sparking. The other dragons by the shore watched, but said nothing.

'The blood-red dragon is under my protection,' Blackrose bellowed, her fierce eyes staring down at the silver and green as they backed away.

'Insect-lover,' sneered the green dragon.

'I beat your father in a fight,' Blackrose growled; 'what makes you think I won't destroy you? Back, both of you, or I'll kill you and leave your bodies for the crows.'

An enormous grey dragon with scars covering his flanks took off from the shore and landed by Blackrose's side.

'The silver one is my daughter,' he said, his eyes on Blackrose. 'If you kill her, then I will do the same to you.'

'Brave words, Deathfang,' said Blackrose, 'but I think you know who would win if I fought you. Tell your daughter and her companion to leave, and no one need die.'

The grey dragon stared at her, then nodded to his daughter. 'Be off with you. Your games are over for today.' He turned back to Blackrose. 'I'll not forget this insult. Be careful, insect-lover. Strong you may be, but you are only one dragon among many here, and you may find the Catacombs a less friendly place, should you be brave enough to return.'

He beat his wings and rose into the air. He hovered for a moment, until the silver and green dragons also took off, then they turned for the southeast and flew away. The other dragons by the shore said nothing, but one by one they took to the air, and sped off after Deathfang, until Blackrose was left standing by the limp body of Sanguino.

She sniffed the wound on his neck, then turned to Maddie, her eyes gleaming with rage.

'Do you know what you have done?'

'It's good to see you too, Blackrose.'

'For a score of days I have been fighting for the respect of the Catacomb dragons, and in one minute you destroy everything I have achieved. I sent you to get a Quadrant, and instead you bring me a boy and...' She turned to Sanguino; 'and this unworthy specimen of dragonhood. Where did you find him; in the gutters of Alea Tanton?'

'He was a pit dragon,' Maddie said, 'and we helped him escape.'

'Why?'

'Because it wasn't right what they were doing to him. They were going to kill him.'

'So? Am I supposed to feel sympathy for this beast? He was out-manoeuvred and out-fought by two mere children, and now I am pledged to protect him.'

Millen groaned, then cried out in pain. 'My leg!' He opened his eyes and saw Blackrose staring down at him. He cried out in terror, his hands raised.

Blackrose looked at him with contempt.

'This is Millen,' said Maddie.

Blackrose's eyes glowed red. 'You found a lover?'

'Eh, no,' Maddie said, 'just a friend. He knows Sable.'

'And where is the Holdfast woman? Let me guess, she let you down? She betrayed you, just as the other Holdfasts have done? Rider, you have failed me.'

Maddie ignored her, and helped Millen into a sitting position. His right leg was broken, and he yelled in pain as Maddie straightened it.

'Millen,' she said, 'say hello to Blackrose.'

He stared at the black dragon, terror in his eyes, then he noticed the body of Sanguino. 'Is he dead?'

'No,' said Blackrose, 'though my life would be considerably easier if he were.' She dipped her head into the reservoir, then turned to the blood-red dragon and sprayed his face with water.

Sanguino spluttered. His eyes opened and he writhed for a moment as if still under attack, then raised his head, the teeth marks on his neck dripping blood over the ground. He caught sight of Blackrose and cowered back.

'I own you now,' Blackrose said. 'I saved your life; you are mine. Bow before me.'

Sanguino limped backwards a few paces, his eyes never leaving Blackrose. 'Who are you?'

'I am Blackrose. Bow, or die.'

Sanguino glanced at Millen and Maddie.

'I am your master,' said Blackrose. 'Say it.'

His lime green eyes widened. 'You are my master.'

'Good. Do not speak again unless I address you.'

Sanguino bowed his head.

Blackrose turned back to Maddie. 'We must return to the Catacombs and start afresh. Know that I cannot guarantee your safety. I will strive to defend you, but dozens of dragons live in the Catacombs, and I cannot be everywhere at once. I advise leaving your friend here to die. He will be nothing but a burden, especially injured.'

'What?' said Maddie. 'Twenty days of living with wild dragons, and you're asking me to leave a friend to die? Is this what life in the Catacomb-place has done to you? What happened to honour?'

'There is no honour among wild dragons,' Blackrose said, but the gleam in her eyes had faded a little.

'But you're not wild,' Maddie said, 'you're a queen; you should know better.'

Blackrose shook her head. 'Do you realise that I have had to fight for my life nearly every day since I arrived here? I have been ambushed, assaulted while I slept, and challenged every time I open my mouth. Do you notice that my rider's harness has gone? It was ripped from my back on my first day in the Catacombs. Eight dragons held me down while Deathfang tore it to shreds. They saw it as proof of my weakness, and every day since I have done nothing but show them their mistake. But now? They watched as I scared off two mere children, and said nothing as I pledged myself to protecting a fat, weak, useless insult to the good name of dragons. They will be laughing at me.'

'Alright,' said Maddie; 'you've made your point, but I'm not leaving Millen.'

'As you wish, but *you* must care for him,' said Blackrose. 'Climb onto my back.'

Maddie stood, and began clambering up the left flank of the black dragon. Blackrose picked up Millen in her right forelimb, her claws tightly pressed around his chest. She glanced at the blood-red dragon.

'Sanguino,' she said, 'if that is truly your name; can you fly? Before you answer, know that if you say "no", I will kill you.'

Sanguino cowered before her. 'I can fly.'

Maddie made it to the top of Blackrose's shoulders, and clung on. The black dragon beat her wings and rose into the air, and Sanguino joined her. His right wing was ripped in places, and Maddie could see the pain in his lime green eyes, but he said nothing. Blackrose sped off, soaring southeast, in the same direction that Deathfang and the others had taken. They crossed the rest of the reservoir, and climbed up and over a high mountain ridge. The barren, rocky slopes rushed beneath them, and Maddie felt the wind against her face. For thirty minutes, Balckrose hurtled through the air, crossing ridge after ridge of featureless mountains. Nothing grew on the slopes, nor in the valleys, and the air had a burnt smell to it. They came to a great rift in the mountains that stretched from north to south.

'This is the pass that used to connect Kinell to Fordia,' Blackrose said, 'though no humans cross it these days.'

On the western edge of the rift sat two towering volcanoes, just a few miles apart, and Blackrose flew between them. Maddie glanced down, and saw great rivers of molten rock flowing down the edge of the ravine and spilling into the valley below. Vapours and steam were rising up, and the air itself felt hot. When they were above the rift, Blackrose turned, and circled lower. Built into the side of the western edge was a series of massive buildings, with pillars and archways, built on many levels. Ancient stairways had been carved into the side of the ravine, but most were in ruins, and many of the arched entrances were blackened.

'This is the Catacombs,' said Blackrose. 'Hundreds of old human tombs, cut into the side of the cliff. The tunnels and chambers stretch back for a mile, and many are wide and high enough to make comfortable homes for my wild brethren. Deathfang occupies the largest – the tomb of an ancient king.'

She spiralled lower, and Maddie started to sweat from the heat rising in waves from the rivers and pools of lava flowing beneath them.

'I, on the other hand,' Blackrose went on, 'have to make do with a lesser chamber.'

She swooped down further, then flew close to the cliff, towards a square opening flanked with ancient pillars. She gestured to Sanguino, and he entered, his limbs landing inside the opening. Blackrose waited until he had shuffled his wounded bulk further in, then followed. The floor and walls of the long chamber were blackened, scorched, and stank, while the heat coming up from the lava flows was almost unbearable. Blackrose pushed Sanguino further in, then turned and set Millen down onto the filthy, broken ground.

Maddie clambered down to join him, a hand covering her nose. 'Is this where you've been living?'

'Yes,' said Blackrose, 'and it took me five victories to earn the right to stay here unmolested. After Deathfang's threats however, I fear what may occur this night, so I shall remain by the entrance. There is food and water in a chamber behind you to the left. Eat, drink and rest.'

She moved up to the square entrance and sat, her dark eyes scanning the outside. Maddie crouched by Millen, and helped him up. He leaned on her, his right leg useless, and they limped along the wide chamber. Ahead of them, Sanguino collapsed in a heap, blood leaking from a dozen wounds.

'Thank you,' said Maddie to the dark-red dragon. 'You saved us; again.'

Sanguino closed his eyes and said nothing, resting his head on his giant forelimbs. Maddie helped Millen into a massive chamber on the left, where the heat and smell weren't as bad, and they sat on a low stone bench by a pile of goat and deer carcasses. Water was flowing down the rear of one wall, coming from a small outlet in the ceiling, and Maddie cupped her hands under it and drank.

She grimaced from the bitter taste, then glanced around in the semi-darkness. A giant sarcophagus sat at the end of the chamber, and other, smaller ones were arranged in a row next to it, lining the wall.

She attempted a smile. 'We made it.'

Millen glanced at her, pain creasing his face. 'I should have stayed in Alea Tanton.'

CHAPTER 5
THE DEADLINE

Falls of Iron, Western Khatanax – 6th Abrinch 5252

Corthie and Aila trudged up the steep stone steps, the sun blazing down at them from the vast blue sky. Crowds had watched as they had walked through the town of the Falls of Iron, after having journeyed all the way from the forests of the Glebe. The cheers that had resounded for Corthie's victory almost a month before had been replaced with a sombre silence, and the townsfolk had worried looks on their faces.

The two of them reached the top of the steps and walked onto the castle forecourt, the whitewashed gatehouse looming up in front of them. No guards or courtiers were there to greet them, and they strode up to the open gates. A handful of militia soldiers on duty stared at them.

'Lady Aila; Lord Corthie,' said one, bowing; 'welcome back to the Falls of Iron.' He glanced around.

'We came back alone,' said Aila, her eyes grim. 'Our guards were murdered in the Glebe.'

The militia said nothing as they entered the castle. They walked through the inner courtyard, passing the entrance to the dungeons, while workers and militia stopped what they were doing to watch.

'I could sleep for a week,' said Corthie as they approached the keep.

'And I'd wrestle a dragon for a bath,' said Aila, 'but I guess we'd better tell Irno that we're back.'

They entered the keep and walked past more guards on their way to Irno's rooms. Aila knocked on the door to his study, and they entered. Inside, the Count of the Falls of Iron was sitting in his favourite chair, while Vana and Naxor were smoking cigarettes by an open window.

All eyes turned to them.

Naxor laughed. 'You're looking rather travel-worn, cousin.'

'You're back, I see.'

'Yes, I returned the same day you left for the Glebe. I was a little bedraggled upon my arrival, but you, my dear? You look like you've been dragged backwards through a bush.'

'It was a long walk,' she said, heading for the side table. She filled two large mugs with cool ale, and handed one to Corthie. Irno got to his feet as Aila and Corthie drained the liquid from the mugs.

'Bad news?' he said, once they had finished.

'The worst,' said Aila. 'Gloag killed our six militia, and tried to kill Corthie. He was going to hold me as a hostage.'

Vana put her hands to her mouth.

'And yet you survived,' said Naxor.

'Only due to Corthie's battle-vision,' she said. 'We were lucky to escape.'

Irno's face paled. 'Did you kill Count Gloag?'

'I didn't kill anyone,' said Corthie, collapsing into a chair. 'We had no weapons, and we were alone in his tower. If Gloag hadn't enjoyed listening to the sound of his own voice so much, I'd be dead and Aila would be in chains.'

'He sold us out to the gods of Implacatus,' said Aila, 'and he told us that Cape Armour and Kaulsnaughton were also against us. We'll get no aid from the other Counties.'

'This is a disaster,' said Vana; 'they were our only hope.'

'Let's not over-react,' said Irno; 'our position remains strong.' He strode to the side table and poured himself a raki. 'Gloag's treachery hurts, but it's not the end, and, once this is over, we will pay him back in full for what he has done.'

'I would have helped,' said Naxor, 'had I known what was happening, but with Kelsey here, I can't vision out of the castle.'

'What happened to Sable?' said Corthie. 'Did you find her?'

'I did, but it's a long story. The short version is that, after I rescued her from certain death, she stole the Quadrant I had found, and abandoned me in Alea Tanton. A charming woman, your aunt. Treacherous, but charming.'

He narrowed his eyes at the demigod. 'I think I'd like to hear her version of what happened.'

'Good luck with that,' Naxor said. 'I doubt she'll be seen in these parts again.'

'And you're saying she has a Quadrant?'

'That is indeed what I'm saying.'

'Where was she going with it?'

'It must have slipped her mind to tell me.'

'Stop squabbling and let me think,' frowned Irno, the glass of raki in his hand as he paced the floor of his study.

'Count Gloag showed us a letter he had received from Alea Tanton,' said Aila.

Irno nodded. 'I have also received a letter, from Governor Felice. It seems she has been promoted, and is now ruling Khatanax.'

'What did it say?'

'Felice is demanding the immediate surrender of three things – our knowledge regarding the salve trade, the Holdfasts, and Belinda. She stated that if I were to hand over all of these, then not only would I be allowed to live, but I would also be generously rewarded with lands and gold.'

'And if you don't hand them over?'

'Then she promised that the Falls of Iron would be utterly destroyed, down to every last man, woman, child and farm animal. The fields would be poisoned, and every building reduced to rubble. Also, my sisters and I would be taken in chains to Implacatus for endless torture, presumably for the amusement of the Ascendants.'

Vana let out a sob.

Aila frowned. 'Was a deadline included?'

'Yes,' said Irno. He glanced out of the nearest window. 'It's due to expire today. Naturally, I have neglected to answer.'

'Are they bluffing?' said Corthie.

'Unlikely. I had Naxor read the minds of a couple of captured Banner officers. Both are convinced that Implacatus will send further forces to Lostwell. It seems we may have celebrated our victory too soon.'

Corthie shrugged. 'If they return, then we do the same thing to them, and we keep doing it until they give up and never come back.'

'If Sable hadn't stolen the Quadrant,' said Naxor, 'then we could all go back to the City, and wait there until things blow over. She's ruined everything.'

Corthie stared at Naxor for a moment, then turned to the others. 'Where are Belinda and Kelsey? If we're discussing what to do, then they should be here.'

'Belinda will be with that filthy animal,' said Naxor.

Aila raised an eyebrow. 'I hope you're not describing Silva.'

Naxor laughed. 'No, though she'll be hanging around close by, no doubt. I was referring to Belinda's cat. I can't abide it.'

'Belinda adopted a stray?' said Corthie. 'She always liked cats.'

'Yes? Well, it loathes me.'

'It's probably a good judge of character.'

'Enough,' said Irno. 'You have a point, Corthie, about Belinda and Kelsey. We should fetch them.'

Aila groaned. 'I know this is urgent, but Corthie and I have been sleeping rough and walking for three days. I need a bath, food, and some sleep, preferably in a bed.'

'You two were sleeping under the stars?' grinned Naxor. 'How romantic.'

'Let's convene in an hour,' said Irno. 'Naxor, fetch Belinda; Aila, take a bath; and Corthie, go and see your sister and bring her down here. I'll order lunch. Are we agreed?'

Corthie glanced at his stained and worn clothes. 'I might need a bath too.'

'As long as we're all back here in an hour,' said Irno. 'Now, I would like to be left alone to think.'

The others got to their feet and walked to the door, as Irno turned towards the open window, his hands clasped behind his back, and his eyes dark.

'Oh, it's you,' said Kelsey as she opened her bedroom door.

Corthie frowned and walked in. Kelsey sat down on the edge of the bed, her gaze lowered, and Corthie took the only chair.

'You should open a window,' he said. 'It reeks of weed smoke in here.'

She shrugged. 'Who cares?'

'So,' he went on, 'I was away for five days, and nearly got killed.'

'You didn't though. I knew you wouldn't.'

'How?'

She squinted at him. 'I, uh, need to tell you something.'

'What?'

She raked around in an over-flowing ashtray until she found a half-smoked weedstick. She wiped the ash and grime from the end and placed it in her mouth, then lit it with a match.

He frowned as he watched her. 'Do you think I might get an answer today?'

'Don't be sarcastic with me, little brother; it doesn't suit you. You're the annoyingly cheerful, optimistic one, or have you forgotten?'

'I may have, recently. What did you want to tell me?'

She glanced at him, her eyes narrow. 'You know how Karalyn can catch glimpses of the future?'

'Aye.'

'Well, the thing is, I can too.'

Corthie's mouth opened and he stared at her.

She took a drag of the weedstick. 'I knew you weren't going to die in the Glebe, because I had a vision of you. It was of nothing important, in fact it was quite mundane. But it wasn't in the Glebe, so I knew you'd survive that.'

'Wow. Alright.'

'You seem to be taking it well.'

'I guess I was used to it with Karalyn. Thanks for telling me, though. Now, can I ask you something? Have you spoken to Naxor?'

'I try to avoid that weasel if at all possible.'

'What did you make of his story about Sable?'

She frowned. 'What did you make of it?'

'I thought he was speaking complete bollocks.'

'Oh. Maybe you're not as dull-witted as I heretofore suspected, brother. I thought you didn't know Sable.'

'I don't. My guess is based purely on Naxor, and the fact that I *do* know him.'

She nodded. 'I believe that she has a Quadrant; I don't think he was lying about that part.'

'I agree. You know Sable – what do you think she'll do with it?'

'Something reckless. She'll go through all of her options, and discard the ones that seem too easy, or anything that would make it look as though she cares. Then she'll settle on the most stupid, risky choice that's left.'

'She has a deathwish?'

'She thinks that she's beyond redemption, but she also thinks that going out in one final act of glorious stupidity will redeem her. She hates the Holdfasts, yet she longs to be accepted as one, especially by mother. It can't be easy being Sable.'

'You have visions, Kelsey; it can't be easy being you, either.'

She glared at him. 'Is that supposed to make me feel better?'

'Just trying to sympathise. I did a lot of thinking on the journey to and from the Glebe, about my purpose; our purpose. The Holdfasts were created for a reason, and I...'

Kelsey shrieked and put her hands to her ears, closing her eyes.

Corthie stared at her, falling silent.

She opened one eye. 'Have you stopped?'

He frowned.

'Good,' she said, removing her hands from her head. 'Never do that again, Corthie. Don't ever talk to me about a higher purpose, or that you think we were created for a reason. Dream mages are a mistake; our bloodline is a mistake; the Creator never meant for us at all. That's the truth.'

He shrugged. 'It's your opinion.'

'You know, I'm not surprised you've started to think this way, not after everything you've done over the last year or so, but believe me, brother, trusting to a higher destiny will do you no good.'

He said nothing for a while, not wishing to prolong the argument. He knew Kelsey was the most intelligent of the four Holdfast children, but maybe that was her problem; she thought she knew everything, and always believed she was right.

'Have you had any other visions?' he said.

She stubbed out the weedstick and coughed.

He waited.

She avoided eye contact with him, keeping her gaze on the floor, her head down.

'I assume you have,' he said, 'but don't want to tell me?'

She shrugged.

'Is it bad?'

'Worse things have happened.'

'Who does it affect?'

She glanced up at him, and he noticed dark lines under her eyes.

'You?' he said.

'I don't want to talk about it.'

'You're worrying me, Kelsey.'

'Really? Well, that can't be helped. I could tell you that it doesn't impinge upon your life in any way, if it makes you feel better.'

'How could something bad happening to my sister not impinge on my life?'

'Because you probably won't think that it's bad.'

He raised an eyebrow. 'Eh? You're speaking in riddles again. Maybe if I knew what was coming, then I could help?'

'There's no point; you know how it works.' She took a breath. 'Did you know that I had a boyfriend in Plateau City?'

'No.'

'We were together for a year and a half. I loved him, well, I did at first, though by the end of it I was sick of the sight of him. He wanted to get married, but I said no. Mother said I was foolish for breaking up with him, but I knew he wasn't right for me. Do you understand? I *knew* it.'

'You mean you've had a vision of someone else? Someone who was right for you?'

'I'm not saying any more. Did you come here for a reason, or just for a chat?'

'We're having a meeting downstairs in Irno's study, and I thought you should be there for it.'

'Is this about the letter he got from Alea Tanton?'

'Aye.'

'Can I ask you something before we go?'

'Sure.'

'Eh, when we were younger,' she said, 'I, um, might not always have been a good sister to you.'

He glanced at her. 'Why are you bringing this up now?'

'It was something that someone said to me, and I've been thinking about it. Me and Keir, we...'

'Made my life a nightmare?'

Her face flushed, and she looked away. Anger surged through Corthie, and he tried to slow his breathing. It was a long time ago, he said to himself.

67

'I can't speak for Keir,' she said, her voice low, 'but I'm sorry.'

Corthie felt sick. For years, he had suppressed all of the painful memories from his childhood, and had concentrated on the happier times, few of which involved Keir or Kelsey; but her words had triggered the tormented feelings he had experienced at the hands of his brother and younger sister.

'I'm sorry, Corthie,' she repeated. 'I want you to know that.'

'It's done now,' he said, forcing the words out.

'Is it? Maybe the way you are is partly my fault; maybe we bullied you so much that it helped turn you into a killer.'

He clenched and unclenched his fists, then shook his head and looked away.

'Is it possible?' she said.

'I'm a Holdfast,' he said. 'Aren't we all killers?'

'I'm not. I've never killed anyone, nor am I likely to.'

'What about Keir?'

She nodded. 'Aye, he's a killer, but he always had a mean streak in him. You were the opposite; cheerful, loving, carefree; that's kind of why you annoyed me so much. Keir once used his fire powers to slaughter thousands in a battle, and when I heard about it, I wasn't surprised. But when I saw *you* fight? It shocked me. Kind, gentle Corthie, transformed into a powerful, relentless killer.'

'It was seven years ago that you last saw me; I was twelve. A lot has happened since then. Four years of training as a warrior, for a start, but even before then, mother was training me in Domm. It was battle-vision that made me who I am, Kelsey; not you, and not Keir.'

She raised her head. 'Are you sure?'

'No. How could I ever be completely sure? A million things go into the making of someone, and I'm far from understanding the person I become when I start fighting. It's a shock to me, too. It's like I'm two people at the same time.'

She gave an approximation of a smile. 'Are we friends?'

'Kelsey, you're my sister and I love you. More than that, you came here, all the way to Lostwell, to look for me and Sable. I'm glad you're here. Let's make a deal. I'll never discuss destiny with you again, if you promise never to bring up what happened between us when we were younger.'

'Alright; deal.'

They stood, and Corthie led the way out of her room. She locked the door behind her, and they went down the stairs of the tower to the floor where Irno's study lay. They said nothing on the way, and Corthie's thoughts were filled with memories of his youth. That was the first real conversation he had ever had with the younger of his two sisters, he realised, and it had been painful. He glanced at her. She was a young woman of twenty-one, far from the girl who had tormented him as a boy. He hadn't held a grudge, and seven years apart had softened his recollections of her. And, it must have taken courage to admit she had been wrong and to apologise.

'One last thing,' he said, as they reached the door to the study. 'I accept your apology. I don't hold anything against you for what you did, and I'm glad we're on the same side.'

She looked a little embarrassed, but nodded.

He opened the door and strode in. Lord Irno was in his chair, while Naxor, Vana and Belinda were seated close by. Aila was standing by the side table, putting some food onto a plate.

'Welcome,' said Irno; 'take a seat.'

Corthie and Kesley walked over and sat, then Irno waited until Aila was also seated.

'I have been thinking over our options,' Irno said. He paused, his eyes glancing over everyone in the room. 'We should evacuate.'

Corthie frowned. 'What?'

The others said nothing, each sitting in silence.

'We cannot withstand a repeated or prolonged assault,' Irno went on, 'and I have the people of the Falls of Iron to think about. Why should they suffer because of salve? I have already begun to make the arrangements.'

'This is crazy,' said Corthie. 'If the gods return, we can fight them; you know that Belinda and I can take on anyone who attacks us.'

'Firstly,' said Irno, 'I believe it is a question of "when", rather than "if". The gods of Implacatus will return, and when they do, they will not merely bring one Ancient and a single battalion, not now that they understand our connections to the salve trade. All it would take is for one of us to be captured, and they would learn of the existence of the City, and of the great reserves of salve that remain buried there. Furthermore, they would learn of your world, Corthie, if they do not already know that it exists. We cannot take the chance.'

Corthie glanced around. 'Why am I the only person who looks shocked by this?'

'You were a little late,' said Irno, 'and we had already begun our discussion when you arrived.'

'Evacuation would be the prudent course,' said Naxor.

'Since when were your actions governed by prudence?' spat Corthie.

'Please,' said Irno, raising his palms; 'above all else, this decision requires cool heads. Let us go round the room, and hear everyone's views.' He looked at Aila. 'Sister?'

'I don't know,' she said. 'I'm torn, if I'm honest. I can see the logic in running, but where would we go, and how would we stop the gods from finding us?'

Irno nodded. 'Vana?'

'I don't want to leave the Falls of Iron,' she said. 'I know I haven't been here that long, but it feels like home. Evacuation should be a last resort. In the meantime, why don't we send out people to hunt for another Quadrant?'

'We should be looking for the Sextant,' said Naxor.

Irno frowned at him. 'Please wait your turn, cousin.'

'Sorry; I thought Vana had finished. As I was saying, the Sextant is the key; the gods know of its existence, and they will surely be hunting for it. If they find it, then they wouldn't even need to come to the Falls of Iron; they could use this device to invade our worlds directly. I say we go, and make for the Southern Cape. Silva can guide us to the tomb of Nathaniel, and we can begin our search.'

Irno turned to Belinda. 'What do you think?'

'We don't have enough information to be certain. If we stay, we risk being trapped here; and if we go, we risk being caught out in the open. And what are we fighting for? To protect the two worlds you all come from? Is that our main goal, or are we just looking to survive? That's what we need to decide first.'

'Thank you. Kelsey?'

The young woman glanced around. 'What?'

'Your opinion, please?'

'About what?'

Irno sighed. 'Have you been listening to our discussion?'

'Not really. I was distracted.'

'By what?'

'None of your business.'

'Can we get back to my question?' said Belinda. 'If we know what we're trying to achieve, then that will help us work out the best course of action.'

'Keeping our worlds safe is the priority,' said Aila.

Belinda nodded. 'Then those among us who know about these worlds, but who are not immune to the power of the gods, should flee, and hide in a mountain cave. The rest of us should search for the Sextant.'

'By that logic,' said Irno, 'we should evacuate.'

Belinda nodded. 'Yes.'

Corthie folded his arms. 'This is defeatist. We can beat the gods; we already have. And we're forgetting Blackrose, Maddie and Sable. They also know about the two worlds, but they're not under our control. We could evacuate, and one of them could be captured, and reveal everything. And what about the hundred and fifty mercenaries we've got locked up all over the town? With them on our side, we could garrison the castle indefinitely. Order the civilians to evacuate if you're worried about them; we should make our stand here.'

'The mercenaries won't help us,' said Irno; 'I've asked.'

'Then we should execute them,' said Belinda. 'They're a drain on our resources, and if we have to evacuate, we can't take them with us.'

'No,' cried Kelsey.

Everyone turned to her.

'I mean, uh, we shouldn't be executing surrendered prisoners.'

'They're enemies,' said Belinda. 'What's the difference between killing them in battle, and executing them for the crimes they have committed? The end result is the same.'

'They're soldiers,' said Kelsey, 'not criminals.'

Irno frowned. 'Do I have to remind you of the numerous atrocities carried out by the Banner of the Golden Fist?'

Kelsey glared at him. 'No. Do I have to remind you not to be an arsehole?'

Irno said nothing as the room quietened. Vana was shaking her head at Kelsey, while Belinda sat and stared at her.

'So tell me, Miss Holdfast,' said Irno; 'since you have, at last, decided to join this conversation, what do you think we should do?'

She pursed her lips. 'There are caves and tunnels behind the castle, aye?'

'Yes. It's where we keep our stores of food and other supplies.'

'And these tunnels are quite extensive?'

Irno nodded.

Kelsey gave a crooked smile. 'Then, unless I'm much mistaken, some of these tunnels will lead out of the cliff, or pass under the town? In other words, there will be secret ways to get out of here if, say, the town was besieged?'

Aila turned to Irno. 'Is that true?'

Irno chewed his lip for a moment. 'Yes.'

Naxor laughed. 'A secret way out? I had no idea you were so devious, cousin, and I've read your mind. You must have buried that little nugget somewhere deep within that thick skull of yours.'

'I reasoned that the fewer who knew, the better. I was going to tell you, if and when we decided to evacuate, but it seems that Miss Holdfast has worked it out on her own. If we departed via the tunnel, then we could leave without causing alarm among the civilian population.'

There was a knock at the door, and it opened.

'My apologies, my lord,' said a courtier, 'but you asked to be informed when it was ten minutes prior to noon.'

Irno nodded. 'Thank you.'

'Noon?' said Vana. 'What happens at noon?'

'It's when the deadline for the gods' ultimatum expires,' said Irno. He stood. 'I am going up onto the roof to take a look.'

'What do you expect to see?' said Aila.

'Hopefully nothing,' he said. 'If noon passes without incident, then perhaps the wild threats of the gods were nothing more than bluster.'

Corthie got to his feet. 'I'm coming too.'

'And I,' said Naxor.

'I'll stay down here,' said Kelsey, 'in case you want to use your powers. Also, I don't need to see what happens next.'

'Very well,' said Irno.

The others stood and started to file from the room, while Corthie glanced at his sister.

'I'll catch you up,' he said to Aila.

He waited until the others had gone, and then sat back down. 'I assume you haven't told the others what you can do?'

She shrugged.

'Why not?'

'They already think I'm a crazy witch; this would just confirm their suspicions. You must promise me that you'll keep your mouth shut about it, even to Aila.'

He nodded. 'Alright. Do you know what happens next? Have you seen it?'

'You'll have to be more specific, brother.'

'Fine. Do you know what they'll see at noon?'

'Aye, I saw it a few minutes ago when I looked into Irno's eyes.'

'What did you see?'

'Sorry. If you want to know, then you'll have to go up there yourself. It's taken me a long time to realise it, but it's better if I keep my visions to myself. After all, there's nothing anyone can do to change them.'

'You can be a stubborn cow at times.'

'You've only just figured that out, brother?'

He stood and walked to the door.

'Be ready to catch Vana,' Kelsey said, smirking.

He sighed and left Irno's study. He hurried along the hallway, and began to climb the steps to the roof of the keep. He caught up with the others as they were emerging from the dark stairwell into the bright sunshine, and he followed them out.

'Is Kelsey alright?' said Aila. 'She seemed preoccupied.'

He shrugged. 'That's just normal Kelsey. She's always preoccupied.'

They walked to the edge of the roof and gazed down over the town, and the fields that stretched outwards from the foot of the cliffs. Corthie filled his lungs with fresh air, his eyes squinting in the harsh light.

'It feels so good to be able to use my powers again,' said Vana. 'Kelsey's presence makes me feel like a mortal.'

'I'll use my vision to range around,' said Naxor.

Irno nodded, his hands held behind his back.

'Everything seems quiet,' said Aila, glancing down at the sun-baked lands.

Corthie said nothing, his nerves jangling.

They waited a few minutes, then Irno glanced at the position of the sun. 'Noon has passed. Perhaps the rumours regarding the might of Implacatus have been somewhat exaggerated. Should we go back downstairs?'

'Not yet,' said Corthie. 'Give it another minute.'

'Alright. Another minute shouldn't hurt.'

'I can't see anyone close by,' said Naxor, 'and I've checked out to a distance of several miles.'

'I concur,' said Vana. 'I sense no powers being used in the vicinity. Perhaps we...' She stopped speaking, and her eyes widened.

On the plains below them, some hundred or so yards from the high wall that protected the settlement, a dark shimmering patch had appeared, as if the air was bending. The patch grew until it measured a dozen yards wide, and the same high, then it wobbled and turned black.

'What is that?' said Aila.

Irno swallowed. 'A portal.'

They stared as the first soldiers began marching through the dark, shimmering void. Four abreast, and clad in heavy armour, they strode from the portal, and began fanning out onto the plain before the town. On and on they came, an unceasing line of steel and leather. Cries rose up from the walls as militia pointed down from the battlements. Tall standards were carried through the portal alongside the unending stream of soldiers; one had a symbol of a flame, another a crown, another with an eagle. Fifty yards from the portal, a further one opened up, and wagons began rolling through, followed by wheeled catapults and ballistae, and then a third portal appeared, and more soldiers poured out into the fields.

Vana put her hand to her mouth, gasped, then toppled over. Corthie ducked to his left and caught her as she fell, then lay her down onto the surface of the roof.

'Is she alright?' said Aila.

He nodded. 'She fainted.'

'Sweet Amalia,' muttered Naxor, his eyes fixed on the army gathering on the plains in front of the town. 'I guess the rumours weren't exaggerated. It looks like they mean business this time.'

Irno nodded. 'It has begun.'

CHAPTER 6

THE BURDEN OF TRUTH

F alls of Iron, Western Khatanax – 7th Abrinch 5252

Naxor rolled over in bed and lit a cigarette, his forehead glistening with sweat. Belinda lay, watching him, her eyes moving up from his lean body to his shoulders, and then to his face. His eyes drew her in, and she felt almost intoxicated.

She must love him, she thought. How else could she explain how she felt whenever he touched her? Her heart would race if he glanced at her with longing, and she missed him, even if they were apart for a short time. What was that, if it wasn't love?

The room began to fill with smoke, which she hated, but she said nothing in case it annoyed him. She didn't want to annoy him, especially after they had lain together.

He flicked ash into a mug by the side of the bed.

'What are you thinking?' she said.

'Oh, the usual stuff; how we're going to deal with the enormous army currently camped outside the walls of the Falls of Iron; that kind of thing. I liked your idea about searching for the Sextant.'

She frowned. 'Have you forgotten the part where I said that those not immune to the powers of the gods would have to hide? That would include you.'

'No, I haven't forgotten; it was all very sensible.'

'You mean you wouldn't mind if we were parted for a while? I'm immune, so I would be one of those looking for the Sextant.'

'Of course I would be upset, my darling, but needs must and all that. Every moment away from you would be agony, but if it helps us in the long run, then it's a burden I would have to carry.'

'Do you want to have children?'

He looked alarmed, then smiled. 'Why not? But there's no rush; we have literally thousands of years ahead of us. Perhaps when this salve business is all over we can discuss it again?'

'Do you think we'll be together for thousands of years?'

'My heart will always be yours, my darling Belinda.'

She smiled, and slipped out of bed, Naxor gazing at her bare skin as she walked to the bathroom. She freshened herself up, then glanced at her reflection in the mirror. Her dark eyes stared back at her, and she shivered. She smiled, to see what she looked like, but it seemed false; worse, it looked as though the woman in the mirror was mocking her. The reflection looked like someone who could be the Third Ascendant, but inside, she just felt like Belinda. She heard a noise from the bedroom and opened the door. Naxor was kneeling on the bed, glowering at the appearance of the cat on the window ledge. He had a book in his hand, and was ready to throw it.

'Don't do that,' she said, her ire stirred.

'Blasted cat,' he muttered. His eyes turned towards her, and she sensed his desire. 'Close the shutters and come back to bed.'

'No,' she said, picking up her clothes from where they lay scattered across the floor. 'He needs fed.'

'Let him catch a mouse or something,' he said; 'it's all he's good for.'

She sat, and began pulling on her clothes.

'Why are you doing that?' he said. 'We don't have to be anywhere; I thought we'd be staying in bed a bit longer?'

She took a breath, and started to worry that she had annoyed him. She couldn't help it; she hated it when he was mean to her cat. She stood, half-dressed, and opened the cupboard under the bedside table.

The cat jumped down from the window, careful to stay out of Naxor's reach, then wound round her legs as she prepared his breakfast. She lowered his bowl to the ground, then crouched by him, stroking his back as he emitted a loud purr.

'I'm jealous,' said Naxor.

She glanced at him. 'What?'

'The way you love that stupid cat. You'd rather stroke him than come to bed with me.'

She frowned. Did he mean that, or was it one of the jokes that he liked to make? His voice had a tinge of bitterness about it, but she knew that if she pressed him, then he would accuse her of having no sense of humour. She stood, and finished getting dressed.

'I want to go up to the roof,' she said. 'I want to see which gods they've sent this time.'

'Why; in case you recognise any?'

'I won't recognise any; you know that. My memories will never return.'

He waved his hand. 'I was being facetious.'

'Why?'

He looked confused for a moment, then stubbed his cigarette out in the mug.

She laced up her boots then walked to the door. 'Please don't hurt my cat while I'm gone.'

He lay back down in bed. 'Of course not, darling.'

She stared at him, wondering if he understood that she was being serious, then opened the door to the hallway.

'Your Majesty,' said Silva, getting up off the chair.

Belinda frowned and kept walking, the sound of Silva's footsteps behind her.

'May I assist you today, your Majesty?'

'I don't know what will happen today, so I can't answer that.' She paused, and turned to the demigod. 'Actually, I want to know your opinion on the siege.'

Silva's eyes lit up. 'My opinion, your Majesty?'

'Yes,' said Belinda as she resumed walking down the passageway. 'I assume you have an opinion. What do you think we should do?'

Silva hurried to catch up. 'You must flee the Falls of Iron at once, your Majesty. If the army outside these walls captures you, you will be taken to Implacatus. The salve trade is of no concern to us, and the fate of the Holdfasts is immaterial next to your own safety. The Queen of Khatanax should not be putting herself in such grave positions of danger without good reason.'

Belinda nodded. That was what she had guessed Silva would say. Her thoughts turned to Naxor, and she started to wish they had parted on better terms. She should have told him that she loved him, and that she would miss him. If only he liked her cat.

They came to the foot of a spiral staircase and started to ascend.

'May I ask, your Majesty, what you thought of my opinion?'

Belinda glanced at Silva. 'I wish you would speak clearly. If you want to ask, then ask; don't ask for permission to ask.'

Silva lowered her eyes. 'Apologies, your Majesty.'

'I don't agree with your opinion,' Belinda said, 'but if I did, where would you advise me to go?'

'Shawe Myre, your Majesty.'

'Where's that? You haven't mentioned it before.'

'I have, your Majesty, though this is perhaps the first time I have named it. Shawe Myre was where we hid for so long after Dun Khatar fell.'

'Our mountain hideout, where Nathaniel died?'

'Yes, your Majesty. It was sacked by soldiers seven years ago, but it remains intact.'

'And why should I go there?'

'It would be a safe place for you to start rebuilding your Realm, your Majesty. There is fresh water, and access to food; and you still have some support in the local towns and villages of the Southern Cape. It was thanks to their loyalty that we survived there for so long.'

'I still have followers?'

'Oh yes, your Majesty. The Southern Cape is sparsely populated, but the people there remained loyal long after the other regions of Khatanax submitted. If you were to appear there in person, volunteers would flood in.'

'How could they flood in if it's sparsely populated?'

'Perhaps I over-spoke, your Majesty; apologies. What I meant was that the people who live there, though few, would flock to you.'

They emerged onto the roof and Belinda lifted a hand to shield her eyes from the glare of the sun. She walked over to the southern edge, Silva a pace behind. Irno and Corthie were already there, both gazing down, Irno with his hands clasped behind his back, and Corthie with his arms folded across his wide chest.

Belinda glanced at Silva. 'Please go back downstairs and wait for me there; I want to speak to Irno and Corthie alone.'

Silva bowed her head, her eyes flickering with irritation. 'As you wish, your Majesty.'

Belinda watched the demigod walk away. She had lied to her; she didn't want to speak to the two men alone, she was just fed up with Silva following her everywhere. She joined Corthie and Irno by the edge of the roof, and looked down. The new army of Implacatus was formed up before the Falls of Iron, spread out in a thick semi-circle from cliff to cliff. Their front ranks made up a continuous shieldwall a hundred yards from the walls of the settlement, and the armour of the soldiers was dazzling in the sunlight. The air above them was bristling with pikes, while large companies of archers and huge throwing machines were dotted among the rear. To the east was a collection of large tents, the tallest of which was flying two standards.

'Good morning, Belinda,' said Corthie.

She nodded to him. 'Have they sent any word to us?'

'No,' said Irno. 'The last of them finally arrived halfway through the night, and they've been arranging themselves ever since.'

'Have you been up here all that time?'

Irno nodded. 'I have.'

'Shouldn't you be down on the castle battlements, organising the defences?'

He narrowed his eyes a little. 'Every ten minutes, a courtier comes up the stairs you have just climbed, to update me on supplies, the disposition of the militia, and the number of civilians who have reached the safety of the caverns; and then they return with my fresh orders. Up here, I can think in peace, or I could until you started asking me questions.'

Belinda frowned.

'Sorry for my tone,' said Irno; 'I'm not myself this morning. There is another reason I'm up here; the roof is out of Kelsey's range. If one of the newly arrived gods wishes to talk, then I am available.'

Belinda nodded. 'Do we know which gods are here?'

Corthie pointed. 'Do you see the large tent?'

'Yes.'

'It has two standards flying from it, different from those held by the companies of soldiers. We think they represent two gods.'

'Lord Renko didn't have a standard.'

'Aye, so we're thinking... maybe more important gods than Renko?'

Belinda gazed at the tall tent in the middle of the camp behind the lines of soldiers. There was no wind, and the two great standards were hanging limp. She could see that both were edged in gold, but no other detail was visible.

'I wonder if they're watching us,' she said, 'just as we are watching them.'

'Probably,' said Corthie. 'Are you ready to fight?'

'I'm always ready.'

'If they're as clever as the stories say,' said Irno, 'then they will have learned from Renko's failure. I doubt they will infiltrate the streets as they did last time.' He pointed at a line of massive trebuchets. 'Those machines took them hours to assemble. They will have brought them for a reason.'

Corthie squinted at them. 'Do they have the range to hit the castle?'

'No, but they are capable of devastating the town, without any need for god powers. That alone tells me that their thinking has evolved.'

'Belinda,' said Corthie, 'any sign of your fire powers yet?'

She frowned. 'No.'

'Pity. They would have been handy against those machines. Never mind; can't be helped. What are your thoughts? What should we be doing?'

Belinda thought for a moment. She appreciated that Corthie treated her with respect. They might not always agree, but he always listened to what she had to say and, unlike the others, he never looked at her as though he thought she was strange.

She eyed Irno. 'You mentioned earlier that you had started making preparations for our evacuation. What does that entail?'

'Ships,' he said. 'Kelsey was right about the tunnel; there's one that leads towards the coast. In the harbour are four fast galleys, crewed and ready to go. I have ordered their captains to pull away from the coast if the army of the gods approaches the port. There's a hidden jetty in a cove five miles to the north of the harbour where they will meet us if that's the case. Within three hours of leaving the castle, we would be sailing upon the ocean.'

Belinda nodded. 'My advice is to give the order now, secretly. We should slip away before the army's preparations for battle are complete.'

'But if the gods think we're still here, they'll begin the assault, and my people will be slaughtered.'

'I don't understand,' said Belinda. 'This goes back to my question in the meeting – what are we trying to achieve? Aila said that keeping the location of the two worlds a secret was the priority. If that is so, then the sacrifice of the townsfolk will be regrettable, but justified. Are you telling me that you disagree? Is our aim to save the lives of the people down there? I need to know what you want before I can offer advice.'

Irno lowered his gaze.

'You should all go,' said Corthie. 'I'll remain to defend the town.'

Belinda shook her head. 'You are meant for greater things than dying here.'

His eyes widened, and he took a step back, saying nothing.

She turned back to Irno, but the demigod was staring out over the edge of the roof, his eyes hazy. He staggered, and Corthie gripped his arm to steady him.

Irno's mouth opened. 'These are the words,' he said, his voice distorted and low, 'of Implacatus. You, Count Irno of the Falls of Iron, were warned, and you have chosen to ignore that warning. Our response will be swift, and devastating. Before you die, know that your death, and the death of all those you hold dear, will be at the hands of the Sixth Ascendant, his Highness Leksandr, and the Seventh Ascendant, her Highness Arete.'

Irno fell to his knees as if pushed, then his head exploded.

Belinda stared, blood dripping down the front of her clothes. Corthie swayed as if drunk, his eyes fixed on Irno's headless body, which slowly toppled to the side. A scream sounded behind Belinda, coming from a courtier who had arrived at the top of the stairs.

'Get down,' cried Corthie; 'the roof's not safe.'

He leaned over and picked up Irno's body by the shoulders. Belinda remained frozen, her mind numb, and she became aware of a series of loud rumbles and crashes coming from beneath them.

'They're bombarding the town,' Corthie shouted as he dragged Irno's corpse towards the stairs.

Belinda's eyes went to the settlement below, and she saw smoke rise. The arms of the trebuchets were arcing through the air, sending massive boulders and flaming barrels of oil into the streets of the Falls of Iron. Her glance went back to the pool of blood on the roof, her mind still disbelieving what had happened.

'Belinda!' Corthie yelled. 'Come on.'

She began to move. She rushed over to Corthie and picked up Irno's legs, and they carried his body to the stairs. The courtier was weeping, her eyes wide in shock. They squeezed past her and stumbled down the steps into the dark stairwell, the roar of the missiles dampening behind the thick stone walls.

A mass of courtiers and militia were gathered at the foot of the stairs, and they fell into silence as Corthie and Belinda brought the body of Irno down. They laid it on the floor amid a hushed and nervous silence.

An officer stepped forward. 'What are our orders?'

Corthie and Belinda glanced at each other.

'We fight,' said Corthie. 'Issue commands to every member of the militia; tell them to get to their posts. The Falls of Iron is under attack.'

The officer saluted. 'Yes, sir.'

Courtiers picked up the body of Irno, and Corthie and Belinda edged past them. She pulled Corthie to the side.

'Should we evacuate?' she said in a low voice.

'Not while we're safe in the castle.'

'There are two Ascendants out there.'

'But they can't get in here. If we flee, they'll catch us out in the open.' He tried to wipe blood from his face, but only smeared it in. 'Damn it all.'

More officers approached. Some were weeping, while others were wide-eyed in shock.

'Sir, ma'am,' said one; 'who's in charge?'

Belinda gestured to Corthie. 'Lord Holdfast,' she said. 'Pass the word; Lord Holdfast is leading the defence. Lord Irno gave his life to save the Falls of Iron, and the castle is secure and can withstand any siege. Ensure the gatehouse is sealed and guarded, and get all civilians into the caverns.'

'What about the town, ma'am?'

Belinda glanced at Corthie, his blood-streaked face giving him a terrifying appearance.

'The town is lost,' he said, his voice almost choking, 'but the castle is impregnable. I... I need to prepare for battle. I will be on the battlements in fifteen minutes.'

'Yes, sir.'

The officers saluted and dispersed.

Corthie turned to Belinda. 'Why did you do that? "Lord" Holdfast?'

'The militia need you,' she said; 'they need a leader they can trust. Get your armour on, and I'll inform the others.'

'And then I'll see you on the battlements?'

'Yes.' She placed a hand on his arm. 'You can do this, Corthie. You're a born leader.'

'What if the others object?'

'Who? Vana? Aila? None of them want to lead, Corthie; it has to be you. Now, go.'

Corthie strode away, a small group of courtiers following. Belinda glanced around and saw Silva, waiting by a wall, her eyes on her queen.

'Your Majesty?' she said.

'This way,' said Belinda, and went back to the stairs. She pushed past the crowd round Irno's body, then took the passageway leading to her room. She quickened her steps. The part of the castle where her chamber was located was, like the roof, out of Kelsey's range, and she realised that Naxor was in danger.

They passed a window, and Belinda glanced at the view. Tall pillars of smoke were rising from every part of the settlement below them, and the noise of screams and destruction was echoing up the cliffside. She carried on, running the last dozen yards, then pulled her door open.

Her room was in darkness, the shutters closed. She closed the door and walked to the bed. Naxor was there, sleeping among the blankets. Belinda gazed at him. He looked so peaceful that she didn't want to disturb him. She glanced down at her blood-soaked clothes. Naxor might panic if he awoke and saw her covered in blood, so she stripped down to her underwear, throwing the soiled clothes into a heap.

Naxor groaned and opened his eyes. He smiled when he saw her.

'Excellent,' he said; 'you've changed your mind and are coming back to bed?' He pulled back the sheet. 'Get in here.'

She stared at him. 'We're under attack.'

'All the more reason to get into bed.'

'No.'

She walked to her drawers and began to pull out fresh clothes. She was desperate to clean the rest of the blood off her skin, but she knew there wasn't time.

'You're teasing me?' Naxor said. 'You stand around in your underwear, and expect me not to react?'

'You don't understand,' she said as she got dressed.

He folded his arms behind his head as he watched her. 'You're a cruel woman, denying me like this. Come on; get into bed, and prove that you love me.'

She turned to him, her anger boiling over. 'No!'

Something changed within her, something in the way she was staring into Naxor's eyes, and without understanding how, she found herself inside his mind, looking out from his eyes at her furious face. Naxor cried out in pain, and she staggered backwards, colliding with the bedside table and falling to the ground. Yet, her mind remained within Naxor.

She could feel his agony as her thoughts trampled over his; she sensed his self-healing powers, and got a flash of terror. He was frightened; frightened of her. His body started to tremble, and she realised that, somehow, he was frozen, his physical form under her control. She began to feel guilty; she was hurting him, but at the same time a euphoric exhilaration was flowing through her.

Inner-vision. At last.

She pulled herself up, and brought her new power under control. She could see Naxor lying on the bed and, at the same time, she could see his thoughts and sense what he was feeling.

He was trying to protect his mind from her intrusion, but she knew in an instant that she was far more powerful than he would ever be, and she pushed his efforts aside. Her power over him intoxicated her, and she lost herself in it, revelling in her ability to see into his mind.

Sable.

He was thinking about Sable. There was something he was hiding. Her anger built. She reached for his memories, and found them – hundreds of years of piled up recollections; the City, Princess Khora, salve, the God-King, the Quadrant, the god-restrainer mask; all jumbled up and shifting like sand under the waves of the ocean. She focussed, her conscious mind forgetting all about Irno and the assault upon the town. The rest of the world faded into insignificance as she plundered his mind.

'No,' he gasped, but she ignored him.

Sable.

Belinda found it; found the memories of his time in Alea Tanton, and she saw the truth. He had lied to her. She replayed the conversations between Naxor and Sable, and felt what he had been feeling. He had offered Sable everything; his love, his future, his loyalty, and she had rejected him. Tears began to stream down Belinda's face, but she couldn't stop; she was too far in. She saw him on the bed, his eyes gazing at Sable, his desire for the Holdfast woman out-shining everything else. Belinda went in deeper, and saw how Naxor truly perceived her. He desired her body, but was contemptuous of her as a person; he saw her as half-mad, a hindrance, a burden. He had been thinking up ways to break it off with her since the moment he had returned to the Falls of Iron, and only his fear of her had stopped him.

She fell to her knees, sobbing, her heart in pieces.

He didn't love her; he had never loved her. He had been willing to run off with Sable, but he didn't love her either; the only person he loved was himself.

Anger swept over her, and she realised that she could obliterate his mind with a single thought. She could do to him what Karalyn had done to her; she could make him suffer; she could implant a terror within him that would drive him mad within days, or... or she could kill him. It would be easy. He had betrayed her, used her, and had been mocking her behind her back. She could see that the others in the castle knew or guessed his true feelings towards her. Why had none of them told her? Even Corthie had suspected, yet he had said nothing. Her betrayal was complete.

She should kill Naxor. She raised her hands and walked forwards. The demigod's eyes were on her, wide with pure fear. She placed her hands on his neck, and squeezed. His eyes began to bulge, but his body remained motionless under her control. He choked, and she sensed the raw panic in his mind.

A scratching noise came from the shutters. She jumped, startled, and released her grip. She stared at her hands; what was she doing? She glanced back at Naxor.

Go to sleep.

His eyes closed, and she sensed his mind fall into oblivion. She withdrew from his head and began to shake, her thoughts seared with his betrayal.

The scratching sound came again, and she leaned up and opened the shutters. The cat jumped down from the window and onto the bed. He sniffed Naxor's body for a moment, then stepped down onto Belinda's lap. He circled round, his claws digging into the skin of her legs as she wept. She stroked him, her tears uncontrollable. He lifted his head and butted her face, then meowed.

'I have to go now,' she whispered to him; 'I'm sorry. Hide in the caverns; the bad gods are coming.'

He butted her again, vying for her full attention. She steeled her heart and pushed him off her lap, then stood. She glanced at Naxor, then turned away, and reached for her armour. She pulled on her coat of mail, then strapped the leather breastplate into position. The Weathervane was lying on a chair, and she picked it up and attached the jewelled scabbard to her belt. The mirror caught her eye, but she refused to look into it, afraid to see her face covered in blood and tears.

There was one last thing she needed to do. She sat on the bed, and prised open one of Naxor's eyes. She couldn't remember how she had entered his mind in the first place, but found it was easy, and she slid her vision into his sleeping thoughts. She went back into his memories, and found the directions through the tunnels to the harbour; as she had suspected, Naxor had read them from Irno's mind while up on the roof the previous day.

She got back to her feet. 'Goodbye, Naxor. Goodbye, cat.'

Silva was sitting in her chair as Belinda left the room.

'Your Majesty!' she cried as she glimpsed Belinda's face. 'Are you well?'

Belinda shut the door behind her as the demigod stood.

'What shall we do?' Silva said, her voice high. 'People are saying that there are two Ascendants outside the Falls of Iron. Nothing will be able to withstand them.'

Belinda glanced at the woman, the only friend she had left. 'We're leaving.'

Silva's eyes widened.

'You were right, Silva; there's nothing for me here. We'll escape the castle, and then you can take me to Shawe Myre.'

Silva bowed, a smile creeping across her lips. 'Yes, your Majesty.'

CHAPTER 7

LUCKY DAY

Falls of Iron, Western Khatanax – 7th Abrinch 5252

Van stared out of the narrow window, gazing at the destruction of the town below, and listening to the continual *thump-thump* of the artillery striking the buildings. Smoke and flames were belching up from the battered settlement, polluting the perfect blue sky above. Outside the walls, the massed ranks of Banner soldiers had remained immobile all day, waiting for the order to advance.

Sohul and he had gone hungry that morning. Their breakfast had not been delivered, and they were running low on cigarettes. Van still had a few of the weedsticks that the strange Holdfast woman had left a few nights before, but he didn't want to risk smoking any while the Falls of Iron was being assaulted.

'The Bald Eagle bastards are down there,' he said. 'I can see them next to the Banner of the Black Crown. The gods must have been scraping the bottom of the barrel to hire that lot.'

Sohul looked up from his bed. 'Any Golden Fist?'

'Not that I can see. Maybe we're in disgrace.'

'But it wasn't the Banner's fault.'

'You know how the gods think; defeat is equivalent to incompetence.'

Sohul nodded. 'Are any soldiers on the move?'

'Not yet.'

'The town must be rubble by now. They can't know that our men are being held down there.'

Van snorted. 'Don't be naïve, Sohul; of course they know. They just don't care. The Falls of Iron has been marked for destruction, and it doesn't matter who's stuck inside. Friends, enemies, everyone is going to die. Do you remember Tankbar on Dragon Eyre? They even killed all of the cats and dogs; we were up to our knees in blood.'

Sohul turned his glance away, his face pale. He had stopped insisting that they were going to be rescued, and Van reckoned the lieutenant was finally coming to terms with the high probability of their impending deaths.

'I hate this,' said Sohul; 'this is worse than combat.'

'Be patient,' Van said; 'and stay ready. If even the smallest opportunity arises, we'll have to grasp at it.' He turned away from the window, and his eyes adjusted to the gloom of the interior. The metal slats on their door were closed, and he wondered if a soldier was posted outside. He walked over and put his ear to the door. He could hear nothing, but that didn't mean that no one was there.

Sohul attempted a smile. 'Where's your little girlfriend when we need her?'

'Shut up about that,' Van said. 'I wish I'd never told you about her visit.'

'You had to explain the weedsticks somehow.'

'I should have made something up.' He walked back to bed and sat. 'I wish I'd been more polite to her. I was being a defiant prisoner, when I should have been wide-eyed and smitten. "Yes, Kelsey, I'd love to drink whisky with you. Wow, has anyone ever told you how beautiful your eyes are?" But no, I basically told her to go away. Maybe Irno will come back and plead with us to sign up.'

'That would be no good; he'd send us to face the Ascendants.'

'Yeah, you're right. Leksandr *and* Arete; I guess Implacatus really wants to get its hands on the salve. Have you ever heard of two Ascendants being sent on an operation?'

Sohul shook his head.

'Exactly. I'm not sure it's ever happened before.'

A harsh grating noise came from the door and they both turned as the slats opened. Outside the chamber, dressed in full battle armour and with his clawed hammer over his shoulder, was the warrior who had slaughtered half of the Banner under Renko. He glanced into the room.

Van got to his feet. 'Yes?'

'I need to ask you a question,' he said.

Van and Sohul exchanged a glance.

'Do you know who I am?' said the warrior.

'Yes,' said Sohul; 'you're the monster that killed hundreds of our men.'

The warrior laughed. 'Was I supposed to stand back and watch as you massacred the townsfolk? If you could fight like me, what would you have done?'

Van walked closer to the door. 'You're Corthie Holdfast, Kelsey's brother, aren't you?'

'And what do you know about my sister? I'd leave her out of this if you want to keep your head on your shoulders.'

'Two Ascendants are attacking the Falls of Iron. I doubt anything's going to keep my head on my shoulders.'

'Funny you should bring them up; they're the reason I'm here. I've noticed that the powers of the gods vary; I've met some with battle-vision, and others with death or flow powers; and others who can control fire. What can these Ascendants do?'

Van gave a bleak smile. 'Everything. All Ascendants have mastery of every power. Vision, flow, life and death, fire, and stone, and all to the highest degree. They're the original gods; they existed before there even were any gods, and every god since is one of their descendants.'

Corthie's expression grew grimmer as he listened. 'I didn't know that.'

'We learned it at school. Some of the Ascendants have had hundreds of children, but they have lived for over thirty millennia, so it's not that surprising.'

'Their powers won't work here,' Corthie said.

'That's partly true. Lady Joaz's vision was blocked, and Lord Baldwin's death powers as well, but that doesn't mean the Ascendants can't kill you up here. Tell me, how would Kelsey block a fireball, or an earthquake, or could she prevent the river from drying up? Lord Renko will have told them everything when he returned to Implacatus.'

Corthie narrowed his eyes. 'You mentioned my sister again, when I asked you not to.'

Van hesitated for a moment, then plunged in. 'She came round here a few nights ago, with whisky and weed. We had quite a chat.'

'What? Kelsey was here?'

'Inside this very cell, though I'm not entirely sure why.'

Corthie stared at him. Van held his ground, but his heart began to race. Had he gone too far?

'You?' Corthie said.

'She came to see me, yes. She asked me all kinds of questions. When you next see her, tell her that I'm sorry that I wasn't as friendly as I could have been. I guessed I was surprised that she turned up.'

Corthie said nothing for a moment. His eyes remained on Van, and he was slowly shaking his head.

'Was that all you wanted?' said Van.

'I have to go. Thank you for telling me about the Ascendants. And thank you for saving Maddie and the dragon.'

'Shh!' Van hissed. His eyes flickered over to Sohul who was lying on his bed, reading.

'I see,' Corthie went on, in a low voice, 'well, thank you all the same. I assume you want to live?'

'I do.'

'Can your word be trusted?'

'Yes,' Van said, raising his voice again, 'which is why I cannot work for you. Count Irno has already asked, and I'll tell you what I told him - the Banner is still under contract.'

'Even though the gods are bombarding your imprisoned soldiers in the town?'

'Yes. That's how it works; you sign a contract, and then you see it out to the end. However, I may be open to an advisory role. No contract; no conditions.'

'Then what's to stop you deserting or turning against us?'

Van smiled. 'Nothing; you'd have to trust me. Obviously, I know you can't do that; that would be...' He paused as Corthie turned to a guard. 'Wait; what are you doing?'

'Releasing you,' said Corthie, taking the keys from the guard.

Van stepped back from the door as Corthie unlocked it. Sohul looked up from the bed. The door swung open.

'Uh,' said Van; 'is this a trick?'

'No trick,' said Corthie, 'but hurry; I have a million things to do and I can't afford to hang around here while you make up your mind.'

'You're letting us go?' said Sohul, getting to his feet.

'Not you,' said Corthie; 'just the captain.'

Van raised his palms. 'Lieutenant Sohul comes with me, or we both stay.'

Corthie said nothing, and for a moment Van was sure he was going to close the door again.

'If he puts one foot out of line,' the huge warrior said, his armour glinting in the lamplight, 'I'll twist his head off.'

Van and Sohul glanced at each other, then hurried for the door. Corthie stepped aside to let them pass.

'Wait,' said Van; 'sorry.' He darted back into the prison chamber, grabbed his cigarettes and the bundle of weedsticks, then rushed back out again. 'Forgot these.'

Corthie gave him a knowing glance, then turned and started walking down the passageway.

'What do you want us to do?' Van said, hurrying to keep up, while a confused-looking Sohul followed behind.

'You said "no conditions".'

'Yeah, but I didn't actually believe you were going to let us out. Are we allowed to run away? Would you try to stop us? And what will Count Irno say about this?'

'Count Irno will say nothing; he's dead. The Ascendants killed him.' He glanced at Van. 'I'm in charge of the defences.'

'You? Excuse me, but, well...'

'Well, what?'

'You may be a mighty warrior and all that, but let's face it; you're a boy.'

'If you try to run away, I will chase you down and kill you, but I don't think you'll try. Stay close to me, and keep your lieutenant out of trouble. I'm holding you responsible for his actions. Do nothing that harms our cause, but if you have any military advice to offer, then I'll listen.'

'This is insane; you have no reason to trust me.'

Corthie stopped, and glared down at Van. 'I don't trust you. I'm not doing this for you; I'm doing it for my sister.'

'That makes no sense. Even if you sister does, eh... have a crush on me, which I'm not saying is true, then I could still be a villain.'

Corthie smiled. 'I've met a lot of villains; you're not one of them.'

'Somehow, that makes me feel a little disappointed.'

They set off again, heading towards the opening at the end of the passageway. Corthie strode ahead, and Sohul caught up with Van.

'What in the name of the Ascendants is going on?' he whispered.

'I have no idea, Sohul.'

'Did you promise to help him?'

'No. I promised nothing, and you heard me tell him about the contract. And yet... he let us go anyway.'

'What do we do now?'

'We keep our heads down and go with it. This may be the only chance we get.'

They went through the opening and emerged into the blisteringly hot sunshine. To their right, the sky was filled with smoke rising up from the town, and the noise of the bombardment pounded on Van's ears. Several militia soldiers marched past on their way to the battlements, and an officer saluted Corthie.

Van and Sohul stood back as Corthie spoke to the officer for a moment. A few of the militia were casting suspicious glances at their Banner uniforms, but no one approached them.

Corthie gestured to the keep. 'This way.' He set off, and was close to the entrance when a woman walked out.

'Corthie,' she said, a grim expression on her face.

'Well?' he said.

'It's true; she's gone. Witnesses in the caverns saw her and Silva leave a couple of hours ago.'

Corthie's face fell. 'And Naxor?'

'He still hasn't awoken. Maybe Irno's... death was too much for her to take.' She started to cry, and Van noticed that her eyes were red from weeping.

'You should go inside and rest,' said Corthie.

'I can't; there's too much to do. Maybe keeping busy will help.'

He put a hand on her shoulder. 'Your brother was a good man, and he didn't deserve what they did to him.'

'For three hundred years I thought he was dead, and now it's come true.' She leaned in closer. 'Maybe we should do the same as Belinda; maybe we should order the evacuation. Vana knows the route.'

'We'll see,' he said. 'For now, stay close to Kelsey. Do you know where she is?'

'She's in the ale room. She says it's the most central point of the castle.' She glanced at Van and Sohul, as if noticing them for the first time. 'Why are they out of their cell?'

'I released them.'

'Have they changed sides?'

'No. You're going to have to trust me on this one; I'll explain later.'

The woman nodded, then leaned up and kissed Corthie. 'Take care. Don't do anything crazy.'

She walked back into the keep. Corthie gazed at the ground for a moment, then turned for the battlements.

'Should we run for it?' whispered Sohul.

Van shrugged. 'Where would we go? From their talk, it sounds like there might be a secret way out through the caverns; and did you hear? The Third Ascendant has deserted. That, and Count Irno's death, must be the reason why the boy's in charge. If we stick with him for now, he might lead us out of here.'

Sohul nodded, and they hurried after Corthie. They followed him up a flight of stone steps to the battlements, and looked out over the plain below them. The army had remained where it was, and the trebuchets were continuing to hurl boulders into the devastated town. Next to the throwing machines, a huge amount of wood had been gathered into great piles.

Van glanced at Corthie. 'You were looking for some advice?'

'Aye. Do you have any?'

He pointed into the distance at the piles of wood. 'As soon as those are lit, the castle will be hit with fire.'

'They're being lit now,' he said.

Van squinted. 'Are they? You have good eyes if you can see that from here.'

Corthie turned to an officer. 'Send word; tell the militia to get ready to put out fires.'

The officer saluted and hurried off. Van kept his eyes on the piles of wood, then caught a wisp of smoke from one. Within seconds, the pile was ablaze, then another followed, the flames rising high. A trumpet sounded, and the trebuchets fell silent. The soldiers on the battlements were all watching, and an eerie silence fell over the town and castle.

Streams of fire burst forth from the two piles. They merged in the air above the settlement, and the thick coil of flames surged towards the castle. It passed over the heads of the soldiers on the battlements and struck the roof of the keep with a deafening roar. Flames spilled down the sides of the building as the surge of fire continued. The paint blistered off the keep, and the rocks glowed red. Fragments split off, and fell to the courtyard below, then a tower collapsed, showering the soldiers beneath with a hail of fiery rubble. Van stared at the keep. The top half was consumed in flames, and screams were coming from those trapped on the upper floors. The jet of flame ceased, and Van glanced back at the twin piles of wood – both were extinguished, their fuel consumed.

His eyes were drawn to the area in front of the stationary army. A crack was starting to open up along the rocky ground. It grew wider, then shot forwards, straight for the half-destroyed town walls. It swept through them, and into the settlement. Van nudged Corthie, who was still staring at the burning keep. The warrior turned back, and gasped.

'What's happening?'

'They're going to obliterate the town,' Van said.

'But there are still dozens of people down there, hiding from the bombardment.'

Van shrugged. 'The Ascendants don't care about that.'

The rift grew wider, and deeper, and buildings began toppling in from either side, the surface of the ground tilting and cracking. The little white-washed houses collapsed into the gaping abyss, then the banks of the river crumbled, and a cascade poured into the dark rift.

'It's coming closer!' Sohul yelled. 'It'll split the cliffside!'

Corthie stared, his mouth open. Behind them, the upper half of the keep was embroiled in an inferno, while down in the town, the rift was rippling its way towards the foot of the cliff. Whole streets were disappearing, and a great cloud of dust was forming in the air. Screams and shouts rang out, then the battlements shook.

'We need to get off this wall,' said Van.

Corthie said nothing, his expression stunned.

'Lord Holdfast!' yelled a soldier. 'What do we do?'

'To the caverns!' he cried. 'Evacuate!'

The soldiers fled down the steps from the battlements as the rift reached the cliffside and started to climb. The dungeon block to their right collapsed and fell away from the cliff, tumbling down to crash into the remains of the town. Van jumped down the stairs. The militia were in a panic, fleeing in every direction, then the great curtain wall fell, the battlements cracking and splintering into fragments that showered down into the town below.

'Run!' someone screamed above the cacophony of flames and grinding rock.

The rift continued on, past the curtain wall, heading for the keep. Soldiers fell in as the ground bucked and rippled, and Van lost his footing, slipping to his knees. A large hand gripped his shoulder and hauled him back to his feet.

'We're going to the keep!' Corthie shouted in his face.

'But...' Van replied, then Corthie dragged him across the ruined courtyard. The rift had reached the tall keep and was running up its southern side, splitting the building in two; and stones rained down on them as they ran. Van turned his neck, but saw no sign of Sohul in the confusion. Corthie pulled Van into the side entrance of the keep, and barged his way past people trying to get out. He burst into a large room, and threw Van inside. The captain skidded across the floor and collided with a table.

Kelsey glanced down at him, an ale in her hand. 'You took your time.'

He looked up from the floor, his eyes wide. Two other women were also there, along with a man who was sitting up, rubbing his head.

'Let's go,' said Corthie from the entrance. 'We've lost. Vana, we need you to guide us.'

One of the women glanced up, her eyes red, and her cheeks stained with tears. She said nothing, but got to her feet, the other woman helping her up. Kelsey finished her ale and joined them.

'My head,' groaned the sitting man.

'Shut up, Naxor,' said Corthie.

Van gripped the table and pulled himself up. He glanced around. There was another door, and no one was paying him any attention, but he checked his urge to run. The group walked to where Corthie was standing, and Van followed.

'I lost my lieutenant,' he said.

'He'll be fine,' said Kelsey. 'Come on.'

They left the ale room and re-emerged into the chaos of the courtyard. The rift had continued past the keep, and was racing up the side of the cliff, sending huge splinters of rock tumbling down into the ruined castle. Corthie led the way, his armoured stature clearing a path through the retreating militia. Ahead of them were several dark cave entrances, and the soldiers were rushing inside.

'I don't understand,' said the woman supporting Vana. 'Why are they trying to kill us? I thought they wanted to know about the salve?'

'They must have read Irno's mind before they killed him,' said Corthie. 'Maybe whatever they found in there was enough.'

'I have a theory,' said Naxor.

'Don't say another word,' said Corthie, glaring at him. 'And if I find out you had anything to do with Belinda leaving, then I'm going to beat you senseless.'

They hurried across the courtyard and entered the dark interior of a cavern. The air was thick with dust and groans, and the stone ceiling of the chamber was cracked.

Corthie turned. 'Vana; lead the way.'

The following two hours were spent in almost utter darkness, as Vana guided them through the tunnels under the cliff. Civilians were trailing after them, along with the survivors of the militia. Much of the way consisted of tight stairs that went endlessly down into the depths of the hill. Vana had a lamp, but it was too far ahead of Van for him to see anything clearly, and he felt his way down the steps, his hand pressed against the wall to his right.

The narrow stairwell opened up into a vast underground chamber full of barrels and crates stacked high. The civilians and militia fanned out through the chamber.

'Remain here,' said Vana, her voice wavering. The people turned to look at her. 'You will be safe here. There is food and water, and the power of the gods cannot penetrate this deep. When they have gone, you can leave by the other tunnels; they come out into a valley a mile north of here.' She turned to Corthie.

'Thank you,' he said.

She nodded. 'Shall I lead us to the harbour?'

'Aye. If we stay here, then the gods won't stop until everyone is dead.'

'Are we going on a boat?' said Kelsey.

Corthie nodded. 'If we make it that far.'

'We'll make it, brother. The gods won't be able to sense us.'

'Alright,' he said. He glanced at their small group as civilians continued to fill the chamber. 'The six of us should leave now.'

'What about my lieutenant?' said Van.

Naxor frowned. 'Can someone explain why we have a Banner officer with us?'

'Later,' said Corthie. His eyes scanned the hall, then he strode off.

'Where's he going?' said Naxor.

The giant warrior reappeared after a few moments, gripping Sohul's arm as he walked.

Van nodded to him. 'You made it.'

Sohul stumbled as Corthie released him. 'Just about, Captain.'

'It seems we're going to the harbour.'

'You two,' said Corthie; 'behave yourselves, and you'll live.' He glanced at Kelsey. 'Did I do the right thing?'

Kelsey nodded, then glanced away. 'Aye, brother. Thank you.'

He nodded, then gestured to Vana. The demigod picked up her lamp, and set off. She led them away from the exhausted crowds and into a stuffy, narrow tunnel, the shadows masking their departure.

The miles passed slowly, and Van's legs and feet were aching as they padded their way through the darkness. The tunnel went on and on, then began to rise in a gentle incline, and widened at the same time. Van listened to the others talk for a while, mostly about Irno's fate, and Belinda's disappearance. He learned that the other woman was called Aila, and that she, Vana and Naxor were demigods from the same family as the dead count. Kelsey, however, remained silent throughout the long march, her eyes never glancing at Van.

After an hour of climbing, they reached the end of the tunnel. It opened out into a narrow ravine facing west, where the sky was a deep red as the sun neared the horizon. Ahead of them, the waves of the ocean were crashing against the rocky coastline.

'This isn't the harbour,' said Corthie.

'No,' said Vana; 'this is the secret cove where Irno had arranged to meet our ship.' She pointed towards the open water, where a ship was anchored. They walked down a rough track that wound through the ravine. A small jetty had been constructed by the water's edge, invisible to any boats that might sail past the ravine, and a sailor hailed them from a rowing boat.

'Lady Vana,' he said, bowing as the group reached the jetty. 'Where is Count Irno?'

Vana began to weep.

'He's dead,' said Aila. 'The Ascendants killed him.'

The sailor's eyes fell, then he glanced at the three other men in the boat. 'Get ready to leave.'

The group filed along the jetty, and each scrambled down into the small vessel. Van saw Kelsey sitting by the rear, and climbed over a bench to reach her.

He sat. 'Hello.'

She turned away.

'Cast off,' cried the sailor, and the rope connecting the boat to the jetty was thrown into the bottom of the vessel. The four sailors took up the oars, and splashed them down into the water. The boat bobbed up and down on the swell, then began moving towards the open sea.

Van nudged Kelsey with his elbow.

'Don't touch me,' she snapped.

'Do you want to tell me why I'm alive?'

'You're alive because my brother saved you.'

'Yes, but why?'

'Ask him yourself.'

'I have. He wouldn't say.'

She shrugged.

The wind picked up as the boat left the relative calm of the narrow inlet, and the sailors got into a rhythm. Van glanced up, watching as the cliffside slowly began to recede. The Falls of Iron was out of sight, some-where a few miles to the east along the ridge, and he wondered when the Ascendants would realise that it had been emptied of its people. On the bench in front of him, Corthie was holding Aila's hand. His eyes were dark and downcast. Vana sat on Aila's other side, and Sohul and Naxor were crammed in behind them, sitting on the planks at the bottom of the boat.

'We got our arses kicked,' said Corthie.

'At least you evacuated the people,' said Aila. 'Hundreds are still alive.'

'Aye, and hundreds are dead. They tore through the town like it was nothing.' He glanced at Van. 'They killed all of your men as well.'

'Yes,' said Van. 'The Ascendants don't get sentimental about the lives of us mortals.'

Sohul opened his mouth, presumably to object, then closed it again, and kept quiet. The boat bucked and dipped on the waves as the sailors rowed, and Van saw the large ship get closer. A rope ladder was being lowered over the side, and the deck was lined with sailors watching the approaching rowing boat.

Corthie put his head in his hands. 'I can't believe Belinda's gone.'

Aila eyed Naxor. 'I'm sure he'll give us an explanation.'

'Yes?' said Naxor. 'Well, I'm still waiting for an explanation of why we have two enemy officers with us.'

'As am I,' said Van. 'Why me?'

Corthie glanced up at him and shrugged. 'It's your lucky day.'

CHAPTER 8

THE WILD DRAGONS

Catacombs, Torduan Mountains, Khatanax – 29ᵗʰ Abrinch 5252

Maddie sat on the ledge at the front of the tomb, her legs dangling over the side of the cliff. Below her, streams of lava bubbled and smoked, the molten rock flowing in two wide channels down from the mountains behind her. The channels ran close to each other, but never met, and the valley was criss-crossed in glowing reds and oranges. Black blobs of solid rock were being carried along, and heaps of dark basalt were piled up all over the blackened valley bottom. An ancient road was visible in places, but long stretches had disappeared under the shifting and broken ground.

Millen sat down beside her, his movements slow and careful. He placed his crutch next to him, then handed her a steaming bowl full of mushed-up green leaves and roots.

'Your weeds,' he said, 'boiled to a pulp as you requested.'

She gazed down into the bowl. Her stomach was rumbling, but the food seemed utterly unappetising.

'This reminds me of sitting on the sea wall of Old Alea,' he went on, 'except there's lava down there instead of the ocean, and you're next to me, not Sable.'

'Do you think it's possible that you might go a single day without mentioning her? I mean, I'm grateful that you make food for me, but if it comes with a side-order of Sable, then I think I'd rather prepare it myself.'

He laughed. 'You don't even know which weeds are edible, and which are poisonous. If you tried to make your own food, you'd be throwing up all over the place, and, let's face it, the tomb smells bad enough as it is.' He lowered his voice. 'Dragons are filthy animals.'

She narrowed her eyes. '*Wild* dragons might be, but Blackrose isn't like that.'

'No, she does seem a little more civilised compared to the others, but that's only because she makes us clean and sweep and mop all the time. She thinks we're her servants.'

'I think that's the whole point,' said Maddie; 'dragons need us to do all of the stuff they can't do, otherwise they end up living like... well, animals. And anyway, you could teach me which plants are edible, and which aren't. Oh, and I saw some weird-looking mushrooms growing and I was wondering if I could eat them. Mushrooms would be nice.'

'Where did you see them?'

She pointed down at the ancient stone path cut into the side of the cliff. It was broken in places, but led down to the valley floor, via many crevices and turns.

'About halfway down,' she said. 'They were orange.'

'Alright. Firstly, that's too far down for me to walk with a crutch; and secondly, I wouldn't touch any fungus that was orange, no matter how hungry I was.'

'I wasn't asking you to walk down there yourself,' she said. 'I remember well what it's like to be on crutches. You're lucky it was such a clean break; I wasn't up and about for a lot longer when I got injured.'

He frowned at her. 'We've been here for twenty-four days, and I'm barely able to hobble around.'

'Exactly. It helps that you're young and fit, I guess.'

'Young? I'm older than you.'

'Not by much. That's another reason you and Sable won't work – you're six years younger than her.'

He gazed down at the valley floor. 'I hope she's alright. This is all my fault; I should have realised that she was in trouble and tried to help her, instead of rescuing Sanguino.'

'Don't let him hear you say that; he's depressed enough as it is.'

'It's true, though. I should have helped her, and then we could have all freed Sanguino.' He groaned. 'What I would do to be back in the merchants' district with her.'

'Don't go on about that again; I want to keep my food down.'

'What are you talking about? I've never told you what happened when Sable and I were in the merchants' district.'

'Yes, you have. You might not remember, but you were pretty delirious for a couple of days after you broke your leg.' She pulled a face. 'You told me all kinds of things, including every detail of what you and Sable got up to.'

Millen's face flushed.

Maddie eyed him. 'Was she your first?'

'No. You might find it hard to believe, but I've had a few girlfriends.'

She nodded and glanced away.

'What about you?' he said.

'What about me?'

'Any boyfriends?'

'None of your business.'

'Come on; that isn't fair. If I told you everything, then you should tell me something in return. We are friends, right? We've been in close proximity for a month and a half; you know me as well as anyone else.'

She frowned as she ate, and not just because of the bitter taste of the food. Would he make fun of her if he knew how inexperienced she was? Her eyes roved over the pools of lava, watching them bubble and flow.

'So we're not friends?' he said.

'I didn't say that,' she said. 'I've had a couple of boyfriends, I guess.'

'You guess?'

'Do drunken fumbles count? I've never had a, you know, proper, um... relationship. And now that I'm a dragon rider, it might never happen. Blackrose is like a fire-breathing chaperone; no boy's going to want to come anywhere near me.'

'Unless you find another dragon rider.'

She narrowed her eyes. She had never thought of that. There would be riders on Blackrose's home world, and she imagined a strapping young man flying on the back of a dragon. In her mind's eye, he looked like a cross between Corthie, Van, and a boy she had once known in Stormshield, with a hint of the gate sergeant who had worked at Arrowhead.

Millen pointed. 'Blackrose is coming back.'

Maddie glanced up. A dragon was circling overhead, descending with each revolution. As the only black-scaled dragon that lived in the Catacombs, Blackrose was easily recognisable. Maddie stood, clutching the bowl. She extended her other hand, and helped Millen stand. He hopped about until he had secured the crutch under his right shoulder, then they moved to the side of the large, square entrance of the tomb, watching as Blackrose landed. She folded her wings and dropped a large pile of torn plants onto the ground that she had been gasping in the claws of a forelimb.

'For you, rider,' she said; 'more weeds.'

'Thanks.'

Millen peered at the pile. 'I'll sift through it, and pick out what's not too toxic.'

Blackrose glanced into the deep darkness of the tomb. 'Has Sanguino stirred today?'

'No,' said Maddie.

'My anger with him grows daily,' said the dragon. 'I think I have been patient enough.'

'Be gentle,' said Maddie; 'his whole world's been turned upside down.'

'So has mine, and so has yours, yet we three haven't despaired. Even Millen has proved himself acceptably resilient after snapping his little insect leg. No, if Sanguino wishes to remain under my protection, then he will have to change his ways. I am on the cusp of attaining a certain degree of power and influence here at last, and I do not wish that to be imperilled by his stubborn melancholy.'

She began to move further into the interior of the tomb, and Maddie followed, leaving Millen to hobble over to the pile of plants.

'What do you mean "on the cusp"?'

Blackrose swung her neck to glance down at her. 'I have been invited to Deathfang's tomb, along with others who hold respected positions in the Catacombs, and I will be allowed to present my case to them.'

'About time! You've fought nearly every dragon in this place.'

'Indeed I have. Respect is slow to win among dragons, but I feel I am nearly there.'

They entered the huge cavern to the right, and Maddie could see the massive bulk of Sanguino in the shadows.

Blackrose turned her neck to gaze at him. 'I know you are awake, red dragon.'

Sanguino remained still, his eyes closed.

'How long is it since you felt fresh air against your face?' Blackrose went on. 'You are not a prisoner here, but you act as if you were in a dungeon. Come out, and we shall fly together.'

'Don't pretend you like me,' Sanguino said, his voice a snarled whisper.

'Who's pretending? I don't like you. You are a pathetic specimen of dragonhood. I am trying to improve you. You are still young, and have many centuries before you; do you want to live out those years in perpetual fear?'

'I am not afraid.'

Blackrose laughed. 'You try to mask your terror with bravado, but I see through you. You are frightened of the wild dragons, even though you are one yourself; or rather, you used to be. For forty years you suffered at the hands of unworthy humans; I, too, know how that feels.'

'You know nothing about me.'

'Unfortunately, I understand you all too well. In a short while, I shall be ascending to Deathfang's tomb, in order to meet with the rulers of the Catacombs. As you are under my protection, I think that you should be there. If you are not, the others will know that you are scared of them. You were shamed in front of them, when you allowed those two child-dragons to maul and humiliate you, but the fact that you attacked them in order to save Maddie and Millen shows that you have some courage. Come, shake your wings and fly with me. Prove to the others that you are not afraid.'

Sanguino said nothing. Maddie glanced up at Blackrose, and saw her irritation grow. Her eyes flashed red and narrowed.

'What will become of you if you remain here, in this tomb?' she said, her voice rising. 'Are you going to hide until you die?'

'I want to die.'

Blackrose bared her teeth and raised a forelimb, her long claws glinting in the dim light. 'Don't tempt me, fool. I could end your life in an instant if I chose, but instead I have shown you nothing but patience. I warn you; it will not last forever.' She glanced down at Maddie. 'Come, rider; let us leave before I do something that cannot be undone.'

The black dragon turned in the wide tomb-cavern, and began to head back towards the light. Maddie glanced at Sanguino for a moment. His dark red scales were filthy, and the chamber stank. Pity flooded her, as well as revulsion, and part of her wished that they had never rescued him from the pits. She shook her head and followed Blackrose out into the main tomb.

Maddie spent the afternoon cleaning the tomb, sweeping and mopping the floor until her arms ached, while Millen sat by a small fire, cooking dinner, his right leg stretched out. His beard had grown, and she felt an urge to cut it off, though they had no blade sharp enough for the job. When the floor was clean, she sat next to him to rest. Blackrose was also resting, taking up the entire rear area of the cavern. Her eyes were closed, but Maddie suspected she was still awake.

'I wish we had brought more clothes,' she said. 'Everything we've got is worn out and falling apart. And beds; I wish we had somewhere more comfortable to sleep than a pile of grass. I'm not made for living rough like this; I hate being dirty, and Malik only knows how I look. If I glanced into a mirror I'd probably keel over in shock.'

'You're a mess,' said Millen, 'but so am I. I've seen urchins living on the streets of Alea Tanton who were in a better state than us. On the other hand, we're alive, so we're better off than Gantu.'

Blackrose stirred behind them. 'Are you ready, rider?'

'Ready for what?'

'Our meeting with Deathfang.'

'What? You want me there with you? I thought wild dragons hated the whole concept of human riders?'

'They do, and yet they know of your existence. If I were to leave you here, they would see that as a sign of weakness on my part, which I cannot allow. Besides, I do not wish to insult the grand tradition of riders; I believe in its great value, and I would be ashamed to deny you in front of them.'

'Will it, eh, be dangerous?'

'Yes. That is unavoidable.'

Maddie nodded. 'Alright.'

'It would be better if you do not speak, however, as your presence will enflame them.'

'Not literally, I hope?'

'That is also my hope, but we must do what needs to be done. Since we are marooned on Lostwell for the moment, we have to establish a power base; a hold over the dragons here that will allow us to build a force to take to Dragon Eyre when the opportunity arises.'

'Where?' said Millen. 'Dragon Eyre?'

Blackrose turned her head to face him. 'I assumed that Maddie would have discussed this with you.'

'She told me you were going somewhere, but never its name.'

'And now you know. Have you heard of my world?'

'It's a different world?'

The dragon glanced at Maddie. 'Please inform him of the basic facts of our situation; he has proven his loyalty, if not his usefulness.'

Maddie nodded, and got to her feet. 'I'll tell him if we return in one piece.'

The dragon edged past the fire and Maddie joined her as she walked to the tomb entrance.

'Do you like him now?' Maddie said.

'Who; the boy?'

'Yes.'

'He is not the lover I would have selected for you, but if you have chosen him, then so be it.'

'He's not my lover!'

'I know. I'm teasing you.'

Maddie frowned. 'Since when did you tease? Living with these wild dragons has done something weird to your brain.'

'Climb onto my back,' she said, a glint in her eye.

Maddie scrambled up the extended forelimb, and got onto Blackrose's shoulders.

'I miss the harness; I don't feel safe not being strapped in.'

'That will have to wait, rider; besides, it is but a short journey.'

She went to the edge of the cavern and beat her great wings, launching herself into the air. The heat from the lava pools struck Maddie like a wave as she clung on, and her eyes were dazzled by the bright glow of the molten rock. Blackrose climbed, and Maddie gazed at the twin flows of lava tumbling down the cliffs on either side of the tombs. Vapours were rising across the narrow valley, shrouding the view in a sulphurous mist. Dragons were watching them from the entrances to a dozen tombs, their eyes following the black-scaled dragon as she rose up to the greatest tomb of the Catacombs. A score of tall grime-stained pillars flanked the great entrance near the top of the cliff. Sitting there was the small golden-yellow dragon that had tried to stalk Maddie and Millen by the reservoir; she had since learned that his name was Burntskull, Deathfang's most sycophantic follower.

Blackrose circled one more time, then landed inside the entrance of the grand tomb. Burntskull remained motionless except for his eyes, which stared at Maddie.

'I see you have brought us lunch,' he said; 'how thoughtful.'

'If you touch her,' said Blackrose, 'you die.'

'Insect lover,' the yellow dragon muttered. 'You shame all dragonkind with your behaviour. This girl should be torn from your back, just as your pathetic harness was.'

'You're a very tiny dragon,' said Maddie. 'I'm not sure you could reach all the way up here.'

Lightning and flames coiled round his jaws as he glared at her. Blackrose ignored him, and walked into the tomb. It was far larger than the one where she lived with Sanguino, and was lined with huge statues of kings and queens, many of which were lying in broken, blackened heaps. A large dark blue dragon was watching them from a side cavern, her eyes narrow. Behind her, three sets of eyes were peering out from under her wing.

'Look,' said Maddie, 'baby dragons.'

The blue dragon growled. 'Tell your insect to stay away from my children, Blackrose.'

'Greetings, Darksky,' said Blackrose; 'you can be assured that we mean no harm to your brood. We are here to see Deathfang.'

'I know why you're here,' the blue dragon said; 'you mean to take Deathfang from me. You want to rule us all.'

'I have no such intention,' said Blackrose, 'and I'd sooner couple with Burntskull than attempt to divide you from Deathfang. I ask only that you listen to what I have to say.'

At the end of the cavern was an enormous hall, with a ceiling so high it was lost in the gloom. In the middle of the hall was a heap of gold and silver, and lying atop it was Deathfang, his head resting on his giant forelimbs. His grey scales were covered in old scars, and half of his right ear was missing. On either side, other dragons were waiting, each staring at Blackrose.

'Greetings to all,' said Blackrose.

Deathfang opened his eyes, and gave her a lazy glance. 'Why are you here?'

'You invited me, Deathfang.'

'Did I?' He scratched his good ear with a talon.

'You did.' Blackrose glanced around the vast chamber 'Most of you, I have already fought, and defeated. If any feel they have been unfairly left out and wish to challenge me, then know that I am ready.'

'You are deep within my lair,' Deathfang said, laughing, 'and outnumbered a dozen to one. If I ordered it, you would be torn to shreds.'

'I do not believe you would behave so shamefully,' she said, 'but if I am wrong, then give the order, and we shall see what transpires.'

Deathfang yawned. 'Say your piece, then leave.'

Blackrose raised her head, her eyes gleaming red in the shadows of the hall. 'This world is sick and dying, ruined by the gods in their arrogance. Here, at the centre of Khatanax, our kin are threatened on every side; the Torduans to the west, Kinell to the north and east, and the wastes of Fordia to the south. The Catacombs are too small to sustain more than the present population, and we are having to fly ever further to hunt. Soon, there will be no wildlife left in the vicinity, and what will we eat then? What kind of life will the three children of Darksky have if we remain here?'

Deathfang emitted a low laugh, but Maddie noticed that a few of the other dragons seemed to be paying attention. Burntskull edged into the hall, but kept out of range of Blackrose's claws.

'You all know that I am from another world,' she went on; 'a world populated by dragons – our true home, the place from where every dragon is descended. It used to be a paradise, but it needs our help. The gods of Implacatus now hold dominion over the fair lands and wide oceans that belong to us, and our kin are in chains; treated as slaves, while greenhides infest many islands. In your hearts, you know that this injustice shames us all; that this is a wrong that must be put right. I shall return there...'

'Good,' muttered Burntskull. 'Make it soon, if you can.'

Blackrose glared at him as Deathfang laughed.

'I propose,' she said, 'that when I return to Dragon Eyre to reclaim what is rightfully ours, I will take with me all who are willing.'

'You're welcome to take any fool who decides to follow you,'

Burntskull said. 'Here, we are our own masters, and you would have us leave in order to fight a war against the gods? A war you have already fought once and lost?'

'Yes. It is true that we were defeated; I was defeated, and cast down from the throne of my father. The pain of that defeat bites deep, but I would rather fight again than live out my days in the squalor of a cave like a rat.'

Deathfang's red eyes stared at her. 'Cease your useless words; I have heard enough. You arrive at the Catacombs, uninvited, and preach to us? You call us rats? Begone, and be grateful you leave alive.'

'Wise words, mighty Deathfang,' said Burntskull, 'but I would add a suggestion. If Blackrose wishes to remain in the Catacombs, then she must give up her insect-loving ways. You recall the harness she was wearing when she first came here? We tore it from her back and threw it into a lava pit, rather than have to endure the sight of it. And here she is today, with that insect on her shoulders. There is another in her tomb, along with that pathetic pit-dragon she is protecting. Both of her pet insects should be treated in the same way as her harness; both should die while she watches. If she is a true dragon, she will not mind shedding the symbols of her weakness.'

'If you try,' said Blackrose, 'then you may succeed, but how many of you will die in the attempt?' She glanced around the hall. 'You have all seen me fight, and you know my teeth will rip out your throats if you touch my rider.'

Deathfang laughed, but his eyes were troubled. 'Go,' he said. 'I have grown tired of listening to you.'

Blackrose tilted her head, then turned and walked from the hall, the eyes of every other dragon on her. Maddie remained silent, watching them. They passed Darksky, who moved back, a protective forelimb shielding her three children, then Blackrose launched herself from the ledge at the front of the tomb.

'Malik's ass,' said Maddie as soon as they were airborne. 'I thought we were going to die in there.'

'Nonsense,' said Blackrose, 'that went very well, I thought.'

'Burntskull threatened to throw me into a pool of lava.'

'Of course he did; I would have been very surprised if he hadn't. Deathfang's reaction was all that mattered, and I could see the fear in his eyes. Eventually, I will probably have to fight him, and when I do, I shall be obliged to kill him. One cannot leave former rulers alive, and he will realise this. He will also realise, if he has any intelligence, that it will benefit him if I depart with several of the dragons that live here. It would solve many of his problems with overcrowding at a stroke.'

'And that pile of gold he was sitting on,' Maddie said; 'that was weird.'

'It's the contents of every looted tomb in the Catacombs. He thinks it makes him seem regal, but it's merely a gaudy, vulgar display that does him no credit at all.'

They circled lower, and Maddie crinkled her nose at the stench from the mist-like tendrils of vapours that were rising around them.

'Down there,' Blackrose said. 'Someone is climbing the path that leads to our tomb.'

'What? A human?'

'Yes, a woman. She has an air of Karalyn Holdfast about her, though it is not her.'

Maddie leaned over and stared through the vapours, her eyes scanning the steep path that led from their tomb to the bottom of the valley. She squinted, and made out a tiny figure against the cliffside. Blackrose swooped down, and Maddie clung on as the dragon descended to the level of the woman.

The woman turned as Blackrose hovered alongside her.

She smiled. 'You must be Blackrose. Maddie was right; you do look like a queen.'

'Sable?' cried Maddie.

The woman glanced up. 'Hello; I didn't see you up there.'

Blackrose's right forelimb shot out, and she plucked Sable from the path, along with the large bag she had been carrying. The dragon soared upwards, and deposited Sable inside her tomb as she landed. Maddie scrambled down, then ran to the woman and embraced her.

'Um...' said Sable; 'nice to see you too, I guess. Where's Millen?'

'I'm here,' came a voice from the shadows of the tomb's interior. Millen came into view, hobbling along on his crutch. His eyes were so wide, Maddie thought they might pop out of his head. She released Sable from her tight grip, and the woman strode up to Millen and kissed him on the cheek.

'Good to see you,' she said. 'Sorry I'm a little late; it's a long walk from Alea Tanton to the Catacombs.'

He flushed, his mouth hanging open. 'I... I...'

Sable raised an eyebrow at him, then turned to Maddie. 'How's Sanguino?'

'Not doing so well. Why are you here? I mean, it's good to see you, and thanks for the help in escaping and everything, but how did you know where we were?'

'I knew you would head to where the wild dragons live, and so I searched. I have vision powers. Why does everyone keep forgetting that?'

Blackrose dropped Sable's bag next to her. 'So we have a Holdfast in our tomb? I'm not sure that I'm pleased about this. The last Holdfast I met betrayed me, and I cursed her family.'

'I've done that a few times myself,' said Sable. 'Karalyn left me behind too.'

'What happened?' said Millen.

'I was captured, for a while.' She lifted her left hand, showing them the stump where her little finger had been. 'They tortured me, but I got away, with a little help from the girls in Renko's harem.'

Millen gasped. 'They cut your finger off?'

'A god called Maisk did that. I killed him ten minutes later.'

She picked up her bag and walked to the fire. 'I have food, wine and cigarettes.'

'But no Quadrant?' said Blackrose.

'Unfortunately not,' she said as she sat. 'One was destroyed, and Lord Renko took the others back with him to Implacatus. There will be other opportunities, though. Two Ascendants have arrived in Khatanax.

They destroyed the Falls of Iron, and they are now searching for the Sextant.' She lit a cigarette. 'We need to find it before they do.'

'And what is a Sextant?' said Blackrose.

'Never mind that,' said Maddie. 'I don't suppose you have any spare clothes in that bag? I've been wearing the same outfit for a month.'

Sable tossed the bag over to her. 'Help yourself; we're roughly the same size. Now, tell me about Sanguino.'

'We helped him escape, just like you told us,' she said as she rooted through the clothes in the bag; 'he brought us here, but then he got his ass kicked by two child-dragons; the equivalent of teenagers, I guess. Since then, he hasn't left the tomb. He's scared, and depressed. He says he wants to die.'

Sable nodded. 'I can fix that.'

Blackrose lowered her head, sniffing at Sable. 'How?'

She smiled. 'I can be very persuasive.'

CHAPTER 9

PRIORITIES

Capston, Southern Cape, Southern Khatanax – 29th Abrinch 5252
Kelsey flicked her cigarette ash over the side of the veranda. 'Corthie,' she said, 'I know we're on the run, and being chased by crazy gods and everything, but I really like it here. We're in a gorgeous little fishing town, with good food; and look at the view. Have you ever seen a sunset like it? The whole sky is red.'

He glanced at her. 'You'd like the City of Pella; the sky's red or pink nearly all day, and at night it glows purple.'

'Aye, Aila was telling me that, but I don't think I'd like to live somewhere surrounded by water and walls.'

'And greenhides.'

'Years ago, I had a vision where I saw you fighting those horrible beasts, did I ever tell you? It confused me for ages; I was starting to think I was going mad.'

Corthie took a sip of raki. Their rented villa spread out behind them on the slope of a hillside overlooking the town of Capston, the capital of the Southern Cape. The harbour was full of vessels, from small fishing boats, to larger ships being loaded with tobacco and wine bound for Alea Tanton. Somewhere among them was the galley that had brought them from the Falls of Iron, tied to one of the long piers.

'On the subject of visions,' he said, 'we should probably talk about Van.'

Her face fell. 'No.'

'Come on. I saved him because I thought he must be the guy you'd seen in a vision, but you've hardly said two words to him, or about him, since we left the Falls of Iron.'

'I don't want to talk about it.'

'But either he is the guy you saw, or he isn't; which is it?'

She lowered her eyes. 'It's him.'

'Then what's the problem?'

'Are you serious, brother? What if I told you that I'd had a vision of you being in love with another woman?'

'Have you?'

'Well, no, but try to imagine how it would make you feel. Would you just suddenly stop loving Aila? And what if you didn't even like the woman that I'd seen you with?'

'You don't like Van?'

'No, I don't. He's arrogant, full of himself, and I don't trust him. I tried to get to know him when he was locked up in the castle, but it was a waste of time. He told me he prefers the company of prostitutes, and yet he's supposed to be the man I spend the rest of my life with? I've often hated the fact that I catch glimpses of the future, but never as much as I do now.'

'Maybe your vision was wrong.'

She glared at him. 'They're never wrong.'

'No, what I meant was, maybe you're misinterpreting it? What exactly did you see?'

She sighed. 'A couple of years ago, I saw myself with another guy, and I could feel that I was in love with him, but I never got a clear image of who it was. I knew it wasn't the boy I was seeing at the time, that was clear enough, and so I broke up with him. Ever since then, I've had that vision in the back of my mind, wondering when I would finally meet him. And then, in the castle, after you killed that Joaz god person, I saw Van, and I had another vision, this time through his eyes. In it, he was looking at me, and from the way he was feeling, I knew he was the one I was meant to be with. But we were in a place I don't recognise, so in theory it could be years from now.'

'He thinks you're infatuated with him,' Corthie said, 'and, from his point of view, I guess that makes sense, though he doesn't understand why.'

'He looks at me like he thinks I'm a crazy woman. I hate him. More than that, I hate the way my prophecies become self-fulfilling. If I hadn't told you about it, then you wouldn't have saved his life, but you had to save his life, otherwise the prophecy wouldn't have come true, and they always come true. It's messed up, and it's driving me insane.'

'I feel sorry for you and Karalyn; this power seems more like a curse. Has it ever actually helped you?'

She shook her head. 'I don't think so, though Karalyn might answer differently; I have no idea what goes on inside our sister's head.'

'We've become strangers to each other. It's been years since the four Holdfast children were in the same room together.'

Kelsey shrugged. 'Mother has her two favourites with her. Do you remember when she used to be scared of Karalyn? That's all changed; and Keir? Mother's always adored him more than the rest of us.'

'You used to adore him too.'

'Aye. I was his faithful little hound, always following him about, even when he was behaving like a right numpty.' She laughed. 'He'd wet himself if he ever saw you again; you'd kick his arse.'

Corthie smiled. The thought of beating up his older brother had been something he had fantasised about when younger.

'Back to Van,' he said.

She groaned.

'What will we do with him? Should we let him go? We have four guards in the villa to ensure he doesn't escape, but if you hate him, then why are we bothering? I know you don't like the word "destiny", but if you and him are going to end up together, then does it matter what we do?'

'All of our choices matter, brother. If we release him, then he could betray our location to the gods. They're still out there, hunting us, though finding the Sextant seems to be their priority at the moment, rather than finding us.'

One of the guards stepped out onto the veranda. Like the others, he was in civilian clothing, but had a sword strapped to his belt.

'Sir, ma'am,' he said; 'Lady Aila has returned.'

Corthie stood. 'Thanks.' He stretched, and finished the raki in his glass as Kelsey stubbed out her cigarette and got to her feet. Lamps had been lit inside the villa, and they walked into a large dining room. Vana was sitting by herself, staring at the floor, while Aila was carrying full bags over to the long table where they ate their meals.

'Did you get everything on the list?' said Kesley.

'Yeah, I think so,' said Aila.

'Did you remember the coffee? You forgot last time.'

Aila frowned as she lifted the heavy bags up onto the table. 'You can do the shopping any time you like.'

'Aye, but you can change your appearance; I can't. Corthie and I aren't supposed to leave the villa.'

'It doesn't mean I'm your servant.'

Kelsey raised an eyebrow. 'A little touchy today, Lady Aila.'

'I had to spend hours queuing up in grocers, butchers, fishmongers, tobacconists...'

'You got my cigarettes?'

Aila narrowed her eyes. 'Of course I got your cigarettes. I knew the fuss you'd make if I forgot them.'

'Stop bickering,' said Vana from her chair. 'I can't stand it.'

'Sorry,' said Aila, as Kelsey pulled a face behind the demigod's back.

Corthie helped unload the shopping from the bags, and eyed the small amount of alcohol that Aila had bought. With her going out every couple of days for supplies, he had been reluctant to ask her to buy more.

'Learn anything interesting?' he said.

'What, from standing around in shops?' she said. 'It's Naxor's job to find out things; I'm apparently just Kelsey's servant.'

'And not a very good one,' said Kelsey. 'I mean, one bottle of raki? You do realise that there are eleven people living here, right? Are we supposed to have a thimbleful each?'

'I'm meant to be a little old lady,' said Aila; 'that's what I look like to everyone in the town. It would be strange if I bought a crate of raki every couple of days; people would get suspicious.'

'Then you should vary your disguise. Pop into the shop as the little old lady, then go back in ten minutes later looking like someone else. Pyre's tits, it's not that difficult.'

'Stop whining,' said Corthie. He picked up a couple of cartons of cigarettes. 'I'm going to give these to our prisoners; try not to kill each other.'

He walked past Vana, who glanced away, and entered the rear of the villa. A guard nodded to him as he approached a door.

'Are you going in, sir?'

Corthie nodded. 'Aye.'

The guard knocked on the door, then unlocked it, and Corthie strode through. Inside, Van and Sohul were lounging on a long couch. The captain was on his back, staring at the ceiling, while Sohul glanced over the top of a book.

Corthie threw the cigarettes at them as the door was closed behind him.

'Thanks,' said Van, catching them. He ripped one of the cartons open and lit two, passing one to his lieutenant. 'Any news?'

Corthie sat and shook his head.

'Tell us what you're doing, and maybe we could help.'

'You'd help us?' said Corthie.

Van shrugged. 'I said "maybe". I can't promise anything, because we have no idea why we're here. When's dinner?'

'Aila's just back from the shops, so it won't be long.'

'You do realise that cigarettes and mealtimes are all that's keeping me from losing my mind? You haven't let us out of this room since we arrived. Is there any weed?'

'No.'

'Surely Kelsey must have some.'

'She doesn't; she ran out days ago, and it doesn't seem that you can buy any here in Capston.'

'Booze?'

'Not enough for you, I'm afraid. Why don't you read a book?'

Van groaned. 'You sound like Sohul. How long will we be here for?'

'For as long as it takes. Unless the gods find us, of course, then we'll have to move quickly. What would you do if I allowed you the freedom of the entire villa?'

Van smiled. 'I'd speak to Kelsey, and ask her the same questions that you refuse to answer.'

'Would you run away?'

Van and Sohul shared a glance, and Corthie got to his feet.

'If I said no, would you believe me?' said Van.

'Probably not.'

Corthie knocked on the door, and the guard opened it and let him out. He watched as the door was locked again, then returned to the dining room. Aila and Kelsey were preparing dinner, while Vana was in the same chair as before, smoking quietly.

'How are our guests?' said Aila.

'Bored,' said Corthie, sitting at the table. 'Not that I blame them.'

Aila glanced at Kelsey. 'When are you going to tell us the truth about Van?'

Kelsey shrugged. 'Never, I hope. It's bad enough that I know.'

'You can't help who you fall for, I suppose.'

'I haven't fallen for him; he's an arrogant idiot, and he's worked for the gods, our enemies, for half of his life. He only cares about himself.'

The back door to the dining room opened and Naxor strode in,

'Good evening, all,' he beamed. He glanced at the meal preparations. 'Something smells wonderful.' He took off his long coat and threw it over the back of a chair, then opened the new bottle of raki and poured himself a large measure.

'Well?' said Corthie.

Naxor raised an eyebrow.

Corthie frowned at him. 'Did you find out anything?'

'Let's see,' said Naxor. 'I read the minds of a dozen people; I found out several things.'

'Anything about Belinda?'

'There are plenty of rumours around town that the Third Ascendant is back on Lostwell, but I think we already knew that. No one I read knows her location, however.'

'You must have some idea where she went.'

'As I have told you many, many times, my dear Corthie, I haven't the slightest notion where she is, or why she took off the way she did. I remember falling asleep, and when I awoke, she had gone. It saddens me greatly that you don't seem to believe me. I loved her; I am the true victim in all of this.'

'Your excuses didn't make sense then, and they don't make sense now. Belinda wouldn't have deserted us without a good reason.'

Naxor reclined onto a couch. 'What can I say? I've already told you everything I know.'

'And what about the Ascendants? Any word on what they're doing?'

'Consolidating their grip on Khatanax. They've subdued Tordue, and Kinell has sent them pledges of undying loyalty. The Four Counties, or should we call them the Three Counties now? Either way, they've also submitted. Oh, and I found one of their agents in Capston.'

'What?' said Aila, turning. 'You found an agent of the gods, here?'

'Yes. He was sniffing around our ship at the harbour, and so I followed him. Unfortunately, he realised I was on his tail, but not before I discovered where he's living.'

'Is he a god?' said Corthie.

'A demigod. He has vision powers, like me. Right now, he's probably telling the Ascendants that he's located our ship.'

The kitchen fell silent.

'Or maybe not,' Naxor went on. 'I did rather a good job of forging the ship's documents, and there are no crew currently on board whose minds he could read.'

'Did he read your mind?' said Kelsey.

'Who's to say? Perhaps. I was just beginning to look into his thoughts when he noticed I was following him. That's how I know he is definitely working for the Ascendants. I imagine his priority is locating the Sextant; finding us would just be a bonus.'

Corthie shook his head. 'Get your coat back on.'

'Why?'

'You said you know where he lives; we're going there, now.'

'But what about dinner? I'm famished.'

'It'll have to wait. Aila, you should come too. Kelsey, Vana, stay here.'

Kelsey frowned. 'I thought you weren't supposed to leave the villa?'

Corthie pulled on his boots. 'I'll make an exception.'

Twenty minutes later, Corthie, Aila and Naxor were walking through the dark streets of the town. A few lamps had been lit, illuminating the front of harbourside taverns, while several of the boats also had lights. Fishing vessels were being unloaded by a quay, their catch being emptied into huge barrels. Corthie's stature had attracted a few glances, but he had pulled a hood over his head and stuck to the shadows. They took a road that led away from the harbour, and Naxor gestured ahead.

'Nearly there,' he said. 'What's the plan?'

'Aila should lead,' said Corthie. He glanced at her. 'Can you make yourself look like one of the town's night-watchmen?'

'Sure,' she said.

'When he comes to the door, tell him that a suspicious-looking man's been seen hanging around outside the front of his house, and we'll follow you in once we know he's there.'

They paused in the shadows, and Naxor pointed to a stone cottage by the roadside. The shutters were all closed, but a soft light was filtering through to the outside.

'Check the rear of the house, Naxor,' Corthie said.

The demigod's eyes glazed over for a moment. 'It's clear.'

Corthie nodded to Aila. She glanced up at him, then crossed the street. To him, she looked the same, but he knew that to everyone else, she would appear like one of the town's night-watchmen. She strode up to the front door of the cottage, and knocked, while Corthie and Naxor waited in the deep shadows on the other side of the street.

She knocked again, then waited.

'Maybe he's not in,' said Naxor.

'Or maybe he's using his vision,' said Corthie. 'Check.'

Naxor sighed, then his eyes glazed over again. He coughed. 'Oh. You're right. He's visioning to someone as we speak.'

'Who?'

'I can't tell.'

'Bollocks,' Corthie muttered. He ran across the road. 'We're going in,' he said to Aila, then he kicked the front door open and charged into the cottage.

'The room to the left,' cried Naxor, as Corthie raced inside.

A man was sitting cross-legged on the floor, his eyes hazy. Corthie strode forwards and slapped him across the face, sending him flying. He fell to the wooden floor, choking and gasping, and Corthie picked him up by the throat.

'Is this him?' he said to Naxor.

'Um, yes,' said the demigod as Aila watched.

Corthie put his other hand over the man's eyes, and forced him onto a chair. Aila glanced around, then picked up a shirt from a table and ripped the arm off.

'Use this,' she said.

Corthie took it and tied it round the man's face to blindfold him. The man struggled, and Corthie pinned him to the chair.

'Don't move,' he whispered into the man's ear, 'or things might get a little painful.'

'Who are you?' the man cried.

Corthie held him in position as Aila and Naxor tied his hands behind his back.

'Are we going to torture him?' said Naxor.

'If we have to,' said Corthie. He slapped the man again. 'Listen carefully. We know you work for the gods of Implacatus. Is that who you were visioning to?'

'I'll tell you nothing,' the man shouted.

'Then we'll break you,' Corthie said; 'piece by piece. We know you're a demigod; we know that your self-healing will fix you, but that doesn't mean you won't suffer first.'

Aila frowned. 'Why don't we just get Naxor to read him?'

'What if he's more powerful than Naxor?' said Corthie. 'How does that work?

Naxor frowned. 'Well, whichever of the two of us has the strongest vision powers will be able to read the other. If we're roughly equivalent, then we'll exhaust each other. If, however, someone were to apply pain to him, that would significantly weaken him, allowing me in.'

'You will pay for this!' cried the man. 'The Ascendants will destroy you all!'

Corthie hesitated. He had been bluffing before, when he had said that he would torture the man. He crouched down next to him, watching as he struggled against the restraints securing him to the chair.

'Listen,' he said, 'I don't want to cause you pain, but I shall. Tell us what we need to know, and you will be unharmed.'

'Who are you?'

'My name is Corthie Holdfast.'

The man stilled.

'Nod if you've heard of my family.'

He nodded.

'You know our reputation; you know we kill gods. You have my word; if you answer our questions, then we will release you. If you don't then... this won't end well.'

'You... you are truly one of the accused Holdfasts?'

'I am.'

The man started to tremble. 'You give your word you won't hurt me?'

'I do. What's your name?'

'Bartov.'

'Hang on a moment,' said Naxor, scratching his chin. He snapped his fingers. 'I thought you seemed familiar.'

'You know him?' said Aila.

Naxor nodded. 'He used to work for Agatha.'

'And you used to supply salve to Dun Khatar,' said Bartov. 'I recognised you when you tried to follow me earlier.'

'So, you're a rebel?' said Corthie. 'Everyone who worked for Agatha was a rebel, like Silva.'

'He might have been a rebel once,' said Naxor, 'but I got a glimpse into his mind before; he definitely works for the Ascendants now.'

'You must have known Belinda,' Corthie said. 'Where is she?'

'No one knows,' said Bartov. 'The Ascendants in Alea Tanton are searching the continent for her, but she's disappeared.'

Naxor frowned. 'We can't trust a word he says.' He pulled a knife from his coat, crouched, and rammed it into the man's foot, pinning it to the floor. 'That should do it,' he said, as the man yelled in pain. 'Take his blindfold off.'

Corthie glared at him.

Naxor shrugged. 'I didn't realise you were so queasy about such things.' He leaned forward and removed the shirt sleeve that was covering Bartov's eyes. He smiled as his eyes went hazy. 'I'm in, well, half in; I can still hear you. Alright, let's see what we have here. Oh, he's a nasty little traitor. He hates Agatha, and loathed Belinda; he blamed Belinda for the gods' invasion of Lostwell. Apparently, she preferred to stay by Nathaniel's side, even after he was dead, rather than fight. It was Bartov who told the gods of Alea Tanton where their secret refuge was, and it was also he who told Renko about the existence of the Sextant.'

'Does he know where the Sextant is?' said Corthie, trying to ignore the agony on the face of the demigod.

'No, but he did see it being loaded onto a ship, here, in Capston, about seven years ago. Belinda and Agatha took it north, but he doesn't know where.' Naxor pursed his lips. 'He was telling the truth about Belinda; they don't know where she is. Finding her is their priority, along with the Sextant. Our family and the Holdfasts come a distant third, I'm afraid. He was in the middle of communicating with Arete, the Seventh Ascendant, when we interrupted him. Fortunately, he hadn't revealed my presence to her, but I'm sure her attention will soon be focussed onto the Southern Cape.'

'I don't understand,' said Aila. 'It was the same with the Falls of Iron; why have they stopped looking for the source of the salve?'

'They haven't,' said Naxor; 'they've realised that they won't be able to figure out its exact location from our heads, and therefore we are expendable. That's why they're after the Sextant – it will lead them directly to our two worlds. The thoughts in our heads are too vague to pinpoint something as distant as another world; only the Sextant, and any Quadrant that has been there will do the trick.'

'Karalyn has one of them,' said Corthie; 'the one that belonged to the God-King.'

'And we know who has the, eh, God-Queen's Quadrant,' said Aila.

Naxor began to pace up and down. 'This confirms my theory. I was puzzled at first when they killed Irno, but now it makes sense.' He stopped by the table, picked up a sword, and removed it from its scabbard. 'Stand back, if you please.'

Before Corthie could react, Naxor swung the sword, slicing through Bartov's neck with a single, powerful stroke. The demigod's head flew through the air, striking the wall and falling to the floor, before rolling to a stop by Corthie's feet.

'I gave him my word,' Corthie said.

Naxor shrugged. 'I didn't.'

'Let's get this straight,' said Aila. 'To find our world, they need either the Sextant, or Queen Amalia's Quadrant?'

'Precisely, cousin,' said Naxor. 'They most likely learned this when they read Irno's mind before killing him. That explains why their hunt for us has been so lacklustre. They don't need us. We'll have to look at a map, and try to work out possible destinations where Belinda might have sent the Sextant.'

'I gave him my word,' Corthie repeated, his voice raised.

Naxor and Aila glanced at him. Naxor laughed. 'I thought your family killed gods for fun? If we'd released him, then he would have contacted Arete the moment we had gone.' He wiped the bloody sword on Bartov's clothes and re-sheathed it. 'Nice weapon; I think I'll keep it.'

He tucked the sword under his coat and strode from the room. Corthie gazed at the corpse.

'He was an enemy, Corthie,' said Aila.

'You're agreeing with what Naxor did?'

'I've done the same thing myself,' she said. 'And so have you.'

'But never after promising someone I wouldn't.'

'We're fighting for the survival of our worlds, Corthie; it's war.' She nodded to the door. 'Come on; let's get out of here before the real night-watchmen turn up.'

He watched as she walked to the door, then turned back to the head-less body tied to the chair. He thought back to the countless times he had slaughtered his enemies; greenhides, and humans, both mortal and immortal. Was Aila right? She had been unhappy when he had killed the soldiers who had surrendered in the Falls of Iron, but what if he had been mistaken about the cause of her sorrow? He had assumed she felt sorry for the dead soldiers, but maybe she had only been concerned about the effect the killings might have on him. He had to remember that, just like Naxor, she was a demigod, and her morality had a different set of rules.

He pulled his gaze from the body, and followed her.

CHAPTER 10

MEMORIES OF SAND AND ASH

Dun Khatar, Southern Khatanax – 29th Abrinch 5252

The sand and ash swirled around the two travellers as they walked along the wide, ruined boulevard. Overhead, the noontide sun was beating down upon them, and the rocks of the city were hot to touch. They reached a dry, barren river course, and climbed down the stone embankment, the nearby bridges having collapsed long before. On the other side rose the bases of the two enormous statues that Belinda remembered seeing when she had been in the city with Aila – King Nathaniel to the left, and Queen Belinda on the right.

They crossed the cracked stones of the riverbed, and scaled the far embankment, Belinda helping Silva climb the last few yards.

'Thank you, your Majesty,' the demigod said, bowing. Silva glanced around, then walked to the base of the Belinda statue. She frowned, and knelt by the side of the huge pedestal. 'With me being away in the Falls of Iron, no one has tended your flowers. I suppose there's less need of them, now that you have returned.'

Belinda walked over, and stood behind her as she tidied away the dead flowers. She felt an urge to tell her about her inner-vision powers, the same urge she had felt many times on their journey from the Four Counties, but her tongue remained frozen inside her mouth. She had barely spoken in days, partly because words made her cry, and she didn't want to embarrass herself again in front of Silva; and partly because her misery seemed physical. She felt as though a weight was pressing down on her, keeping her mouth closed, while her chest had a tightness that caused her pain. Naxor's betrayal had made her doubt everything, and even her own thoughts seemed untrustworthy.

Silva glanced up at her. Belinda hadn't told her the reason for their sudden departure from the Falls of Iron, and she wondered what the woman made of it, though her curiosity wasn't enough to make her want to read the demigod's mind. After what she had seen in Naxor's head, she didn't want to risk looking in anyone else's, worried about the unpleasant truths she would find there.

'I'm here, your Majesty,' Silva said, 'if you ever want to talk about what's upsetting you.'

Belinda frowned, then realised that she had been crying. She turned away and wiped her face, angry with herself. She took a long breath, then another, trying to calm her thoughts, but her anger only increased. Why had she ever believed in that lying rat? Why had she trusted him? She must be so stupid, so stupid. Everyone would be laughing at her. Stupid Belinda. She clenched her fists, suppressing a scream of rage.

'I want to show you something, your Majesty,' Silva said behind her.

Belinda's anger dissipated, replaced by the heavy feeling again. She turned.

'This way,' said Silva, and she set off along the embankment by the side of the Belinda statue. They walked in silence, heading towards the large, ruined palace.

'I know you've been to the palace before, your Majesty,' Silva said as they got closer to the great edifice; 'I sensed a trace of your powers within its walls, but you didn't go into the rooms that I want to show you.'

They crossed the plaza in front of the palace and entered through its wide, broken doors. To the left, Belinda noticed shards of the brandy jug that she had smashed after getting drunk with Aila lying scattered over the ground. Silva led her to a staircase to the right of the large hall, and they ascended the worn steps to the highest level still standing. The roof was missing in parts, but Silva pointed to a more intact wing of the palace.

'Your quarters were in here, your Majesty,' she said. 'Of course, the palace was rebuilt and remodelled many times over the centuries, but this wing was your home for the longest period, right up until Implacatus invaded Khatanax.'

They went through a ruined opening, and entered a long hall, with rooms opening off either side.

'This was your audience chamber,' Silva said, 'and my rooms were to the right.' She pointed at a rough stone platform that rose a few feet above the rest of the floor. 'Your throne sat there, your Majesty, right next to that of King Nathaniel. Ah, the sight of you sitting side by side was the most glorious and regal spectacle I ever saw; their Royal Majesties; a wondrous splendour to behold.' She sniffed, and a tear snaked down her cheek. They walked onwards and passed through an arched opening behind the throne platform. Silva led Belinda through a series of passageways, until they came to a large chamber with another square platform, measuring several yards in length. There were no windows in the room, but a hole in the ceiling was letting in the sunlight.

'This is what I wanted to show you, your Majesty,' said Silva. 'It may look like another throne room, but that platform was used to support something else – the Sextant.'

Belinda gazed down, and noticed grooves and holes cut into the surface of the platform. They were weathered but still deep. From them, Belinda guessed that the Sextant stood on six circular feet, and was two yards in width, and three in length. She turned back to the entrance, and saw that the stones above the doorway had been neatly removed.

Silva caught where she was looking and smiled. 'They demolished half of that wall to get the Sextant out of the palace. I remember that you didn't want to leave, but Lady Agatha insisted, and she was right; the gods of Implacatus arrived a few days after our departure and destroyed the city. The carnage was the worst I have ever heard of. Every civilian who remained behind was slaughtered like animals. They lay where they fell, until the sand and wind reduced their bones to dust. Your people, your Majesty.'

Belinda glanced back at the platform. Was Silva trying to provoke a reaction from her? She tried to imagine the slaughter of the inhabitants of Dun Khatar, but it left her feeling cold, as if she was listening to a story rather than the truth of what had occurred.

Silva gave her a sad smile. 'Is any of this stirring any memories, your Majesty?'

'There are no memories in me, so none can be stirred.'

Silva nodded, but her eyes looked doubtful, as if she couldn't quite believe that Belinda's memories had gone forever, no matter how many times she had been told.

'This last room,' she said, pointing towards a dark entrance by the far wall, 'was where you looked after King Nathaniel when he fell into the long sleep.'

They walked to the opening, and Belinda gazed inside. It was empty, and its window had crumbled into a gaping hole. Sand was piled high in drifts by the other walls, and the wind was swirling it around the stone floor.

'It's hard to picture it now, your Majesty,' Silva said, 'but you spent over a century in this room. The King's bed was on the right, and you nursed him here, day after day, while you left Agatha to rule Khatanax. There was a stool, just there on the left, where I used to sit, ministering to your needs as best I could. It was here where I gave you the salve that restored your youth. We gave some to King Nathaniel too, in an effort to revive him. His body was rejuvenated, but his spirit never returned to us.'

She fell silent, and Belinda watched her face for a moment as her tears fell.

'After the Sextant had been removed from the palace,' she went on, 'the time had come to carry the King's unconscious body to the prepared refuge of Shawe Myre. You and I followed the guard of honour that bore him away, and we walked the entire route through the mountains. We still had hope, back then, that his Majesty would awaken.'

'Why didn't I stay and fight?'

Silva turned, her eyes dark. 'Lady Agatha urged you to. The salve had brought you back to your full strength, she said, and as the Third Ascendant, only you had the power to resist the might of Implacatus. You refused, your Majesty. You said that all things were fleeting, even a city as magnificent as Dun Khatar, and that the only important duty was to watch over King Nathaniel until he awoke. It was when you told Lady Agatha this that she ordered the evacuation. Many who had remained loyal for millennia deserted you at that point; they fled, scattering far and wide. Some made their peace with Implacatus, while others were hunted down and destroyed.'

They left the chamber, and began to make their way back down to the ground floor of the palace. Instead of walking back outside, Silva led Belinda through a series of passageways until they came to another set of stairs, which went down. They descended into the dark gloom of the basements beneath the palace, and Belinda made a low glow of sparks appear from her fingertips to light the way. Silva pushed on, deeper into the underground caverns, until they heard the sound of running water.

'There is an ancient spring here,' said Silva, 'where we can fill our waterskins. It's not fresh, in fact it would kill any mortal who tried to drink it, but it will suffice for us.'

They walked along a tunnel, until they came to a stone spout emerging from the side of a wall. From it, a flow of cloudy water was spilling into a cracked and worn basin, before seeping into the ground. Silva filled their waterskins, then picked up a fresh torch from a bundle that lay close by.

'Could you please light this, your Majesty?'

Belinda raised her hand, and sparks shot out, igniting the torch and filling the cavern with a warm glow. She glanced around. Along the opposite wall was a row of massive, stone sarcophagi, and there were also signs of recent habitation – blankets, packs, and dark patches where fires had been lit.

'This is where I stayed, your Majesty,' Silva said, 'whenever I came to visit the city. It is the only place in Dun Khatar with water of any kind, and it offers shelter from the sandstorms, eruptions and earthquakes that plague the area.'

She picked up the two full waterskins and made her way to a pile of blankets between two tombs, then sat. Belinda remained standing, her eyes scanning the intricate carvings on the row of tombs. On top of each were life-sized stone figures lying in repose, warriors and nobles. Safe from the winds, the carvings had retained much of their detail, and she could see the individual features on the faces of the figures.

'Who is buried down here?' she said.

Silva glanced up at her. 'Those of the royal family who perished before the final invasion. For five thousand years, you ruled this world with King Nathaniel, your Majesty, and the forces of Implacatus went to war with Lostwell many times.'

'The royal family? You mean, my family?'

'Yes, your Majesty.' Silva turned to the sarcophagus next to her, and Belinda noticed that several candle stubs were arranged by its base. 'This tomb belongs to Lord Gaudin, who died over two thousand years ago defending Estinax, a continent far to the west that is now overrun with greenhides. His body was brought back here after he fell, and was given full honours.' She looked into Belinda's eyes. 'He was my father, your Majesty, and your grandson.'

Belinda stared at her. 'You... you are my granddaughter?'

'Your great-granddaughter, your Majesty.'

'Nathaniel and I had children?'

Silva smiled, but there was no joy in it. 'Dozens, your Majesty. You were partners for many millennia.'

Belinda walked over, and crouched by Silva. 'Where are they all?'

'Some lie entombed in this chamber, your Majesty, while others were born before you rebelled against the other Ascendants, and presumably still live on Implacatus, along with their descendants.'

'Some are buried here?'

Silva nodded. 'Yes.'

Belinda stood. She lit one of the spare torches, and walked alongside the long row of tombs. On each was carved a name that was unknown to her. Were some of them the resting places of her children? She took a closer look at one that had the figure of a woman carved onto its massive lid. At the end of the tomb, words had been carved into the stone.

Lady Bethan, beloved daughter of King Nathaniel and Queen Belinda
Born in the year 871, Died in the year 2199, Aged 1317
Rest in Peace, Little Flower

Belinda sank to her knees, overcome with the weight of her history, and she wept, crying for a daughter she couldn't remember.

At Belinda's insistence, Silva took her by every tomb in the long cavern, pointing out how each person had been related to her. They passed sons, daughters, and over a dozen grandchildren. Belinda's tears dried up after the fifth or sixth sarcophagus, her mind numbed by the enormity of what she was witnessing. It wasn't only the dead who haunted her thoughts; the knowledge that she almost certainly had descendants still alive and living on Implacatus and other worlds was overwhelming. After a while, the names and lineages started to blur together, and when they had completed their tour, she sat on a blanket spread over the ground, her eyes lowered as Silva prepared them some food.

Next to the magnitude of what she had learned, her troubles with Naxor seemed almost insignificant; trivial even. She had been hurt by him, but he was unworthy of her tears. She was the Third Ascendant, and Naxor was nothing but a shallow fraud compared to her. Despite knowing this to be true, her chest still ached from his betrayal, and she promised herself that she would never give her heart to anyone else without first understanding their true feelings.

She glanced at Silva. 'I have inner-vision.'

The demigod's eyes widened as she turned to face Belinda. 'Excuse me, your Majesty?'

'I have inner-vision.'

'That's... that's excellent news. When did your power re-appear?'

'In the Falls of Iron, not long after Count Irno was slain by the two Ascendants who attacked us. I found out by accident; I went into Naxor's mind without meaning to.'

'I see. Should I assume, your Majesty, that what you saw in there was instrumental in your decision to leave?'

'Yes.' She shook her head. 'I was a fool to think he loved me.'

'You're not a fool. Love can trick even the wisest into making mistakes.'

'So you agree that Naxor was a mistake?'

'It's true that I didn't like him, your Majesty. I always felt him to be untrustworthy, and unfit to be your partner. However, whenever I mentioned such things to you, you would rebuke me, so I learned to keep my mouth closed.'

'He also lied to me about Sable Holdfast. Do you remember he told us that she had betrayed him? The truth is that he offered her everything in return for the Quadrant. He asked her to return with him to the City of Pella, and promised to be her lover, and shower her with palaces, gold and riches.' She gave a wry smile. 'And Sable refused. She rejected his advances. She used her vision powers and saw right through his lies; he didn't want her either, he only wanted the Quadrant that she possessed. I almost killed him.'

'Perhaps you should have, your Majesty.'

She shrugged. 'Maybe. Part of me is glad I didn't, glad that I didn't sully my hands with his blood.'

'He is unworthy to kiss your feet, your Majesty.'

'Another part of me wishes to make him suffer, watch him writhe in pain, listen to him beg for his life; part of me desires to see his blood on my hands. I want his last words to be "I'm sorry" before I cut his throat.'

Silva said nothing for a moment, then passed Belinda a bowl of food.

'With every power that is restored to you,' she said, 'you are becoming more whole again. I freely admit that I doubted the promise of Karalyn Holdfast, but you were correct, your Majesty. First sparking, and now inner-vision.' She paused for a moment. 'Have you used it since?'

Belinda glanced at her. Something about the demigod's tone was making her wary. 'No.'

Silva nodded. 'May I ask why not?'

Belinda frowned. 'You may.'

'Apologies,' Silva said, her face flushing; 'I forget how you detest such prevarication.' She took a breath. 'Why haven't you used your new power again?'

'I'm afraid. If the man I loved was lying to me, then what else are people hiding? I longed for this power in particular, so that I would be able to distinguish friend from foe, but now I just worry that I have no friends, that everyone I know thinks I'm stupid. That's why I couldn't face Aila and the others; what if I went into their minds, without meaning to, and discovered what they truly thought of me?'

Silva glanced away, her eyes troubled.

'You're worrying me, Silva. Are you hiding something?'

The demigod swallowed. 'I, too, am unworthy, your Majesty.'

The anger within Belinda began to rise to the surface again. 'What lies have you told me?'

Silva edged backwards. 'None, your Majesty, I swear it. I have never told you a lie.'

'Then what do you have to fear? Why are you being evasive? Speak, or I will go into your mind and find out for myself.'

Silva burst into tears. 'I'm sorry, your Majesty!' she wailed. She bowed her head, lowering her body until she was prostrating herself before Belinda. 'I am unworthy.'

Belinda stared at her, her eyes narrow. She moved back from the demigod in disgust, and felt the hilt of the Weathervane jab into her waist. She glanced at the sheathed sword, and in a moment of uncontrolled rage, she drew it, and the dark blade glistened in the lamplight.

Silva let out a cry.

Belinda stood, and pointed the sword at the back of Silva's neck.

'Speak, or I will kill you here, next to the tomb of your father. What are you hiding from me?'

'My beloved Queen; my beloved great-grandmother, please, I beg you, let not your anger with your worthless servant end my life, even though I may deserve it.' She glanced up, her face streaked with tears. 'You were not the first god I sensed in the ruins of Dun Khatar this summer.'

Belinda frowned. 'Who else did you sense?'

'A god I had almost forgotten about, your Majesty; a god who fled Dun Khatar thousands of years ago to become the ruler of Nathaniel's salve-world; the Queen of the City of Pella – Amalia.'

'You sensed the presence of Amalia?'

'Yes, your Majesty, and then I tracked her down. She was attempting to flee across the Shinstran desert, alone, with no food or water. She was weak, and grievously wounded, her right arm shorn at the elbow. I did what I thought was right; I brought her back here, to the safety of these tombs, and tended her wounds.'

Belinda glanced around. 'She's here?'

'No, your Majesty; she departed the ruins before you arrived with the others from the salve-world. I assisted her; helped her travel to the refuge of Shawe Myre. She is there now, awaiting us.'

'This was all a trick? You betrayed me to Amalia? What was your plan – that she would ambush me to exact revenge? You loathsome creature; I should kill you now.'

'No!' Silva cried. 'Amalia doesn't want revenge; she still loves you as a friend. She told me everything, all about your arrival in the City of Pella, and that you had lost your memories and were allied to the Holdfasts. She even told me that you had betrayed her trust, and almost killed her, but she has forgiven you, your Majesty. All she wants is a chance to talk with you again. I spoke to her after I sensed your return to the ruins here, and she asked me to go to the Falls of Iron, to try to persuade you to reclaim what is rightfully yours, and to try to separate you from the others, none of whom are worthy of your friendship. I did as she asked, but not because she or

I wish any harm upon you. The opposite is true; we want to help you.'

Belinda kept the point of the sword against Silva's throat. 'If you wanted to help me, then why didn't you tell me any of this?'

'Because Amalia warned me that your memory loss had... confused you, your Majesty. She told me that if I was honest with you, then you would most likely kill me rather than listen to me. She knows that you hate her, and it pains her more than any wound. She wept ceaselessly, but not because of her arm, or because she had lost power in the City of Pella. No, your Majesty, she wept for you.'

'Amalia is a liar,' Belinda said. 'I saw the way she ruled the City of Pella; power is the only thing she cares about.'

'She told me that you would say that. She urged me to keep her presence here a secret for that reason. I believe her, your Majesty; I believe that she is genuinely sorry for the ill-feeling that developed between you on the salve-world. She wishes to make amends, she wishes to talk to you; most of all, she wants to be your friend again.' She stared into Belinda's eyes. 'Read my thoughts, my Queen, and you will see every conversation I have had with her. Judge for yourself, and if you are not satisfied, then take my head; I will deserve it.'

Belinda stared back. 'She truly wishes to be my friend, after what I did to her?'

'Yes, your Majesty. She knows it wasn't the true Belinda who acted that way.'

'She's wrong. I am the true Belinda, and there is no return to who I was before.'

Silva sobbed. 'Then all hope is lost.'

Belinda sheathed her sword. 'Maybe not.'

'Your Majesty?'

'If Amalia has forgiven me, then perhaps I can forgive her. I'm not sure I can forgive you, though.'

'I'm so sorry; I did what I thought was best for you; everything I have done has been for you, my beloved Queen.'

'You hid this from me, which is the same as lying. You were right, however. If you had told me this when we were in the Falls of Iron, then I would have dismissed you from my sight, or maybe I would have killed you. I assume Amalia remains in possession of her Quadrant?'

'I assume so, your Majesty.'

'Then get off your belly; I hate it when you grovel like that.'

Silva shuffled into a sitting position, her back to her father's sarcophagus. 'Will I ever receive your forgiveness for what I have done, your Majesty?'

'I don't know.'

'I will never hide anything from you again; I swear it.'

'How far away is Shawe Myre from here?'

'Ten days' walk, your Majesty, through the mountains.'

'Then gather your things; we're leaving.'

CHAPTER 11

BROKERING A DEAL

S outhern Cape, Southern Khatanax – 31ˢᵗ Abrinch 5252

'Do you reckon you could swim to shore from here?'

Sohul glanced at Van. 'I'm not sure, sir. The currents are powerful; do you see the way the ship is straining on the anchor? And those rocks, sir; they look pretty dangerous.'

'Come on, Lieutenant,' Van said; 'you'd make it.'

'Is that, um, an order, sir?'

Van leaned on the railing at the side of the galley as the vessel swayed back and forth on the swell. 'Technically, you're not under my command any more, Sohul. Our contract's up; it expired at midnight yesterday.'

Sohul frowned as he flicked cigarette ash over the side of the boat. 'So it did, sir; I mean, Van.'

They watched as a rowing boat approached. Their ship was anchored two hundred yards from a small bay with a jetty, beyond which a fishing village lay spread out along the hillside. The harbour was too small for the galley to dock, so Corthie had sent Naxor and two of the sailors in the rowing boat to pick up supplies and news.

Sohul shook his head. 'That means we've been prisoners for fifty days. I wonder if our death dues have been paid to our next-of-kin yet. My old mother will think I'm dead.'

'You'll get back home one day.' He gestured towards Corthie, who was standing with Aila near the bow of the ship. 'Our captors would have killed us by now if they had any intention of doing so. And look at us, we not chained up, or locked in the brig.'

'I don't think this boat has a brig.'

'You know what I mean. At the next sign of civilisation, I'm going to ask them to let you go. It's me they want, though I still haven't worked out why.'

'We have a pretty good idea, Van. It's that Kelsey girl; she's clearly fallen for you, even if she has an odd way of showing it.'

Van shook his head. 'I'm not buying that. She didn't speak to me once when we were staying in the villa in Capston, and the only thing she's said to me since we got back on the ship is "Get out of my way", and then she called me a numpty, or something like that.'

'Maybe in her language "numpty" is a term of endearment.'

'Regardless, they have no reason to keep you a captive any longer, especially now that you're unemployed.'

'It wouldn't feel right, deserting you like that. We've been through a lot over the years, Van. How could I ever face the officers and men of the Banner if I walked out? Contract or no contract, we're Golden Fist, and we stick together.'

Ropes were thrown down the side of the galley as the rowing boat pulled alongside. A small crane was pushed into position and secured to the deck, then sailors swung its arm out over the side. Naxor got to his feet inside the rowing boat, and began to climb a rope ladder, while two sailors attached the first water barrel to the crane's hook.

'I hate boats,' said Sohul.

Van raised an eyebrow. 'Why?'

'They remind me of Dragon Eyre. We seemed to spend half our time on boats there, sailing from one lizard-infested island to the next.'

'Funny, I don't mind them. I like the smell of the ocean, well, not the ocean by Alea Tanton, but it's clean on this side of Khatanax.'

Naxor climbed onto the deck, and Van watched as the demigod spoke to Corthie and Aila.

'I wonder how many times he's read our minds,' muttered Van.

Sohul narrowed his eyes. 'Several, I'd imagine.'

'If we could get rid of him, we could escape.'

Sohul glanced at the hilly countryside opposite the boat. The land was rocky and barren, and a series of high mountains were stretching away to the north. 'And go where?'

'It's only fifty miles back to Capston; we could walk it in a couple of days. From there we could get a ship to Alea Tanton.'

A cough came from behind them. Leaning against the side of a cabin was a sailor, his crossbow held in both hands, and a cigarette hanging from his lips. 'I can hear you, lads,' he said; 'just thought you should know.'

Van smiled. 'Why; are you interested in coming with us? The Hold-fast boy not paying you enough?'

'I'm paid enough to watch you clowns. Easy money, and with the added bonus that if one of you tries to run, I'll have the pleasure of shooting you.'

'Then you'll be the first sailor I've met who can shoot straight,' said Van, lighting a cigarette. He offered one to Sohul and then to their guard, who grinned, tossed the butt he was smoking over the side, and took it.

'Naxor seems a little agitated,' said Sohul, gesturing to the demigod, who was waving his arms about in Corthie's face.

'Maybe he's highly strung,' said Van, leaning back against the railing.

'Or maybe there's been bad news.'

Van frowned. 'Look at the size of that village; and it's in the middle of nowhere. What possible news could have reached here? They probably still think Nathaniel's the king.'

Corthie, Aila and Naxor walked across the deck, and disappeared down a wide hatch by the bow.

'I wonder if that means we'll be going soon,' said Sohul.

'I wouldn't get your hopes up, lads,' said their guard. 'The rowing boat will need to make a few trips back and forth yet to bring everything we need. It's about five hundred miles to the next harbour after this one, and another three hundred after that to get to Kinell.'

'Is that where we're headed?' said Van. 'Are we going to Kinell?'

The sailor shrugged.

At that moment, another sailor emerged from a hatch near the rear of the boat, and rang a bell hanging from a chain by the deck cabin.

'Lunchtime at last,' said their guard. 'Come on, lads, move it.'

They threw their cigarettes into the ocean and walked to the bow hatch, the sailor following them with his crossbow. They went down the steep flight of steps, then turned back towards the stern and entered a long room with tables bolted to the deck. Corthie and Naxor were arguing at the far end of the room, while Aila, Vana and Kesley were sitting close by.

Van and Sohul took their places on a bench as they waited for their meal to arrive.

'We have to go,' Corthie was saying. 'If there's a chance she's there, then we can't leave her.'

'But she already left us,' said Naxor, 'and we have no guarantee that Belinda will actually be there.'

'Where are you talking about?' said Kelsey.

'A place called Shawe Myre,' said Naxor.

Corthie nodded. 'It's the secret refuge where Belinda and the others hid for ages after Dun Khatar was destroyed. It turns out that it's not too far from here, maybe twenty or thirty miles. That's where Belinda will have gone.'

'We don't know that,' said Vana, 'and if it's so secret, then how did Naxor learn about it in that tiny village?'

'I read it from an old man's mind,' said Naxor, 'though I'm regretting telling you all about it. The old man remembers being in this Shawe Myre; the locals around here were supportive of Belinda and the other rebels, and they used to provide them with food and other supplies before the gods found it. But that's the problem, the gods *did* find it, seven years ago, and they sacked the place. Why would Belinda go back there?'

'Because that's what Silva would have wanted,' said Corthie, 'and I think Belinda will want to see Nathaniel's tomb.'

'I'm sorry,' said Aila, 'but I have to agree with Naxor on this one. There's a good chance that Belinda won't be there, but even if she is, we have to find the Sextant before the gods do; that's our mission. Belinda made it clear what she thought of us by walking out in the middle of a siege.'

Corthie glared at her, and the demigod glared back.

Van's attention snapped away as a bowl of fish and vegetables was placed in front of him by a sailor. He glanced at Sohul, but he was busy listening to their captors continuing to argue.

'I'm not abandoning her,' said Corthie, 'not after everything we've been through.' He scowled at Naxor. 'And, let's be honest here, I've never believed Naxor's story. He knows more than he's letting on about Belinda's disappearance. If I could just speak to her for even a moment I could straighten it out. I could be there and back in a few days.'

'We don't have a few days,' said Naxor. 'If we know that the Sextant was put onto a ship, then so do the two Ascendants in Alea Tanton. If they find it first, then both of our worlds will be destroyed.'

Van shared a sideways look with Sohul.

'You don't want me speaking to her,' said Corthie, prodding a finger into Naxor's chest, 'admit it. Because if I did, then she'd tell me what happened, and that's the last thing you want.'

'Boys, boys,' said Vana; 'I have a headache. Must you shout?'

'I'll go,' said Kelsey.

The others turned to her.

Kelsey shrugged. 'I could go. If the Sextant was last seen in this place, what was it called again?'

'Shawe Myre,' said Naxor.

'Aye,' said Kelsey. 'The Sextant was there, before it was put onto a ship. There might be clues about where it was taken. And I think

Corthie's right; it's the likeliest place for Silva to take Belinda. I can ask her what happened, and then I can follow you all north.'

Corthie shook his head. 'And how would you do that?'

'Get another boat, I suppose. I'm fairly resourceful. Just lend me some gold, and I could be on my way.'

'No,' said Naxor; 'out of the question. You, my young Holdfast, are what's keeping us safe from the Ascendants. Without you, they would be able to find us.'

'It's a pretty big ocean,' said Kelsey; 'they won't find you.'

'I refuse to allow it,' Naxor went on, 'you know what they did to Irno; they would do the same to us.'

'For a moment, Naxor,' said Corthie, 'I almost agreed with you, right up until the point where you seemed more worried about your own safety than my sister's. Who would look out for her on the road? She can't fight.'

Van coughed. 'If I may?'

Everyone in the group turned to look at him.

Van stood. 'If you are looking for someone to provide an armed escort, then allow me to offer you my services. It happens that Sohul and I are no longer under contract to the gods. For a suitable price, I would be prepared to guard any one of you.'

Naxor snorted. 'You? A dirty little mercenary? Forget it.'

'I am a mercenary,' said Van, 'and a damn good one. I have never once in thirteen years of service broken any contract that I have agreed to. For ten gold a day, plus expenses, I would be available to travel to Shawe Myre, and then to any location of your choosing. I can fight, ride, cook, hunt and, like Miss Holdfast, I am also fairly resourceful. I ask only that you consider my offer; thank you for listening.'

He sat, picked up a fork, and began to eat his lunch as the others continued to stare at him. Sohul chuckled quietly by his side, and he avoided meeting his glance in case he started to laugh. Out of the corner of his eye, he saw Kelsey get up from where she had been sitting and whisper something to Corthie. He frowned and shook his head, then the two of them strode from the room.

'What was that about?' said Naxor.

'Who knows?' said Aila.

Vana narrowed her eyes. 'The Holdfasts are keeping secrets from us.'

'You, my dear Vana,' said Naxor, 'have elevated stating the obvious to an art form. Of course they're keeping secrets. What about; that's what I want to know.'

'Corthie was right about one thing,' Aila said, 'you really don't want us finding Belinda, do you? If you loved her, you'd be desperate to find her.'

'She walked out on us; are you surprised that my feelings toward her have soured a little?'

'And Kelsey made a good point about the Sextant,' said Vana; 'perhaps there are clues to be found in Shawe Myre.'

Naxor gave a stony stare to the two women. 'Whose side you are on?'

'I hadn't realised there were sides, Naxor,' said Aila, 'but if you're asking me to choose between you and Corthie, then you lose.'

Naxor snarled and stormed from the room.

'You should have seen their faces,' said Sohul back in their cabin, 'especially when you mentioned ten gold a day.'

'And that Naxor,' Van said, smiling; 'what an asshole. It'd be funny if Corthie threw him overboard.'

Sohul nodded. 'What do you make of the boy?'

'He's too young to lead, but he'll get there.' Van gave a wry smile. 'Not so long ago, you were calling him a beast, not a boy.'

'He seems like a different person from the monster I watched slaughter his way through the Banner. It was like he'd taken too much salve and gone on a rampage. He'd be an officer in the Golden Fist within six months.'

'If he's any good at taking orders as well as giving them,' said Van. 'Something tells me that doing what he's told might not be his strong point.'

There was a thump on the cabin door and it opened. Their guard poked his head through and pointed at Van.

'Up you get,' he said.

Van stubbed out his cigarette and walked to the door. 'Why?'

The sailor opened the door wider, and Van saw Corthie standing outside in the narrow corridor.

'Yes?' said Van.

'I need a word,' said Corthie. 'Come with me.'

Van glanced back at Sohul, shrugged, then left the cabin. The sailor locked the door, and Van followed Corthie down the corridor and into another room, where Kelsey was sitting, looking embarrassed.

'Take a seat,' said Corthie, shutting the cabin door.

Van raised an eyebrow, then sat by the small porthole. He glanced at Kelsey, but she had her eyes lowered.

'I need to know,' said Corthie; 'were you serious before?'

'About what?'

'Your offer.'

'Um, what? You're actually considering taking me up on it?'

Corthie nodded. 'If you meant it.'

Van laughed. 'You want me to escort your sister? Me; a man you don't know? I thought you didn't trust me.'

'I don't. That's why I would be holding on to Lieutenant Sohul while you were gone. You two are good friends, and you know each other well. If you break your contract, then I'll kill him. How does that sound?'

'For a start, you are insulting me, and I don't like it. I have never broken a contract and I never will. Secondly, by holding Sohul as a hostage, you would be coercing me, which would actually allow me to break my contract, as it would be invalid.'

'I wouldn't be coercing you,' said Corthie, 'because you'd be entering into the agreement willingly. You can refuse it if you wish, but if you were to accept it, then that would be one of my conditions.'

Van smiled. 'You have me there. I have a condition of my own, then. Upon completion of the contract, you will pledge to let Lieutenant Sohul go free. His mother will be mourning him right now, thinking he is dead. He's a good man, and I think he should be allowed to return home.'

'And what about your mother? Don't you want to go home?'

Kelsey glanced up. 'His mother is dead.'

Corthie blinked. 'Sorry. Regarding Sohul, though; I can agree to that condition.'

Van rubbed his forehead. 'Are you serious? What about the guards on the ship? Why don't you send one of them?'

'The ship is already running at minimum strength; I can't afford to lose another crewmate, especially if we have to guard Sohul for the remainder of the journey.'

Van turned to Kelsey. 'What do you have to say about this?'

She shrugged. 'Nothing I say now will make any difference to what happens.'

'Why? Do you think your opinion doesn't count? Has your brother become the bully?'

'That's not what I meant,' she said. 'If you agree, then I'll tell you everything once we're underway.'

'Oh,' he said; 'now I'm curious.' He took a slow breath. 'I would do a lot to help Sohul; he's done the same for me many times, and I owe him, so I'll listen. What would you need me to do?'

'Escort my sister to Shawe Myre, protect her, and then accompany her north, with or without Belinda.'

'And if we find the Third Ascendant?'

'Then obey my sister's commands. I trust her judgement.'

'Alright. Next, "north" is a little vague. As far as I know, north of the mountains where I assume this Shawe Myre lies, is the Shinstran Desert, followed by the Fordian Wastes. Where in the north do you mean? Kinell?'

Corthie took a map from his pocket and unfolded it on the table. 'Are you familiar with the geography of Khatanax?'

'A little.'

Corthie pointed to a place on the map on the east coast of the continent, close to the mountains that divided the Fordian Wastes from Kinell. 'Do you see this port, here?'

'I see where you're pointing, but I have no idea if there's a port there. As far as I know, there are no towns in Fordia, except for ruined ones.'

'Naxor says that there is a functioning port a few miles south of these mountains on the map.'

'Do you believe him?'

Corthie laughed. 'As a matter of fact, I do.'

Van frowned. 'What is the Sextant?'

'You don't need to know that.'

'Fifty days should suffice,' Van said, 'which would equate to five hundred in gold, and I'm talking Implacatus-standard weights here, plus the expenses will probably amount to the same, especially if we have to charter another ship. Can you afford me?'

'We brought the contents of Irno's treasury with us,' said Corthie; 'we can afford you.'

Van glanced away, his eyes finding the waves through the thick glass of the porthole. He went through Corthie's words, trying to find where he was being tricked. They shouldn't be trusting him. If he agreed to the contract, then the irony would be that they would be able to trust him; but how could they know that? Agreeing would tie him to Kelsey for fifty days, thereby hampering his ability to escape, but if it would win Sohul's freedom, then he would regret refusing.

'What do you want?' he said. 'I mean, what is your ultimate aim? I've signed contracts in the past for gods who were cruel and rapacious, and I've always done my duty, but I'd like to think that I'm a little more picky these days about whom I select as an employer.'

Corthie frowned. 'I'm not sure I understand.'

'He wants to know,' said Kesley, 'if we're the good guys or the bad guys.'

Van smiled. 'Nicely put. I've had my fill of working for assholes. Are you assholes?'

'Alright,' said Corthie; 'we want to stop the gods of Implacatus from invading and destroying our worlds. It's as simple as that. The Sextant will allow them to locate our worlds, and we have to find it before they do.'

'That's it? You're trying to defend your worlds?'

'Aye. You know the gods; you know what they're capable of.'

Van nodded. 'Then this operation to Shawe Myre seems superfluous to your aims.'

'It is,' said Corthie, 'which is why I have agreed with the others that we should press on northwards. But, Belinda is my friend and I care about her deeply.'

'She's the Third Ascendant,' Van said, shaking his head; 'gods like that don't have mortal friends.'

Corthie said nothing for a moment, his eyes heavy. 'We have to try.'

Van nodded. An image of Dragon Eyre flashed through his mind. He had assisted the gods in their brutal invasion and subjugation of a world that had posed no threat to anyone; maybe it was time to repay a little of the debt he carried around in his salve-ridden heart.

'I'll do it,' he said. 'I'll agree to your terms if you do also.'

Corthie smiled. 'Do we need to write something up?'

Van paused for a second. As willing as he was to agree to the terms, perhaps it would be prudent to keep any deal informal.

'No,' he said. 'I can remember everything you said; I just need to hear you swear that you'll abide by the terms.'

'I swear it. Fifty days, five hundred in gold, and Sohul will be released, alive and unharmed.'

'Plus expenses, up front.'

Corthie nodded.

Van stuck his hand out. 'Then we have a deal.'

⁂

Three hours later, Van and Kelsey climbed down a rope ladder into the rowing boat, and two sailors began pulling on the oars, drawing them away from the side of the galley. Up on the deck, Van could see the eyes of everyone on board gazing down at them. Apart from Corthie, no one looked happy. Sohul was incredulous, and was glaring down at the rowing boat, his expression enraged. He had accused Van of abandoning him, despite the promise of freedom, and seemed to think that Van would use the agreement to flee. He would understand in time, Van thought. Along the railing from Sohul stood Aila, Vana and Naxor, who had all voiced their objections about sending a captured mercenary off with Kelsey. Naxor in particular seemed embittered by the prospect of losing the woman who could block the powers of the gods, and had only begrudgingly provided a rough map of how to get to Shawe Myre. He had taken the information from the mind of the old man in the village that he had read, and had repeated several times that he could not be held responsible for its accuracy. Aila was also aggrieved, but her anger had been directed at Corthie rather than Van. The young leader was keeping secrets from her, Van suspected, and she didn't like it one bit.

The rowing boat bobbed up and down on the waves as the sailors pulled them closer to the rocky shoreline, and Van turned to Kelsey. The young woman was gazing back at the galley, her expression unreadable.

'I have a couple of questions,' he said.

She frowned. 'Can they wait?'

'Some can, but this one won't; can you ride a horse?'

Kelsey burst into laughter. 'Can *I* ride a horse? The Holdfasts own an enormous number of horses on my world. It's what we're known for, and I grew up surrounded by them. I owned five by the time I was fourteen. It's a sure bet that I'm better at riding a horse than you are, Mister Mercenary.'

'Good to know,' he said. 'Can you cook?'

'You already bragged about being able to cook.'

'Yes, but I'm not your servant; that needs to be made clear right now. I will die to protect you, but I'm not going to run around cleaning up after you. We share the mundane tasks; washing, cleaning, cooking, mending clothes, stuff like that. Agreed?'

She shrugged.

'Do you know how to use a crossbow?'

'I thought you were going to do the fighting?'

'I am, but there might be times when you need to be able to defend yourself; if I get injured, for example.'

'No.'

'Alright. I can teach you.'

'Shouldn't you be calling me "ma'am", or "my lady" or something?'

'I will if you insist, otherwise I'll call you by your name. Do you insist?'

Kelsey pursed her lips. 'Let me think about it. Try it; I want to hear what it sounds like coming from you.'

'Very well, my lady. How's that?'

She frowned. 'Try "ma'am".'

'Certainly, ma'am.'

'Nah,' she said. 'Kelsey will do.'

'Alright. Now, what about a cover story for us? It's probably best if you lose the Holdfast name. I doubt many round here will have heard of it, but we should be careful right from the start.'

She squinted at him. 'Then just say "Kelsey". You don't need to use my family name.'

'And you should just use "Van". It's best if you don't call me "Captain".'

'I wasn't intending to. I have a few names for you – numpty, bawbag, smartarse... Should I go on?'

'You can call me what you like if it makes you feel better. I'm the one that's getting paid.'

The small boat pulled in close to the little harbour, and one of the sailors climbed up onto the wooden planks of the jetty and secured the ropes. A line of filled water barrels sat there, awaiting transfer to the galley, and a few locals were standing around with goods to sell. Van clambered up from the boat, then leaned down, extending his hand. Kelsey ignored him, and climbed up on her own. They glanced back at the galley in the distance, then turned for the village.

A villager approached. 'Would you be looking to buy anything, sir? We have food, water, wine...'

Van handed him a list. 'I want everything on here.'

The villager's eyes widened as he glanced at the list. 'This will all come to quite a price, sir.'

Van smiled. 'Don't worry about it; it's not my money.'

'I'll see what I can do, sir.'

Van watched the sailors unload their bags and gear from the rowing boat as the villager walked away to talk to the other locals, the list clutched in his hand. Van crouched by one of the bags, and withdrew the sword he had been given. It was of poor quality compared to the weapons he was used to carrying with the Golden Fist, as was the cheap leather armour, but he had lost all of his kit in the Falls of Iron. He attached the scabbard to his belt, then picked up the bags. One of them was heavy, containing the gold he needed for expenses, and he slung it over his back with a grunt, then walked to the end of the jetty, Kelsey a pace or two behind him.

'I didn't know you had a list,' she said when she caught up with him.

He winked at her. 'This is not my first operation.'

'Urgh,' she groaned. 'Don't ever wink at me; it makes you look like an oaf. I hope you put cigarettes on the list.'

'Of course I did.'

'What about weed and booze?'

He nodded. 'I think I've covered pretty much everything we could need. After all, your brother is paying.'

'He sure is.' She glanced at him. 'You think he's mad, don't you? For trusting you.'

'I don't know if mad is the right word. Naive, maybe.'

'But you think I'm mad.'

He looked at her. He did think she was mad, but felt it might not be best to say it out loud.

'Let's just say that I don't understand your motivations. You stopped your brother from killing me in the Falls of Iron, and then you got him to save my life when the Ascendants attacked. At first I thought you might have a crush on me, but since then I've realised that you don't actually like me one bit. I'd be lying if I said I wasn't a little confused.'

The villager walked over to them, the list still in his hand. 'We think we should be able to get most of the items here, sir.'

'What about the horses?' Van said. 'They're my priority.'

The villager nodded. 'That should be fine, although there aren't too many horses in these parts, and as I said before, they won't come cheap.'

'What about the weed?' said Kelsey. 'That's *my* priority. I'm going to need some if I have to spend the next fifty days in this guy's company.'

The villager smiled. 'That should be no problem, ma'am.'

CHAPTER 12

FROM THE HEART

C atacombs, Torduan Mountains, Khatanax – 1st Lexinch 5252
Sanguino unfurled his great wings by the entrance to the tomb and sniffed the air.

'You can do it,' said Sable, placing a hand against his left flank; 'you're strong and brave, and we're proud of you.'

He turned his neck to face her. 'I don't know; maybe tomorrow?'

'Today,' said Sable; 'now. Look, Blackrose is up there, waiting for you. It's time to show the other dragons that you are the mighty Sanguino.'

He tilted his head. 'I am the mighty Sanguino.' He closed his eyes for a moment, then launched himself off the edge, beating his wings as he ascended.

'That's it!' Sable cried, her hands to her mouth. 'Well done!'

Maddie shook her head from the side of the tomb. 'The "mighty Sanguino?"'

Sable laughed, and flashed a smile at her, making Maddie wish she had a smile like Sable's. She walked over to join Maddie and they sat by the wall of the tomb, watching as Blackrose and Sanguino circled each other in the sky above the Catacombs.

'You can mock,' Sable said, 'but it worked.'

Maddie frowned. 'Only because you were using your mind powers on him; admit it.'

'Sure, I admit it,' Sable said, shrugging; 'only a little, though. Dragons are much harder to persuade than people. That's why it's taken me three days to get him back in the air.'

'Yeah? We were trying for over twenty days, and he never left his cavern.'

'And now he has, I guess we should clean it. The smell in there would knock out a gaien.'

Maddie groaned.

'Come on,' said Sable; 'imagine how pleased he'll be if he comes back to a clean cavern, and imagine what this tomb will be like without the stench.'

'I've been cleaning all morning. Let's have five minutes to sit down first.'

'Alright,' Sable said, lighting a cigarette.

Maddie glanced at her. Sable drew in her attention, as if the woman was magnetic. There was something about her that seemed too good to be true, and it was starting to nag at the back of Maddie's mind. It wasn't just how pretty she was, though there was that, it was her whole demeanour. Millen had been a gibbering wreck since her return.

'Why are you looking at me like that?' she said. 'Are you sure you don't want a cigarette?'

'No, thanks. I told you, after smoking all of Van's I felt really sick. I've still got his little silver case.'

'Do you? Can I see it?'

Maddie got up and wandered over to her pile of possessions. Millen nodded to her from where he was preparing dinner, and she delved into her bag and retrieved the case. She took it back over to the wall and dropped it into Sable's lap.

Maddie sat as Sable examined the case.

'It's very nice,' Sable said.

Maddie nodded. 'I almost sold it at one point, but I figured he might want it back.'

'I doubt we'll ever see him again. The Banner of the Golden Fist was destroyed at the Falls of Iron.'

'So he's probably dead?'

'Probably.'

'Shame. He seemed alright.'

'Yeah. He was a good-looking guy.'

'That's not what I meant,' said Maddie. 'Why do you have to twist my words?'

Sable looked surprised. 'I didn't think I was.' She frowned. 'I get the feeling you don't like me much, Maddie. Why is that?'

'I guess I'm a suspicious person. For all I know, you might be using your powers on me.'

Sable laughed, which annoyed Maddie even more. 'Trust me,' she said, 'if I was using my powers on you, you wouldn't be suspicious of me; you'd be believing every word I said. The fact that you're wary of me is proof that I'm not manipulating you in any way.'

'I don't like the way Millen has been acting since you got here.'

'Ah. You're not jealous, are you? Do you like him?'

'Yes, but not like that. He's a friend, and I worry that he's so madly in love with you that he'd crawl over broken glass just for one of your smiles. Did you make him be like that? Did you make him love you?'

'I didn't need to,' she whispered. 'To be honest, I thought he would have been over his infatuation by now. Things would have been much simpler if he didn't love me.'

'You shouldn't have slept with him.'

'Excuse me? What business is that of yours? The day I start to judge you for your choices is the day you can say things like that to me.' She took a draw of her cigarette. 'Having said that, you're probably right. It was spur of the moment; I didn't realise that he would... take it so seriously. Alright, so you're suspicious of my powers, and you don't like that Millen is in love with me; anything else? Let's get it all out into the open, Maddie; after all, we're going to be spending a lot of time together and, frankly, I can't be bothered tiptoeing around your feelings.'

'Well,' said Maddie, 'there is something else.'

'Yeah?'

'I haven't mentioned any of this to Blackrose, but something about your story doesn't add up.'

'Go on.'

'Millen and I travelled here with Sanguino, right? It took us ages to get here, round the coast and then over the mountains.'

'So?'

'Well, you must have had a similar kind of journey, except that you say that you walked all the way from Alea Tanton.'

Sable narrowed her eyes.

'I don't believe it,' said Maddie; 'I don't believe that you were walking for twenty-odd days before getting here. You arrived in clean clothes, with your hair looking perfect; even your nails are in great condition. And you were carrying that enormous bag with you, with plenty of cigarettes and wine, and more clean clothes? Sorry, Sable, but I think you're lying.'

'I see.'

'To my mind, there's only one way you could have got here looking like that.'

'Oh. You suspect that I lied about not having a Quadrant? You think that I have concealed the truth from you, Blackrose, Millen and Sanguino?'

Maddie flushed, and she began to wonder if she was making a fool of herself. 'Yes.'

Sable smiled. 'You're right.'

'What?' Maddie cried. 'You... you...'

'Hush, please,' said Sable. 'Before you freak out and run around screaming that I am the great betrayer, I want you to think it through. Consider, please, why I may have acted in that way.'

Maddie stared at her. 'Bloody Holdfasts!'

Sable sighed. 'That's not thinking it through. Come on; put yourself in my shoes for a moment. Imagine you were me, and you were walking through the streets of Alea Tanton with a Quadrant in your possession. What were my options? I could have gone home, back to my half-sister and her charming children. I could have looked for my nephew Corthie. I could have travelled around Khatanax, using my powers and the Quadrant to amass great riches; or, I could put myself in grave danger and come here, to find you. Of all the options available to me, coming to the Catacombs was probably the least wise, as far as I'm concerned; yet here I am. Now, imagine if I had announced to Blackrose that I had a Quadrant; what would have happened next?'

Maddie frowned.

'She would have taken it, wouldn't she?' said Sable. 'Poetic revenge for what Karalyn did to her. And your plans for gathering support among the wild dragons would have come to nothing, as she, and you, would right now be in Dragon Eyre, alone. I came here to help you, but letting you both get killed needlessly is not what I would call helpful.'

'You devious little liar.'

'Maybe, but I happen to be correct. You can insult me all you like, but in your heart you know I'm right. The question is – what are you going to do now, Maddie Jackdaw?'

'You can read minds; why don't you tell me?'

'Do you want me to read your mind?'

Maddie snorted. 'As if you haven't already done it a hundred times since you arrived.'

'Don't flatter yourself; you're not that interesting.'

Maddie clenched her fists. 'I should punch you in the face.'

'Let's conduct a little experiment, Maddie. I'm going to use my powers on you for a moment, just so you can get a small taste of what I can do. Maybe once you've experienced that, you might give me a little more credit, and believe that I'm not manipulating you.'

'Give me a cigarette first.'

Sable smiled. 'Why? Do you really want one?'

'Yes. I mean... what? No. I don't know. I thought I did, but... Wait, was that you?'

'Yes. I made you crave a cigarette.'

'But I didn't feel you in my head.'

Sable nodded. 'I'm pretty good. Now, you saw how easy that was for me, yeah? All those feelings of anger you have towards me that are floating around your mind; I could get rid of them in an instant. I could make you adore me, and follow everything I say. If I wished, I could force you to agree with me about keeping the Quadrant a secret from Blackrose a little longer. I could even, if I wanted to, remove your memory of this conversation, and squash all of those little suspicions you had, so that you would become a nice, obedient girl. But I won't. You know, I'm tired of living like that.' She stood. 'I'm going to start cleaning Sanguino's cavern. You can stay here if you want, and think about it. I want you to be free to make your own decisions, Maddie.'

She strode away, leaving Maddie leaning against the wall. She bowed her head, thinking about Sable's words. She was starting to understand why the Holdfast woman aroused such hatred and distrust among others; if no one could tell if their feelings were genuine, then every feeling became suspect. Sable could be playing a complicated game of double bluff, telling her that she was free to decide, while having already set up what her response would be. And she could remove memories? The thought horrified Maddie.

She glanced towards the entrance to the tomb, wondering when Blackrose would return, and trying to come to a decision about what she should do when she did. If she told the dragon the truth, then Sable's life would be in danger, but if she lied, then she would be betraying the bond they shared. What would Blackrose do with a Quadrant? Maddie would advise her to stay a bit longer, to try to win over as many wild dragons as possible to her cause, but she knew Sable was right. Blackrose wouldn't listen to such reasoning; she would want to leave immediately.

She got up and wandered over to where Sable was picking up a bucket of water and a mop that Maddie had made out of rags and a stick. She noticed Millen watching them from the far wall, his eyes fixed on Sable.

'Hey,' Maddie said to the Holdfast woman.

Sable nodded, her eyes wary.

Maddie picked up another mop. 'I have more questions,' she said in a low voice.

Sable pointed at a shadow approaching the tomb entrance. 'It might be a little late; here she comes.'

Maddie turned, then blinked. The dragon that was landing by the entrance was silver-grey, and much smaller than Blackrose or Sanguino.

'Insects!' the dragon called out as she walked into the tomb. 'Your protectors seem to have flown away to the east, leaving you unguarded.'

'That's Frostback,' whispered Maddie; 'Deathfang's daughter. She was one of those who beat up Sanguino.'

Sable strode forward into the centre of the cavern. 'Good afternoon, Frostback, and how can we help you?'

'It occurs to me,' said the silver dragon, 'that I could eat all three of you, and Blackrose would never know it was me.'

'Yes, she would,' said Sable, getting ever closer to the dragon's head, 'because I have vision powers, and right now I'm telling her that you're trespassing in her tomb.'

Millen pulled himself up with his crutch and started to hobble forwards. 'Sable! Stay back.'

'Don't worry,' said Sable, a hand on her hip as she confronted the silver dragon. 'Our guest was just leaving.'

'Do you think I'm afraid of you, insect?' laughed Frostback. 'You are no god, therefore you possess no vision powers.'

Maddie caught up with Millen, and together they stood behind Sable.

'You seem like a fine dragon,' said Sable; 'your scales gleam like the moon, and your eyes are like burning coals. You long to be respected, but you'll never find fulfilment here, not while you live under the shadow of your father. Join us, and make your peace with Blackrose and Sanguino; we are in need of mighty allies such as you. Rise above your base instincts, Frostback; I know you have a noble heart.'

Frostback took a step back, her red eyes widening. Lightning pulsed and flickered round her jaws, and she groaned as if in pain. She shook her head violently, and her long claws dug into the stone floor of the tomb, gouging out rough channels of rock.

'What are you doing to me?' she cried. 'Witch! You are a witch! Get out of my head!'

The tomb rang and shook with Frostback's rage as she slammed her forelimbs down onto the ground. Millen toppled over with a cry, his crutch skittering away, but Sable stood her ground, her eyes fixed on the dragon.

Frostback closed her own eyes. 'No more, witch; I'm shutting you out. I do not need my eyes to find you; I can smell the stench of your filthy lies from here.'

Sable dived to the left as Frostback's claws reached out for her. The dragon moved fast, and brought a forelimb down, pinning Sable to the ground. She leaned over her, her jaws open.

'You will die for what you tried to do to me, witch,' Frostback said, her voice low and filled with menace.

'No!' cried Millen. 'Leave her alone.'

'Blackrose is on her way back,' gasped Sable, her waist and legs held to the ground under the heavy limb. 'I told her you were here.'

'It matters not,' said Frostback. She curled her talons round Sable and lifted her from the ground, then she raised her head and opened her eyes. She glared down at Maddie and Millen, keeping Sable out of her line of sight. 'Blackrose is finished when the others hear of this.'

She backed out of the cavern, then turned and beat her silver-grey wings, the undersides glowing red as they reflected the light from the lava pools. Maddie ran to the entrance of the tomb and watched Frostback as she began to circle.

'Behold!' the silver dragon cried, her voice echoing off the cliffside. 'Come and see! See what I have found.'

Maddie leaned out of the tomb and glanced up. All over the Catacombs, dragons were approaching the entrances, sticking their heads out of their tombs to look at Frostback, and the human she was carrying in her forelimb.

'Behold the witch!' said the silver dragon. 'Blackrose had a witch in her tomb, and I caught her.'

'A witch?' came Burntskull's voice from above. 'What nonsense is this?'

'I speak the truth,' said Frostback, turning to hover in front of the entrance to her father's tomb. 'She may be mortal, but she was in my mind, trying to change my thoughts.'

'Impossible,' said Burntskull.

'Put her back,' said another dragon, though Maddie couldn't tell which; 'she is under Blackrose's protection. If you kill her, the black dragon will cause us nothing but trouble.'

'You must believe me,' said Frostback; 'Blackrose has been harbouring this insect; she must know of her wicked powers. The black dragon must be cast out, along with those she is protecting.'

'Daughter,' cried a powerful voice; 'cease this ridiculous charade. Blackrose has earned our respect through the victories she has won. Making up stories about her pet insects does you no credit.'

'But, father...'

'Enough. I have spoken.'

Frostback cried out in frustration. She wheeled through the air, then plunged downwards, passing the tombs and heading for the bottom of the valley, Sable still clasped between her claws. Maddie felt Millen appear by her side, and he let out a cry.

'She's going to kill her!'

Maddie stared, frozen to where she stood. None of the other dragons were reacting as Frostback hurtled lower and lower. She pulled up above a vast pool of lava and beat her wings, hovering over the bubbling and steaming rock.

'Witness me!' she cried. 'The witch must die.'

She extended her forelimb, dangling Sable out over the lava, then dropped her.

A shape appeared, soaring through the mists of vapour. It raced down, and clutched Sable from the air as she fell.

'Sanguino!' shouted Millen.

The dark red dragon turned in a tight circle over the lava flows, Sable held in both forelimbs. Frostback screamed in frustration, and attacked, sending a blast of fire down at Sanguino. He curled in his neck and limbs to protect Sable as the flames rushed across his wings then, before he could react, Frostback had her jaws round his throat. Two other young dragons rushed down to join her in the attack; the green dragon from the reservoir, and an orange dragon with black stripes across its wings. The green dragon fastened its claws into Sanguino's back, while the orange dragon went for his head. With his forelimbs sheltering Sable, and his neck in the grip of Frostback's teeth, Sanguino was unable to resist, and the group fell, crashing into the jagged land-scape of black basalt between the lava flows. The orange dragon raked its claws across Sanguino's face, and he let out a roar that shook the cliffside.

Without knowing what she was doing, Maddie started to race down the old, worn steps that led from the tomb entrance, her feet leaping down the uneven stairs. She was barely a third of the way down before a large, dark shadow swooped past her. Maddie glanced over as she ran. It was Blackrose, hurtling from the sky like lightning. She reached the melee, and ripped the green dragon from Sanguino's back with her claws and threw him to the ground. She turned to the orange dragon and blasted a great jet of fire into his eyes, forcing him back. Frostback released her grip on Sanguino's neck.

'You!' cried the young silver dragon. 'You brought a witch into our homes.'

Blackrose raised her claws, but didn't strike. Instead, she moved into a defensive position over Sanguino's body. The green and orange dragons backed away, but Frostback held her ground. Maddie kept running, jumping down the stairs two or three steps at a time, and she passed out of sight of them for a moment. When she turned again, the sky over the valley was filled with dragons. Deathfang himself was beating his enormous wings as he hovered over his daughter, while Burntskull and over a dozen others were close by, ready to intervene. Maddie reached the bottom of the steps and sprinted along the side of the nearest lava flow, as Blackrose stood guard over the still body of Sanguino, her eyes never leaving Frostback.

'Daughter!' bellowed Deathfang from above. 'You have disobeyed my direct order. I commanded you to release Blackrose's insect, and you have dishonoured me.'

Blackrose lowered her claws a fraction. 'Is that so?'

'It is so, Blackrose,' said Deathfang. 'My daughter claimed that one of your insects was a witch. We told her such a thing was impossible, and that she was to do no harm to anyone under your protection. We may have our disagreements, black dragon, but we are not without honour. If you let my daughter live, you will have my thanks, and my assurance that she will be appropriately punished.'

'And the others? The green and the orange? Will anyone speak for them?'

'The green dragon is my son, Halfclaw,' said a female dragon hovering amidst the others. 'What Deathfang has pledged regarding his daughter, I pledge the same for my son. He shall be punished; you have my word.'

Maddie reached the edge of the stretch of basalt where Sanguino was lying, and stopped, fearful of going any further.

Blackrose turned to the orange dragon, who was starting to edge away. He glanced up, but the dragons above were blocking any chance of escape.

'And this one?' said Blackrose.

No one spoke.

With a speed and aggression that Maddie had never seen from her, Blackrose sprang at the young orange dragon. Her claws tore into his flank, and she ripped out his throat with her teeth, snapping his neck so that his head hung limp and lifeless from her jaws. She flung his body into the closest pool of molten lava, where it sank as flames licked the blistering scales. Frostback and Halfclaw cowered back at the sight, whimpering.

'Has justice been done, Blackrose?' said Deathfang.

Blackrose gazed upwards, her jaws bloody. 'It has, Deathfang.'

'Then this is over,' said Burntskull. 'Frostback, Halfclaw, return to the lairs of your parents for punishment. Everyone else, go home.'

The dragons began to disperse. Frostback and Halfclaw took off, keeping their eyes on Blackrose as they ascended, and within a minute, the sky was clear again. Maddie raced forwards.

'Blackrose!' she called.

The black dragon turned. 'You shouldn't be down here, rider; you could have been hurt.'

She reached the body of Sanguino. 'Malik's ass, oh no. Is he dead?'

'No,' said Blackrose, 'he lives, though he has been badly wounded, again.'

She sniffed him, and prodded him with a forelimb. His wing was covering his face, and his limbs were curled into his right flank.

'I assume Frostback was referring to Sable?' said Blackrose. 'Where is she?'

Maddie pointed at Sanguino's bundled limbs. 'In there.'

Blackrose prodded Sanguino again. 'Release her. We are safe.'

Sanguino let out a groan of agony, opened his claws, and Sable fell to the ground in a heap. Maddie raced to her side and crouched by her. Her eyes were closed, but her chest was rising and falling.

'Sable!' Maddie yelled.

The Holdfast woman opened her eyes and glanced around. 'Sanguino,' she gasped, 'he saved me.'

'He did,' said Maddie; 'he was very brave, but he got hurt.'

Sable sat up, rubbed her head, then saw Sanguino coiled up behind her. Her eyes widened.

'How bad is he?' she said, trying to scramble to her feet.

Maddie helped her stand, and they gazed at the still form of the dark red dragon.

'I'm not sure,' said Blackrose. 'Sanguino, show me your face.'

He groaned again, a pitiful sound full of sorrow and pain, then moved his wing, revealing the deep claw marks across his face. Blood was pouring from his left eye socket, and his right eyeball, usually a lime-green colour, was a milky white, and scored across the centre.

Blackrose's expression darkened. 'He has been blinded.'

Sable put her hands to her mouth. 'No.' She started to cry. 'I did this; this is my fault.'

'Is it?' said the black dragon.

'No,' said Maddie, putting her arm round Sable's shoulder as she wept. 'Frostback came into our tomb when you were away; she was going to kill us. Sable tried to use her powers to stop her, but they didn't work, and Frostback took her away.'

Sable stumbled forwards, and placed her hands onto Sanguino's face as he lay in pain. She ran her fingers up close to the edge of one of the claw marks, then leaned her head against him.

'I'm sorry, Sanguino; I'm so sorry.'

Maddie turned her glance towards Blackrose. 'Will he heal? You told me dragons heal better than us. Maybe his sight will return?'

'Maybe,' she said; 'maybe not. Killing the young orange dragon gave me no pleasure, but if he was the one that dealt the blow that blinded Sanguino, then Deathfang was right; justice has been done. It is over. Rider, take Sable back to the tomb; I shall carry Sanguino.'

Maddie walked up to Sable, and gently removed her hands from the dark red dragon's face. Sable fell into Maddie's arms, her tears unabated. Maddie turned her round, and began to lead her towards the foot of the stairs that led back up the cliffside. As they walked, Maddie noticed that almost every tomb had a dragon at its entrance, and each one was gazing down at them. At their own tomb, she could see Millen, the crutch under his right shoulder.

'It was my fault,' whispered Sable as they crossed the basalt towards the path.

Maddie held her tight. 'No, Sable, it wasn't.'

'I should never have filled him with courage; I did that. I told him he was brave and strong, and now he's blind.'

'No, Sable, don't you understand? Your powers don't work on dragons; what happened with Frostback proves that. When Sanguino saved you, it wasn't because you had manipulated him; it wasn't because of your powers.'

'Then why did he do it?'

'Because you believed in him, Sable; because you cared. Because to him, you're worth saving.'

CHAPTER 13

TRUSTING TO FATE

O ff the Fordian Wastes, Eastern Khatanax – 2nd Lexinch 5252
    Corthie glanced at Aila, but she had her back to him as she
brushed her hair, and was avoiding his eyes.

'I'm sorry,' he said.

She didn't respond.

'I want to tell you, but I promised Kelsey I wouldn't say anything.'

'It's fine,' she said. 'You've obviously made your choice.'

'It's not like that; I didn't choose my sister over you. She made me
swear not to tell anyone; what would you do in my position?'

She turned to glare at him. 'I would tell you.'

'But that would break my promise.'

'You also promised not to keep secrets from me, or have you
forgotten?'

'No.'

'You make promises too easily,' Aila said. 'Remember the trouble
your promise to Blackrose caused? It nearly ended with the destruction
of the City. If you're not careful, then at some point no one will trust you
any more. You shouldn't have made any promises to your sister; you
should have told her that you had already made a promise to me. It's

clear where I rank in your priorities, Corthie – in second place, behind your family.'

Corthie lowered his eyes and stared at the wall of their cabin.

'It's painfully obvious, anyway,' Aila went on, as she resumed brushing her hair. 'Kelsey is besotted with that mercenary. That, I can sort of understand, even though I fail to see the attraction. What I don't understand is why you would trust him to look after her. Right now, she could be lying dead in a ditch, while Van runs off with the gold you gave him.'

'He won't have done that.'

'Why not? Because we're holding onto his lieutenant? Don't be so naïve. The fact that Van deserted his colleague should tell you all you need to know about his sense of loyalty. At the very least, you should have made Naxor read his mind before they departed. You could have sent the two of them away in the rowing boat until they were out of Kelsey's range, and then we could have had a clearer idea of his motives. But no; instead, you decided to entrust a complete stranger with the safety of your sister. If it had been Karalyn, I wouldn't have worried, but Kelsey? That girl won't be able to defend herself if Van decides to turn on her.' She shook her head, her fist gripping the brush so tightly that her knuckles turned white. 'I just don't understand how you could be so... stupid.'

Corthie said nothing. Aila's words stung, but he could take being called stupid. What disturbed him far more was the fact that he had broken his word to the woman he loved. She was right; he had made two contradictory promises, and had chosen to keep his word to Kelsey, rather than Aila. If Kelsey had still been on board the galley, then he might have felt comfortable telling Aila the truth about his sister's powers, but with her gone, Naxor was once again able to read his cousin's mind, and the secret would be out.

He stood, as the conversation seemed to be over.

'Is that it?' said Aila. 'Have you nothing else to say?'

He shrugged. 'I could say, "trust me, it'll all be fine", but I don't think you'd believe me.'

'Then go. Right now, I think I'd rather be alone.'

Corthie gazed at her for a moment, then stepped out of the cabin and closed the door. He walked to the aft stairs and climbed up onto the deck, where a cool breeze was blowing. He took a deep breath and glanced around. It was another perfect, sunny day, with no clouds in the sky. To the left of the ship, the barren wastes of Shinstra, or perhaps Fordia, were gliding by, featureless and empty, while on the right lay the vast ocean. Sailors were busy at their tasks, and the three large sails were full with the wind.

He heard a chuckle and turned to see Naxor glancing at him.

'I know that look,' the demigod said. 'Has my cousin been giving you a hard time?'

Corthie said nothing.

'I'm actually grateful to you,' said Naxor, his smile broadening, 'as for once, I am not the object of everyone's ire. Your recent, somewhat baffling decisions have taken the pressure right off me. And, it's nice to be able to use one's powers again, though I'm frankly a little shocked to find out what goes on inside the mind of a sailor.'

'Have you done what I asked of you?'

'Naturally,' said Naxor. 'I have ranged my vision up and down the coast, and located the ancient capital city of Fordia.' He pointed northwest. 'The ruins should be visible within an hour or so.'

Corthie nodded. 'We'll anchor close by, and then I want you to take a more detailed look.'

'That may take a while.'

'The ruins are a possible hiding place for the Sextant. I don't want us to pass them by without checking.'

Naxor inclined his head.

'If we assume that the Sextant isn't there,' Corthie went on, 'then the next place along the coast is that port town by the mountains you mentioned, correct?'

'Yes.'

'And after that, Kinell?'

'Indeed, though I would be greatly surprised if the Sextant had been hidden anywhere within that realm. Kinell has been allied to Tordue ever since the gods invaded; if it were there, it would surely have been discovered by now.'

'What about islands, or other continents?'

'Unlikely, as the ship was seen leaving north from Capston. If it had been heading due east, then we could have considered the large island of Druinax, which happens to be infested with greenhides; or if it had been heading south, then we could have looked into Oanax.'

'Is that also overrun?'

'No, Oanax is covered in plantations farmed by indentured prisoners. It's where we get all of our coffee and sugar from. It's like the Tarstation of this world, only a damn sight hotter.'

Corthie leaned on the railing and shook his head. 'We don't seem to have many options.'

Naxor smirked. 'Feeling the pressures of leadership, are you? That's why I've never fancied the role; it's always the leader who gets the blame when things go wrong. Perhaps if you were a little more... honest with those whom you are trying to lead, it would stand you in better stead.'

'Don't lecture me about honesty, Naxor.'

'It's for your own good, you know. I'm not sure how much patience Aila has with those who deliberately keep the truth from her.'

Corthie considered throwing the demigod over the side of the galley, but instead turned and began to walk away.

'Where are you going?' said Naxor.

'You can let me know when we reach the ruined capital; I'm going to check on Sohul.'

'Why? Are you intending to send him off into the wilderness with Aila, or Vana, perhaps?'

Corthie kept walking, ignoring Naxor's laughter. He reached the bow stairs and descended. A sailor was on guard outside the prisoner's cabin, and he saluted Corthie as he approached, then unlocked the door.

Corthie nodded to the sailor then went inside. Sohul was sitting in a chair, his arms folded across his chest, while an unopened book lay close by.

'Good morning, Lieutenant,' Corthie said. 'How are you today?'

Sohul glared at him.

'Still angry, I see.'

'Angry?' snapped Sohul. 'I'm bloody furious.'

'He did it for you, you know. Van; he did it to earn your freedom.'

Sohul snorted. 'And you believe that, do you?'

'Aye, I do.'

'Then you're a fool.'

'Regardless, when we reach the next inhabited port, I'm letting you go.'

Sohul's glare turned into a more puzzled expression. 'Why?'

'Because I promised Van I would.'

'But I thought he had to fulfil the terms of your deal for that to happen?'

'I have every confidence that he will.'

Sohul groaned and put his head in his hands. 'How could someone this gullible be put in charge?'

'I thought you mercenary officers kept going on about how you never broke your contracts, yet you think that Van will break his?'

'There is no contract, you idiot; you didn't make him sign anything. He told me that you agreed the deal with a handshake.'

'So?'

'He tricked you. Handshakes count for nothing among the Banners. Nothing, do you understand? No contract is binding unless it's written down and signed by both parties.'

'You're starting to sound like you don't want to be released.'

'How can you be so nonchalant about it? Don't you care that you've been fooled?'

'I knew exactly what I was getting myself into. Do you honestly believe that I would have sent my sister away with him if I hadn't?'

'Based upon the evidence at hand, yes. As for the offer of freedom, that remains your decision, but I would very much like to be free.'

'Then maybe you should stop telling me how stupid I am.'

Sohul's face fell a little. 'Yes, of course. Perhaps my, uh, emotions have been running a little high recently. My apologies for any offence.'

Corthie laughed. 'My skin's as thick as a gaien's, which is just as well, seeing as how everyone on board this ship seems to think that I've lost my mind. We'll be anchoring in about an hour. Take some time to stretch your legs and get some fresh air.'

Sohul watched as he went back to the door and left the cabin. The sailor saluted again, and locked the door, then Corthie went back up on deck.

He watched as the landscape passed by, wondering what it had looked like before the gods had poisoned it. It had been green and fertile once, or so he had been told, but it was hard to imagine. After a while, he made out the beginnings of a great city stretching along the coastline. Like Dun Khatar, it was in ruins, and sand was half-covering many edifices. Corthie ordered the ship's captain to take the galley in closer, and they sailed into the wind, drawing nearer to the shore, then adjusted course again, so that they were moving parallel to the coast. An ancient harbour came into view, its old breakwaters still intact, and beyond, Corthie could see the quays and ruined buildings along the waterfront.

'Take us into the harbour,' Corthie called to the captain, 'then weigh anchor fifty yards from shore.'

The captain nodded, and ship began to turn again. Naxor appeared by Corthie's side.

'Quite a sight, isn't it?' the demigod said. 'Over a million people once lived here.'

'Did you ever visit before the invasion?'

'No. Pre-invasion, my trips were limited to the palace in Dun Khatar.' He gestured to his side, and Vana approached. 'I took the liberty of asking my cousin along, so she can scan the area for any sign of gods.'

'Good idea,' said Corthie. 'Hi, Vana.'

She nodded in his direction, but said nothing. At least she wasn't calling him stupid, Corthie thought.

They stood at the railing as the ship passed between the two massive, stone jetties and into the calm waters of the harbour basin. The stumps from old wooden piers were poking up through the clear water, and small, silver fish were darting among them. The captain gave the order to halt, and the anchor slid into the depths, while the sailors gathered in the canvas from the three sails.

'There are no signs of any god powers being used in the vicinity,' said Vana.

'Thanks,' said Corthie. 'Can you tell if any of them have been here recently?'

'No. Lady Silva has that particular ability, not I.' She turned, and walked back towards the stern.

'Don't take it personally,' said Naxor, 'she's been that way with everyone since we left the Falls of Iron.'

'I don't blame her; her brother died there.'

'Are you implying that Aila and I should put more effort into mourning Irno?'

'I'm not implying anything.'

'You have to remember that Aila and I have been through wars; we've seen death in all its variety, whereas Vana was always a little sheltered from that. I know that Aila feels her brother's loss keenly; she just chooses not to show it.'

'And how do you know that? Have you been inside her head?'

'Do you really expect me to answer that question?'

'You must have hated Kelsey being here; you must have felt half-blind not being able to pry into everyone's thoughts.'

'Yes, but you have to balance that with the impossibility of having your head blown off by an Ascendant. Your sister had her uses. And besides, I can't read everyone's thoughts. Your thinking is a profound mystery to me.'

'I thank Karalyn daily for protecting my mind from people like you.'

Naxor chuckled. 'Leaving such pleasantries aside, I think I shall begin my sweep of the city. I'll start in the centre and work my way out. I must warn you, even if the Sextant is here, it could be buried under any one of those buildings, or covered in a decade's worth of sand. There's a good chance my vision could pass right over it and I wouldn't know.'

'I understand. Take your time; if you spot anything, we can use the rowing boat to take a closer look.'

Naxor nodded, then sat on a bench by the railing, his eyes glazing over. Corthie watched him for a moment, then went to the bow hatch and descended the stairs to the lower deck. He walked along the passageway, then went into the cabin he shared with Aila.

She was sitting on the bed with her legs crossed, smoking.

Corthie frowned.

She glanced at him.

'Do you smoke now?' he said.

'It's weed,' she said.

'What kind?'

She raised an eyebrow. 'There are different kinds? I don't know; I got this off a sailor. I tried one of Vana's cigarettes, but it was horrible and I couldn't see the point. Weed, on the other hand?' She shrugged. 'Do you want some?'

He sat. 'No, thanks. You know I hate it. Are you doing this to annoy me?'

'Partly, though also because I felt like it. Back in the City, I always thought that I'd enjoy travelling. Well, it turns out that I don't. Are you going to get drunk in retaliation?'

'No.'

'Hmm, I've noticed that you haven't been drinking since we left Capston.'

'That's right; I'm trying to keep a clear head. What we're doing is important.'

'But you used to get drunk every day when you were fighting the greenhides. Was that not important?'

'That was different. I don't need a clear head to fight.'

'But your recent decisions don't seem to have been very clear-headed.'

He nodded. 'I'm aware that everyone on this ship thinks I'm an idiot for sending Van off to Shawe Myre with my sister. I don't care, to be honest; I know I did the right thing, and that's what matters.'

'Meaning I don't?'

'It hurts that you don't trust me.'

'It hurts that you won't tell me the truth, so I guess we're even.'

'I guess we are.'

Aila glanced away, her eyes narrow. Corthie was about to stand up to leave when there was a knock at the cabin door.

'Sorry for interrupting,' said a sailor as he opened the door, 'but Lord Naxor wants to see you up on deck, sir.'

'Thanks,' Corthie said. He turned back to Aila, who shrugged. 'See you later,' he said.

He left the cabin and went up the stairs to the deck, where Naxor was sitting by the railings.

'How's it going?' Corthie said.

Naxor pursed his lips. 'I found... something; just not what I was expecting.'

'What?'

'People,' he said, as Corthie reached the railing. 'People, living in the ruins. Fordians, to be exact.'

'Are there many of them?'

'I saw a few dozen, at least, though there are presumably more. There must be a source of fresh water somewhere, perhaps a well. They seem to have settled close to the city's main square, about a quarter of a mile from the harbour.'

'What can they possibly be eating? I haven't seen any signs of life along the coast.'

'They're Fordians; their needs differ.'

'Do they?'

'Yes. They have skin that is similar to that of greenhides, although not as thick, of course. It allows them to survive for long stretches without food. They can live off water and sunlight for surprisingly long periods, although they do need food now and again.'

'They're related to greenhides?'

'No. The Fordians were created by Nathaniel as the original inhabitants of Lostwell, and designed by him to be more efficient than other humans. A bit like you were, I suspect. They only thing they share with greenhides is the colour of their skin.'

Corthie glanced at the ruins stretching out across the water of the harbour basin. 'They were allied to Belinda, weren't they? That's why their lands were destroyed?'

'Indeed, yes.'

'Then she might have trusted them to look after the Sextant.'

'Perhaps.'

'Can you read their minds from here?'

Naxor frowned. 'I can access their minds, but they think in a language that I'm afraid I don't understand. It must be a tongue used only by the Fordians. I met several in the palace in Dun Khatar, and they all spoke the same language as you and I.'

Corthie frowned. 'Why do we speak the same language?'

'Is this the first time that this has occurred to you?' Naxor said, laughing. 'We both speak the Divine Language, which is the same tongue spoken by the gods of Implacatus. The "why" is a little complicated – Nathaniel created both of our worlds; on yours, he must have designed it into at least one of the peoples who live there, whereas on mine it was brought to the City by the God-King and God-Queen, who enforced its teachings over many millennia, until all of the original languages had died out. Lostwell's creation predated either of our worlds, but I'm not sure why Nathaniel didn't make the Fordians speak it. Perhaps they did for a while, and it changed over time.'

'Do you think the settlers in the ruins would know how to speak it?'

'Possibly.'

'Then we should go and talk to them. They might be able to give us some information.'

'I'm sorry, "we"?'

'Yes. Get ready for a little trip ashore, Naxor; I'll get the rowing boat ready.'

An hour later, the rowing boat pulled alongside the empty quay of the harbour, and Corthie and Naxor climbed up onto the weathered stone. The two sailors who had been rowing started to follow them but Corthie raised a hand.

'No,' he said; 'you both stay in the boat. We don't want to alarm the locals.'

'Yes, sir,' one nodded.

Corthie glanced at the ruins of the harbour front. Once-grand buildings were lying half-collapsed, their roofs long gone, and their windows were like dark eyes staring back at him. Everything had been constructed from a red sandstone, and the wind had scoured the facades, rubbing smooth any details that had existed. Next to him, Naxor was wearing a sullen expression, and had a sword strapped to his waist.

The demigod caught Corthie's glance. 'What? I can fight too, you know, if I have to.'

'Let's hope we don't have to.'

'So, what's your great plan?'

'We find someone who speaks the same language, and we talk.'

'Do you think these Fordians have survived here this long by being hospitable to strangers? If you get yourself killed, then I'm the one who'll have to tell Aila.'

'I'm not going to die here.'

Naxor raised an eyebrow. 'Certain of that, are you?'

'Aye, I am.' He gestured to the ruins. 'Take me to the Fordians.'

They walked along the wide quayside, then Naxor led them down a street, the flagstones half-covered in drifting sand. A silence hung over the city, deep and still, broken only by their footsteps. They turned a corner, and the galley in the harbour basin behind them slipped from view; they carried on, surrounded by the remains of what had clearly been a rich and prosperous city. Some of the ruins were still several storeys high in places, rising up like jagged brown teeth from the sand.

'We are being watched,' Naxor whispered, as they approached a large, open plaza.

Corthie felt for the strap that was keeping the Clawhammer on his shoulder. 'How many?'

'Dozens. They've must have seen the ship; they know we're here.'

'Good.'

They strode into the centre of the plaza. It was enclosed on all four sides by high ruins, while the ground was covered in a jumble of broken pillars, pediments, archways and giant ashlar blocks of sandstone.

Corthie halted in the middle of the plaza, and took the Clawhammer from his shoulder. He raised it into the air, then slowly placed it onto the ground in front of him. He lifted his hands, palms extended to show they were empty.

'I am Corthie Holdfast,' he called out into the silence. 'I am not your enemy. I am here only to talk. I have no armour, and my weapon lies at my feet. If you hate the gods of Implacatus, then maybe we could be friends.'

'Go back to your ship!' cried a voice from the shadows of the ruins. 'Go back, or we will kill you.'

'I am a friend of Queen Belinda, the Third Ascendant,' Corthie said. 'I am looking for her, and I am looking for her Sextant. The gods of Implacatus are also searching for the same things. If you wish to stop them, then help me, please.'

A spear flew through the air towards them, striking the flagstones a yard from where Corthie was standing.

'That was your last warning,' the voice called out. 'Go.'

Corthie shook his head. 'No.'

'I think we should take their advice,' said Naxor, his hand on the hilt of his sword, and his eyes tight. 'There are too many of them, and they are all around us. Maybe if you had worn your battle armour, but without it, you'll be cut to shreds.'

'Come out and face me,' Corthie cried, ignoring the demigod.

There was movement in the shadows in front of him, and then to the left and right. Corthie channelled his battle-vision, just enough to clear his mind and remain alert, his muscles and limbs poised and ready. The first Fordians came into sight as a group of a dozen or so began to emerge from the ruins. They were armed with spears, but it was their skin that Corthie noticed first. It was green, just as Naxor had told him, but paler and duller than the skin of the greenhides, and other than that, they looked entirely human.

'Queen Belinda has returned to Lostwell,' he said, keeping his hands raised as more groups of Fordian warriors stepped out from the shadows of the ruins. 'She and I have fought side by side many times, and...'

'You lie!' shouted a man to the right. 'The Queen of Khatanax has departed these lands, never to return. She abandoned us to the gods of Implacatus, and allowed our country to be destroyed.'

Corthie watched as the warriors formed a circle around him and Naxor, their spears bristling towards them.

'You may be a god,' the Fordian man shouted, 'but know that we will fight to the end.'

'I am not a god,' said Corthie.

'Then you will die, and your blood will be spilled here, to join that of our slaughtered ancestors.'

The man raised his hand, and the warriors charged, their spears lowered. Corthie pulled on his reserves of battle-vision, taking in everything around him in an instant, as if time had slowed down. His hand began to reach for the Clawhammer, but he forced himself not to, fighting his instincts to kill. He felt a bloodlust surge through him, and knew with a certainty that if he were to raise his weapon, then every Fordian in the plaza would die at his hands. A spear was flung at him, and he stepped aside to avoid it, then another grazed the back of his left calf muscle, its stone tip ripping through his skin.

Then they were upon him. He pushed Naxor to the ground and stood over him, his battle-vision bursting to be free, but he controlled it, using it to defend himself only. Spears jabbed at him, and he ripped them from the grasp of the Fordians as he turned and ducked and swayed, as if locked in a dance with his attackers. Part of him longed to unleash his full powers against them, and it took all of his concentration not to kill. He parried and blocked, disarming the Fordians one by one as they surged around him. One he punched in the face, sending him back to land in a heap, his nose broken, and he calmed himself. It was exhausting, far harder than killing, he realised. When he had been out in front of the Great Walls of the Bulwark, he had been able to completely lose himself in a frenzy of death, as if in a trance, but fighting while not killing was sapping his energy far quicker, as every blow, every block, and every movement required a higher level of control and discipline. Wounds from their stone-tipped spears began to appear, on his torso, back, legs, and his arms, and he suppressed the pain, not allowing it to distract him. He ripped another spear from the hands of a warrior and snapped it like a stick, as sweat poured down his face. He reached for another, but the warrior retreated, and as he did so, the others pulled back as well. Over a dozen Fordians were lying on the flagstones, groaning, and of those still on their feet, more than half had been disarmed.

Corthie panted. 'Do you see the blood? My blood? You know I'm not a god, but you also know that I could have killed every one of you had I wished to.'

The Fordians stared at him.

'What do you want?' cried the man who had spoken before.

'I am Corthie Holdfast,' he said, 'and I have come to Lostwell to defeat the gods of Implacatus. I have already killed two of them with my own hands, and I will not rest until every god that threatens this world is dead.' He paused, glancing at the faces of each of the Fordians. 'I have been chosen to do this; this is my purpose; my destiny. If the Sextant falls into the hands of the Ascendants, they will use it to destroy my own world, and others, and nowhere will be safe from them. Help me. If you know where the Sextant is, then help me.'

The man who had spoken raised his hand, and the other warriors lowered their spears.

'You fight like a god, Corthie Holdfast,' he said, 'but from your wounds we can see that you speak the truth; you are mortal, like us. Go back to your ship and leave us in peace.'

'I cannot; I need your help.'

'We cannot help you; the Sextant is not here.'

'Do you know where it is?'

'We do, but that secret will not be revealed by any one of us; we gave an oath to Queen Belinda.'

'Would you rather it fell into the hands of the Ascendants? What use is your oath if it destroys you?'

The Fordians said nothing.

Corthie lowered his hands and closed his eyes. 'Help me, or kill me. Lead me to the Sextant, or cut me down, and lose the last hope this world has to be free.'

He calmed his breathing and waited. His thoughts went to Aila, and then to Kelsey, and he was glad they weren't watching. Neither had believed him when he had spoken of having a destiny, and both would be cursing his stupidity if they could see what he was doing. It didn't matter. He wasn't fated to die in the ruins of an ancient, desolate city in the desert. He would confront the Ascendants, and win.

'Open your eyes, Corthie Holdfast,' said the voice of the Fordian.

Corthie did so. The warriors around him were staring in awe, and some had their heads lowered.

'My name is Gurbrath, and I am the chief of the people here,' said the Fordian. 'Do you truly intend to defeat the Ascendants?'

'I do,' he said.

And has Queen Belinda truly returned?'

'She has.'

Gurbrath nodded. 'You have a mighty spirit dwelling within you, Corthie Holdfast. Take me back to your ship, and I shall lead you to the Sextant.'

Corthie nodded in relief, then the pain of his wounds flared and he almost stumbled. Naxor scrambled to his feet, and dusted himself down.

He eyed Corthie and shook his head. 'You're insane. Aila will not be happy when I tell her about this.'

Corthie leaned on him. 'You don't have to tell her everything.'

'Of course not,' he smirked, 'but I will.'

CHAPTER 14

SHAWE MYRE

Shawe Myre, Southern Khatanax – 8th Lexinch 5252

Belinda paused on the forest track to wipe the sweat from her forehead. The heat was intense despite the altitude, and the humidity felt oppressive. For ten days, she and Silva had been walking. For the first six of those, they had crossed the barren wastes of the dusty, black, basalt fields, through winding ravines and over bleak mountainsides, before they had passed beyond the reach of the volcanoes and entered the heavily forested region bordering the Southern Cape. Even with range vision, Belinda would have been lost without Silva as her guide within the rippling folds of the mountains. Hidden passes and almost invisible ridges and precipices criss-crossed the area like a labyrinth, and any map would have been useless.

'Are we close?' she said to Silva, who had paused on the track ahead of her.

'Yes, your Majesty; not long now.'

'How did the gods ever find this place?'

'It was betrayed, your Majesty, by a demigod who once worked for you in Dun Khatar. He sent a vision to Governor Latude in Alea Tanton, and showed him the exact location of our refuge. They had searched for it several times before, but had never been successful.'

'I'm not surprised. These mountains are worse than any maze.'

'It was the perfect hiding place, your Majesty. No one has ever found it without being shown the way.'

Belinda took a drink of warm water from the skin she was carrying. 'Why did the demigod wait so long before betraying us? You said that we hid for two centuries.'

'We remained safe in Shawe Myre for two hundred and thirty-eight years, your Majesty, from the moment we left Dun Khatar, to the day we were discovered, and you departed Lostwell with Lady Agatha. Our betrayer felt that your plans to leave this world amounted to abandoning your realm, and he succumbed to anger and spite. His name is Bartov, and may he be cursed for all eternity.'

'He's still alive?'

'I don't know, your Majesty; I never saw him again after Shawe Myre was sacked. He would never dare to step foot anywhere near the refuge. I heard a rumour he was living in Capston, on the coast of the Southern Cape, but I don't know if that's true.'

Belinda nodded. She was conscious that she had started to use words like 'we', and 'us' more often since they had left the ruins of Dun Khatar, as if part of her was coming to terms with her past, but it still felt a little false. Had this Bartov really betrayed her, or had he betrayed the old Belinda? She shouldered her waterskin and they set off again, following the forest track as it snaked along the bottom of a deep ravine. A stream ran to the right of the path, gushing down from the mountains behind them, and she longed to jump in to cool off. The branches above them were thick with birds calling to each other, and she had seen more than one lizard sitting motionless in the undergrowth, staring at them with unblinking eyes.

The path began to climb, winding upwards and crossing the stream via a shallow ford. Though Silva insisted on calling it a 'path', Belinda would not have awarded it such a title; to her, it seemed indistinguishable, as if the demigod had been choosing random directions in which to turn. On either side, the steep cliffs of the ravine towered above them, forbidding, but also teeming with life. Insects buzzed around their heads, but their powers healed any bite within seconds.

They ascended for another hour, until they climbed above the tree-line, and Belinda gasped in relief as a cool breeze swept over the face of the mountainside. Then she noticed the view. She glanced at the way they had come, and saw the vast forest stretching away across the slopes, shielding the ravines and gullies from sight, while beyond, to the west, the row of volcanoes sat. Two of them were smoking, sending pillars of fumes high into the deep blue sky. Belinda turned to face the south. Over the edge of a sharp ridge, the land began to fall away in a succession of folded valleys and slopes towards a plain.

'Down there is the Southern Cape,' said Silva. 'The port town of Capston lies about fifty miles from here. Other than that, the region is thinly populated.'

Belinda sat on a large boulder and relaxed for a moment, letting the breeze blow through her dark hair. She pulled on her range vision, and set it free, feeling a rush as her sight shot out towards the plain. She left the mountains behind, and dived low to the ground, passing over terraced vineyards, and huge plantations where tobacco grew. Tiny villages and farm cottages lay dotted around, but no sizeable towns. Her vision reached the coast, passing the southernmost tip of the continent of Khatanax, then she wheeled to the north-east, and reached the port town that Silva had mentioned. Ships and small fishing vessels were tied up in the harbour, and it had an idyllic look to it. After so many days of not meeting anyone else on their journey, Belinda felt a twinge of loneliness as she watched the people strolling by the harbour, or eating at the little cafes next to the quayside. They had been her people, once, before she had abandoned them.

She closed her eyes, and her vision returned to her body.

'It's beautiful,' she said.

'It's what Shinstra and Fordia used to look like,' said Silva; 'and Tordue, before all of the refugees arrived there. It's a glimpse of the past, as well as what the future could hold.'

'The future? Do you believe that the wastes could flourish again?'

'In time, your Majesty, and with the correct policies. The government in Alea Tanton doesn't care about the people or land of Khatanax; they rule it as if it were their personal playground. Even with Governor Latude in jail, I doubt that the two Ascendants who have arrived will be responsible stewards.'

'What do you know of Leksandr and Arete?'

'Very little, your Majesty; I have met neither. Of all the Ascendants, only you and King Nathaniel governed with any concern for those under your rule.'

Belinda smiled. 'You would say that, though.'

'But it's true, your Majesty. Implacatus called us rebels, but we were in the right.'

'I've met a few rebels since I lost my memories – Agatha, and Amalia, for example. I wouldn't have called them responsible rulers. Neither cared about mortals. Of the six gods who accompanied me from this world, none of them were in the right, as far as I could see. They wanted total dominion over the world where the Holdfasts come from, and were prepared to kill anyone in their way.'

Silva's eyes darkened. 'Lady Agatha could be ruthless, it is true.'

'So was I,' Belinda said, 'before I... changed.'

'It was Nathaniel's death that truly changed you, your Majesty. After his passing, you became... bitter and angry, and consumed with a desire for revenge, but you weren't always like that. The "wise old queen", that was what the people called you. Would they have done that if you were evil?'

Belinda glanced at her. 'Be honest with me; what did you truly think of Agatha?'

'She hated me, your Majesty, and, though I do not like to speak ill of the dead, the feeling was mutual.'

Belinda frowned. 'So, are you saying that my nature, I mean the way I am now, is similar to what I was like before Nathaniel's death?'

'No. Before he fell into the long sleep, perhaps. It's hard for me, your Majesty, to talk about you as if you were two people. You're very different from the person you were in Shawe Myre, but... I don't know, your Majesty; I don't think I can give you an answer to that question. I'm sorry.'

'It's fine. I'm not sure I understand what kind of person I am now, so I shouldn't expect you to know.'

'It's not far now, your Majesty; should we go?'

They stood, and Silva led them down from the ridge. They re-entered the cover of the forest, and Belinda started to sweat again in the thick humidity. She followed Silva down a steep track, and into the depths of another ravine, this time on the southern side of the mountains. Twenty minutes of walking brought them to a stream, which was racing down the slopes in a noisy torrent. Beyond was a cliffside, with a series of narrow caves in the rockface. The one on the far left, closest to the river, was the smallest, and Silva guided her towards it. They waded across the fast-flowing stream, and stepped inside the dark, narrow cavern. Silva pushed on, plunging them into darkness. They followed the cave as it twisted into the side of the ridge, then Belinda saw a dull, green light ahead. The end of the cave opened out into another valley, the way hidden by thick undergrowth, through which the sunlight was filtering. Silva pushed her way through it and Belinda gazed around. They had emerged into a deep ravine, hidden from the outside world. Unlike the other ravines they had passed, it had been cleared of undergrowth, and fruit trees were arranged in neat rows, along with a small vineyard and vegetable gardens. Tiny cottages dotted the grassy floor of the valley and, higher up, wooden structures were suspended on thick chains from the over-hanging cliffsides, like birdcages. Slender rope bridges connected the structures, and long ladders dangled down to the ground beneath them. A stream wound its way through the centre of the ravine, over which little wooden bridges had been laid. Birds were singing from the branches of trees, and bees were buzzing over the countless flowers in bloom.

Silva smiled. 'Shawe Myre, your Majesty.'

Belinda glanced around, amazed that such a place could exist so deep within the mountains.

'It is completely invisible from above,' Silva went on. 'Someone could be standing on top of that ridge over our heads, and they wouldn't see a thing. The cave we walked through is the only way in, unless you had a Quadrant, of course.'

'It all seems so new,' Belinda said, 'as if it has been freshly built.'

'The gods of Alea Tanton destroyed most of it seven years ago, your Majesty. It has taken us that long to rebuild it.'

Belinda noticed movement, and her hand went to the hilt of the Weathervane. Several people were coming out of the cottages on the valley floor, having noticed their arrival.

Silva raised her voice. 'People of Shawe Myre! I have done what I promised to do.' She got down to one knee and faced Belinda. 'Behold our Queen! Behold the Third Ascendant; she has returned to us as if born again.'

Cries came from the people by the cottages, and more emerged. Some ran out from the little orchards, or from within the vineyard, while others stared down from the houses hanging from the underside of the cliff. Within moments, the entrance to the cave was surrounded by people, many of whom were weeping openly, while others threw themselves to their knees, their hands raised in supplication.

Belinda gazed at them all. The noise was increasing, a cacophony of voices exclaiming thanksgivings and praise.

Silva glanced at her. 'Your Majesty, do you have anything to say to your people?'

'Thank you,' she said, her voice lost in the cries around her.

'Silence for the Ascendant!' bellowed Silva, and the crowd went quiet.

'Thank you,' Belinda repeated, as every face turned to her. 'Your welcome is... overwhelming. I don't deserve it. Seven years ago, I left this world, and today I have returned to Shawe Myre a changed woman. Your loyalty humbles me. I hope I can live up to your expectations.'

A young girl approached, a flower in her hands. She offered it to Belinda with a shy smile.

Belinda took it, then started to cry. 'I don't deserve this.'

Silva stood. 'Give the Queen some space; she has been on a long and arduous journey. Let her through so she can rest, and then she will speak to you again.'

The demigod pushed forwards, clearing a path through the thick crowd. Belinda followed, with the flower in her hands and tears on her face. The crowd stood to either side, hushed and watching as she was led by Silva to the other side of the ravine, crossing a wooden bridge on the way. They went to an opening in the rockface, where stairs had been cut from the stone, and started to climb, leaving the crowd behind them on the grass.

They ascended the steps in silence, as Belinda's thoughts whirled. Narrow, slit openings in the rock provided light from outside as they climbed, and every time she passed one, Belinda could see that the crowd had grown, and by the time they reached the top, it seemed as if the entire valley floor was filled with people. They came to a long gallery that ran along the side of the cliff, about halfway up. It was open on the side facing the ravine, and several slender rope bridges were connecting it to the wooden houses that hung suspended from thick chains. They turned to the right and walked until they came to the largest hanging structure, and crossed the bridge.

'This is your home, your Majesty,' said Silva, as they walked into a large room that took up an entire floor of the building. 'We rebuilt it exactly as it was.'

The room was open on all four sides, with slim beams supporting the upper storeys. Two wooden, spiral staircases rose from near the centre of the room, and a series of couches, cushions, low tables and reed mats covered most of the floor.

'I hope you like it, your Majesty.'

Belinda said nothing, her eyes scanning every detail of the room. She felt like a stranger, yet somehow the room, and the house, seemed right. She walked to the far edge of the room and placed her fingers onto the railing that ringed it. From there, she could look up and down the length of the ravine. It was about a quarter of a mile long, and barely fifty yards across at its widest, narrowing at some points to barely ten. Not a single inch of ground space was wasted. Paths wound past gardens and trees, crossing the river back and forth in sinuous lines. Above the valley, there were at least a dozen hanging houses, though hers was the largest and grandest.

'Would you like a drink, your Majesty?' said Silva. 'I would love you to try the wine we make here.'

Belinda slid the bags and waterskins from her shoulder and walked back to the middle of the room, where Silva was opening a clay jar.

'Yes,' she said; 'I'd like that.'

'Then sit, please, your Majesty.'

Belinda selected a chair and sat.

'You will, of course, have more servants shortly,' Silva said, 'but maybe we'll let you settle in a bit first, your Majesty. Some of the servants you had seven years ago are still alive, and I'm sure they'll be keen to rejoin your service. Upstairs, there is a kitchen and dining area, and some guest rooms, and on the top floor is your bedroom and bathroom, along with a few other private rooms.' She passed her a glass of white wine. 'It's not exactly the same floor plan as you had in the old house, but...'

'Where is Amalia?'

Silva paused. 'I'm not sure, your Majesty. I didn't see her among the people by the valley entrance. Do you want me to summon her?'

'In a moment.' She took a sip of wine. She didn't like it, but thought better of mentioning it. 'It's wonderful.'

Silva beamed. 'I'll tell the vine mistress; she will be very pleased.'

'Silva, who are all those people?'

'I'm sorry?'

'I didn't know there would be people here. I was expecting a dusty old tomb.'

'They are your subjects, your Majesty.'

'Sit down, Silva. Talk to me. Explain it.'

A tiny frown passed Silva's lips as she sat. 'Explain what, your Majesty?'

'Who are those people?'

'They are a mixture of the survivors from seven years ago, and some new volunteers who came here to help us rebuild the valley after the sack. Most are mortals, but some are demigods.'

'What are their numbers; break it down for me.'

'I think, your Majesty, that there are around a hundred and thirty people living in Shawe Myre. Eight are demigods, including me.'

Belinda swallowed. 'Are any... are any of them related to me?'

'Some of the mortals are distantly related, your Majesty, but I am the only demigod who is a direct descendant of yours.'

'Oh. I don't know if I'm relieved or disappointed.'

'The wars and invasion took a heavy toll on our family.'

Belinda said nothing, embarrassed that she had admitted feeling relieved that she didn't have a son or daughter living in Shawe Myre. As she had seen in the crypt under the palace in Dun Khatar, many of her descendants had fallen in battle throughout the time she had ruled Lostwell. She wondered how she had managed to harden her heart to the loss at the time. She had heard lots of people say that immortals had a differing set of morals to mortals; if that was so, she still felt like a mortal. How long would it take before she lost that feeling? Did she want to lose it?

She put the glass down onto a table. 'I want to see Nathaniel's tomb.'

'Now, your Majesty? Wouldn't you prefer to freshen up first? We have been on the road for many days.'

'No. I want to see it now.'

'Of course.'

They stood, and Silva led her back across the slender bridge to the stone gallery. They walked along it to the end, where it turned and bore straight into the cliffside. Belinda followed Silva down the passageway, their way lit by a series of small lamps burning a fragrant oil that reminded Belinda of sandalwood. The corridor opened into a chamber with multiple exits.

'The tunnels extend quite a way into the hillside,' said Silva. 'There are storerooms, wine cellars; all sorts of things, even a room where cheese is matured. There are no cows here, but we have a few goats.'

'And the tomb?'

Silva nodded. 'This way, your Majesty.'

She took a passageway to the right, and they walked along it for a minute, ignoring several doors and other corridors that branched away. They entered a large chamber with rough walls, and Belinda noticed a large stone platform with six postholes dug into it.

'Was this where the Sextant was kept?'

Silva looked startled. 'Yes, your Majesty; how did you know? Do you remember it?'

Belinda shook her head and pointed at the platform. 'Those holes match the same pattern as the platform in Dun Khatar.'

'I see,' Silva said, her expression falling.

'How was it transported in and out of here?'

'You removed the roof, your Majesty. A couple of yards above our heads is the top of a small ridge. You used your powers to move the stone, and then reformed it afterwards. As you know, the Sextant lay here unused, and no one was allowed to touch it.' She pointed at one of the two other entrance ways. 'King Nathaniel lay in there during his long sleep. The chamber is bare and empty now.' She gestured at the last entrance. 'His Majesty's tomb was in there.'

Belinda strode forwards and entered the chamber. In its centre was a great stone sarcophagus, its lid lying in broken fragments on the ground. Scorch marks stained the sides of the tomb, and there was nothing inside. Sitting on a wooden bench by a wall was a woman, her right arm swaddled in bandages, who turned as she entered.

Belinda narrowed her eyes. 'Amalia.'

The former God-Queen got to her feet, her mouth opening. She stared at Belinda for a moment, then a smile crept over her lips.

'You're back,' she said.

'Silva brought me, just as you asked her to.'

'She told you, did she? And yet you still came; that gives me hope. Am I right to feel hope, Belinda?'

Belinda drew her sword, and the dark metal of the Weathervane glimmered in the lamplight.

'If you're going to kill me,' said Amalia, 'then please do it now and make it quick. I don't need a lecture, or a reprimand, or to be told how wickedly I behaved. I am well aware that you disapproved of the way I ruled the City, and I would be lying if I said I had changed. I am seven thousand years old, and I am unlikely to alter my ways now. So, get it over with.'

Belinda took a step forward, the Weathervane extended in her right hand, then hesitated.

Amalia smiled. 'I'll make it easy for you.' She knelt before Belinda and bowed her head, exposing her slender neck. 'My head is yours to take.'

Belinda stared at her, then raised the sword over Amalia. With one stroke her enemy would be dead, and the God-Queen's Quadrant would be hers.

'Your Majesty?' whispered Silva from the chamber's entrance, fear running through her voice.

'Stay back, Silva,' said Belinda; 'this is none of your business.'

She positioned the sword above Amalia's neck. Mercy had always been a concept she had struggled with. If someone had committed a terrible crime, then why should they be allowed to get away with it? Amalia had committed many terrible crimes, including the slaughter of thousands of her subjects, and yet, something was giving Belinda pause. It wasn't pity, for she felt none towards the god kneeling before her. Part of it was curiosity; she wanted to hear what Amalia had to say, but mostly it was because Amalia's death would sever yet another link to Belinda's past.

'Where is your Quadrant?'

Amalia glanced up. 'I don't have it.'

'Why not?'

'Because I hid it when I arrived in Dun Khatar. At the time, I presumed that you or Yendra would be coming after me, to finish me off, and I needed something to bargain for my life. My arm was causing me great pain, and I was in no condition to resist. Then Silva found me, and I decided to leave it where it was. It's perfectly safe; no one will find it.'

'Where?'

'No,' said Amalia. 'I'm not answering any more questions with a sword over my neck. Either kill me, or let me speak without the threat of death.'

Belinda kept the Weathervane steady. From Amalia's words, it was clear she had no idea that Belinda had acquired inner-vision. She thought about reading the location of the Quadrant out of the former God-Queen's mind, but didn't know if that would alert Amalia to her new power, and it might prove more useful if she continued to believe that Belinda was blind to her thoughts.

'Please, your Majesty,' Silva said from the door. 'I beg you, my beloved Queen; please listen to what Lady Amalia has to say. If it displeases you, then you are free to do as you wish.'

'I'm free to do as I wish now.'

'Of course, your Majesty; but nevertheless, I beg you; please listen first.'

Belinda glanced into her great granddaughter's eyes and entered her mind.

Say nothing, she said inside her head, *about me having inner-vision. Amalia doesn't know, and I want to keep it that way.*

Silva bowed her head.

Belinda turned back to Amalia. 'I'll give you a day,' she said. 'You have Silva to thank for that. Despite lying to me initially about your presence here, she has been kind to me. She is family. For her, I will give you one day to convince me not to kill you.'

She sheathed her sword.

Amalia stood, and smiled. 'Very well. In the Royal Palace in Ooste, we once sat for hours, talking, while you plied me with opium in the hope that I would fall asleep, so you could rescue my dreadful grand-daughter Aila. Regardless of that betrayal, I will sit with you again, and I will try to talk you round. You will find that I haven't changed. I can only hope that you have, my old friend.'

CHAPTER 15
FOREST FLAMES

Mountains of the Southern Cape, Southern Khatanax – 8th Lexinch 5252

Kelsey's voice rang out through the forest, sending birds up into the air calling and screeching. Van turned, his hand on the hilt of his sword. Behind him, Kelsey was waving her arms about.

Van frowned. 'What is it this time?'

'These bastard flies!' she shouted. 'I'm covered in bites. And don't say "this time," as if all I've done is complain.'

He rolled his eyes and turned back to face the direction they had been travelling. Ahead of them, the undergrowth was thick and seemingly unending, and only the position of the sun was telling him anything about their location.

'We're lost,' Kelsey said, as he set off again; 'admit it.'

'I told you we were lost yesterday, so it wouldn't be much of an admission. If we can make our way up this hillside, then we might be able to get our bearings.'

He pushed his way past a tumble of bushes, each step taking him a little higher.

'You've been saying that for an hour,' muttered Kelsey as she followed.

'It was true then, and it's true now.'

They came to a massive outcrop of rock, and scrambled up the slope to its side. It was surrounded by the forest, but the top of the rock was clear, and he climbed up onto it, the pack on his back weighing him down. He reached the top, and stood, gazing around at the vast sea of green on all sides. Kelsey joined him, slid her pack off and sat on it, panting.

'Let me see the stupid map,' she said.

He pulled it from a pocket and handed it to her.

'I'm going to slap Naxor repeatedly the next time I see him for drawing this piece of crap,' Kelsey said as she looked at it. 'It's completely useless. A four-year-old could have done a better job.'

Van turned in a full circle, his eyes trying to pick out the folds of the landscape. Mountains rose up all around them, and the ground between was rippled and twisted, and the forest cover made it even harder to distinguish anything.

'Shawe Myre could be anywhere,' Kelsey went on, scratching one of the insect bites on her arm. 'We could be going round and round this hideous forest forever and still not find it.'

'Do you want to go back to the coast?'

'What? Why are you saying that?'

'We could try to get some decent intelligence from the villagers, or a guide, if possible. We could return to the farmstead where we left the horses, and stock up on some supplies.'

She stared at him. 'Are we low on supplies?'

'We have plenty of food and gold, but you've smoked nearly all of our cigarettes.'

'You're just looking for an excuse to run away.'

He laughed. 'I could run away now if I wanted to, and leave you to die in this forest. You'd never make it out on your own.'

'Pyre's arsehole, you're a dick.'

He glanced at her. 'Are all the Holdfasts so foul-mouthed?'

'No, just me. My mother blushes if she says "damn". Anyway, I thought tough mercenaries would be more thick-skinned.'

'The Banners are highly disciplined units; they don't tolerate sloven-liness of any kind, especially among the officers.'

'So slaughtering civilians is alright, but swearing is frowned upon? Idiots.' She rummaged in her bag, then lit a cigarette.

Van frowned. 'I didn't say it was time for a break.'

'Kiss my arse.'

'No thanks; I would need a lot more gold for that.'

She paid him no attention, so he unslung his pack and sat on the surface of the large outcrop of rock. He wiped the sweat from his face and checked the position of the sun.

'It'll be getting dark soon,' he said. 'We should be thinking about finding somewhere to camp for the night.'

'Another day wasted,' Kelsey said. 'I thought you were some kind of expert tracker?'

'I never said that. The Golden Fist had its own specialised scout platoons – they were expert trackers, and highly paid for their skills.'

Kelsey squinted at the hand-drawn map. 'What are these weird squiggles next to where Shawe Myre is supposed to be?'

Van shrugged. 'Caves, maybe? And the line could be a track or a river; I don't know. We should have brought Naxor with us.'

'Are you stupid? He wouldn't have been able to use his powers with me here.'

'Right. I forgot that.'

She shook her head. 'Numpty.'

'You really hate me, don't you?'

'Whatever gave you that idea?'

'Perhaps the fact that you haven't stopped insulting me in six days.'

She flicked ash onto the rock. 'I don't particularly hate you. There are worse things I could call you aside from "numpty". I enjoy annoying you, though.'

'You're not worried that my patience will snap?'

'Nope.'

'Perhaps you should be. Your brother gave me enough gold to live on for quite a while. I could easily kill you, and be back in Capston within four or five days. From there I could get a ship to Alea Tanton, and rejoin my old employers.'

'Aye,' she said; 'you *could* do all that. But you won't.'

He glanced away, the smirk on her face starting to anger him. He knew she was right; despite the shaky basis of the deal he had reached with Corthie, he had still given his word to the young warrior. He would face no sanctions from the Banners for reneging on a handshake, but it didn't matter; his word was his word. He stared out over the forest, trying to pick out anything that might signify the presence of people, and felt a cooling breeze wash over his face.

'Can we stay here tonight?' said Kelsey. 'I can't face going back into the trees again today. There are no insects up here on the rock, and that wind feels great.'

He checked the sun, and judged that there was an hour of daylight remaining. 'Alright.'

'Can we build a fire?'

'I wouldn't advise it.'

'Why not?'

'Because, up here, it'll be seen for miles around. It would be like lighting a huge beacon, telling everyone where we are.'

'So?' She gestured towards the forest. 'There's no one out here. Surely it's worth the risk to avoid getting eaten alive by the flies? I saw your bites this morning; they're as bad as mine. Could we not have one night without them bothering us?'

Van nodded. 'Alright. I could do without being bitten for a night, but only if we can pick a location that's a little less open. Stay here; I'll have a look around.'

He eased himself to the edge of the rock and dropped down the side to the forest floor. He glanced around, then worked his way round the circumference of the giant outcrop, picking up a collection of fallen branches as he walked through the thick undergrowth. On the far side of the outcrop was a shallow indentation in the rockface, and he dumped his pile of wood onto the earth next to it, and started clearing a space, hacking down the wiry branches of a thorn bush, and trampling the long grass. Sweat poured down his forehead as he worked, but he could feel the air begin to cool as the sun neared the horizon. He picked up stones and made a circle of them on the ground by the indentation. The outcrop would shield any fire from most onlookers, and the smoke would be invisible when night came. When he was finished, he whistled upwards, and Kelsey peered over the side.

'Pass me our bags,' he said.

She nodded, then lowered the two bags down to him. Once he had laid them to the side, she began clambering along the edge of the outcrop. She dropped, and he caught her as she landed.

'Get off me,' she muttered, pushing him away.

'Just trying to help.'

She glanced down at his handiwork. 'That wood will last about ten minutes.'

'I hadn't finished collecting it. Get some food ready. I'll be back in a bit.'

Van held off lighting the fire until the sun had set behind the mountains to the west. The insects were out in full, and Kelsey was sitting cross-legged on the ground with a tunic draped over her head to keep them away. They had eaten a meal of hard biscuit soaked in water, and some dried fruit while waiting for it to get dark. Van knelt by the circle of rocks, and lit the wood with a match. There was no wind, but much of the wood had retained its moisture, and it was some time before the flames took hold and he could sit back.

He glanced at Kelsey. 'Happy now?'

'Marginally less unhappy.'

'That'll do for me,' he said, stretching out his legs and watching the low fire burn. He had collected a large pile of wood, and had arranged it on one side of the fire to help it dry out. The damp wood was generating a lot of smoke, but it helped drive the insects away, and they had some peace from them as they sat and stared at the flames.

Kelsey took a weedstick from a pocket and lit it off a burning stick. She was sitting on a blanket, and had another one cushioned between her back and the side of the outcrop of rock.

He glanced at her as she sat smoking, her face reflecting the glow of the fire.

'Do you keep your promises?' he said.

She frowned. 'What?'

'Well, do you?'

'I try to.'

'Then don't you think it's time you told me why you saved my life?'

'I didn't promise that.'

'When we got off the ship, you told me that you would tell me.'

'But I didn't promise.'

'What's the difference? You said you would tell me "when the journey was underway".' He glanced around. 'It seems to be underway.'

'There's no point; you wouldn't believe it.'

'I might.'

She took a long draw of the weedstick, then exhaled a plume of smoke. 'Why do you think I saved you?'

He laughed. 'Would I be asking if I knew the answer to that? I told you before; at first, I harboured the delusion that you might have had a crush on me.'

'Aye, I remember. A little presumptive of you, don't you think?'

He shrugged. 'Maybe. It wouldn't have been the first time someone had developed a crush on me. It's the uniform and the rank that does it, I guess.'

'I thought you only went with prostitutes?'

'I knew you'd bring that up. I wish I'd never told you. Anyway, that's for when I'm off duty. On duty? That's a different story. Do you remember that god Corthie killed – Joaz?'

'Aye. You told me that you weren't going with her.'

'No, I told you that I didn't love her. But she and I... well, she had her needs, and I guess she felt that I could fulfil them for her.'

Kelsey grimaced. 'Eurgh.'

'The gods can be like that,' he went on. 'A lot of the male gods have harems, and many of the female ones think that we officers are fair game. I was getting a bit tired of it, to be honest.'

'Poor you.'

'You can mock, but being at the beck and call of a god can have its drawbacks. They can be very demanding.'

'Let me get this straight; your sexual history consists of bedding prostitutes, and prostituting yourself to insatiable gods?'

Van frowned. 'I admit, it doesn't sound great if you put it like that. What can I say? I'm a mess. It's not my only fault; I have plenty of others too.'

'Such as?'

'Oh, let's see. Pass me that weedstick first.'

She leaned over and handed it to him, and he took a draw.

'Drink,' he said, 'weed, opium, salve...'

'Salve?'

'Yes.'

'I don't understand. I thought salve was what keeps the gods looking young.'

'That's right; that's why they want it so badly.'

'And it heals mortals, right?'

'It does that too.'

'So why would you mention it in the same breath as weed and drink?'

'Because, if you take enough of it, it's better than either of those. Much better. It makes you feel... alive, truly alive. It can also heighten aggression, which is why it's given out to soldiers in the Banners; they take it before battle. When I first saw Corthie fight, he reminded me of soldiers on a salve rampage. Suffice it to say that I've had my problems with addiction in the past.'

'And now?'

'Now I steer clear of it. If I don't, then I could become addicted again, and it will probably kill me. Half of my company are amazed that I'm still alive, and it's the one area of my service record that gets me into trouble.' He smiled. 'I've had several "final" warnings about it.'

'I'm surprised the gods allow mortals to have any.'

'It's not available to the general population, but the Banners are provided with enough before major operations. There's always been a steady supply as far as I know; the gods will do anything to keep it that way.' He passed the weedstick back to Kelsey. 'How did I end up talking about myself? Weren't you supposed to be telling me something?'

'You like talking about yourself.'

'I'd rather hear about you. I've gone over every time we've met, looking for clues to explain why you and your brother acted the way you did. It doesn't make sense.'

She gazed into the fire. 'It's true; I have a crush on you.'

He snorted.

'I told you that you wouldn't believe it.'

'Alright, I'll humour you for a moment; let's say that's true. It still doesn't explain why your brother is paying me to escort you to Shawe Myre. Corthie's young, but he's not a fool.'

'I don't want to tell you; it'll ruin everything. Right now, we're getting on well and...'

'Are we? Is this your idea of friendship? We constantly bicker, and you insult me a dozen times each day before breakfast.'

'Believe me, that's better than if I told you the truth.'

He narrowed his eyes as he glanced at her, trying to imagine what could make their relationship any worse than it already was.

'How do you think I would react,' he said, 'if you told me everything?'

She turned to him, meeting his eyes. 'You'd think I was insane. You might desert me here, in the middle of the forest.'

'I made a deal; whatever happens, I wouldn't leave you to die.'

'I wouldn't die. I've no idea how I'd get out of the forest, but I wouldn't die.'

'Do you have healing powers? I know that sounds like a stupid question, but if your brother has battle-vision, and you can stop the gods from visioning into our heads, then maybe it's not so stupid.'

'No. I can't heal myself, or others. You're getting closer though.'

'Ah,' he said, drawing his legs in and edging a little nearer to her; 'so we're talking about powers? You *do* have another power. It's not battle-vision or healing. I'll be annoyed if it's fire, especially as I just spent an hour getting ours ready.'

She smiled. 'It's not fire.'

'Wow, you actually smiled. Not smirked, smiled.'

'Shut up.'

'Then it's rock or flow, I guess, which, I have to say, is not outlandish enough for me to think that you're insane. The idea of mortals with powers would have seemed utterly ridiculous only a short time ago, but I've seen what you and Corthie can do.'

'It's not flow or stone.'

'So, it's something weird? That could make sense, seeing as you can block powers, which is already pretty weird. Hang on, can you make memories disappear?'

She raised an eyebrow. 'Why do you ask that?'

'Because for a while I was convinced that someone had been messing with my memories back in Alea Tanton. I freed Maddie Jackdaw from prison, but can't remember any of it.'

'My aunt did that to you.'

His mouth fell open. 'What?'

'Aila told me. Sable Holdfast, my aunt; she can mess with people's memories. More than that, she can persuade people to do stuff that they don't want to do; a power that she has been known to abuse from time to time. She was working as a spy in Alea Tanton, and had you wrapped round her little finger.'

'Sable Holdfast?'

Kelsey chuckled. 'Aye. She's rather badly behaved for an aunt. I think she was pretending to be a servant or something.'

'A servant? I don't remember suspecting any servants.'

'She would have gone into your mind and told you not to worry, so you wouldn't have. Let me tell you the worst thing she did – she once went into my brother-in-law's mind, and got him to use his fire powers to slaughter hundreds of civilians and burn down a hospital. That was before he was my brother-in-law, but still. And he never knew; he blamed himself for it right up to the day he died. Getting you to free Maddie Jackdaw was charitable in comparison.'

He shook his head. 'That's impossible.'

'If you think that's impossible, then there's no chance you'll believe what I can do.'

Van leaned over and threw some more wood onto the fire. 'Have you got any weed left?'

She took out another smokestick and lit it. 'My family are pretty strange,' she said. 'My mother is an excellent vision mage, from battle right up to inner, and my father could spark. His twin sister was this famous fire mage called Keira, but she died before I was born. At that time, the peoples of my world didn't get along, and my parents were among the first from different nations to marry. They had four children. Corthie, you've met, of course. He has my mother's battle-vision, but also our father's height and build; then there's Keir, my older brother, who has upper vision and fire powers, and some weird ability to combine the two so he can control lightning.'

'I've heard the Ascendants can do that,' said Van; 'they all have vision and fire powers, and they mix them just like you said. They can mix other powers, too. Like stone and flow, for example, to make a tough compound that is impervious to fire and bombardment. They use it to coat buildings on my world; fortifications and such like.'

Kelsey nodded. 'Aye, we have clay mages and flow mages who work together to do that. Anyway, that leaves my sister, Karalyn. Her powers are… considerable. Mine are puny in comparison; everything I can do, she can do better, and she can do a lot of stuff that I can't. She can make herself invisible.'

Van laughed.

'I knew you'd be an arsehole about it, but it's not that far-fetched.

You've heard of gods who can fool people into seeing them as looking different, as if they're altering their appearance?'

'I guess.'

'Well, Karalyn makes people think they can't see her. She isn't really invisible; she just convinces people's eyes that she's not there.'

'And she can block powers as well?

'Aye, and sense when others use them. I can do that too, up to about a mile away or so.'

'That sounds useful.'

'It is. The other power I share with my sister is far from useful, however. It's more like a curse.' She passed him the weedstick. 'Are you ready?'

He nodded.

'I'm going to regret this, but here goes. You know how vision mages, or gods, can go into your head and look out from your eyes?'

'Yes.'

'I can do it too, but I can't read anyone's thoughts, and I can't see their memories. Instead, sometimes, not that often, but now and again...'

'Yes?'

She lowered her head and closed her eyes. 'Sometimes, I can see what's going to happen.'

Van fell silent. Of all the answers he was expecting, that wasn't one of them.

'Nine times out of ten,' she went on, 'it's things that are about to happen in the next few minutes, like when Sohul elbowed you in the eye. Do you remember that?'

He did, but he kept his mouth closed, his eyes on the young woman sitting by the fire.

'Often,' she said, 'I have no idea what I'm seeing; it's just a tiny glimpse of events that make no sense to me, and sometimes it's only when the event has happened that I realise it corresponded to something I saw. There's only one thing consistent about them – they always come true. That's the hardest part to come to terms with; for years I tried to thwart the events I saw, but it only made it worse. I presume it was the same for Karalyn, though we've never sat down and really talked about it. We've never got on, not since she wiped Keir's mind when he was a baby.'

Van smoked. 'You see the future? Is that what you're saying?'

'It's exactly what I'm saying.'

He nodded.

'Well?'

'What?'

'Do you think I'm insane?'

He passed her the weedstick. 'I don't know. I'm the type of person who needs proof.'

'And the elbow in the eye wasn't proof?'

'It could have been a coincidence. It seems quite a leap to go from that to an ability to predict the future.'

She shrugged as she took a draw. 'There's nothing I can do to make you believe me.'

'Could you not predict something that's going to happen in five minutes?'

'No. I can't do it on command; it happens randomly. I'm looking into your eyes right now, and I'm seeing nothing.'

She held his gaze for a moment, then looked away. She seemed sincere, he thought, but that only proved that she believed it, not that it was true.

'I assume,' he said, 'that you're telling me this because... well, because you've seen my future? You've seen something happen in my future, and that's why you and your brother saved me? I mean, your brother knows this, yes?'

'Aye, he knows. We've all known about Karalyn's abilities, ever since she was little, but I kept mine a secret after seeing how everyone treated her. They were all scared of her, and I didn't want people looking at me in the same way. But, I had to tell Corthie, and now I'm telling you.'

'So? What did you see?'

'Do you promise you won't freak out?'

'I'll try. Wait, was it my death?'

She squinted her eyes at him. 'Why does everyone assume I've seen their death? No, it wasn't your death, though you might wish it was after I tell you. Alright, here we go – you are sitting in a garden, next to a large building; I don't recognise it; I don't know where you are. It's sunrise or sunset, I think, because the sky is red, and you're looking at someone. At that moment, I could feel what you were feeling, and you are... oh bugger. You're in love with the person you're looking at. She's holding a baby, but, wait – I don't know if the baby's yours, but you feel love for him too, so I'm guessing he might be.' She swallowed. 'The person you're looking at, is me.'

Van stared at her, but said nothing. Was she trying to trick him? Was this a convoluted way to trap him into staying with her? He remembered thinking that she had fallen for him, but it seemed clear that she could barely stand him, so why would she make up something like that?

She sighed. 'Your silence is telling. Are you trying to decide whether I'm crazy or a liar?'

'Look, Kelsey, I, uh, need to tell you... I don't know what you want from me, but I'm not in love with you.'

She glared at him. 'I know that! I'm not in love with you either, you stupid twat. You're marginally less of an arsehole than I thought you were when we first met, but you still don't make my top twenty list of guys I could see myself being with. You are handsome, but there doesn't seem to be much going on beneath your looks; you're shallow, vain, self-centred, and you don't even read books. Pyre's arse, you're the opposite of what I imagine to be my type. And yet? Somehow, in the future, I'm going to love you.' She clenched her fists as a tear slid down her cheek. 'I don't even want to have children, but that baby boy might be mine – he might be ours. It's so unfair.'

'Does Corthie believe this?'

'Aye. He's used to Karalyn's power, so he accepted it better than I'd hoped. That's why he trusts you to look after me.'

'What about the others; Naxor, Aila?'

'The only people on Lostwell who know I can see the future are Corthie and you. Keep it that way – tell no one.'

The fire began to die down. Van gazed into it, watching the embers glow against the dark background of the forest. Fifty days, he thought. He would fulfil his end of the deal, and then run, get as far away as possible from the young woman sitting a yard from him. He felt sorry for her in a way, as she seemed to actually believe the nonsense that was coming out of her mouth, but he would never love her.

'I hate you,' she muttered.

He glanced at her. She looked more miserable than ever, her expression a blend of anger, frustration and sorrow. She was damaged, disturbed, even, and that meant she was unpredictable, dangerous. If she believed her own story, then what might she be capable of doing in an attempt to make it come true?

He rolled out his blanket onto the ground and lay down. 'I'm getting some sleep.'

She laughed, but it was bitter. 'You do that. Never mind that I've bared my innermost thoughts to you; you go to sleep, Van. Sweet dreams.'

He turned so that he was facing away from her. For a moment he wondered if she would cut his throat as he slept, but she needed him to get out of the forest alive, so he reckoned he was safe enough. What had he done to deserve her for company? Of the fifty days, six had already passed; just forty-four to go, and then he would ditch her somewhere her brother would be able to find her. Between them, they had saved his life in the Falls of Iron, so that was the least he could do. Dig deep and be a professional, he told himself. He closed his eyes, and for some reason an image of kissing her entered his thoughts. Just as she had said about him, he realised that he found her attractive on the outside; it was what was on the inside that alarmed him. He banished her from his mind, and tried to think about what they would do when the sun rose. It was going to be awkward; there was no getting away from that.

He listened to the sounds of the forest over the crackling of the fire. The birds were quiet, but the insects were buzzing, and he could hear a rustling in the undergrowth from the small animals that had approached because of the light from the flames. Lizards, probably, he thought.

Something made a clicking noise, and he realised his mistake. He shot up, his hand reaching for his sword.

'Don't move!' cried a voice from the shadows. 'Hands in the air; you are surrounded.'

Kelsey frowned at him as they raised their hands. 'Some bodyguard you are.'

CHAPTER 16

DISOWNED

Catacombs, Torduan Mountains, Khatanax – 8th Lexinch 5252

Sable pointed a stick at the crude drawing on the ground. 'And this line here controls distance; you move a finger along it to tell it how far you want to go.'

Maddie frowned. 'But don't you have to be facing in the right direction?'

'No. The Quadrant knows which way north is, regardless of how you're holding it.'

'Oh. That's probably just as well, as I get confused about where north is.'

Sable moved the stick. 'These little lines here govern altitude. I think the central line is sea level, but I haven't tested anywhere below it to find out.'

'I'm quite impressed you've managed to learn so much about it.'

'I had a third, I mean, a month, to practise. That's all I was doing after escaping Alea Tanton. I still haven't figured out how to get it to take you to another world, though.'

'That's all I've done. Well, that's what I did the one time I have used it. It was simple.' She pointed. 'There are squiggles over there, and if they're triggered, then the Quadrant goes back to the location where the world you are standing on was first made. That's how we got from my world to this one.'

Sable smiled. 'I'm glad I didn't inadvertently trigger that. I've no idea where Lostwell was created; I might have ended up on Implacatus. Here's an easy one for you.' She pointed again. 'There's a symbol by this jewel. Trigger it, and the Quadrant takes you back to the last place it was used. Very handy if you appear in a tricky situation and you need to retrace your steps in a hurry.'

Maddie nodded, then heard a noise. 'Millen's coming,' she whispered.

Sable drew her foot over the drawing and wiped the ground clear.

'Hi, Millen,' she said as he approached. 'How's your leg today?'

His face reddened, as it always did whenever Sable spoke to him. 'Fine. A tiny bit better, I suppose.' He leaned his crutch against the wall and eased himself down to sit with them by the entrance of the tomb. 'Did you come all the way over here to avoid me?'

Sable laughed. 'Of course. We girls have to keep some secrets.'

'And it's good exercise for you,' said Maddie. 'When my leg was broken, I...'

'Yes, yes,' said Millen; 'you've told me a million times. If I have to listen to another story about your recovery I'll throw myself off the edge of the tomb.'

Maddie scowled at him. 'You do that, then. At least I wouldn't have to hear you whine any more. And we could watch as the dragons eat you.'

'Not if I take you with me.'

'Don't fight,' said Sable as she lit a cigarette. 'We three are the only humans within a hundred miles; we need to stick together.'

Millen lowered his eyes. 'Sorry.'

'I'm not,' said Maddie. 'We should have brought Gantu along instead of you; he couldn't possibly be any worse at cooking.'

'You met Gantu?' said Sable.

'Briefly. He punched Millen, and then a greenhide cut his head off and ate it.'

Sable laughed.

'Hey,' said Millen; 'are you forgetting he was my cousin? I hated him, but he was still my cousin. Plenty of Blue Thumbs will have been upset by his death.'

'He was a horrible brute,' said Sable; 'and boring. I hated having to pretend to be interested in his endless stories about that stupid team. Don't look at me like that, Millen. You lived in fear of him; don't deny it.'

Millen flushed and glanced away. Maddie shook her head, dismayed at the effect a word or look from Sable could have on him. The Holdfast woman had shown no interest in resuming any kind of romantic relationship with him, but that hadn't seemed to dampen any of his feelings towards her. He worshipped her, no matter how mean she was to him.

Sable glanced up at the blue sky outside the entrance. 'Blackrose is on her way back.'

'Good,' said Maddie. 'It always worries me a bit when she's not here.'

'She's bringing back food,' Sable said, turning her eyes to Millen.

'I should make a start on lunch,' he said. 'Are you hungry?'

'Ravenous,' she said. 'Try not to overcook the meat again; yesterday's meal gave me terrible heartburn.'

'Sorry.'

He pulled himself to his feet, grabbed the crutch, and hobbled off into the interior of the tomb.

Sable glanced at Maddie. 'What?'

'Nothing.'

'Come on; you've giving me one of your disapproving looks, Miss Jackdaw. What have I done now?'

Maddie sighed. 'It's just, whenever I bicker with Millen, he gives back as good as he gets, which is fine; it's what I'd expect. But, whenever you say anything to him, he's all "sorry" and bashful glances. You have him eating out of your hand.'

'I can't help it,' she said; 'it sounds like you're annoyed with him rather than me. Listen, we're starting to run out of wine, and I have almost no cigarettes left. Tomorrow, when Blackrose goes off on her daily flight, I'm going to need you to distract Millen for a while.'

'Why?'

Sable smiled. 'Do I have to spell it out? I plan on popping back to Alea Tanton to stock up on supplies. It will only take twenty minutes. Help me out, and I'll bring back a few treats for you; what would you like? Clothes? Food? I know an excellent bakery that does these amazing little cakes; I could bring you a tray of them, and we could hide them from the others.'

'I don't know.'

'Fine, no cakes. Maybe something savoury?'

'That's not what I meant. I know I agreed to keep the Quadrant a secret, but this seems wrong. I don't like having to lie to Blackrose.'

'Have you actually lied to her about it?'

'Well, no, but I'm not telling her something she would very interested in knowing, and that amounts to the same thing. And besides, what if she notices that we never run out of things? She might get suspicious.'

'It'll be fine. Dragons don't care about how many packets of cigarettes I might have stashed away in my bag, and it would be stupid not to use the Quadrant to make our lives here a little bit more comfortable. Aren't you sick of eating that green mush every day? It looks and smells utterly foul. Come on,' she said, smiling; 'don't make me "persuade" you.'

Maddie narrowed her eyes. 'You'd better be joking. If I find out you've been rummaging about in my head making me do things, then I'll get Blackrose to dangle you upside down over that lava pit again.'

'All you need to do is keep Millen busy for twenty minutes; half an hour at the most. If it all goes wrong, then I'll take the blame. You can tell Blackrose that I made you do it.'

'And how am I supposed to distract Millen?'

She got to her feet. 'I don't know; use your imagination.'

'Where are you going?' said Maddie.

'Sanguino needs his dressings changed, and Blackrose will be back in a moment. You know I'm not her favourite person.'

She walked off, disappearing into the gloom of the cavern. Maddie shook her head as feelings of guilt gnawed at her insides. Part of her was determined to say no to Sable, but another part of her really wanted to eat some cake.

A shadow blocked out the light from outside as Blackrose swooped down and landed inside the tomb. In her left forelimb were the bloody corpses of two deer, while her right clutched a mass of vegetation.

'Rider,' she said, angling her neck to gaze down at Maddie.

'Hi, Blackrose. Nice time out flying?'

'Yes, though it would have been more enjoyable with you on my back.'

'It's too dangerous without the harness.'

'Indeed. Its replacement will be one of the first things we should attend to when we leave the Catacombs. Unfortunately, that may still be some time away. I am making progress, but slowly.' She glanced around. 'Where are the other humans?'

'Millen's starting on lunch, and Sable's with Sanguino.'

Blackrose tilted her head. 'I often think it would be better if it were just the two of us here. Sanguino is in an even worse state than before, Millen is equally without use, and Sable is a bad influence on you.' Her eyes glowed red. 'The blind, the lame and the wicked, and somehow I am responsible for them all.'

'That sounded cruel.'

'Life is cruel, rider, and I have no regrets. Were I truly as callous as Deathfang, I would have slain all three of them by now.'

'You said that Sable is a bad influence on me; well, I think living here is a bad influence on you.'

'Your opinion is noted, rider.'

'In other words, you're going to ignore it.'

'Precisely. Now, let me drop off today's food that I was cruel enough to spend time gathering for everyone, and then we can talk some more. I want to discuss various ideas I have about convincing Deathfang to allow me to hold some talks on the history of Dragon Eyre for the younger dragons that live here.'

She walked through the interior of the tomb, and Maddie hurried to keep up. They reached the circular hearth where Millen was sitting. He was warming a large pot of water over the flames, and he glanced up as Blackrose laid down the two deer and the vegetation.

'You may remove enough meat for you and Sable,' she said to him, 'the rest is to remain raw for myself and Sanguino.'

Millen nodded. 'Yes, ma'am.'

Another shadow flitted over the entrance to the tomb.

'Blackrose!' cried Burntskull as he landed, keeping his limbs perched on the lip of the cavern. 'May I enter?'

Blackrose turned. 'You may.'

Burntskull strode forwards, tucking his yellow wings in. 'I bear some news.'

'Then speak.'

'As you are aware,' he said, coming to a halt in front of Blackrose, 'Deathfang exiled his daughter following that unfortunate incident some days ago. Frostback removed herself from the Catacombs, and took up residence in the caves on the far side of the valley from here.'

Blackrose tilted her head. 'None of this is unknown to me.'

'Have you ever spoken to the dragons who dwell on the far side of the valley?'

'I have not. I have seen them while out flying, but I restrict myself to mixing only with Catacombs dragons. You once told me that only exiles and criminals dwell on the other side of the valley.'

'That is so. Frostback has been telling all and sundry there about what happened, and today, one of the other exiles arrived, demanding permission to approach.'

'Who?'

'A dragon named Grimsleep. Deathfang exiled him some years ago for the murder of a young female who had refused his advances; he had his wings ripped and was lucky to leave with his life.'

'And what does this Grimsleep want with the Catacombs? Does Deathfang require a volunteer to drive him away, or kill him? I would be happy to do so.'

'The exile has made an interesting claim. He says that he is the father of Sanguino, and he wishes to see his son.'

'I see.'

'Deathfang has told me that the decision is yours. He will tolerate a short visit from Grimsleep, but only if you allow it. If you say no, then Grimsleep will be driven off. If you say yes, then Deathfang will allow him to stay for one hour, but after that, he must go.'

Blackrose said nothing for a moment as the yellow dragon kept his eyes on her. 'Tell me, Burntskull, if I were to acquiesce with this Grimsleep's request, would I face any repercussions if I lost my patience with him and ended his life?'

A smile crossed Burntskull's face. 'None whatsoever, Blackrose. He is an exile; he has forfeited all of his rights.'

Blackrose glanced down at Burntskull. 'And didn't you wish for me to be exiled also?'

'I did,' he said; 'I would be liar to deny it. Your arrival upset the delicate balance that we had established here, but I have realised my mistake; you have proved yourself worthy, and you have my respect. You would be a powerful and noble leader, were anything to happen to Deathfang.'

'I will allow this Grimsleep to enter my tomb.'

Burntskull tilted his head. 'As you wish.'

He turned, beat his wings and flew out of the entrance.

'I have several questions,' said Maddie.

'I thought you might.'

'First, does that mean Burntskull likes you now?'

'He does not like me. He fears and respects me, which is far better. Above all, dragons admire strength; not necessarily physical strength, but strength of will and purpose. We are drawn to those who display it.'

'Second, why are we letting Grimsleep in? He sounds horrible. Should I and the other humans hide while he's here?'

'Certainly not. If he harms a hair on your head I will eviscerate him and hang his corpse from the edge of the tomb. Of course, I may end up doing that regardless. To hide you would be to imply that I fear for your safety, and I refuse to show fear in front of such an unworthy beast. We shall let him in because he is the father of a dragon under my protection, and he has a right to know how his son is being treated in my care. Go now, and inform Sable.'

'Why Sable? Why not Sanguino?'

'The Holdfast woman is closer to him than you are, and he is beginning to develop a bond with her. This, I would like to encourage. Together, they would elevate each other. Once you have spoken to her, remain in Sanguino's cavern; I will lead Grimsleep there personally.'

Maddie nodded, then rushed off. She gestured to Millen to stay where he was, and sped off into Sanguino's tomb. The smell hit her the moment she entered. The dark red dragon was lying on the ground, his tail coiled round his body, and his head resting on his forelimbs. Sable was standing next to his massive head, dabbing at his eyes with cloths smeared in ointment.

'Hi, Maddie,' she said; 'what's the hurry?'

'We have a guest arriving. Another dragon.'

Sanguino flinched, his head jerking up.

'It's alright,' said Sable, her hand on his neck. 'No one's going to hurt you.'

Maddie came to a halt a yard away. 'Burntskull was here. He says that Sanguino's father has come to the Catacombs; he wants to see him.'

Sanguino groaned, and the claws of his forelimbs scraped across the stone floor. 'He is not welcome.'

'Blackrose is going to allow the visit,' said Maddie.

'Why?' said Sable.

'Dragon politics,' said Maddie; 'it would be bad form to refuse. Blackrose has permission to kill him if he misbehaves. He's an exile; a nasty piece of work by all accounts.'

Sable turned to Sanguino. 'Do you remember your father?'

'Yes, though I have often wished I could wash my memories of him. But if Blackrose has allowed it, then I must accept it. Sable, please stay with me.'

'Of course.'

'I'm staying too,' said Maddie.

'Thank you,' said the dark red dragon.

Voices came from the main part of the tomb, low dragon voices, but Maddie couldn't make out what was being said. She glanced at Sable, but the woman's attention was on Sanguino, and she watched the two of them together for a moment, thinking over Blackrose's words. Were they developing a bond? Maddie felt a little bit jealous, as if her bond with Blackrose was unique, but she also saw how the Holdfast woman and the dark red dragon could be good for each other.

Blackrose entered the cavern, keeping to one side. 'Sanguino,' she called out; 'your father is here.'

A red dragon with mottled black patches stuck his neck into the cavern. His huge head was covered in scars, and his teeth were stained and ragged. He stared into the tomb, his eyes ghosting over Sable and Maddie before settling on Sanguino.

He pulled his enormous bulk into the tomb. 'I am Grimsleep. I fathered you, boy. My last recollection of you was of a weak and bleating coward. I had vainly hoped that you would have improved yourself, but I see you continue to bring shame to me. Are you blind? A blind dragon cannot fly, and a dragon that cannot fly is nothing but useless meat. You should throw yourself in the lava pools below so that others will remember nothing but your end, and perhaps that would redeem my name somewhat.'

Maddie opened her mouth to speak, but Sable beat her to it.

'You shame no one but yourself with those words,' the Holdfast woman said. 'Your son has great courage, and outweighs you in every regard. You, on the other hand, do not deserve the name of dragon, you disgusting reptile.'

Grimsleep opened his jaws in rage and raised a forelimb, the claws extended.

'Remember my words at the tomb entrance, Grimsleep,' said Blackrose in a calm voice. 'Recall that I am hoping you dishonour yourself, so that I can tear you limb from limb.'

'You? The supposed protector of my son?' Grimsleep said. 'What kind of protector allows those under their charge to be blinded? Did you do it to him yourself?'

'I killed the dragon responsible,' said Blackrose. 'I snapped his neck and threw him into a fiery pit. He was lucky; with you, I would not be so quick. Say what you have come to say, then be gone.'

Grimsleep turned back to Sanguino. 'Your association with insects leaves you lower in my estimation than I had thought possible. Like a dog, you have been domesticated. Soon, they will have you performing tricks for them. Speak to me, boy, or do you have to seek their permission first?'

'I have not spoken before,' said Sanguino, 'because I have nothing to say to you. For the first time, I am grateful for my blindness, so that I cannot see you.'

Grimsleep laughed. 'The young silver dragon that told me you were here said you had a new name; a name not given by myself. "Sanguino", she said you were called. It amazes me that you allow yourself to be called by this name – who thought of it? Your human captors in that vile city by the sea? Have you even told the others your true name?'

'I am Sanguino, for I disown you and recognise Blackrose as my sole protector. She is my mother now. May worms eat you from within; may they burrow their way beneath your rotten scales and putrefy your flesh.'

Grimsleep tilted his head a fraction. 'May you never fly again; may you slowly rot in this cavern without ever seeing the moon, or feeling the wind under your wings.' He turned to Blackrose. 'I shall now take my leave. You can have the boy; he is of no use to me.'

Grimsleep dragged his huge form from the cavern, and the sound of his departure filled the air.

'It is done,' said Blackrose. 'If he returns, I will kill him without warning. Sanguino, you are now my son.'

The dark red dragon bowed his head. 'Thank you, mother.'

Maddie and Sable shared a glance as Blackrose withdrew from the cavern.

'That was... intense,' said Maddie. She glanced at Sanguino. 'Are you alright?'

'I am fine,' said the dragon. 'I am free of my old father, and now owe him nothing.'

'He was wrong,' said Sable; 'you will fly again; I promise it.'

'You shouldn't make promises like that,' said Sanguino. 'In time, my left eye may heal a little, but I fear that the sight in my right eye may be gone forever, and I need both to fly.'

Sable raised her hand to his face. 'Trust me. You will fly. Now, let's back to work; I need to finish dressing your wounds.'

She nodded to Maddie, who took it as a request to leave. She turned, and hurried from the cavern. Blackrose was sitting by the square entrance, and she walked up to her.

'I imagine you have questions?' the dragon said.

'You imagine correctly. Are you really his mother now?'

'Yes. The solemn curses you heard formally severed the link between Sanguino and his father. That was the real reason for Grimsleep's visit, I now believe. Parents have responsibilities, and Grimsleep wanted none of it, so he rushed here to be done with his son. Naturally, as the boy's protector, I filled the gap.'

'So those curses, they didn't actually mean them?'

'They may have meant them for all I know, rider, but not necessarily so. They are part of the ritual of disownment. First the insults, then the renunciation, and finally the curses. It was all part of a dance, one which both father and son seemed eager to follow to the end. And now they are father and son no longer; if someone wounds or slanders one, then the other no longer has any obligation to seek recompense or revenge. It will free Grimsleep from all of his fatherly duties.'

'And what was that business with the name?'

'Grimsleep was correct – Sanguino is the name given to him by the human followers of the Bloodflies; a pit name; just as Buckler was.'

'What? Buckler was a pit name?'

'Indeed. He too fought for the Bloodflies, and he would have been

Sanguino's junior for a while; an apprentice, you might say, though I never heard Buckler mention him.'

'Haven't you asked Sanguino about him?'

'No. My guess is that there was bad blood between them, and I do not wish to open old wounds. Perhaps, as the older dragon, Sanguino bullied Buckler; tormented him. The young dragon that you knew in the Bulwark was very different when he was first taken from the pits. He was broken, fearful and nervous. I do not wish to face the possibility that my new son might have behaved badly towards him, so I choose to let it lie. I advise you do the same, rider.'

Maddie frowned. 'I'm not sure I'll be able to. I loved Buckler.'

'Yes, but he is dead, and it is the living who now need our care and attention. If my suspicions are correct, then whatever Sanguino did to Buckler occurred over ten years ago; tell me, what use would it be to cast up old offences, when there is no way for them to be made right?'

Maddie walked up the edge of the entrance and sat, her legs hanging over the drop to the valley floor. She thought back to Buckler. She had always known him as cheerful and full of life, and it was hard to imagine the state he had been in when he had first arrived in the Bulwark.

'Back to the names,' she said. 'If Sanguino had an original name, then what is it, and did Buckler have another name as well?'

'I will not answer your first question. Sanguino has indeed told me what his father had named him, but only he can tell you that. I will not betray his trust. The answer to your second question is no. Buckler was born in captivity, and was named at birth by humans. Buckler was the only name he ever possessed.'

She nodded. 'That seems a shame.'

'It is a shame, a dreadful shame. To have been raised by humans as a slave, fit only to fight for the entertainment of a mob. The word "shame" hardly begins to cover it.'

'One last thing,' she said. 'Sable promised Sanguino that he would be able to fly again. Do you think he will?'

'No.'

'That's it? Just "no"?'

'His right eye will never fully heal. Sable should not use words as if they are cheap things that can be tossed around. Her promise will only hurt them both.'

'I don't know; she seemed pretty sure.'

'That woman lies as easily as breathing, rider. If I could get into her head to play the truth game, this fact would be revealed to all in an instant. Do not trust her promises, and do not enter into any deal with her without my knowledge. I trust you, Maddie, but I fear you will be led astray by her honeyed words, just as Millen is rendered a fool in her company. Promise me you will be careful.'

Maddie's heart began to race with an anxious trepidation. 'Sure, Blackrose,' she said. 'I promise.'

CHAPTER 17
FIRE AND WATER

Yoneath, Eastern Khatanax – 8th Lexinch 5252

Corthie stopped on the hillside and glanced back down the track. Aila, Vana and Naxor were lagging behind, and were still a few minutes away.

'Demigods,' said Sohul next to him; 'they've never enjoyed physical exercise. What with Quadrants and carriages, I don't think they're used to walking long distances.'

'You could be right,' said Corthie.

Sohul sat on a rock by the side of the steep path and lit a cigarette.

Their Fordian guide frowned. 'We should be hurrying,' said Gurbrath. 'This track is exposed, and we might be seen.'

'By whom?' said Sohul, glancing around at the empty hills. 'There's no one here.'

'By Ascendants with vision powers,' said Gurbrath, looking at the officer as if he was stupid.

'Is it much further?' said Corthie, sliding his heavy pack to the ground.

'Just another mile or two,' said Gurbrath. 'We need to get over this ridge and descend into the wide valley beyond, where we will be hidden by the shield that surrounds Yoneath.'

Corthie stared into the distance. On the horizon to the east, he could just make out the ocean, where they had anchored the previous morning, opposite a small, half-ruined port. To his right, the south, spread the Fordian Wastes, an unbroken wilderness of parched earth and desert, while behind and to his left rose the mountains that separated the wastes from Kinell. The hillsides were covered in dusty brown earth and gnarled bushes, with tufts of grass here and there, but compared to the wastes, they were positively teeming with life.

Sohul shook his head as they watched the demigods struggle up the incline.

'Are you wishing you'd stayed on the boat?' said Corthie.

'Absolutely not,' said the lieutenant. 'I'm not overly fond of ships and the ocean, and I'm glad to have solid ground under my feet again. I even enjoyed camping out under the stars last night.'

'You didn't have to come with us,' Corthie said. 'You're free to leave.'

Sohul chuckled. 'And go where? I appreciate the gesture, but I think I'll stick with you for now if it's all the same. Perhaps when we get to this Yoneath place, someone will be able to show me the way through the mountains to Kinell.'

Gurbrath scowled. 'Be careful what you say, mercenary. Kinell is our mortal enemy. Their soldiers hunt down and kill any Fordians they find in these hills. The shield is the only reason Yoneath has remained safe and hidden for so many years. Once you've been there, you will never be allowed to travel to Kinell.' He stared at Corthie. 'You should have ordered him to stay on the ship.'

Corthie nodded. 'We can blindfold him if it'll put your mind at ease.'

'It would, but his fate will be out of my hands once we arrive. There is every possibility that the city leadership will not look upon me kindly for having brought strangers into our hidden domain. A friend of Queen Belinda and three rebel demigods they might accept, but a mercenary in the pay of Implacatus?'

'I'm not in the pay of Implacatus,' said Sohul. 'I currently have no contract.'

Gurbrath laughed, a low mocking sound. 'I doubt the leadership will see any difference.'

Corthie glanced from the Fordian to the officer. 'What if he works for me? Would they find that acceptable?'

'Perhaps,' said Gurbrath.

Corthie stuck his hand out towards Sohul. 'Ten gold a day for tactical and military advice; for a dozen days. Agreed?'

Sohul frowned at the offered hand. 'Have I not already told you about the invalidity of such deals?'

'Shut up, Sohul, and shake my hand. Unless you want to be arrested when we arrive?'

'Fine,' Sohul muttered. He reached out, and Corthie gripped his hand tightly.

'Swear it,' he said.

'Ow!' Sohul grimaced. 'Alright, alright; I swear it. We have a deal.'

'What's going on up here?' said Aila, as she reached the crest of the ridge.

Corthie released Sohul's hand. 'Say hello to my new employee.'

She rolled her eyes and took a swig from her waterskin.

Naxor staggered up the slope, panting, then collapsed in a heap close to where Sohul was sitting. Behind him, Vana came last, her face red.

'I don't understand,' said Corthie, gazing at the exhausted demigods. 'Haven't you all got self-healing? How can you be tired out already?'

'It doesn't work like that,' said Aila, 'we can still be unfit. We've walked the equivalent of the entire length of the City so far today, and we did the same yesterday; and we're going uphill.'

Naxor struggled into a sitting position. 'And we have a lot further to go. I've scanned these mountains with my vision; there are no settlements out here; no farms, no nothing; just empty hills.'

Gurbrath smiled, but said nothing.

They rested for a few minutes then carried on. Gurbrath led them over the spine of the dusty ridge, and down into a sheltered valley on the other side, following a narrow track overgrown with grass and wiry shrubs.

Corthie squinted into the distance. At the bottom of the valley, he began to see the start of narrow strip fields, neatly arranged between irrigation channels on terraces cut into the south-facing side of the hill. Workers were out, tending the crops, and some stared as they approached.

'This Yoneath must be underground,' Sohul said to Corthie as they descended the slope, 'but even so, I'd expect to see farms and fields soon, otherwise how would it feed itself?'

Corthie frowned. 'What? Look over there; what do you see?'

Sohul shielded his eyes from the sun. 'Where?'

Corthie pointed at the fields and a cluster of small cottages.

The lieutenant shrugged. 'Nothing; just barren slopes.'

Gurbrath laughed again, then halted on the path and glanced at Corthie. 'You have many talents, Corthie Holdfast,' he said. 'Tell them what you can see.'

'I see farms, houses, fields, stretching all the way along the side of the hill.'

The others stared and frowned.

'Is this a trick?' said Naxor. 'This valley is as barren as the last ten we've walked through.'

'It is the shield of Yoneath,' said Gurbrath. 'When the gods invaded Khatanax two and a half centuries ago, it was first used only to hide our ancient sacred site of Fordamere from the armies that ravaged the land. But as time passed and more refugees settled in the valley, it was expanded to cover a much larger area – the city of Yoneath. Come. Once we pass through the shield, you will see what Corthie Holdfast can already see.'

He set off again, and they followed him to the floor of the valley. As they walked, Corthie began to see more signs of life, from dogs guarding sheep in the fields, to children playing by the irrigation channels. In the far distance, the valley came to an abrupt end. A vast wall of rock loomed up over the clustered houses and streets, with a great archway in its centre. They followed the path along the valley bottom, until they reached a stone marker, with a weathered carving of the sun on its face.

Gurbrath halted again. 'This is the edge of the shield. Once we pass this point, all will become visible to you. I must warn you; the location of the city of Yoneath is a secret that the Fordians have kept from the outside world for centuries. Only Queen Belinda knew of its existence, which is why she chose it as the hiding place for the Sextant. Once we enter, you may not be allowed to leave.'

They passed the marker stone, and Corthie heard the others gasp.

'You could see this all along?' said Aila as her eyes roved over the settled hillside.

'Aye,' said Corthie. 'It must be done with vision powers, which is why I'm not affected.'

'You are correct,' said Gurbrath.

'Then there must be a god in Yoneath,' said Naxor; 'a powerful one.'

'You will see,' said their guide.

They got another hundred yards along the track before their progress was halted by a group of armed Fordian soldiers. Gurbrath raised his empty palms and strode forward to meet them, and they talked in a language Corthie didn't understand.

'It's just as well Kelsey isn't here,' said Aila. 'I'm guessing she would block whatever powers are creating the illusion.'

Naxor laughed. 'Good point. I'd love to learn how it's being done. It's remarkable. I scanned this very valley with my own powers and saw nothing.'

'I can sense the powers being used,' said Vana, 'but I couldn't before we passed through the shield. It's a type of vision, just as Corthie said; like an expanded version of what Aila can do, but instead of cloaking an individual, it's cloaking the entire area for miles around.'

'Oh,' said Aila. 'That makes me feel a little inadequate.'

Gurbrath returned to the small group. 'I have spoken to the patrol,' he said. 'They are displeased that I have brought strangers into Yoneath, but are prepared to allow Corthie Holdfast to carry on. The others must remain here, under guard. It will be up to the leadership to decide your ultimate fate.'

Naxor groaned. 'You mean we've walked all this way in the heat of summer for nothing?'

'Not for nothing,' said Gurbrath. 'The leadership may decide to kill you for having learned our secret.'

'Let me talk to them,' said Corthie. 'I'll convince them that we're all on the same side. Once they understand why we're here, I'm sure everything will be fine.' He glanced at Gurbrath. 'But first, I want to know my friends will be safe.'

'They will not be harmed,' the guide said. 'A decision will have to be taken by the leadership before anything happens. For now, they will be escorted to a place where they will be given food and water.'

Corthie walked up to Aila. 'What do you think?'

'You're asking for my advice? This makes a pleasant change.'

'Do you think we should trust them?'

'I thought you'd already made up your mind.'

'I know my own mind; I want to know what you think.'

She sighed. 'Alright. It could be a trap, but if they have the Sextant, then it might be worth the risk. If they've been hiding here for so long, then I understand why they're wary. Just be careful what you say, and don't promise them anything rash.'

He nodded, then dropped his pack to the ground.

'Sohul,' he said; 'help me get my armour on.'

The lieutenant came over and started to pull the pieces of steel plate from the pack.

'Your armour will not be necessary,' said Gurbrath.

'I say it is,' said Corthie, as he stood with his arms out-stretched. 'You're separating me from my friends. No doubt you'll say you're being cautious; well, so am I.'

'I've told you that they will be safe; do you doubt my word?'

'No, but as you've said, it's not up to you. If any harm comes to my friends, I will avenge them.'

Gurbrath and the Fordian soldiers watched, but did nothing as

Sohul strapped the armour onto Corthie's frame. A small crowd of onlookers stood a short distance away, their green faces gazing at the strangers. When the last piece of armour had been attached, Sohul passed Corthie his helmet.

'Thanks, Lieutenant. If trouble comes, I'm counting on you to earn your pay.'

Sohul nodded. 'Just make sure it doesn't come to that.'

Corthie knelt by the pack and assembled the Clawhammer, fastening the handle to the end. He lifted it, and pulled the strap over his shoulder. He noticed that several of the soldiers and onlookers were staring at him, a mixture of fear and awe in their eyes. He nodded to the others, then stepped towards Gurbrath, whose expression remained dark.

'Don't be surprised if the people here eye you with hatred,' the guide said. 'To them, you look like a god; an enemy. You are making this very difficult for me, Corthie Holdfast, but so be it.'

He gestured to the soldiers, and they split into two groups. Half remained with the demigods and Sohul, while the others flanked Corthie and Gurbrath, and they began walking towards the huge rock-face at the end of the valley.

As they got closer, Corthie realised that the valley floor branched before the wall of rock, and the side valley was also packed with houses and more farms. People were flooding out of their homes to watch Corthie as he strode along the track, and he drew on his battle-vision to keep him alert.

'The ridge ahead of us,' said Gurbrath, 'contains the sacred shrine of Fordamere. It is entered by that archway, runs for a mile through solid rock, then emerges into a similar valley on the far side. It is the beating heart of all Fordians, our most treasured place. If you draw your weapon inside its walls, then you will die; do you understand?'

Corthie nodded.

More soldiers ran out of the archway as they got closer, and moved into position surrounding Corthie. They passed through tidy, well-kept streets flanked with cottages and market gardens, then came to a halt a few yards from the giant archway. There, Corthie waited a few moments as a heated argument went on around him in the Fordian language. Fingers were pointed at him, and from the angry tone of many, Corthie guessed that his presence wasn't being welcomed by all. Gurbrath stood his ground, arguing back, until a group of older men and women walked out from under the archway, dressed in fine robes. More words were spoken, then a path was cleared, and the group approached Corthie.

They regarded him for a moment, then one spoke. 'Prove you are mortal.'

Corthie frowned.

'Do it,' said Gurbrath, 'otherwise they won't believe it.'

Corthie slid the armour from his left forearm, and showed them a scar he had picked up fighting the Fordians in their abandoned capital by the ocean.

'That is not enough,' said one of the robed men. 'We must see you bleed.'

Corthie extended his hand. 'Give me a knife.'

Gurbrath put his hand into the folds of his cloak, and passed Corthie a short blade. He took it, and ran the point an inch down his arm. Blood seeped from the wound, and the crowd pressed in to take a closer look, their voices growing louder. An old woman in robes poked the cut with her finger, and examined the blood.

'Very well,' said a robed man. 'You may enter. Lord Gellith has been watching your approach, and awaits you. Come.'

The soldiers pushed the crowds out of the way, and Corthie followed the group in robes, Gurbrath by his side. They passed under the tall archway, and entered a cavern, its floor and walls smooth. It ran in a straight line, and ahead, Corthie could see a red glow. After a hundred yards, the cavern opened up into a vast space. On the right, buildings lined the cavern walls, while a single ancient-looking structure sat alone on the left. To either side of the lone building were vast pools, one of still, clear water, the other of bubbling, red lava.

'The way of fire,' said Gurbrath, pointing, 'and the way of water.

Between them stands the temple of Fordamere, where my people have worshipped for millennia. Once, it was the only building within this cavern, but Lord Gellith has governed from here since our lands were transformed into the wastes.'

They were led to the largest building on the right, a structure that reached up to the roof of the cavern. As they walked, Corthie saw the twin channels that fed the pools – two flowing streams that emerged from the rock. They crossed a wooden bridge over the water channel, which lay only twenty yards from a stone bridge over the river of lava. They entered the building and went into a large hall, where an old man was sitting on a throne, his white beard resting in his lap. His skin was green, as was everyone's within the cavern except for Corthie. The robed group approached the throne and bowed, then moved to either side to flank the ruler.

Gurbrath stepped forward as Corthie halted.

'This is Corthie Holdfast, my lord,' he said, bowing low; 'a mortal who has the powers of the gods. His abilities are such that he saw through the illusion of the shield, and with my own eyes I witnessed him defeat and disarm forty soldiers. He bleeds, yet he has battle-vision. Condemn me if I have done wrong, my lord, but I felt I had to bring him here. He claims friendship with Queen Belinda, and seeks to warn us about the Ascendants.'

'The Divine Queen?' said the old man. 'Are the rumours true? Has she returned to Lostwell?'

Gurbrath nodded to Corthie.

'She has,' said Corthie. 'I arrived with her.'

'Then where is she?'

'Shawe Myre, I believe. I have sent my sister there to discuss her plans. May I ask who you are?'

A few of the nobles in robes stared at him with contempt, but the old man simply nodded.

'I am Lord Gellith, ruler of Yoneath these past centuries. It is my privilege and duty to protect the remnants of Fordian culture and civilisation from those who wish to harm us. Tell me, how were you able to see through the shield that cloaks the valley?'

'The powers of the gods do not affect me. I come from a world where there are no gods, and it is the mortals who have powers.'

At this, several nobles cried out as if Corthie had uttered a blasphemy.

The old man raised his hand. 'Quiet. Corthie Holdfast, this world that you speak of, is it where the Blessed Queen Belinda chose to go when she left Lostwell? The world that caused the death of Nathaniel, the Divine King?'

'It is. He tried to destroy his own creation, and we stopped him. When Belinda, Agatha and the others came to avenge him, we stopped them too. All except Belinda were killed. With my own hands I ended the life of Gregor, whom you may remember?'

'I recall Gregor,' said the old man, his eyes narrowing. 'Why was Queen Belinda spared this carnage?'

'Because she chose to side with us against our oppressors, just as we should unite to resist Implacatus.'

'Fine words,' said Gellith, 'but they ignore the reality of the situation. Two Ascendants are currently in Alea Tanton, plotting our destruction. To resist them would mean our deaths. They are already searching for Yoneath, and my powers will not be able to deflect them forever. When they come, which they shall, I will be faced with a choice – give them the Sextant, or be forced to watch the slaughter of my people.'

'There is a third option,' said Corthie; 'give the Sextant to me, and I will ensure it never passes into the hands of the Ascendants.'

'No. Not only have you claimed to have killed the Divine King, but you also say that you annihilated the companions of the Blessed Queen. The only way I would pass the Sextant into your keeping is upon the express order of her Divine Majesty, the Third Ascendant, who entrusted it to me. Without that, I would refuse any such request.'

'Then, by your inaction, the Ascendants will try to take it from you by force. If they succeed, they will use it to destroy my world. I will not allow that to happen. You should know, Lord Gellith, that I am here for a purpose, and that purpose is to destroy the gods, and forever free this world and all other worlds from their tyrannical grip. I advise you not to stand in my way.'

The murmurings from the robed nobles grew into a tumult, their voices shouting out in anger and shock at his words. Corthie remained still, his hands by his sides, and his head held high. The old man on the throne remained silent and calm amid the rising cacophony in the hall, until, at length, he raised his hand.

'We shall take your words into consideration, Corthie Holdfast, for you have given us much to ponder.' He turned to Corthie's guide. 'Chief Gurbrath, I do not fault your decision to bring this man to Yoneath, but at the same time I wish it had not occurred. His presence here endangers us all, for once the Ascendants become aware that he has entered our territory, their fury will be difficult to assuage. While he remains our guest, you will be responsible for him. Show him the Sextant, then ensure he and his companions are provided with comfortable rooms and plentiful provisions, while we, the leadership of this city, decide what is to be done.'

Gurbrath bowed low. 'I shall do as you order, my lord.'

He tugged on Corthie's sleeve, and they turned to withdraw from the hall. As they walked away, Corthie heard the bitter arguments resume behind him. Soldiers moved to flank them, and they were escorted back out into the cavern.

'You have doomed me, Corthie Holdfast,' said Gurbrath. 'Your words will mean my death, despite Lord Gellith relieving me of any blame, as others will not see it that way. I will be lucky to return to my home after what you said in there.'

'I said what had to be said. Will Gellith hand the Sextant to the Ascendants? If he does so, my entire world will fall. What would you have me do? Say nothing?'

Gurbrath muttered something in his own language as he led Corthie towards the temple. They were between the two rivers, and the two pools; the water to the left, and the lava to their right. Gurbrath strode down the gentle slope towards the temple in the centre of the cavern. It was ringed with soldiers, and they came to a halt a few yards away.

'I thought you were supposed to show me the Sextant?' said Corthie. 'Is it inside the temple?'

'The Sextant is in plain sight,' he said, pointing at the temple roof.

Corthie squinted. In the middle of the roof, a platform had been constructed amid the red tiles, and upon it was... something. It was the size of a wagon, and made from glass, metal and wood, with six thick columns holding it up. Its interior was lost in a web of metal wheels and cogs, with glass fittings and wooden panelling, and the entire thing gleamed as if it were brand new. One glance was enough for Corthie to know that he would never be able to move it on his own; it would require a team of workers, with pulleys and ropes, and enough gaien or horses to shift its weight once it had been taken down from the roof.

'Is that it; that's the device that can create new worlds?'

Gurbrath nodded. 'It is.'

Corthie took a couple of steps toward it, but the soldiers in front of the building lowered their spears, while others pointed longbows at his chest.

'Go no further,' said Gurbrath, 'for the land upon which the temple is built is sacred, and none but Fordians are allowed to approach.'

Corthie gazed at the ancient structure. 'Are gods worshipped there?'

'Two gods in particular. Old gods, who predate the creation of Lostwell and the Fordian people. Gods that each one of us held dear in our hearts for millennia.'

'That sounds like you don't worship them any more.'

'Many here still do, but whether the gods are worshipped or not, the temple that commemorates them is one of the few relics of the olden times that still exists. So much was lost in the invasion; libraries, temples, schools of learning, that we cherish anything that remains. The Fordian refugees that fled to Alea Tanton have debased themselves. They don't remember their culture or their language, and they act like mere Torduans nowadays. Only here is the spirit of Fordia kept alive.'

Corthie looked beyond the temple. Upon the rear cavern wall was a vast mosaic, made up of thousands of coloured tesserae, depicting two figures; a man and a woman. Both looked young and in their prime, and while the man was holding an open book and a quill, the woman wielded a long, dark-bladed sword.

'King Nathaniel the Creator, God of Water and Life,' said Gurbrath, 'and Queen Belinda the Warrior, Goddess of Fire and Death. The ancient deities of Fordia. Corthie Holdfast, destroyer of gods, do you now see why your words have not only doomed me, but your mission also?'

Corthie said nothing, his steel armour glimmering blood-red in the light from the burning pool.

CHAPTER 18

AT HOME

S hawe Myre, Southern Khatanax – 8th Lexinch 5252

'Let's try again,' said Belinda. 'Amalia will be here soon and I want to get it right.'

'Very well, your Majesty,' said Silva from where she sat on a wicker chair.

Belinda stared into the demigod's eyes and concentrated. She sent her inner-vision into Silva's head, and tried to remain as quiet as possible. She caught the number eight in the demigod's mind, then pulled out again.

'Eight,' said Belinda.

'Correct, your Majesty; however, I felt the same thrumming behind my temples as in the previous attempts.'

Belinda frowned. 'Damn it. I need more practice.'

She sat back on the low couch, and glanced through the railings at the valley of Shawe Myre. A few lanterns had been lit at sunset, but all were small and downward-facing, just as the lamps in her hanging house were. Insects were flitting around the little lights, and occasionally one would find its way under the glass canopy and burn out with a sizzle.

'May I speak, your Majesty?'

'Of course, Silva.'

'I was wondering if this is perhaps the best course of action. Would it not be better to tell Lady Amalia that you have inner-vision? Then she would be more likely to tell the truth.'

'But I want to know if she's prepared to lie to me; I want her to think that I can't read her, to see what she says.'

'Are you trying to entrap her, your Majesty?'

'No, but I acknowledge that it might happen. She says that she's my friend; if that is so, then why would she lie to me? I need to know if she really is my friend, Silva.'

'Is it right for friends to test each other like that?'

'I don't know; I've never had any.'

Silva glanced down.

'Fetch Amalia,' said Belinda.

'Yes, your Majesty.' Silva rose, bowed, then walked from the large open room, crossing the rope bridge and disappearing into the shadows of the gallery.

Belinda sipped from her glass of water and tried to prepare herself. She intended to listen rather than talk, and thought about what Amalia might say. Her gaze drifted over the chairs, tables and lamps around her. She had rearranged the furniture after her bath, and had a perfect view from her couch; she could see the whole open floor of her house, and she could still glance down at the valley. Her eyes caught on the flickering flame of a lamp. Someone had forgotten to replace the glass canopy after lighting it, and the naked fire was visible. She stared at it for a moment as a strange feeling pulsed through her. It was almost as if the flame was calling to her, wanting her to connect and become one with it. She narrowed her eyes and lifted a finger, and the flame rose an inch. She gasped, and the flame dropped back down again.

Fire powers, she thought. Could it be true?

'Good evening, Belinda.'

She turned, and saw Amalia approach, her soft shoes making no sound on the reed mats covering the wooden floor. Silva was a pace behind, and held back as Amalia walked into the square of couches and chairs that Belinda had laid out before her.

'Leave us, Silva,' Belinda said. 'If I need you, I will call.'

The demigod bowed, and retreated from the house.

'May I sit?' said Amalia.

'Yes.'

'Thank you.' She gestured to a table where drinks and food were spread. 'I assume I should help myself to refreshments.'

'Yes.'

Amalia poured herself a glass of wine, a smile tracing her lips. 'You rarely waste words, I notice. There is never any beating around the bush when you are conversing.'

Belinda frowned, wondering why anyone would want to beat around a bush. And with what? A stick?

'You used to be so talkative as well,' Amalia went on, 'but enough of the past. When we had our long talk in Ooste, I spent hours going over little incidents that we shared many years ago. I think I was trying to trigger something in your memory, but it was also for the sheer nostalgia of it; after all, it had been a very long time since I had been able to talk about the old days with anyone.' She took a drink. 'Hmm. A rather peculiar vintage, this one. However, I digress. For our chat this evening I am going to avoid the past if that's alright with you.'

'Was that a question?'

'Let's say it was.'

'Then that's fine with me. I don't feel like talking about a past that I don't remember, and I've had Silva telling me stories about it ever since she arrived in the Falls of Iron.'

Amalia nodded. 'You know, this is the first time I've seen you dressed informally since you returned. In Ooste, you were looking all soldierly, and earlier today, you were besmirched in the grime that comes from trekking across deserts and through forests for days. You clean up well, Belinda; that dress suits you, and your hair is making me slightly envious.'

'Thank you. What did you want to talk about?'

'As I said, in Ooste I tried to appeal to the past, and I failed, so today I want to talk about the present, and the future. In Tara, just before I departed the world of the City, I was consumed with rage, and all I could think about was making Aila suffer for the death of Marcus. And then Corthie Holdfast cut my arm off, and a few seconds later I was on my knees in the ruins of Dun Khatar, with blood everywhere. I was sure that I had only hours before you or Yendra would make an appearance, and I was in agony. My powers were so focussed on my injury that I wouldn't have been able to kill a fly, let alone Yendra. I hid the Quadrant and waited, but no one came, and the rage I felt began to give way to self pity.' She gazed into the distance. 'Things got better after I was led here by Silva, and I started to make plans for how I could make my way on this world, but those ideas were wrecked by the untimely arrival of gods and Ascendants from Implacatus.'

'You know about that?'

'Yes. It can take time for news to reach Shawe Myre, but one of the demigods here has range-vision power, which allows her see as far as Capston, and I have her read the news for me. Renko's arrival was bad enough, but Arete and Leksandr? The Ascendants mean business this time, and Lostwell is no longer safe. More than that, they are hunting the source of the salve, and the world I ruled for three and a half thousand years is no longer safe either.'

'I thought you didn't care what happened to that world?'

'I care.'

'The world I went to with Agatha is also in peril.'

Amalia shrugged. 'That, I don't care about. Do you know where the Sextant is?'

'No. Do you?'

'I have no idea. Silva told me that you and Agatha hid it somewhere. If it hasn't been smashed to pieces, then it represents a grave threat to my world.'

'Your world? You might as well call it Emily's world, as she is now the ruler.'

'Who? Wait, that awful Aurelian girl who was really an Evader? Please don't tell me that she's in charge.'

'She is the Queen, and Daniel Aurelian is King.'

Amalia scowled in obvious disgust. 'Mortals? Has the City sunk so low? My foolish daughter Yendra has finally had her way.' She shook her head. 'Pathetic.'

'You were talking about a threat.'

'Yes, I was. If the Ascendants find the Sextant and learn how to operate it, they could use it to locate *my* world. I would be greatly interested in preventing that from happening.'

'Why? And don't say because you care – I don't believe it.'

'Because, my dear Belinda, my options have rather narrowed of late, but your arrival has opened up a new opportunity. Your presence here signals to me that you are no longer bound to any obligation you felt towards the Holdfasts. Is that true?'

'Yes. I brought Corthie back to Lostwell, and reunited him with his sister.'

'Well done. Splendid, in fact, as I assume that he has returned to his own world?'

'No. They fell out, then Karalyn stole the God-King's Quadrant from Blackrose and went back to her world alone.'

Amalia laughed. 'Really? How droll. It's nice to know that my family is not the only one that suffers from dysfunction. Unfortunately, that means that Corthie is still on Lostwell, and I'd rather not bump into him again if I can help it.'

'He is your ally when it comes to the Sextant; he also wishes to stop it falling into the hands of the Ascendants.'

Amalia groaned. 'I am unwittingly in league with the Holdfasts? My enemy's enemy?' She sighed. 'On the bright side, I can leave him to do all the hard work; let's hope the young chap's successful. Now, back to that opportunity I was talking about. I have a little plan. If you are no longer tied to the Holdfasts, then perhaps you would like to consider listening?'

Belinda narrowed her eyes. 'Isn't that what I've been doing?'

'Indeed. I shall press on. I propose that you and I return to the City, evict Emily from my throne, and take over control. We could defeat Yendra, and come to an arrangement with Montieth, and then rule the City between us. I'd take Maeladh in Tara, naturally, and you could have your pick of the other palaces, or we could split Auldan and Medio between us? A few of my grandchildren would have to go, especially that treacherous little bitch Yvona in Icehaven, but the rest would easily be cowed into submission. Then, we dump a truly massive amount of salve somewhere on Lostwell, and let the gods fight over it. That should keep them off our backs for a millennium or so.' She smiled. 'Well, what do you say?'

'I'm already a queen, the Queen of Khatanax, and of Lostwell.'

'Yes, dear, but this world is doomed. If the Ascendants don't destroy it, then all the damn earthquakes and volcanoes will soon render it uninhabitable. Would you really want to rule over a desolate, volcanic wasteland?'

'But almost all of your world is uninhabitable,' said Belinda. 'One half is ice, the other desert, and greenhides control the rest.'

'Yes, but Malik and I spent millennia building a rather large city where we could live in peace. You don't have millennia to spare; the Ascendants are here. Do you think Leksandr will stand by while you rebuild Dun Khatar? Besides, if we returned to my world, we could spend a few centuries destroying the greenhide nests, one at a time, fortifying as we go.'

Belinda leaned forward and picked up a handful of raisins from a bowl. 'Alia told me something about the greenhides.'

'Did she indeed? And what did my idiot granddaughter have to say?'

'She said that Marcus told her that you and Malik brought the greenhides to that world; that you invented the threat to keep the mortals under control.'

'Yes. I admit it. We opened a portal and let a queen and her workers pass through. Originally, our plan had been to keep the beasts as a weapon of last resort – we calculated that we could unleash them upon any invasion force that arrived from Lostwell or

Implacatus, but none ever came. Controlling the mortals was a secondary benefit.'

Belinda shook her head. 'That level of cruelty is beyond what I'm capable of.'

'It wasn't always so.'

'What do you mean? Was I once that cruel? Tell me, do you think I am a different person now? How does my nature compare with who I was before?'

'Oh, that's not easy to answer. Were you once that cruel? Hmm. No, you weren't cruel as such, but you were ruthless, and sometimes you did what had to be done, even if it resulted in the suffering of many. On one hand, I would say that you are quite different from the Belinda I once knew, but, I don't know, there are certainly flashes of your old self in there too. Of course, I didn't see what you were like after Nathaniel's death, but Silva has told me that you were a terrible and vengeful Queen at that time.'

'And why would you want me to go back to the City of Pella with you? Why me?'

Amalia laughed. 'Who else could I choose? I am alone here, friendless and vulnerable, while you are strong and powerful. On one level, I would need you simply to counter Yendra while I am still recovering from my injury; and you would also be immune to Montieth's powers, nullifying the threat from that quarter. Of course, we could also take Silva, and the other demigods that live in Shawe Myre – that girl with vision powers would be handy, and Silva could perform the role that Vana used to do, keeping an eye on the movements of all those with powers. An injection of fresh blood might reinvigorate my family line, and we could encourage the production of children to create a new generation of demigods to help us rule.'

'No, stop. Go back a bit. Are you saying that the only reason you want me to go with you, is because I would be useful?'

'Oh, Belinda, do you really want me to beg? Should I go down on one knee and tell you that I love you, that you were my best friend? It's true, but I tried that approach in Ooste, and failed utterly. I thought that appealing to your practical side might be more fruitful this time. You know, you have changed; you are not quite the same person that you were when we met in Ooste, which is strange, considering that was only a few short months ago.'

'Really? What's different?'

'You seem less sure of yourself. Less single-minded, and perhaps more open to new ideas.'

'Why is that strange?'

Amalia raised an eyebrow. 'I know of gods whose personalities have remained stable over thousands of years. I think I know the reason, though; you can only remember events since the Holdfast woman wiped your mind. To you, everything seems new, and you are still growing. I know that sounds a little patronising, but don't dismiss it out of hand. How many years of memories do you have? Three? Or was it four? Regardless, it is a mere speck of time compared to the long millennia that you have been alive for. Have you come to terms with immortality yet?'

'No. I cannot fathom what it means for me. I am still getting used to the rhythm of each year, whereas you and Silva talk about centuries as if they were nothing. The future frightens me. Not tomorrow, or the next day, but the idea that we could meet again in a thousand years, and look the same, and think the same? It's terrifying. I'm not ready to think about that, not yet.'

'Then let me help you. You have strength, I have experience. As co-rulers of the City, we could be a perfect partnership. Sure, we'd disagree, but I believe we could find workable compromises to any problem that arrived at our door.'

'But we would first have to overthrow the order that has been established there, and imprison or kill the Aurelians. The people would hate us.'

'So? The attitude of mere mortals should be of no concern to an Ascendant.'

'It would be wrong.'

'Wrong? Don't make me laugh. We are gods, Belinda; we dictate what is right and what is wrong. Mortals crave strong government; they need rules in order to live productive lives. They would worship you, and fear you. Statues and monuments to your beauty and glory would spring up all over the City, and they would fight each other to have the privilege of kneeling at your feet. You could have the pick of any man you desired; they would kill each other for the honour. Me, they would hate, but I could live with that.'

'And I would be your equal?'

'No. What I have in mind is a partnership, yes, but you would lead. I am prepared to live in the shadows, while you became the figurehead. I want Tara; that is my condition. Within the bounds of the territory of the Rosers, my will would be law, but in the rest of the City, you would be the Queen; the Ascendant Queen. If you're worried about the reaction of the mortals, then try to think of the longer term; in a few short decades, most of the citizens would have forgotten all about the year-long rule of the Aurelians. We would control the history books, and our version of the truth would become ingrained within their tiny minds. Then, you could be as nice as you like; a benevolent and loving Queen, who cares for her people.'

'I don't know, Amalia.'

The former God-Queen smiled. 'That's fine; it's far better than the flat-out rejection I was fearing. Think about it. I am open to changing any part of the plan that irks you. I need you for this to work; I cannot deny it, so I am prepared to compromise. Come up with ways to make it work that you would be happy with, and we can talk again.'

Belinda glanced at her, then turned to gaze down into the dark valley. Did she want to return to the City of Pella, Tara and the Bulwark? Part of her did; part of her welcomed the new beginning it would establish. She was known there and, despite its small size, she liked it. She would never agree to overthrowing Emily, Daniel and Yendra, but maybe a compromise could be reached that would satisfy everyone. She went through Amalia's words, looking for lies, but the god had seemed honest enough. She thought of Shawe Myre, and Khatanax; she had already abandoned it once before; could she do so again? But maybe

Amalia was right about the memories of mortals – give it a few centuries, and they would have forgotten the past as each generation succeeded the one before.

That left the Sextant, and the Ascendants, who weren't likely to cease their search for the source of salve. And the Holdfasts. Was she capable of running off to Pella, and ignoring the consequences that might fall upon the world of Corthie, Daphne and Karalyn? She owed them nothing, but she still cared. She turned back to Amalia, who was waiting with an expectant look on her face.

It was time to delve into the former God-Queen's mind, and uncover whatever lies or omissions she had said or left unsaid. She focussed her vision powers... but nothing happened. She blinked. She felt for her battle-vision and it thrummed into life. She tried again, concentrating, but no vision left her eyes.

'Are you alright?' said Amalia. 'You look as if someone has placed a cold hand upon your back.'

'I'm fine,' she said.

Amalia raised an eyebrow. Belinda turned, and gazed at the lamp that was missing its little glass canopy, feeling for the flames. Nothing. A terrible feeling crept over her; had her new powers disappeared? She was close to panic, she realised; what could make her powers vanish?

She groaned. 'Silva!'

The demigod appeared from the shadows opposite the hanging house and crossed the bridge.

'Your Majesty?' she said, bowing as she approached. 'How can I be of service?'

'Have the patrols been out tonight?'

'Of course, your Majesty; as always.'

'Could someone explain to me what's happening?' said Amalia, looking bemused.

'Go down to the valley,' Belinda said, ignoring the former God-Queen, 'and find out if any of the patrols have returned. If they have, ask if they have found anyone out in the forest.'

Silva nodded, though her eyes remained dubious. 'Certainly, your Majesty. And if they have found someone?'

'Then have them brought here.'

'Yes, your Majesty.' She bowed again, then walked away towards the bridge.

'Well?' said Amalia. 'Do you want to share what just occurred with me? Who do you think is out in the forest?'

'I have a suspicion, nothing more,' she said. 'Please leave. I promise I will think about everything you have said tonight. I'm not saying yes, but I'm not saying no, either.'

Amalia finished her wine, and placed the glass back onto the table. 'Very well. I shall return to my quarters, lie on my bed, and over-analyse every word I said. You have given me just enough hope to feel that all is not yet lost.' She stood, and inclined her head slightly. 'Good night.'

Belinda nodded. 'Good night.'

Amalia strode to the other side of the large, open room and crossed the bridge. Belinda got to her feet as soon as she was out of sight, and began pacing up and down. She stared at the naked flame again. Nothing. She lifted her left hand and tried to create sparks between her fingers. Nothing.

She hoped that she was right, otherwise her powers had disappeared for no reason, but at the same time her heart began to race with anxiety, and she felt the tightness in her chest return. Kelsey, she could deal with, but what if Naxor was also there? She clenched her fists. One thing at a time. The minutes passed, slow and painful as the ache in her chest increased. She sat, then stood again, unable to settle, her eyes flicking down to the deep shadows of the valley where the entrance to Shawe Myre was located. There was the faint glimmer of a bobbing lamp, then low voices drifted up.

She took a breath. Shawe Myre was her place; her home, even though she had only arrived earlier that same day. She sat, and waited.

Silva appeared, crossing the rope bridge. She walked over to where Belinda was sitting, and bowed.

'Your Majesty, you were quite right. One of the patrols has just returned, and they have brought two travellers that were apprehended in the forest a few miles from here. One of them is Kelsey Holdfast, and the other appears to be a soldier assigned to protect her.'

Belinda sighed in relief. 'No one else?'

'No one, your Majesty.'

'Alright. Bring them up.'

'They are on their way as I speak, your Majesty. Should I remain here?'

'For the moment, though I may want to speak to Kelsey alone. We'll need to find them somewhere to stay, as they won't be able to leave until dawn at the earliest.'

'Yes, your Majesty; I will see to it.'

A group emerged from the shadows of the gallery – six soldiers, who were flanking Kelsey and a man. Silva dismissed the soldiers, and led the two others into the hanging house. Kelsey's eyes were wide as she glanced around, then she saw Belinda, and smiled.

'There you are,' she cried.

'Good evening, Kelsey.'

'Wow. Belinda in a dress. Somehow you still look dangerous.'

'Is that a good thing?'

Kelsey laughed.

'Take a seat,' Belinda said. She glanced at the man. 'I recognise you. Aren't you a captain in the Banner of the Golden Fist?'

'I was, ma'am,' he said, bowing. 'I am now contracted to Corthie Holdfast. My name is Van Logos.'

'That's right,' said Belinda.

'Are we your captives, ma'am?' he said.

'My guests,' she said. 'Sit.'

Kelsey and Van sat on a couch opposite Belinda. Both of them looked tired and their clothes were travel-worn and stained. There was also an air of something between them; an awkwardness, as if they were uneasy in each other's company.

Belinda smiled. 'Welcome to Shawe Myre. Why are you here?'

'Straight to the point as always,' said Kelsey. 'The simple answer is that my brother sent me. He's worried about you, and was concerned when you ran away like you did. I think he wants to make sure that you're still friends, and he said that whatever happened to make you leave, he still cares about you.'

'You came all the way from the Falls of Iron to tell me this?'

'No. The Falls of Iron, well, it fell. The Ascendants ripped it apart with earthquakes and fireballs. We fled by ship, and sailed round to Capston, looking for the Sextant. Then, at a little village on the coast, Naxor read the location of Shawe Myre out of an old guy's head, and that's when Corthie sent me.'

Belinda's face fell at the mention of Naxor.

'Everyone's got a different explanation about why you left,' Kelsey went on. 'Hey, is it alright if I smoke?'

Belinda nodded.

'Thanks. Anyway, Naxor insisted he had no idea why you walked out, but to be honest, Corthie and I didn't buy it. No offence if you still like him, but Naxor's full of crap. Is he the reason you left?'

'Yes.'

Kelsey lit a cigarette. 'I knew it. That lying little arsehole. What did he do?'

'He betrayed me. He tried to seduce Sable.' She felt her eyes start to well, but steeled herself. 'He didn't love me.'

'Sable?'

'Yes. She had a Quadrant, and he offered her everything in exchange for it.'

'And what did she say?'

'She said no.'

Kelsey nodded. 'Good for her.'

'She didn't do it for my sake.'

'No, but at least she wasn't stupid enough to believe him.'

Belinda glared at her.

'That came out wrong,' said Kelsey. 'I'm not saying you're stupid; it's that Sable would have been able to see into his mind, whereas you can't. It's not your fault. Though, I kind of wish you had told us. Corthie would have flung Naxor from the battlements if he'd known the little rat had hurt you.'

Belinda glanced away. 'I feel stupid.'

'Love makes people do stupid things; that's different from *being* stupid. I guess Naxor was your first love, I mean, your first love since you had your mind wiped. Believe me; no one will blame you for falling for him. You actually saw through him fairly quickly if you think about it. I'd bet he's managed to string some girls along for ages.'

'I think this is the nicest you've ever been to me, Kelsey.'

'Aye? Oh. I'm not sure I like being called nice.'

Van suppressed a laugh, though his eyes seemed far from happy.

Belinda frowned. 'Are you two...?'

'No,' they both said at once.

Belinda said nothing for a moment, then she glanced up at Silva. 'Please escort Van back down to the valley and find him somewhere to sleep. Also, make sure he has food and any other provisions he needs.'

'Yes, your Majesty.'

'I, uh, my job is to protect Kelsey, ma'am,' said Van. 'I'll need to stay close to her.'

Belinda smiled. 'Kelsey is under my protection, and she will be staying with me, here in my house. No harm will come to her. Good night.'

'This way,' said Silva, gesturing to the bridge.

Van frowned, glanced at Kelsey, then got up and followed Silva out of the large room.

'Thanks,' said Kelsey, once they had gone. 'That guy is driving me mad.'

'I can lock him up if you want.'

'No, though that would be funny.' She shook her head, her eyes distracted.

'Do you want to tell me about it?'

'You know, I do. You seem a little different from normal, Belinda. Less... uptight.'

Belinda smiled and sipped her water. 'Somehow, Shawe Myre feels like home. I like it here.'

'It's certainly a beautiful house, and I can't wait to see the valley in daylight. It was lucky your soldiers found us, otherwise we'd have been wandering around the forest forever. Is it all right if we stay for a few days?'

'I hope you will. Pour yourself a drink, Kelsey. I have one rule about smoking – you can do it here, on this floor, but nowhere else in the house; agreed?'

'Sure.'

'So, you and Van?'

Kelsey took a breath. 'Alright, here goes. Where do I start? Oh, I know. You're aware, of course, that Karalyn can see the future? Well, let me tell you a little secret...'

CHAPTER 19
NOT AN INTERROGATION

S hawe Myre, Southern Khatanax – 8th Lexinch 5252

The demigod led Van across the rope bridge and away from the hanging house. He glanced back over his shoulder, but his view of Kelsey and Belinda was blocked by a spiral staircase that stood near the centre of the large room.

'There is an empty cottage on the valley floor that will be suitable,' the demigod said as they walked along a gallery, passing other houses suspended by thick chains from the over-hanging cliffside. 'Do you have any particular needs?'

'I'm sorry, what?'

The demigod gave him a look. It was civil, but beneath it, Van could sense an air of slight hostility. 'I meant dietary requirements, or perhaps you would like some wine?' she said. 'We make our own here in Shawe Myre.'

'Yes, thank you. Any food will do.'

He shifted the weight of the pack on his shoulder as they started to descend the same stairs they had walked up ten minutes before. He swore under his breath. He should have insisted on staying close to Kelsey; it was what he was being paid for, after all, though he felt fairly certain that the young Holdfast woman would be safe.

They emerged from the bottom of the stairwell into the dark valley, where a tall woman was striding past.

'Hello, Silva,' she said.

The demigod inclined her head. 'Lady Amalia.'

'What a coincidence meeting you here,' Amalia said, her eyes glancing at Van as she spoke. 'Have Queen Belinda's guests settled in?'

Silva looked uncomfortable for a moment. 'This is one of them,' she said, gesturing to Van. 'I was just about to take him to the old cottage by the orchard, where he will be staying.'

'Ah, I see. Will the other guest be residing with the Queen?'

'Yes, my lady.'

'I won't keep you much longer, Silva, but I would be very grateful if you would tell me who it is. I used to know many of the Queen's old friends.'

'Her name is Kelsey Holdfast, my lady.'

'One of the Holdfasts? How delightful. I was quite close to Corthie at one point. I shan't intrude on their privacy tonight, but I hope I will be able to make Kelsey's acquaintance come the morning. Good night, Silva, and good night...?' She glanced at Van.

He bowed. 'Van Logos, ma'am.'

'Good night, Van Logos. It was a pleasure meeting you.'

She swept past them and disappeared into the gloom.

'Is she a god?' said Van, as he and Silva resumed walking.

'Yes,' said Silva.

'What happened to her arm?'

'She sustained an injury.'

Van frowned in the shadows. Fine, he thought, so everyone was going to keep him in the dark about what was going on. He glanced up at the hanging houses, and could see a dim light spill out from the one where Kelsey and Belinda were. They passed a twin row of orange trees, and came to a squat, stone cottage. Silva took a key from a pocket and unlocked the door, then gestured for Van to enter. He went inside, and Silva came in behind him and lit a lamp to reveal a small room, furnished with a couple of chairs and a table that stood by the only window.

'There is a bedroom through that door,' Silva said, pointing to the rear of the room, 'and a bathroom off it. Make yourself comfortable, and someone will be along shortly with provisions. If there's anything else you need, you can let them know. Do you have any questions?'

'Yes. Are you going to lock me in?'

Silva looked surprised. 'Of course not. You are our guest.'

'Am I free to go where I please?'

'No. The houses and cottages here are dwelt in, and it would be rude to go barging in. Also, the hanging houses are out of bounds without an invitation from one of the occupants. Apart from that, you can walk the length of the valley. Oh, one more thing; do not attempt to leave Shawe Myre. The soldiers will stop you, and you might get hurt.'

Van nodded.

'I will leave you now. Good night.'

He waited until the demigod had left the cottage, then he dropped the heavy pack onto the wooden floor. The cottage had a musty smell, as if it hadn't been lived in for a while, and the walls were rough and in need of some repair. He pushed open the door to his bedroom and glanced inside. A low wooden-framed bed sat on the floor, with a mattress, but other than that, the room was empty. To the side was another door, which he assumed led to the bathroom. He went back into the main room and paced the floor for a moment, then sat in one of the rickety chairs.

He lit a cigarette, and Kelsey popped into his mind. He had been so focussed on making sure she got to Shawe Myre in one piece, he hadn't gone over what had occurred between them before the soldiers had appeared by their camp fire. The camp fire. It had been a stupid idea, and he should have vetoed it, but, on the other hand, it had got them caught, and the first part of his mission had been fulfilled. They had been lucky the soldiers had been friendly, otherwise their whole trip would have ended messily.

He heard a knock, and the front door opened. A young man walked in carrying a loaded basket.

'Good evening,' he said. 'I have brought food and wine.'

'Thanks,' said Van. 'Set it down on the table.'

The young man took the basket over to the shuttered window, and placed it onto the table.

'Was there anything else you needed?'

Van shrugged. 'I don't think so.'

The young man bowed, then left, closing the door behind him. Van got up from the chair and walked to the table. Inside the basket were jugs of water, and others of wine, and neat little parcels of food. He looked over it for a moment, then picked up a wine jug and opened the shutters a little to let in some air. Outside, the orange trees were close to the cottage, and he could almost reach out and touch some of the ripening fruit. He pulled the stopper out of the jug and swigged a large mouthful of wine. It was hardly up to the standards of Implacatus, but it would do.

He sat, and again his thoughts went straight to Kelsey. Damn it. Why did he feel worried for her? She was perfectly safe up there in the hanging house. He had seen Belinda fight, and knew she was far quicker with a sword than he was.

'May I come in?'

He glanced at the front door. Through a narrow gap, he could see that the god from before, the one with the injured arm, was standing outside.

'Sure.'

She opened the door and entered. She too was bearing a basket, and was carrying it with her good arm. She had changed clothes, and was wearing a dark red dress, with a black robe over her shoulders to conceal her injury.

'I thought I'd check that your accommodation was up to scratch.'

He shrugged. 'I've been in worse places.'

'Quite. Would you mind if I sat for a moment?'

He gestured to the other chair.

'Thank you,' she said, walking across the small room. She sat on the wooden chair. 'Hmm. Not exactly the most comfortable. So, how are you?'

'I'm fine, ma'am.'

'Good. That's good. Now, I am a very old friend of Queen Belinda; in fact, our relationship goes back thousands of years. Please don't consider this some sort of interrogation, but Shawe Myre is not used to receiving visitors, and one must be cautious.'

'I understand.'

'You are a soldier, I believe?'

'Yes, ma'am. A mercenary, if we're being strictly accurate.'

'I see. And you have been contracted to guard Miss Holdfast?'

'I have. Corthie Holdfast is my current employer.'

She nodded then placed the basket onto the floor and withdrew a bottle. 'Don't look so worried, Van. Just a few questions, that's all. And you can put that wine down; I've brought something a little less tart for us to enjoy.' She opened the bottle. 'Brandy from Kinell. Have you ever tasted it?'

'Many years ago, ma'am.'

She waved her hand. 'Dispense with the "ma'am", if you please. This is an informal chat.' She placed two glasses onto the table and filled them with brandy. 'I take that you are aware of the Queen's identity?'

'Yes. I learned it in the Falls of Iron.'

She nodded as she passed him a glass. 'It's not every day a common mercenary gets an audience with the Third Ascendant. You are honoured. From your look, I would say that you are an officer. Am I correct?'

'I'm a captain.'

'Excellent. It's nice to know that Corthie sent such a qualified soldier to be Kelsey's guard.'

'You said you knew him?'

'Oh yes, I know Corthie very well. We are allies, in fact. Both of us are trying our best to prevent the Sextant from falling into the wrong hands. Do you know what will happen if Leksandr and Arete get to it first?'

'I do.'

'Then you'll understand the seriousness of our purpose. You see, I come from the world where Corthie fought so valiantly against the greenhides.'

Van nodded, unsure what to make of the god's presence. Had Belinda sent her to check his reliability? Did they think he was a spy?

'Tell me,' she said; 'how is Aila?'

'She's fine. Naxor too.'

She crinkled her nose slightly at his name, which made Van like her a little more.

'And Vana is also well,' he said, 'but her brother Irno died.'

'Yes. I heard he was killed by an Ascendant. Another grandchild gone before his time.'

He glanced at her. If she had been mortal, he would have guessed her age to be late twenties, roughly as old as he was; but she wasn't – she was a god.

'Lord Irno was your grandson?'

'He was, as Aila, Vana and Naxor are my grandchildren. I have several others who are currently on my world, blissfully unaware of the threat they are currently facing; the threat Corthie and I are trying to oppose. I assume he hasn't mentioned me to you; my presence here on Lostwell remains unknown to the Ascendants.'

He took a taste of the brandy.

She smiled. 'How is it?'

'It's very nice; the best I've had in a long while.'

'I'm glad you like it. Are you loyal to Miss Holdfast?'

'I never break a contract.'

'Are you close to her?'

Van hesitated. Had Kelsey told them about her crazy vision? He tried to utter a banality, but it was too late; Amalia was smiling at him with a knowing look in her eyes.

'I, uh... I...' he stammered.

'It's quite all right. Guards and those they are protecting can sometimes get a little more intimate than perhaps they should; I imagine it happens all the time.'

'I swear, no matter what she's told you, nothing improper has taken place.'

'Of course. One wouldn't want any word of this to get back to Corthie; he might not be too pleased to discover that the guard he contracted to protect his sister harboured any sort of illicit feelings towards her.'

Van narrowed his eyes a fraction. He wondered if she could read his mind, for if she could, she would know that Corthie would probably approve of any relationship that developed between him and Kelsey. He groaned to himself. Kelsey. Her presence would block all of Amalia's powers. He was safe, and Amalia was merely guessing, which meant she wasn't there on Belinda's behalf. She wanted something. He wondered what else she had told him that might be untrue.

'Don't worry,' she said; 'I won't tell him, well, not if you answer my questions.'

He nodded.

'First, why is Kelsey here? What does she hope to achieve?'

'As far as I know, she's passing on a message from her brother to Belinda.'

'That's *Queen* Belinda to you; our chat may be informal, but it's not irreverent. And what is this message?'

'I wasn't privy to it.'

'Come now. Do you mean to tell me that such an important message was entrusted to a single person? Was Corthie really so remiss to take the chance that it might not be received?'

'I can't speak for Corthie's motives. I'm just a mercenary; I was never part of any strategic discussions. My mission was simply to escort Miss Holdfast here, and then escort her to our next destination.'

'Are you also contracted to escort Queen Belinda to this destination?'

'I was ordered to do whatever Miss Holdfast commands.'

She frowned at him, as if realising he had seen through her attempted deception.

'So,' she said, smiling again; 'how is Corthie getting along with the search for the Sextant?'

'I don't know. Miss Holdfast and I left his company some time ago, and I've not heard anything from him.'

'You know, I'm a good reader of people, and there's something about you that doesn't add up. You are an officer who claims to know nothing, and you are trying to seduce the young woman you're supposed to be guarding. If you mean any harm to Kelsey I would have to kill you.'

He drained the glass. 'You should know that I've been interrogated by gods several times in my career. During the course of those, I have learned to tell when someone's fishing for information, and when their threats are empty. I've had enough of this charade. Either tell me what you want in plain words, or get out.'

Amalia simmered for a moment, her expression as dark as her dress.

'In plain words, then,' she said; 'what does Kelsey want with Belinda?'

'If she wants you to know, she'll tell you.'

'I have plans, and if that little bitch interferes with them, my wrath will come down upon you as well as her. I want you out of Shawe Myre as soon as possible, do you understand?' She stood. 'Stupid mortals. I'll see myself out.'

She strode through the door and slammed it behind her. Van picked up the bottle of brandy, refilled his glass, then put his feet up on the chair where she had been sitting.

'Van!' Kelsey shouted through the bedroom door. 'Are you in there?'

He groaned, and put a hand to his aching head.

'Van!'

'I'm in here,' he said, his voice hoarse.

'Get up; come on, it's a beautiful day.'

He opened his eyes and instantly regretted it. Despite the darkness in the room, his head was splitting. He slid his legs out of bed, and stood, his balance shaky. He pulled on his clothes and opened the door.

'Woah,' Kesley said, squinting at him; 'you look like death. Don't tell me you got drunk on that wine? One glass of that stuff almost put me off alcohol for life.'

He staggered past her and grabbed his cigarettes from the table in the main room. There was one left in the packet, and he lit it, then coughed, doubling over for a moment, wheezing.

'Pyre's tits, Van. Is your hangover raging?'

He sat. 'I've felt better.'

She glanced at the table. 'What's this?' she said, picking up the half-empty bottle of brandy. 'This looks better than that wine.'

'Brandy,' he muttered; 'from Kinell.'

'That was generous of them. It looks like our nights were spent a little differently,' she said, sitting in the other chair. 'I had a great talk with Belinda. Wow, I can hardly believe I just said that. Belinda, who would have guessed? In fact, that was the first time I've ever really talked to her properly.' She passed him the jug of water. 'Drink some of this.'

Van swigged from the jug. He nearly retched, but managed to hold it in. 'Sorry,' he mumbled.

'For what?'

'I got drunk, when I'm supposed to be on duty.'

'You're allowed a night off. I was perfectly safe, safer than I was with you, to be honest. So, did you just sit here all alone and drink? Sounds a little... sad.'

He glanced at her as he smoked.

She frowned. 'What are you hiding?'

He was going to have to tell her about Amalia's visit. He needed to warn her not to trust the god.

'Well?' she said.

'Someone was in here last night.'

'Aye? Who?'

'Amalia.'

Her expression immediately turned serious. 'What? The god? The former God-Queen of the City? She was here last night?'

'Yes.'

'You spent last night getting drunk with Amalia?'

'She brought the brandy.'

Kelsey glared at him. 'I'm sure she did.'

She got up and strode towards the door.

'Wait,' he said; 'where are you going?'

'You just couldn't help yourself, could you? The same day that I tell you about the vision, and you go back to your old ways of sleeping with the first god that will have you? You make me sick.'

'What? I didn't sleep with her; I didn't even get drunk with her. She was asking me all these questions, but she was full of crap and I told her so. She stormed out, and *then* I got drunk.'

She paused, glancing down at where he sat.

'She was fishing for information,' he went on, 'wanting to know why you were here, and what your plans were. She made a few half-hearted attempts at threatening me when I wouldn't answer, and then she left.' He felt a familiar ache in his chest. 'That's it; that's all that happened.'

'Oh.' She stood for a moment, then returned to the chair. 'I, uh, thought that...'

'I know what you thought.' He shook his head. 'But why would you be angry about it, even if I had? You don't like me; we're not going together.'

'I know.'

'So?'

She lowered her eyes. 'But we will be together, one day. And when we are, I don't want to look back and... Pyre's arse, I don't know what I'm trying to say.'

'You're expecting me to be faithful to you, even though we're not a couple?'

'Not expecting, just... hoping. I know it's stupid. I know you think I'm crazy. Sometimes I wish I was crazy, and that my visions were nonsense, but they're not. I should never have told you.' She glanced at him. 'Give me a cigarette.'

He shrugged. 'That was my last one.'

She slumped in her chair.

He glanced at his half-smoked cigarette, and passed it to her. 'Have the rest of this.'

'Thanks.'

They sat in silence for a moment, Van watching her as she smoked. She seemed sincere, but how could he possibly accept that his future had been mapped out? Still, if she genuinely believed it, then she was bearing a burden greater than he would be able to cope with.

'I told Belinda,' she said after a while. 'So, that's four of us who know.'

'Did she believe it?'

'Aye, Van, she did. She's known Karalyn for years, and is well aware that she has the power to see the future, so it wasn't much of a leap for her to believe that I can do it too. I hope you didn't tell Amalia.'

'No, though she guessed there was something going on between us. That's when I knew she was lying; she threatened to tell Corthie that I'd acted inappropriately towards you.'

Kelsey half-smiled.

'Don't trust her. She was all smiles and brandy when she first arrived, but after I refused to tell her anything, she called you a little bitch and threatened revenge on us if we ruined her plans.'

'What plans?'

'I don't know, but they involve Belinda. She also said that she wants us to leave Shawe Myre as soon as possible. Is she really a friend of your brother's?'

'Is that what she said? It was Corthie who cut her arm off; Belinda told me. A "little bitch", eh?'

'Belinda mentioned Amalia to you?'

'Aye. She told me that she was living here, and filled in a bit of her background for me. They used to be friends, a long time ago.'

'And now?'

'Belinda isn't sure. She isn't sure about a lot of things, to be honest. She doesn't know what she wants to do.'

Van nodded. He wasn't sure he cared what the Third Ascendant did next; his job was now to get Kelsey safely back to her brother.

'How long do you think we'll be staying here for?'

'I don't know,' she said.

He gave a bow. 'I await your orders.'

'Let's go for a walk,' she said, standing. 'I have more cigarettes in my room, but we can go the long way; I want to take a look at the valley.'

He laced up his boots and pulled himself to his feet, feeling the various aches and pains throughout his body. At least his nausea was starting to pass. He glanced at the brandy on the table. He had been very close to drinking the entire bottle, and he remembered making a conscious decision to stop when he had reached the halfway point, despite an urge to continue drinking. Some small part of his brain had been able to tell him to go to bed, and for that he was grateful.

She shook her head at him. 'Hopefully the fresh air will do you some good.'

They went through the front door, and Van flinched from the bright sunlight, his head pounding. As his eyes adjusted, he started to take in their surroundings. The valley was narrow but long. Grass covered much of the ground between the vegetable gardens, orchards and cottages, and the little river was rushing past, its sound the loudest noise in the valley. Butterflies and bees were flitting about among the beds of wild flowers, and the trees were heavy with hanging fruit.

Kelsey led him along a path, and they crossed the river on a wooden bridge. Workers were out, building a series of dome-shaped mounds on a stretch of burnt gravel, where large piles of wood sat.

'That must be how they avoid sending smoke up from the valley,' said Kelsey, watching the workers.

Van frowned.

'They're making charcoal,' she said, glancing at him.

His mind drifted away as she began to explain to him the intricacies of charcoal production, and the construction of kilns. He had noticed during their journey that she seemed to have an almost encyclopaedic knowledge on a wide variety of subjects. He had very little in common with her, besides drinking and smoking. He knew he was smart, but her breadth of interests was far wider than his, and, he had to admit, she was cleverer than him as well. He wasn't intimidated by that, but wondered how they could possibly be fated to be together. Her type would be more of a bookish college professor, rather than a cocky army officer.

She nudged him with an elbow as they approached a narrow terrace of vines. He glanced up, and saw Belinda and Amalia on the same path, coming towards them. They were deep in conversation, and hadn't noticed Van and Kelsey.

'Hey!' Kelsey cried.

The two gods looked up. Belinda smiled, while Amalia rolled her eyes.

'Good morning,' said the Third Ascendant, then she frowned as she noticed Van's complexion. 'Are you ill?'

'He's hungover,' Kelsey smirked. 'Too much brandy.'

'Oh. Well, would you mind if I tried something?'

Kelsey laughed. 'It depends what it is.'

'I have a theory about your blocking powers,' Belinda said, as they came to a halt on the path. 'We know that they stop vision and so on, but what about physical contact?' She extended her hand towards Van. 'May I?'

'Uh, alright,' he said, not really understanding what she meant.

Belinda took his hand in hers and closed her eyes. Van frowned for a second, then felt a surge of healing power rip through his body. He staggered, and would have fallen if not for the firm grip of her hand clutching his. In an instant, his aches and pains disappeared, and he felt whole again. It was just like salve, and he gasped at the tingling euphoria that enveloped his body.

'Did that work?' said Kelsey. 'What am I saying? It clearly worked.'

She glanced away, and Van noticed something that looked almost like jealousy in her eyes.

'Thank you,' he said to Belinda. 'I mean, thank you, ma'am.'

The Third Ascendant smiled. 'You're welcome.'

Amalia rolled her eyes again.

Kelsey turned to her. 'You must be Amalia.'

'I am,' she said.

'So, I'm a little bitch, am I?'

Amalia smiled. 'Is that what this worthless mortal told you? If I were you, I'd dismiss him from his post at once. He behaved disgracefully towards me last night when I welcomed him to the valley. He is slovenly, untrustworthy and has the morals of a sewer rat.'

'Aye?' said Kelsey. 'Well, I'd trust him over you any day. Aila told me lots of stories about you, about how you married her off to her thuggish cousin, for example, and about how you let the greenhides in through the gates of that City of yours. And now you're trying to trick Belinda into agreeing to some plan or scheme or something. My brother should have chopped your head off instead of your arm.'

'How dare you?' cried Amalia. 'You know nothing.'

'No,' said Belinda; 'what Kelsey said is true. You did do those things, Amalia.'

She turned to Belinda, a look of fear in her eyes. 'No, I...'

'And yet,' Belinda went on, 'we now find ourselves on the same side. If we are to prevent the Ascendants from destroying Lostwell, and the worlds that you and Kelsey come from, then we will need to put aside our differences. If we fight among ourselves, we will lose.'

Amalia and Kelsey glared at each other.

'We should have breakfast together,' said Belinda. 'If we can sit round the same table and eat without trying to kill each other, then maybe there is hope. Van, please join us.'

He bowed. 'I would be honoured, ma'am.'

'Fine,' muttered Kelsey, her eyes narrow.

Belinda turned to Amalia.

'Very well,' said the god; 'you are the Queen of Shawe Myre, and we are at your service.'

Belinda smiled. 'Good; now, follow me.'

CHAPTER 20
THE SUPPLICANT

Catacombs, Torduan Mountains, Khatanax – 10th Lexinch 5252

Maddie coughed as the wind blew vapours from the lava flow into her face. Going for a walk had seemed like a good idea, especially after being stuck for so long inside the tomb, but she was starting to regret it. She glanced up, and saw the square entrance fifty feet above her. Not far to go. The ancient steps were cracked and worn under her boots, and she needed to keep her concentration to avoid slipping and falling back down the cliffside. As she trudged up the slope, a shadow hurtled over her head and she shrieked in fright. A dragon rushed past her, so close she could almost touch its scaly underside, and for a moment she thought it was going to pluck her from the steps and carry her off. She huddled against the rock with her hands over her head as the shadow passed by. The dragon was silver-grey, the same one that had broken Millen's leg and then dangled Sable over the lava pool.

Frostback. Maddie frowned. Wasn't she supposed to have been exiled? She watched as the silver dragon entered Blackrose's tomb and disappeared into the interior, then quickened her pace. She ran up the last few steps and clambered into the tomb, then came to an abrupt halt. Ahead of her, Blackrose was blocking the silver dragon's approach, her claws extended. Maddie rushed to the far side of the entrance, but Frostback's long tail was swishing back and forth.

'You are not welcome here,' Blackrose growled. 'Get out, now.'

Maddie's eyes widened. If there was a fight, then there was a good chance she would be pushed out of the tomb by accident. She tried to edge round Frostback, avoiding her tail, then she noticed the angry wounds down the silver dragon's flank, and across her limbs and neck, which were covered in bites and claw marks.

Frostback lowered her head. 'Please,' she said, her voice low. 'If I return to the other side of the valley, I will be killed, or worse.'

'That is of no concern to me,' said Blackrose. 'Your father punished you for trying to kill a human whom you knew was under my protection, and you led those who blinded Sanguino.'

'I know,' said the silver dragon, as she bowed her head almost to the ground. 'I am sorry. Please take me under your protection; I have nowhere else to go.'

Blackrose lifted her head, her eyes glowing a deep red. 'You ask for *my* protection? You?'

'I place myself at your feet, Blackrose; protect me, or kill me.'

The black dragon hesitated and little sparks of lightning leapt across her bared teeth.

'You are young,' she said, 'but strong. Why do you need my protection?'

'The dragon named Grimsleep wants to mate with me,' Frostback said, her eyes closed; 'he has learned that my father is Deathfang, and he pursues me day and night, and nearly killed me this morning. It was I who told him that Sanguino was in your tomb, under your protection, and now he will not leave me alone. If I return to the caves on the far side of the valley, he will kill me if I refuse him again.'

Blackrose said nothing.

'I surrender myself to you, Blackrose, and place my life at your mercy. Protect me or kill me, but do not send me away.'

'Was it Grimsleep who gave you those wounds?'

'It was. I went to my father before coming here, and asked him to show pity upon me, but he disowned me instead, and told me that I was no longer worthy to share in his bloodline. I heard that you adopted Sanguino, and the only way I can live with any honour is if you do the same to me. If you refuse my plea, I will throw myself into the molten rock below, for I would rather die than become Grimsleep's mate.'

'You wish to become my daughter?'

'I will do anything you ask, mighty Blackrose. I humble myself before your majesty, and beg you to shield me as you have shielded Sanguino.'

'Excuse me,' said Maddie.

The two dragons turned their necks to stare at her.

'Um, can I squeeze past, please? I'm a bit worried that I might get knocked off the cliff.'

'Let her pass,' said Blackrose.

Frostback bowed her head again, and moved her body to the left. Maddie hurried by, and noticed that Sable and Millen were standing by Blackrose. She rushed over to them, then turned so that she was facing Frostback. The silver dragon had closed her eyes again, and her head was bowed before Blackrose.

'I will need to consider this,' said the black dragon. 'There is an empty cavern to your left; await me in there.'

'Yes, Blackrose,' she said. She opened her eyes and walked through an archway and into the dark chamber beyond.

'What are you going to do?' said Maddie.

'That is what I am trying to decide, rider.'

'She tried to kill me,' said Millen. 'I was lucky I only got a broken leg.'

'I am aware of that,' said Blackrose. 'Come; I wish to include Sanguino in our discussions.'

The three humans followed her into the dark-red dragon's cavern, where he was sitting, his ears pricked up.

'Did you hear what transpired a moment ago?' said Blackrose.

'I did.'

'And what is your opinion?'

'I will do as you command. Mother.'

'I would have it debated first,' said Blackrose. 'Rider; what do you say?'

Maddie frowned. 'Do you believe what she told us about Grimsleep?'

'I do,' said the black dragon. 'From her words, I would guess that Sanguino's former father is trying to shame and anger Deathfang by forcing himself on his daughter. To retaliate, Deathfang has therefore disowned her, so that no dishonour may fall upon him.'

'That's terrible,' said Maddie.

'Deathfang's only alternative,' said Blackrose, 'would be to lead a raid on the far side of the valley, to hunt down and kill Grimsleep.'

'Then that's what he should do. He's her father.'

'Not any more, it seems.'

'The coward.'

Sable leant against the wall of the cavern and lit a cigarette. 'I think we should take her in.'

'But she dropped you into a lava pit,' said Millen. 'It's her fault Sanguino got blinded.'

Blackrose turned her gaze upon the Holdfast woman. 'I want to hear your reasoning.'

'Aren't we looking to recruit others to the cause of liberating Dragon Eyre?' Sable said. 'One has come to us, begging to be accepted into our little group; why should we turn her away? I know that she tried to kill me, but as Maddie often says, that's dragon politics.'

'What about Sanguino's eyes?' said Millen. 'She's an enemy.'

Sable glanced at Blackrose. 'It would be magnanimous, and wise, to turn an enemy into a friend. As your daughter, she would be under your authority, and obligated to you for saving her life. Could you conceive of a better way for her to pay off the debt she owes to Sanguino?'

'You speak with cunning, Holdfast witch,' Blackrose said.

'Could it be a trap?' said Maddie. 'Maybe she's trying to infiltrate us, so that she can wreck our plans, or do us some harm.'

'I grant that there is a slim possibility that she intends to betray us,' said Blackrose, 'but her wounds tell another tale. She has been attacked, several times. From what I gather, life on the far side of the valley is lawless and hard, and the weak and young are preyed upon.' She turned to the dark red dragon. 'We have now debated the matter in question, and wait only to hear what you have to say.'

'I told you,' said Sanguino; 'I will do as you command.'

'That is not an acceptable response. I am the matriarch of this group, and all those in it have a duty to offer their counsel when requested. You wish to be my son? Then you will have to act like a son.'

Sanguino lowered his head. 'Frostback is much younger than me. I am heavier, and stronger, and yet twice she has defeated me in combat. Twice she would have slain me, were it not for your intervention. In the Southern Pits of Alea Tanton, I thought I was the mightiest dragon that had ever lived; I slaughtered greenhides, and defeated the dragons and warriors of the Blue Thumbs and the Deadskins with ease; but here? Here, I am weaker than a young girl. Frostback's presence would humiliate me. She... frightens me. I am blind, and she would be able to torment me at will.'

'I see,' said Blackrose.

'Wait,' said Sanguino, 'may I continue?'

'Proceed.'

'Even taking into account all that I have said, I agree with Sable; we should take her in. For I loathe Grimsleep more than I fear Frostback, and I would be shamed to think that my fear was the cause of his victory over her.'

Blackrose tilted her head. 'Thank you. The final word goes to my rider.'

'Me?' said Maddie. 'Alright. I don't much like the idea of Frostback living here in our tomb if I'm being honest. That day she came round, she would have eaten us if Sable hadn't, you know, annoyed her so much that she decided to do the whole dangling over the lava thing. She hates humans; that seems clear enough. I'm guessing that she would have to swear oaths and things like that, but would she stick to her word?' She groaned. 'I don't know. Yes, I suppose, because, as Sable said, we need others to join us and it would hardly look good if we refused the first dragon that asked us for help.'

'Very well,' said Blackrose.

'Is that it?' said Maddie. 'You've decided?'

'It's not as simple as that, Maddie.'

'Why not?'

Blackrose's eyes gleamed. 'Dragon politics. I cannot unilaterally decide to take Frostback under my protection, as she has been exiled by the leader of the Catacombs. Deathfang might justly feel that I am acting against his express wishes; he may even suspect that I am fomenting rebellion. In order to preserve the peace, I must speak to him first.' She glanced round the chamber. 'I will fly up to him now. While I am gone, do not attempt to provoke Frostback or seek any vengeance against her.'

'I'm not going anywhere near her,' said Millen. 'If she knows you've gone, then what's to stop her eating us?'

'She knows I will kill her if she does so.'

'Stay in here with me, Millen,' said Sanguino. 'If Frostback approaches, I will bathe her in flames.'

Blackrose turned, and strode from the cavern. Millen frowned, adjusted his crutch, and limped over to stand by Sanguino's side.

Sable eyed Maddie. 'You coming?'

'Where?'

The Holdfast woman lowered her voice. 'To speak to Frostback, of course.'

'What about what Blackrose said?'

'I'm not going to provoke her, or seek vengeance; I promise. Happy now?'

Maddie sagged. 'Alright. I'll come, just to stop you doing anything crazy.'

They began to walk from the cavern.

'Hey,' said Millen, 'where are you going?'

'To get some fresh air,' said Sable; 'it's a bit stuffy in here.'

He narrowed his eyes as they walked out into the main area of the tomb. Blackrose had departed, and they crossed the cavern to the chamber where Frostback had been sent. Maddie paused by the entrance, but Sable walked right in without any hesitation.

Frostback turned her long neck to stare at them. 'You have come to mock me, insects?'

'No,' said Sable. 'We've come to plot Grimsleep's death with you.'

The silver-grey dragon said nothing as Sable and Maddie approached. Her wounds looked raw, and dried blood was streaking her face.

'If your bid is successful,' Sable went on, 'then we shall have three dragons, enough to kill that vile lizard.'

'Three?' said Frostback. 'One of those three cannot fly, because of my actions. I tried to tell the truth to my father about you, witch, and when he refused to believe me, I grew bitter and angry. You are the cause of my misfortunes.'

'No, you are,' said Sable. 'I tried to stop you from eating us; I was acting in self-defence. Justice was on *my* side that day, not yours. Against your claws, teeth and fire, how are we humans meant to protect ourselves? My powers are my defence.' She gestured towards Maddie. 'Blackrose's rider and I have both counselled the black dragon to let you stay.'

Frostback's head lifted as she regarded the two women. 'This does not make me obligated to you.'

'You're right, it doesn't,' Maddie said, 'and I'm glad about that, because I wouldn't want any favours from you. I don't like you much; you've been nothing but mean and spiteful to us.'

'I will forbear from killing you, insect, but only because I respect Blackrose.'

'You mean you fear her.'

For a moment Frostback looked as if she were about to strike, and her eyes glowed brightly, then she slumped down, her head lowering.

'Yes; I fear her. Everyone in the Catacombs fears her, even my father; or should I say my former father. Blackrose could tear Deathfang to shreds if she wished, and I hope one day I will have the opportunity to see that happen.' She closed her eyes. 'He disowned me. Darksky has borne him new children, and I am of no more use to him. I curse him.'

'How old are you?' said Sable.

'I turned seventy-three at the last equinox. If Blackrose refuses me, I will not live to see seventy-four.'

'Where's your mother?' said Maddie.

'Darksky chased her off when she became Deathfang's new mate. She hasn't returned. I looked for her across the valley, but no one had seen her or heard from her. I have had enough of your questions, insects. I don't know what you want from me; if you are hoping to ride upon my back, then you will be disappointed. I shall never lower myself to become a beast of burden to a mere insect.'

'We don't want that,' said Sable. 'Maddie has Blackrose, and I'm rather fond of Sanguino.'

'But he will never fly.'

Sable smiled. 'We'll see about that.' She nodded to Maddie. 'Let's go.'

The two women turned and walked from the cavern.

'See?' said Sable. 'That was fine. Frostback now knows that we support her bid, even if she still doesn't trust us. It'll stand us in good stead if Blackrose accepts her, and if she doesn't, well, it won't matter anyway.'

Maddie glanced at her as they walked. 'Why are you persisting with this "Sanguino might fly" stuff? His right eye will never work again.'

'But his left is starting to heal.'

'He needs both to fly, Sable.'

She smiled. 'Maybe it's time to show you what we've been working on.'

Maddie frowned as Sable led the way back into Sanguino's cavern. Millen was sitting on a stool to the dark red dragon's right, his crutch leaning against him.

'Sanguino,' said Sable. 'I think we should let Maddie and Millen know what we've been doing.'

He raised his head. 'Are you sure?'

'Yes, but if you aren't, then I'll keep it a secret for a bit longer.'

Sanguino said nothing.

'What secret?' said Millen.

'Very well,' said Sanguino, 'but they must promise not to laugh.'

Sable raised an eyebrow. 'Why would they laugh?'

'I would be displaying my weakness for all to see; many would mock a dragon for being so dependent upon a human.'

'Another dragon might laugh,' said Sable, 'but Maddie and Millen aren't dragons.' She walked up next to him, and laid her hand on his side. 'Maddie,' she said, 'go over to the far corner of the cavern and hold up some fingers, but don't say how many.'

'Um, alright.'

She did as Sable asked, and lifted her hands, raising eight fingers.

'Sanguino,' Sable said, 'concentrate, then tell us how many fingers you can see Maddie hold up.'

The dragon remained still for a moment, then exhaled. 'Eight.'

Maddie laughed. 'You're right.' She changed the number of raised fingers. 'What about now?'

'Five.'

'Correct again. Malik's ass, how are you doing this?'

'Through me,' said Sable. 'I am connecting to his mind, and allowing him to see out through my eyes.'

Maddie gasped. 'You can do that?'

'It's difficult, but we've been practising a lot. The first time gave us both a headache.'

'I remember,' said Sanguino, his jaws curling into a smile.

'Our minds have to be locked together,' Sable said. 'I have to go into his mind, and draw his consciousness into mine; it's a dream mage thing. At the moment we have to be in physical contact, but maybe in time close proximity will suffice.'

'And he'll be able to fly,' said Maddie, 'you know, if you're on his back, say?'

'On its own, it's still not enough to allow Sanguino to fly. Imagine, if

I'm on his back, then how could he see what's under him? But if his left eye heals as well, it should work. No, it will work.'

'That's amazing,' said Millen. 'Does that mean you're his rider?'

Both Sable and Sanguino glanced away, as if embarrassed.

'That's quite a forward question to ask a dragon,' said Maddie. 'Before I became Blackrose's rider, we had to form a close bond; the type of bond that will last until one of us dies. There has to be love, and trust, and loyalty; it's not something you can take lightly.'

'It sounds like quite a commitment,' said Millen.

'It is,' said Sanguino, 'and it is also a difficult one for me. As much as I respect Blackrose, I was brought up to despise the notion of human riders. Sometimes, my pride is my greatest enemy.'

'But no one laughed,' said Sable.

'Of course not,' said Maddie. 'It was... well, I thought it was quite beautiful, actually.'

Sable gave her a smile, and for once it looked heartfelt. 'Thank you.'

'Yeah,' said Millen; 'it's great news, but it makes me a little jealous. Maddie has Blackrose, and Sable has Sanguino. I feel a little bit left out.'

Sable laughed. 'There's always Frostback.'

An hour passed, and Blackrose had not returned. Maddie left the others in Sanguino's cavern, and went to sit by the square entrance to the tomb, watching the skies. She hadn't mentioned it, but she felt a little jealous too, and she wished she could connect to Blackrose's mind the same way that Sable could do with Sanguino. But then, she guessed, Blackrose would learn the truth about the Quadrant, so maybe that wouldn't be such a good thing.

Maddie Jackdaw.

She jumped as the voice in her head spoke her name.

It's taken me a few days, but I've found you at last.

Who... who are you? she said inside her head.

It's Naxor; you do remember me, I hope?

Oh, right. Yeah. Hello, Naxor.

I am in the company of Corthie Holdfast, and he asked me to send out my vision to try to find you. The location of the Catacombs is well known, although it is at the very limit of my powers.

I heard what happened to the Falls of Iron, she said. *Where are you?*

We are in a hidden city to the east of your location, populated by Fordians. I'll need to be quick, as my powers are already fading at this distance. Corthie wants you to pass on a message to Blackrose.

Yes?

He asks that she be ready. We have located the Sextant, and the Ascendants will be coming soon. He asks for her aid in resisting them. Banner troops and soldiers from Kinell are in the mountains, searching for the hidden city. If united, we shall have a greater chance of defeating them.

Are you joking? After everything that's happened, Corthie's expecting Blackrose to help?

He has no expectations, Maddie; he merely pleads for assistance. Pass on the message, and I will try to speak to you again in a few days.

The presence vanished from her mind, and she frowned, before pulling herself to her feet. She walked to the entrance of Sanguino's cavern, and gestured to Sable, who glanced up.

'I need you for a minute,' said Maddie.

Sable nodded, put down the mop she had been carrying, and strode over. Maddie led her into the shadows of the main tomb, and Sable glanced around.

'Is Blackrose back?' she said.

'No,' said Maddie; 'this is about something else. Do you know a demigod called Naxor?'

She gave a crooked smile and nodded.

'He's just been in my head.'

Her face fell. 'Oh. I see. Then he knows all about my plans, because you know about them. Damn. I hadn't taken into account that someone like him might come looking for us.'

'I didn't say anything about our plans.'

'It doesn't matter; he will have read through your memories. Did he mention me?'

'Uh, no.'

'What about Belinda?'

'No, he didn't say anything about her, either.'

Sable nodded. 'What did he want?'

'He says he's with Corthie, in a hidden city. They've found the Sextant.'

Her eyes lit up. 'They have? A hidden city? Did he say where?'

'Somewhere to the east, he said. He wants me to tell Blackrose; Corthie has requested her help.'

'Help with what?'

'The Ascendants are looking for the hidden city, and he wants her to help fight them. You mentioned the Sextant when you first got here. Why is it so important?'

'It's the most powerful device on Lostwell, maybe the most powerful device anywhere in existence. It can make and destroy worlds, and it can find them. If the Ascendants get to it, they will be able to locate the world you come from, and you know what that means.'

'They'll use it to invade the City?'

Sable nodded. 'If Corthie's found it, then we should help. The Ascendants will have Quadrants – we can use the idea of them to persuade Blackrose.'

'You mean lie to her again?'

'Not at all; we can be completely open about this. Surely you agree? We have to keep the Ascendants from getting their hands on the Sextant, otherwise your world will be devastated; do you want that to happen?'

Maddie glowered. 'No.'

'And can you think of another way to persuade Blackrose to help? I'm aware that she doesn't trust the Holdfasts, but she might be willing to help if she thinks there's a Quadrant waiting for her if we're successful. Also, she might relish an opportunity to take on the Ascendants; she could get some revenge for Dragon Eyre.'

'But we're not ready; we're supposed to be gathering an army of dragons, and all we've managed is Sanguino, no offence, and maybe Frostback. How is Blackrose meant to take on two Ascendants?'

'It's not ideal timing, I'll admit, but what else can we do? If we wait until we're ready, it might be too late.'

Maddie raised an eyebrow. 'You seem awfully concerned about my world. What are you getting out of this?'

'It's not just your world that's at risk, Maddie; mine is too. The Ascendants would love to destroy a world where mortals with powers exist, and the Sextant will lead them to it. I may have my disagreements with my family, but I don't want them to be obliterated. Look, I'll leave it up to you; Naxor was in your mind, after all. Pass on his message to Blackrose and we'll take it from there.'

A shadow flitted across the entrance to the tomb and Blackrose alighted. She tucked in her great wings and strode forwards.

'I have news,' she said.

'Uh, so do I,' said Maddie.

'Mine takes precedence, rider. Come, I wish to speak with Frostback.'

The black dragon turned and entered the cavern where the silver-grey dragon had been waiting. Sable and Maddie glanced at each other, then hurried after her. They went under the high archway to stand by Blackrose's side. Ahead of them, Frostback had her head lowered, her eyes avoiding the black dragon's gaze.

'Frostback,' she said, 'I have spoken with Deathfang and the others in his circle, and we have come to an agreement. It wasn't easy, and compromises had to be reached by both parties, but the immediate news is that you shall be allowed to remain here, in this tomb, under my protection.'

Frostback let out a strangled gasp of relief, her shoulders dipping and her eyes closing.

'There are conditions, however,' Blackrose went on. 'For now, you will not be allowed to leave the tomb for any reason; if you do, you will be driven off, and I will be expelled from the Catacombs. Do you understand? If you flout this rule, then I will also suffer. Deathfang could not be moved on this point, and I had to agree to it in order for you to remain. For his part, he will not interfere with your stay here, and he will respect my authority over you. We also agreed that if Grimsleep comes looking for you, then we will band together to defeat him. You are safe.'

'Thank you, Blackrose,' said Frostback, her voice low. 'You have put yourself at risk because of me.'

'I have. You should know that I do not take my responsibilities lightly; I will protect you, but I will also expect certain things from you – your respect and your obedience being the most important. You will also refrain from antagonising Sanguino, and you will treat him and the three humans who live here as part of your kin. This you must swear.'

'I swear.'

'Do it properly, Frostback.'

The silver-grey dragon opened her eyes. 'I swear on my life that I will treat Sanguino and the three humans who live here as part of my kin. I swear that I will not leave the tomb without your permission, and I swear to respect and obey your authority. If I break my word, may worms eat me from within; if I prove false, may you rip out my throat with your jaws. I submit to you, my queen, my mother.'

'Very good,' said Blackrose. 'This chamber is now your home. I must leave to go hunting, as there are now six mouths to be fed. When I return, we can talk about the future.'

Blackrose turned and left the huge cavern, and Maddie ran to keep up.

'Sable?' said the black dragon, glancing around as she strode towards the tomb entrance.

'Yes?' said the Holdfast woman.

'Deliver the news to Sanguino and Millen.'

'Of course.' She eyed Maddie for a moment, then hurried off towards the cavern where the dark red dragon lay.

'Can I have a minute?' said Maddie.

'For you, rider, always,' said Blackrose, halting by the entrance.

'Do you remember Naxor?'

'That sly little salve-stealing, double-crossing demigod? Of course I remember him.'

'He spoke in my head while you were talking to Deathfang.'

'Did he now? What does he want? Whatever it is, my answer will be no.'

'He passed on a message from Corthie.'

'I see. You have a love for guessing games, Maddie, so allow me to participate. Corthie is in trouble, and he wishes me to assist him?'

'Um, yes.'

'And he has given a vague promise that I shall be rewarded, perhaps with a Quadrant, if I come to his rescue yet again?'

'He didn't actually promise anything this time.'

Blackrose laughed. 'Tell me, rider; would helping him further our purpose of liberating Dragon Eyre from the oppression of the gods?'

'Not directly, no. But...'

The dragon's eyes burned red. 'But what?'

'Well, the Ascendants, they will have Quadrants with them. If we helped, then we might be able to get one, and we do need one, don't we?'

Blackrose tilted her head. 'Is Corthie opposing the two Ascendants that arrived on Lostwell?'

'Yes, well, he will be soon, he thinks. They're after that Sextant thing, and he's found it. Sable says it's the most powerful device in the world.'

'What's going on, Maddie? You sound like you're trying to talk me into accepting this one-sided alliance with the Holdfasts. I don't have the time or the inclination to offer my assistance to a boy notorious for his failure to honour his promises, and I'm a little disappointed that you think I should. What are you hiding?'

'Nothing. It's just that, well, Sable says the Ascendants could use the Sextant to find my world; the world of Pella and the Bulwark.'

'I see. You wish me to fight once again for the City that imprisoned me for a decade. Haven't I saved it enough times already?' She began to unfurl her wings. 'This conversation is over, rider.'

'But...'

'I beseech you; do not bring it up again. My days of pandering to the whims of the Holdfasts are long over.'

She launched herself off the edge of the tomb, and soared up into the blue sky.

Maddie noticed Sable lurking close by.

'She said no, I assume?'

Maddie nodded. 'This is wrong. I tried to persuade her by saying that she might get a Quadrant out of it, when you already have one with you. She's going to roast me alive if she finds out I knew and didn't tell her.'

'Don't worry; keep your nerve. If we're clever about this, then we'll all get what we want. You and I will help keep the Ascendants away from the Sextant, and Blackrose will have a following, and a Quadrant. We can all win.'

'A following? You mean Sanguino and Frostback? How is that going to be anywhere near enough to retake Dragon Eyre?'

'Baby steps, Maddie,' Sable said, glancing at her. 'Everything will be fine; trust me.'

Maddie nodded, and relaxed a little. Sable was right, she was worrying about nothing. Everything was going to be fine.

CHAPTER 21

COOPERATION

Y oneath, Eastern Khatanax – 10th Lexinch 5252

'I didn't promise her anything,' said Corthie.

Aila frowned at him. 'Are you certain about that?'

'I explicitly told Naxor not to. I asked her for help, that's all.'

'But surely you don't believe that she'll agree? You remember how hard it was to get Blackrose to help us last time?'

Corthie kept his eyes on the flowing river of lava in front of them. 'I had to ask.'

'Corthie, she cursed your family.'

'She can't hate us that much; Naxor said that Sable is staying with them in the Catacombs.'

'Sable? What's she doing there?'

'Helping them, or so Naxor said. I'm guessing he read Maddie's mind, but he's been fairly vague about the details. The thing is, Naxor told us a while back that Sable had a Quadrant in her possession but, if that's the case, why hasn't Blackrose used it to travel to Dragon Eyre? Naxor said that she's trying to raise an army of wild dragons to help her, but I still find it hard to believe that she wouldn't have left if she'd been able to.'

Aila frowned, her face glowing in the reflection from the lava.

'Still,' Corthie went on, 'Maddie and Sable's presence there can only help us. Both of them have homes that are at risk from the Ascendants; maybe they'll be able to persuade the dragon.'

'Let's get back out into the fresh air,' said Aila; 'my eyes are starting to sting.'

They got up from the stone bench where they had been sitting and turned away from the lava flow. Ahead of them was the heavily guarded temple, and the soldiers eyed them as they passed. Gurbrath was waiting for them by the bridge over the stream of water; he was under orders to escort them whenever they entered the caverns of Fordamere. He inclined his head as they approached.

'I would rather you didn't come in here,' he said as they crossed the wooden bridge; 'not only does it inconvenience me, but it encourages the crowds to come out to stare at you.'

Corthie glanced around at the many faces watching them. 'It's the same wherever I go in Yoneath.'

'Yes,' said Gurbrath, 'but people tend to get nervous when you are so close to the temple. For every Fordian who supports you, there are five who would like to see you thrown into the pool of fire.' He frowned. 'And me too, I presume.'

'Every day, the soldiers of Implacatus get closer to finding Yoneath. I don't care about a few disgruntled Fordians; they'll thank me if the enemy breaks through the shield and I'm all that stands between them and the Sextant.'

'There are many who think surrendering the Sextant to the Ascendants is a small price to pay for the survival of Yoneath.'

'How do we persuade them otherwise?' said Aila. 'If we were allowed to remove the Sextant, we could take it out of Yoneath before the Ascendants get here.'

'Lord Gellith has refused to consider it, ma'am,' said Gurbrath. 'If my information is correct, he believes that only a full submission to the Ascendants will save this city.'

'He's a demigod, isn't he?' said Corthie.

'Yes. His mother was a Fordian woman, but his father was a god.'

'Who?'

'I don't know. Lord Gellith has always kept that a secret from us. Whoever it was, our lord inherited his shielding power from him.'

'Is that all he can do?' said Aila.

'It's his only god power, if that's what you mean, ma'am.'

They left the huge cavern and the two pools behind them and strode along the tunnel towards the daylight. Wherever they passed, Fordians would stop what they were doing to stare, some with curious expressions, others with downright hostility.

'Perhaps, Corthie,' said Gurbrath, 'if you didn't walk around in armour carrying that fearsome weapon, people would look at you less.'

'I want them to look at me; I want them to know I'm armed and ready to fight. Also, if I left the Clawhammer in the house where we're staying, someone would steal it.'

Gurbrath looked like he was going to object, but closed his mouth and said nothing. They emerged into the bright sunshine and walked through the clusters of Fordians doing business by the entrance to Fordamere. Farmers and merchants were selling their wares, while others were strolling around with baskets, looking for items to buy.

'God killer!' someone shouted, and a murmuring rippled through the crowd. People began moving away from Corthie, some bristling with rage. Mothers ushered their children away as a group approached. A few were armed with makeshift weapons, and they blocked Corthie's path.

Aila, Corthie and Gurbrath came to a halt.

'If you're here to ask me to leave Yoneath,' Corthie said, 'then the answer is no.'

'We don't want you to leave,' said a man holding a pickaxe. 'You should be locked up, so that when the Ascendants get here, we can give you to them.'

'You might wish to kneel before tyrants, but I never shall. I will fight the Ascendants, and I shall defeat them.'

'You are but one man,' the pickaxe-wielder sneered.

Corthie unslung the Clawhammer and gripped it in both hands. 'Then try to arrest me.'

Gurbrath stepped forward into the gap between them. 'There is no need for violence. Lord Gellith has forbidden any Fordian to lay hands on Corthie Holdfast or his companions.' He stared at the group. 'Go home.'

A woman holding a long knife spat on the ground at Gurbrath's feet. 'Your part in this won't be forgotten; it was you who led this foreigner into our most sacred shrine. There will be nowhere to hide when the Ascendants get here.'

A whistle blew behind them, and a squad of regular soldiers appeared at the edge of the crowd, pushing their way through. Corthie shouldered the Clawhammer, and the armed group dispersed.

'Everything's fine, officers,' said Gurbrath as the soldiers approached. 'I was just escorting our guests to their accommodation.'

The lead soldier frowned, his eyes darting over the crowd as his comrades cleared a space around Corthie.

'Get them out of here,' he said to Gurbrath.

'At once,' Gurbrath said, bowing his head. He gestured to Corthie and Aila and they passed through the rest of the crowd into a wide street. Gurbrath hurried them along and they came to the guarded house where they were staying. It was detached from the other buildings on the street, and soldiers were ringing it. A young man rushed up to them as they neared the front door.

'We're with you, Corthie,' he cried.

Corthie glanced at him as they walked.

'Not all of us want to kneel before tyrants,' the young man said. 'If you resist the Ascendants, you will have the support of many. I would rather die than be a slave.'

'That's good to know,' said Corthie. 'Stay strong, and get ready.'

The young man nodded and raised a fist in salute. They reached the front door of the single storey wooden-framed house, and guards parted to allow Aila and Corthie to enter, while Gurbrath remained outside.

There was no hallway, and the front door opened onto the largest room in the house, where Naxor, Vana and Sohul were sitting.

'Enjoy your walk?' said Naxor.

'It was delightful,' said Aila. 'We were only accosted by an armed band once this time.'

Naxor laughed as he glanced at Aila, then stopped abruptly.

'Get out of my head,' she said, her eyes narrowing.

Naxor looked away, then laughed again, but it sounded hollow. 'I shall, eh, yes, I shall perform a sighting, I think. It's time for my daily check of the mountains.'

He got up and strode into one of the house's back rooms.

'What was that about?' said Vana.

'Nothing,' said Aila. 'Ignore him.'

'It didn't look like nothing,' said Corthie. 'Was he reading your mind again?'

'Only for a moment; I think he sensed my hostility.'

Sohul glanced out of a window. 'Quite a crowd is gathering in the street.'

Vana got up and peered past the half-open shutters. 'They look angry.' She turned to Aila. 'I don't like it here; we're not welcome. I think we should leave, and return to the ship.'

'And go where?' said Corthie. 'Where could we sail that would be safe?'

'Almost anywhere would be safer than here.'

'There would be nothing to prevent the Ascendants from taking the Sextant if we leave.' He paused for a moment. 'But maybe you should go back, Vana. You could wait on board the ship for us. Sohul could escort you to the coast.'

Vana's face brightened a little. 'That's not such a terrible idea. I could make sure the ship is ready to go, especially if you come fleeing down from the mountains with a thousand soldiers at your heels. Aila, you will come with me, yes?'

'No,' she said. 'I'll stay with Corthie and Naxor, but I agree; you should go. It's going to get dangerous here soon and, let's face it, you're no good with a sword.'

Corthie glanced at Sohul. 'Get your things together and be ready to depart. I may need to contract you for a little longer.'

The lieutenant nodded. 'I'll make sure Lady Vana gets to the ship safely.'

'I feel like a coward for deserting you all like this,' Vana said, 'but Aila's right; I would be useless in a fight, and I'd only hinder you if I stayed.'

'You might have to wait until the crowd outside dies down,' said Aila as she glanced out of the window. 'There are too many out there to get past.'

Naxor hurried into the room, his eyes wide.

'Sohul's going to take Vana back to the ship,' said Aila.

'What?' he said. 'Uh, no; that won't be happening, I'm afraid.'

'Why not?' said Vana.

'Because hundreds more Banner soldiers have entered the mountains; they're everywhere, sweeping through the valleys all around us. The road back to the coast is blocked.'

Vana's face paled.

'It's only a matter of time before the shield is breached,' Naxor went on. 'One of the Banner patrols is bound to stumble through it, and when they do, the illusion will be as good as useless. We might be able to fight our way through them, but there's no way we could sneak past.'

'Any sign of the Ascendants?' said Corthie.

'None that I could see. Troopers from Kinell are to the north of us, and Banner soldiers are on the three other sides, closing in.' He glanced towards the window. 'What's that noise?'

Aila frowned. 'Just a few hundred Fordians demanding Corthie's head on a stick.'

Naxor walked to the window. 'Oh. I'm not altogether sure that the soldiers guarding us are there in adequate numbers. If the crowd rush the house, they won't be able to stop them. On the other hand, quite a few civilians appear to be punching each other, so perhaps they're not all opposed to us.'

'Maybe I should speak to them,' said Corthie.

'You can't go out there,' said Aila; 'you'd be lynched.'

'I was thinking of the roof,' he said. 'I could climb up through the hatch in the kitchen.'

'And what would you say to them?' said Naxor. 'You would calm them down, I hope, rather than rile them up further?'

'I'm sure I'll think of something.' He glanced at the demigod. 'Can you read Lord Gellith's mind from here?'

'I guess so, but he tends to think in his own language.'

'Do it anyway. Try to find out what his plans are.'

Corthie strode into the kitchen without waiting for a response. His height allowed him to reach the hatch in the ceiling without needing a ladder or a chair to stand on, and he opened it, revealing the blue sky above the flat roof.

'Are you sure about this?' said Aila from the doorway.

Naxor glanced at her. 'Maybe, cousin, it's time to tell...'

'No,' she snapped.

Corthie frowned. 'Am I missing something?'

Aila shook her head. 'Just be careful.'

He nodded, raised his arms, and heaved himself up through the hatch. He brought his knees up, then stood, his steel armour shining in the bright sunlight. The volume of noise increased as the hundreds of Fordians packing the street noticed him. Howls of outrage mixed with cheers, and the crowd surged forwards, pressing the soldiers back against the walls of the house.

Corthie raised his right arm into the air. 'People of Yoneath,' he cried, letting his voice carry across the street. 'The armies of the Ascendants are approaching, and they have surrounded this city. It will not remain hidden for much longer, and the time has come to make a decision.'

The noise from the crowd barely abated while he spoke, but many were looking up at him, listening to his words over the cacophony.

'You, the people of Yoneath,' he went on, 'must choose. Will you submit to your oppressors, the same gods that destroyed the green lands of Fordia, or will you get off your knees and fight? Did your ancestors struggle so that you could forever live in fear; did they fight and die for nothing? What do you think will happen if you cravenly allow the Ascendants to walk in here and take the Sextant? Do you really believe they will let Yoneath live in peace? They will trample over your sacred shrine of Fordamere, and enslave you all!'

Fights began to break out all over the street, and the volume rose as the violence spread. Weapons were drawn, and the first soldier went down amid blows from the mob as they surged round the house. More soldiers were trying to reach the street, whole companies of them, armed with shields and clubs. The mob retaliated with stones, raining them down on the soldiers, who pushed forwards in thick lines. Screams rose as the street became a battlefield, and blood was spilt as, slowly, the soldiers started to gain control.

'Are you slaves?' Corthie cried. 'Or are you free? Will you kneel before your enemies, or will you fight?'

The crowd broke as the soldiers pushed them back, and the fighting spread into neighbouring alleyways and streets. Groups of those opposed to Corthie were more numerous than his supporters, but there were enough of the latter to prevent anyone from getting through to the house. Bodies lay scattered across the paving slabs by the front of the house, and Corthie could feel his battle-vision straining to be unleashed. He imagined himself leaping down from the roof and laying into the mob of those who wished to surrender to the Ascendants; they were cowards, all of them.

'Corthie!' yelled a voice behind him. He turned. Aila was at the hatch, standing on a chair. She was staring at him, her eyes wide. 'Get down!"

He strode to the hatch as Aila got out of the way, then he dropped back down to the kitchen floor. The three demigods were staring at him.

'You are actually insane,' said Naxor, a slight smirk on his lips; 'completely insane.'

'What were you doing up there?' said Aila.

'I was telling them the truth,' he said.

'You incited a riot!' she yelled. 'There is a riot happening outside the front door of this house; people are getting hurt because of what you said. How is that supposed to help?'

'What was the alternative?' he said. 'Do you want me to sit here and do nothing?'

'I want you to use your head, Corthie; think. We're supposed to be persuading people, not rousing them into killing each other.'

The sound of the front door opening came from the main room, and Corthie walked through. Gurbrath had entered the house, looking shaken. He glanced at Corthie.

'Soldiers have sealed off the street,' he said, his voice low. 'They have orders to escort you all to a... safer location.'

'Where?' said Corthie, as the demigods joined them in the main room.

'This house is too exposed,' Gurbrath said. 'If you remain here, there will be more fighting, or someone might try to set it on fire. For the sake of keeping the peace, I ask that you please cooperate.'

'Where?' Corthie repeated.

'Fordamere,' said Naxor; 'I can see it in his mind. Rooms have been set aside for us in the most heavily guarded part of the shrine, and we won't be allowed to leave them.'

'We'll be prisoners?' said Vana.

'You are still our guests,' said Gurbrath, 'but Naxor is correct; you will not be permitted to leave your rooms.'

Corthie folded his arms as he glared down at Gurbrath. 'No.'

'Lord Gellith does not want to risk more episodes of violent disorder,' their guide said. 'If you refuse to cooperate, then the soldiers have been ordered to force you into going.'

'Let them try.'

'What?' said Vana, her eyes wide.

'There are a hundred armed and angry soldiers outside,' said Naxor. 'I think we should listen to them.'

'You're demigods,' Corthie said; 'what have you got to worry about? You'll heal from any injury.'

Aila glared at him, but said nothing.

'If you don't tell him,' said Naxor, 'then I will.'

'Shut up,' said Aila.

'What's he talking about?' said Vana.

'None of your business.'

'May I say something?' said Sohul. 'I'm inclined to agree with the others, Corthie. We can't hold out here; the soldiers have the house surrounded.'

Corthie glanced at Aila. 'Are you keeping something from me?'

She shot a glance of anger at Naxor, then turned to him. 'Maybe we should go into the kitchen for a minute.'

He followed her through into the other room.

'What is it?' he said. 'Are you breaking up with me?'

She squinted at him. 'Why would you ask that?'

'I know you're still angry with me for sending Van off with Kelsey, and about other things.'

'Do you think we should break up?'

'No. I love you, Aila. Just because we've been arguing about everything recently doesn't mean I want to end it.'

She said nothing, her eyes lowered.

'If it's not that,' he said, 'then what?'

She glanced up at him. 'I'm pregnant.'

His mouth opened, and he stared at her.

'I didn't want to tell you,' she said, 'but Naxor read my mind earlier and, well...' She shrugged. 'Now you know.'

He continued to stare at her, his mind blank.

'You appear to have lost the ability to speak,' she said. 'Does the prospect of becoming a father fill you with so much dread?'

'No, I mean... I... I don't know; I'm still trying to take it in. Why didn't you want to tell me?'

'Because I hadn't decided what to do.'

'I don't understand.'

'I'm a demigod. I can end the pregnancy any time I wish. It has something to do with our internal self-healing powers.'

'You want to end it?'

'I said I hadn't decided. Look where we are; look what's going on around us. We have nowhere to live, and we're in the middle of a war. You'd admit that the timing is not ideal. Also, I don't know how I feel about having children. No, that's not true. The thought of giving birth to a mortal child makes me feel terrible; worse than terrible. Losing you will be bad enough, but how could I face out-living my own child?'

'And what about my feelings?'

'In a thousand years, you'll be gone, but I will still be breathing, and I will remember.'

'Do you even know if the baby is mortal?'

'It's too early to tell, and it's not a baby; not yet. Right now, it's just a small collection of cells.'

'I don't believe that.'

'No? Well, I have to. It's the only way I can cope with whatever decision I'll end up taking. It would be different if we were on your world, living in peace, and if you were a little older. You're only nineteen, Corthie; maybe you're too young to be a father.'

'I'm not too young.'

'You just stood on a roof and incited a riot; that doesn't seem mature, or responsible. And now you want to fight a hundred soldiers. You were right about us demigods; unless they chop our heads off, then we'd heal from whatever injuries the soldiers gave us, but what about our child? Would you risk it being harmed?'

'So you call it a child when it suits you?'

'Don't avoid the question, Corthie. You need to decide what's important to you.' She reached up and touched his face. 'I'll leave you to think for a moment.'

Aila walked from the kitchen, closing the door behind her. Corthie stared at the floor, his thoughts like thick treacle. Pregnant? His brother Keir flashed into his mind. He had got a girl pregnant when he had been sixteen, and had run away to escape having to deal with the consequences. Corthie had despised him for that. The mother, Jemma, had come to live in the Holdfast mansion on the estate, and Corthie had got to know her more than Keir ever had. He remembered swearing to himself that, if and when the day ever came, he would be a better father than his arrogant, selfish brother; he would be a better man.

He opened the kitchen door and walked into the main room, where everyone turned to glance at him.

'Gurbrath,' he said; 'tell the soldiers that we will cooperate. Tell them I won't cause any trouble.'

Corthie's room was fairly comfortable for a cell. It had a proper bed, and a wardrobe, and there was a toilet in a tiny chamber at the back. A slit window overlooked the cavern, and the lava pool gave the room a red glow. The Fordians hadn't referred to it as a cell, of course, as the fiction of them being guests was upheld; their new accommodation was for their own protection, they said, to prevent them coming to any harm. Despite their words, Corthie had been disarmed, and his steel armour had been stripped from him and taken away, along with the Clawhammer.

The stout, iron-framed door had been locked, and Corthie could see the shadows cast by two soldiers through the gap by the stone floor. The room had been carved from the side of the cliff, and was directly above the barracks where the Fordamere garrison resided, to the right of the high building where the leadership of the city sat. Corthie wasn't certain, but he guessed that Naxor was in the room to his right, and Aila was in the next one along. Aila. He had traded his freedom to ensure that she, and the child within her, were safe, but they had not been given a chance to speak again since being taken from the house, and he had no idea what she had decided to do, or if she had even reached a decision.

Did he want to be a father? Yes, but Aila had been right about the timing. How was he supposed to fulfil his destiny if he had a child to care for? Could he concentrate on fighting the Ascendants while having another person in his life who would require his love and attention? He closed his eyes as he sat on the bed. He knew he was being selfish, but he had always imagined children coming at some distant, peaceful, point in the future.

A key grated in the lock and the door opened.

Standing outside in the lamplit hallway was Lord Gellith, with armed soldiers flanking him. Bows were pointed into the cell as the Fordian demigod gazed down at him.

'Thank you for cooperating, Corthie Holdfast,' he said. 'I'm sure you understand my reasons for relocating you and your companions today; I cannot afford another outbreak of violent disorder in the streets of Yoneath. I wish it hadn't been necessary, but I also wish that you had never come here.'

Corthie said nothing.

'As a courtesy,' Gellith went on, 'I want to inform you of my plans. As you are no doubt aware, soldiers of several Implacatus Banners have been hunting for Yoneath throughout these mountains. It is a mere matter of time before they penetrate the shield and find us, so I have decided to forestall that eventuality. One hour ago, I sent a message to their commanders, revealing the location of our city, and inviting them to enter, peacefully. They agreed.'

'You're surrendering?'

'No, we are cooperating, just as you did earlier today. I have decided that the best way to ensure the safety of my people is to allow the Ascendants and their soldiers to take what they want – the Sextant. I have an agreement from the Banner commanders that no one will be harmed when they arrive. They have also promised to respect the sanctity of our shrine.'

'Do you believe them?'

'I don't know. What I do know, is that there is more chance of Yoneath surviving if I cooperate rather than resist. Your foolish words to the crowd, if followed, would result in our annihilation. I have also agreed to one other condition laid down by the Banner commanders, and when they get here, I will be placing you into their custody. You have a few days yet; the Banners are concentrating their forces before entering Yoneath. They showed no interest in any of your companions, but they want you, Holdfast.'

Corthie laughed, but it was bitter. 'You betrayed a guest? Are you not ashamed?'

'Yes, I am. You have my apologies, but your life is outweighed by the many that have lived here in peace for so long. I swore to keep them safe to the best of my abilities, and if the Sextant and you are the price, then so be it.'

'The Ascendants will not honour any agreement,' said Corthie, 'and when they get here, I will fight them.'

'You will not fight them; you will be locked in this chamber.'

'You're wrong,' Corthie said. 'Don't you understand? I have been chosen to do this; I have been chosen to confront the enemies that besiege our worlds. I *will* fight them; and I'll win.'

CHAPTER 22
OLD FRIENDS

Shawe Myre, Southern Khatanax – 12th Lexinch 5252

Belinda watched Kelsey light another cigarette. Her legs were crossed beneath her on the long couch, and she was glancing down at the workers in the valley.

'I thought you'd run out of those,' she said.

'Eh?' said Kelsey. 'The cigarettes? I've been rationing them. Van ran out days ago, but I still have a couple of packets hidden away. I'm just going to fit one more in before he gets here.'

'I like him.'

'Aye?'

'Yes. He seems honourable, especially compared to Naxor. He refused to say anything to Amalia when she tried to trick him.'

'Did she tell you about that?'

'I insisted. She said she was worried that you were trying to entice me away, and she went round to squeeze whatever information she could out of Van. She knows it was wrong, but that's Amalia.'

'And yet you still trust her?'

'No, but I'm considering her offer. Her injury means that she needs to conserve all of her powers, to focus them on healing her arm. She needs me.'

'And what happens when her arm grows back? You'd be stuck in that City with her, and Aila told me what she was like the last time she was the queen there.'

'I'd make sure she stayed in her palace and didn't get into any trouble.'

'How?'

Belinda leaned over the low table. 'My powers have started to return. Before you arrived, I'd just been practising with fire, and I can spark too. But, much more importantly, I have inner-vision. That was how I finally saw through Naxor.'

Kelsey's mouth opened. 'Why didn't you tell me?'

'Only Silva knows. I've kept it from Amalia. I'm telling you now, so that you'll understand why you don't need to worry about me. I'll be able to read Amalia, and see what she's planning. But the truth is that I haven't decided. I would feel like I was abandoning Lostwell for a second time.'

'Wow. You have the full range of vision and fire abilities, as well as healing powers. Ha, you've overtaken Keir. You know, I'm glad Karalyn wasn't lying to you about restoring your powers; I had my doubts, I'll admit. I wonder what will be next.'

'If it's death or flow, then I'll be able to kill people from a distance, and I'm not sure how I feel about that. Back in Plateau City when I was working for the Empress, death powers were what I craved the most, but now? I watched Thorn kill, and it changed her.'

'It didn't change her that much,' Kelsey said, 'and I doubt if she's used them since the war ended. Looking after Karalyn's twins has domesticated her a fair bit, but now that their mother's back, who knows what she'll do? I agreed with the others back then; I thought Karalyn was right to keep those powers from you. But now? Maybe you're ready.'

'I don't know if I want the responsibility.'

Kelsey laughed. 'See? You're definitely ready.'

'Can I try something?'

'Depends.'

'Hold your hand out.'

'Uh, alright.'

Kelsey extended a hand over the table and Belinda clasped it between her fingers. She closed her eyes, feeling for Kelsey's life force, but felt nothing, as if the young woman wasn't there.

Kelsey raised an eyebrow. 'Well?'

'Nothing.'

Kelsey laughed. 'What were you expecting?'

'I wanted to see if powers could affect you by touch, you know, like the way I was able to heal Van even though you were standing right next to him. You can block powers that move through the air, but I could sense him through his skin. But you? It's like you don't exist. I'll never be able to heal you.'

'Aye, but I'll never be killed by a god's touch, so you win some, you lose some.'

'Then why was Corthie able to be healed by touch? I saw Yvona heal him in Icehaven after he'd been wounded fighting the greenhides.'

'Corthie's protections were put in place by my sister; he wasn't born with them. It's the same with Sable and Keir; because they have dream mage blood, Karalyn was able to block powers from reaching them, but for me and Karalyn it's different. We block powers naturally.'

'I'm going to spend some time practising my new powers when you and Van leave; I can do that while I try to decide what to make of my life.'

'So you're definitely not coming with us? Corthie will be disappointed.'

'I know, but for the first time since I awoke, I'm free to choose my own path. I want to help prevent the Ascendants from destroying your world, and the world of Pella, but I'm not ready to face them yet. Tell Corthie that I love him, that he'll always be like a brother to me, but that I need to figure out who I am.'

'Fair enough.'

'What about you?'

'What about me?'

'What are you going to do about Van?'

Kelsey shrugged. 'That's just it; I don't need to do anything. What I saw, will happen; there's no stopping it.'

'Then shouldn't you start to act like it? I mean, if you're going to end up in love with him, then why don't you spend more time with him? And maybe, you know, you could go a day without squabbling with him and calling him names.'

'Don't start with that,' she said, groaning. 'This is the problem right here; this is exactly how my visions become self-fulfilling. When he told me that Amalia had been round to the cottage, I was flooded with jealousy, even though it was irrational. The idea of him being with another woman makes me feel sick, even though I don't love him. I guess part of me wants to resist the inevitable, part of me wants to cling on to some sense of autonomy. I have free will, except I don't, not when it comes to the future. It drives me crazy just thinking about it.'

'Have you ever had any visions about me?'

'No. Well, that's not strictly true. Yesterday, I saw you spill that glass of water five minutes before you did it, but that's probably not the kind of thing you meant. Thankfully, the far-into-the-future type of visions are rare.'

Belinda turned as two servants came down one of the staircases from the upper floors of the hanging house. They bowed low before her, then walked to the rope bridge.

'You have servants now?' said Kelsey.

Belinda frowned. 'Yes. Silva insisted. Apparently, I'm not allowed to make my own bed any more, or tidy up after myself.'

'I hope they weren't rummaging through my stuff.'

'I'm sure your cigarettes are safe.'

Kelsey gestured to the bridge, where Van, Amalia and Silva were approaching. 'Remember, don't tell Van about those.'

They watched as the small group approached.

'Have a seat,' said Belinda, 'and help yourselves to drinks or food.'

'Thank you, ma'am,' said Van, as Silva bowed.

Amalia sat on a couch to Belinda's left, and filled a glass with wine.

'I have come to a decision,' said Belinda. 'I will not be leaving with Kelsey and Van when they go.'

Amalia's face broke into a smile.

Belinda turned to her as Silva and Van also sat. 'It doesn't mean that I've decided to go to Pella; I've still to make my mind up about that.'

'Of course,' said Amalia. She reclined on the couch, the tension visibly lifting from her shoulders.

'When will we be leaving?' said Van.

'In a day or so?' said Kelsey. 'We'll go back to the coast, I think, and catch a boat north.'

He sniffed. 'Have you been smoking?'

'No. Certainly not,' she said. 'Are you suggesting that I've been keeping a supply of cigarettes hidden from you? Frankly, I'm shocked that you would accuse me of such skulduggery. Shame on you.'

'I see,' said Van. 'It's like that, is it? After I shared my last cigarette with you?'

'You shouldn't have smoked all yours when you were drunk.'

'Don't quarrel, mortal children,' said Amalia. 'Let me revel for a moment in the news that you will soon be gone.'

'Revel away, donkey brains,' said Kelsey. 'I can't wait to tell Aila and Corthie that you were actually less pleasant than their stories had made out.'

'I can think of a few messages for them that you can take back with you,' the former God-Queen said. 'Tell my granddaughter that I still have a restrainer mask in her size.'

Kelsey laughed, then her face fell.

'No response to that?' said Amalia. 'How disappointing.'

'Shut up,' said the Holdfast woman.

Belinda frowned. 'What is it?'

Kelsey glanced up. 'Gods.'

Silva raised an eyebrow. 'I can't sense anything.'

'Of course you can't, you numpty,' snapped Kelsey. 'I'm blocking your powers.' She stood, and walked to the railings that surrounded the open level of the house. She gazed down into the valley, then turned back to Belinda. 'Two gods. They're using vision to scan Shawe Myre.'

Belinda and the others got up and joined Kelsey by the railings. Belinda glanced up and down the valley.

'I don't see anything,' she said.

Kelsey pointed to their left. 'Maybe a quarter of a mile that way.' She gasped. 'Look!'

Belinda stared into the distance. To the left of a small terraced vineyard was a stretch of grass, and on it a shimmering light had appeared. It formed into a black circle, several yards high and wide.

'What is that?' said Belinda.

'A portal,' said Van and Amalia at the same time.

'Silva,' said Belinda; 'go downstairs and alert the guards. No, wait; we'll all go down.'

'Soldiers,' said Van, pointing.

They glanced back at the portal. A double column of armoured troopers were running out of the portal and spilling onto the grass. Within moments dozens were through, and more were following.

'A Banner,' said Van; 'they've found us.'

Belinda rushed back to where she had been sitting and strapped the Weathervane to her belt. She was wearing no armour, but knew she had to fight.

'What are you doing?' cried Amalia. 'We need to hide.'

'No,' she said. 'I'll not flee again.' She turned to the others. 'Follow me, and stay close.'

She raced for the bridge, and ran across it, heedless of whether the others were coming. She rushed down the stairs and emerged onto the path at the bottom. Shawe Myre soldiers were standing there, waiting for her.

'Your Majesty,' one shouted; 'are we under attack?'

'We are. Protect Kelsey Holdfast, and keep her close to me.' She drew the Weathervane, and ran towards the vineyard. Workers were staring at the soldiers as they piled through the shimmering blackness of the portal. At least a hundred had come through, and more were coming.

Belinda halted by a bridge, the dark-bladed sword grasped in both hands.

'Stop,' she cried. 'This is my home.'

The soldiers ignored her. Squads were forming up, and fanning out to occupy the narrow valley, blocking the central area where it reached its narrowest point.

'Stop, or I will attack,' Belinda said.

The last soldiers came through the portal, and it fizzled, then vanished. Standing on the grass where it had been were two figures – a tall man with white hair, his skin pale and almost shining, and a dark-skinned woman with red hair. Both looked young, as if in their twenties, and each was holding a sword. They stared at Belinda for a moment, then bowed their heads.

'Third Ascendant,' said the white-haired man; 'it is an honour. Now, surrender if you please, or these soldiers will slaughter every living thing in this valley.'

Belinda glanced around. Silva was by her side, and a small cluster of soldiers was gathered round Van and Kelsey behind her.

'Where's Amalia?' she said.

'Gone, your Majesty,' said Silva; 'I don't know where.'

Belinda turned back to face the two gods as they approached. 'Who are you?'

'I am Leksandr,' said the man; 'the Sixth Ascendant. Do you not recognise us?'

'The rumours must be true,' said the red-haired woman. 'I am Arete, the Seventh Ascendant. We have been hunting for you, Belinda. Lay down your weapons, unless you wish this valley to be drenched in blood.'

'I'm not afraid of you,' said Belinda. 'Your powers won't work here.'

The woman laughed. 'Why do you think we brought soldiers? And look, I am holding a sword in my hand for the first time in centuries. We are well aware of the power of the Holdfast girl; we sensed her at the Falls of Iron. Weigh it up, Belinda. You have, what, twenty armed guards against our three hundred? We know your battle-vision will still be working, but Leksandr and I also possess that skill. You are out-numbered, so unless you wish this fertile little valley to be utterly devastated, you will surrender.'

'We are here to talk, Belinda,' said Leksandr. 'Ascendant to Ascendant. You have lost your way, and we desire to bring you back to the light.'

Belinda remained motionless, her sword held out, her battle-vision thrumming within her.

'If you submit,' Leksandr went on, 'then none of your mortals will be killed. We have no interest in Lostwell; it is dying. We wish only to save you.'

'What do you want?' Belinda said. 'Speak plainly.'

'Order your guards to lay down their weapons and return to their homes,' said Arete, 'then kneel before us and submit.'

'Submit? If I am the Third Ascendant, shouldn't you be kneeling before me?'

Arete and Leksandr laughed.

'You are a renegade and a rebel,' said Arete. 'You were deprived of your rights millennia ago. Have you truly lost your memories?'

'If I do this,' Belinda said, 'what happens next?'

'We will order our soldiers to occupy the valley,' said Leksandr, 'but no one will be harmed. Then, we shall retire to your home, sit down, and talk.'

'But we require your submission first,' said Arete, 'otherwise we shall still be in a state of war with you. This is your decision, Belinda, Queen of Khatanax, God of Fire and Death, and only you can take it.'

Belinda stared at them, her mouth dry. She knew how good she was with a sword, but what could she do against two who were equally skilled? And, while she was fighting them, the Banner soldiers would be slaughtering everyone else. She swallowed her pride; what good would it do if Silva or Kelsey were killed? The inhabitants of Shawe Myre were staring at her from the vineyards and orchards; she had a duty towards them.

'Do you even know why we were fighting a war?' said Arete.

Belinda shook her head.

'Then don't throw your life away for a cause you don't remember. His Divine Majesty, Edmond, the Second Ascendant, is prepared to welcome you back into our ranks. Today, Belinda, you can finally end a war that has raged across the worlds over thousands of years. If you submit, then it will be to him, not to us, that you will pledge your allegiance.'

'You can even keep your sword,' said Leksandr; 'join us.'

Belinda glanced back, and locked eyes with Kelsey. The Holdfast woman looked weak and frail compared to the armoured ranks of soldiers; her powers might be great, but she was still mortal. She turned back to the Ascendants, lowered her eyes, and sheathed the Weathervane.

'Throw down your weapons,' she said, her voice sounding tired.

Behind her, she heard the sound of spears and bows being dropped onto the path.

'Your Majesty,' whispered Silva; 'don't trust them.'

'I have no choice, Silva. I'm sorry.'

She bowed her head and knelt on the bridge.

'Swear your allegiance to the Second Ascendant,' said Leksandr. 'End the war.'

Belinda closed her eyes. 'I swear.'

'Mark this day,' cried Arete. 'Soldiers of the Banner of the Undying Flame, bow your heads towards the Third Ascendant and rejoice! The God of Fire and Death is one with us again, at last.'

The Banner soldiers let out a roar, their cheers reverberating off the high sides of the ravine. Leksandr sheathed his own sword, strode forward and extended his hand.

'Get up,' he said.

She took his hand and stood. He embraced her, then Arete

approached with her arms outstretched, and the two Ascendants clasped Belinda tightly, while the soldiers continued to cheer.

Arete kissed her on the cheek. 'Welcome back, sister.'

Over twenty Banner soldiers accompanied the three Ascendants up to Belinda's hanging house. They took up positions by the railings as Belinda, Arete and Leksandr sat down on the long couches. Kelsey, Van and Silva were being guarded a few yards away. The mercenary had been disarmed, but they hadn't been hurt. Servants served wine from bottles that had been carried through the portal on a cart. Arete and Leksandr were both smiling, but Belinda had never felt so lost, so powerless.

'I have so many questions,' said Arete, 'that I barely know where to begin.'

'I'm sure Belinda has questions too,' laughed Leksandr.

'I do,' she said. 'How did you find me?'

'Lord Renko reported your return to Lostwell,' said Arete. 'Most of us thought you were dead, but after we'd examined Renko's mind, we knew he was telling the truth.'

'We have been searching for you ever since we arrived in Khatanax,' said Leksandr. 'You were at the Falls of Iron, were you not? After that, we lost track of you for a while, but Lord Latude, the former governor, knew the rough location of Shawe Myre, and so we focussed our hunt in this vicinity.'

'But we still couldn't find you,' said Arete. 'It was only when we detected faint signs of vision and fire powers being used that we were able to narrow our search down. The Holdfast girl's presence slowed us again, but we persisted, until finally, we found this valley. Our search for you has delayed our other plans.'

'Yes,' said Leksandr. 'Right now, we should be in Yoneath to collect the Sextant. Our troops there are ready to move in; they can secure the site before we need to arrive in person.'

'You found the Sextant?' said Belinda.

'We have. Once it is in our possession, then we can move onto the next phase of our plan; to secure the supply of salve. Do you remember anything about salve?'

'My memories are gone forever, but I am aware of salve.'

'We guessed as much,' said Arete, 'otherwise how could we explain your presence at the Falls of Iron? You are a friend of the Holdfasts, and a friend of those responsible for smuggling salve to this world. You don't need to answer that; we know it's true.'

Leksandr glanced over at Kelsey. 'Come here, girl.'

Kelsey got up, and two soldiers brought her over to stand in front of the Ascendants.

'Over what area,' said Leksandr, 'do your blocking powers extend?'

'Screw you,' she said. 'I'm telling you nothing.'

'It was a simple question, mortal,' Arete said. 'Answer, or you will be tortured until you speak.'

'My brother's going to kick your arses for you.'

'Are you referring to Corthie Holdfast?' said Leksandr. 'Perhaps you haven't heard; your brother is currently sitting in a dungeon in Yoneath. His capture was part of our price for allowing the Fordian rebels to live. He won't be kicking any arses.'

'The war is over,' said Arete. 'We won. We shall take the Sextant back to Implacatus, and you and your brother will be coming with us. We wish to carry out a few experiments on you, to discover how it is possible for mortals to possess the powers of the gods. You are at the beginning of a long journey, mortal girl, and the path you are on will be filled with pain. Why don't you spare yourself some, and cooperate?'

'Her range covers a hundred yards or so,' said Belinda. 'There's no need to cause anyone any pain. Kelsey Holdfast is not up for negotiation; she stays with me.'

'A hundred yards?' said Leksandr, glancing at Arete. 'Impressive. Perhaps we should move her to the other end of the valley, then you, I and Belinda can merge our minds. We will discover everything we need to know far quicker that way.'

'No,' said Belinda.

Arete raised an eyebrow. 'Are you rebelling again? Already?'

'I cannot merge minds with you,' said Belinda. 'Kelsey and Corthie's sister, Karalyn Holdfast, sealed my mind long ago. No one can penetrate it. You will never be able to read my thoughts, whether or not Kelsey is here.'

Leksandr frowned. 'I see.'

'This will not please the Second Ascendant,' said Arete.

'There is nothing I can do about that,' said Belinda. 'What's done is done.'

They turned as a group of soldiers trooped down the stairs from the upper floors. One of them was holding Kelsey's pack in his hands.

'Hey,' she said. 'Leave my stuff alone.'

The soldier bowed in front of Leksandr and Arete, and withdrew a Quadrant from the pack.

'Oh my,' said Arete, taking it.

'It appears damaged,' said Leksandr. 'How did this happen?'

'My mother whacked it with a sword,' said Kelsey. 'Oops.'

Arete closed her eyes as her fingers glided over the surface. 'It used to belong to Lady Agatha, and before that, Belinda herself.'

'Give me my pack,' said Kelsey.

The soldier glanced at Leksandr, who nodded. 'As long as it doesn't contain any weapons, she can have it.'

He passed the pack to Kelsey, who took it and sat down next to Belinda. She raked about inside, then pulled out a packet of cigarettes and lit one, blowing smoke into Leksandr's face.

'Perhaps if she were to lose an eye,' he said, 'she might be more pliant.'

'Control your mortal, Belinda,' said Arete, 'otherwise I would be more than happy to pluck an eye from her head.'

'Don't touch her,' yelled Van from where he was sitting.

Leksandr glanced at Belinda. 'Who is he? Is he important?'

'He is Kelsey's guard,' said Belinda.

'Bring him over here,' said Arete.

Two soldiers gripped Van by the arms and hauled him over.

'Perhaps if we torture him, then the Holdfast girl would be more cooperative?'

'That's what I was thinking,' said Leksandr.

Arete raised a finger. 'Get him on his knees.'

The soldiers pushed Van down, until he was kneeling on the reed mat in front of the couches.

'I am a Captain in the Banner of the Golden Fist,' he said. 'I have rights.'

'You have no rights, mortal,' said Leksandr. 'You are nothing, a speck of humanity adrift in the vastness of time.' He gestured to the soldiers. 'Beat him.'

The soldiers bowed, then one punched Van across the face. The other weighed in, striking the captain until he fell to the floor.

'Stop!' cried Kelsey.

'We will make them stop if you promise to behave,' said Arete.

Belinda stared as the soldiers continued to beat Van. One stamped on his hand, and the other kicked him in the stomach. What had she done? She glanced at the Ascendants, and then at the soldiers ringing the room. Kelsey jumped up and tried to pull the soldiers off Van, but one slapped her across the face with the back of his hand, sending her toppling backwards.

Belinda stood. 'Enough.'

The soldiers hesitated, and Kelsey rushed to Van's side, her arm raised to shield him.

'You told me that no one would be harmed,' Belinda said to Arete and Leksandr. 'Were you lying?'

'My dear Belinda,' said Arete; 'are you siding with a mere mortal over us, your true friends? I remember watching you do much, much worse to mortals, and now you baulk at a beating?'

'She has changed,' said Leksandr, 'and not for the better. The situation is worse than we had hoped.'

'We go back to the very beginning, Belinda,' Arete said; 'over thirty thousand years, to a time before we were gods, to the time we ascended and became gods. There were twelve of us, the first, the eternal. We wrote the rules by which every world now lives; we made the worlds, and the mortals who inhabit them. We create, we destroy, we endure. Next to us, the suffering of a million mortals means nothing.'

'I don't care,' said Belinda. 'I remember none of that, but I will tell you this. If you kill this man, or hurt Kelsey, then I will fight you. I might not be able to kill you both, but at least one of you shall not be returning to Implacatus alive.'

Arete smiled. 'Now, that sounded like the Belinda I remember. Perhaps there is still hope, Leksandr.'

'Perhaps,' he said. He glanced at the soldiers. 'Take this man and Kelsey Holdfast, and secure them down in the valley. We shall be remaining here this evening, and will depart at dawn.'

The soldiers bowed. Two grabbed hold of Van's shoulders, and another pushed Kelsey along.

'Get off me!' she yelled as the soldiers led them away.

Belinda sat and watched as Van and Kelsey were taken over the bridge.

'If we cannot merge minds,' Arete said, 'then we shall have to talk.'

Leksandr nodded, then turned to Belinda. 'Start at the beginning and tell us everything; everything you can remember.'

Belinda suppressed the fear in her heart and made her face expressionless. They couldn't read her mind, she told herself. Whatever she said, they wouldn't be able to tell if she was lying or telling the truth. It wasn't much, but it gave her a glimmer of hope. She could hide her real thoughts, her real feelings, and bide her time.

'Very well,' she said. 'I will tell you everything.'

CHAPTER 23
BOUNDARIES

Shawe Myre, Southern Khatanax – 12th Lexinch 5252

Van grunted and rolled onto his back, his eyes opening to darkness. Pain shot through his body, and he stifled a cry.

'Van?'

It was Kelsey. Van shuffled backwards, then sat up.

'Van, are you alright?'

He touched his jaw before trying to speak. A tooth was loose, and his tongue was bleeding, but no bones in his face had been broken.

He spat blood onto the ground. 'I've had worse.'

'Your hand?'

He lifted his swollen left hand onto his lap. 'Don't worry about me. I saw that bastard slap you; are you alright? Where are we?'

'We're in a small cottage, not far from where you've been staying. Why couldn't you have kept your mouth shut? If you'd stayed quiet, then they wouldn't have beaten you up, and you'd probably be free right now, instead of being locked in here.'

He shrugged. 'I have a contract.'

'You mean a handshake?'

'It doesn't matter; I gave my word to your brother to do my best to protect you for fifty days, and there's still thirty-seven to go.'

'Getting beaten up isn't protecting me; it makes you less able to protect me, you daft twat.'

'I needed to stick close to you; I knew the risks.'

'You mean you did that even though you knew you'd probably get a thrashing for it?'

'What can I say? I'm a professional.'

'Aye, a professional arsehole.'

'Come on; are you saying you'd rather be alone in here right now?'

She hesitated. 'No.'

'Then, you're welcome.'

He heard her tut as his eyes adjusted to the gloom. He could make out a dim outline of a doorframe, but there were no windows, and no furniture that he could see.

'That was a nice touch,' he said.

'What?'

'You blew smoke into an Ascendant's face in front of Banner soldiers. They'll be gossiping about that for years in the barracks.'

'He was annoying me.'

'You got any of those cigarettes left?'

'It's been four days since you had one; maybe you should quit? After all, you've made it this far.'

'That's the cruellest thing you've ever said to me.'

'Sorry. I'll try to be crueller in future.'

'Come on, don't hog them. We could be dead in an hour.'

He heard her rummage through her pockets, then saw the spark of a match. He glanced away from the tiny flame, and took the lit cigarette.

'Thanks,' he said. 'Damn it, my hand is going to be useless for a while; one of the fingers might be broken.'

'Serves you right.'

'I notice you didn't contradict me when I said that we might be dead in an hour.'

'That's right,' she said. 'I try to ignore stupid comments, though with you that can be difficult, seeing as most of what you say is stupid. No,

Van, we're not going to be dead in an hour, though perhaps we might wish we were.'

'In your vision,' he said, 'did both of us still have our eyes, and our teeth? What about our ears; still there? Any massive facial scarring going on?'

'I seemed the same,' she said. 'I couldn't see you; I was looking out from your eyes, remember?'

'Eyes, plural?'

'I don't know how that aspect works. It might have been one eye, I guess. I wasn't gazing at you with outright horror, so there's a fair chance you'll come out of this with your pretty boy looks intact.'

'Urgh, don't ever say that. Handsome, rugged, yes, I'll accept those, but "pretty"? Give me a break.'

'Excellent. Once again you tell me your weak spot. Now I'll be sure to call you pretty at least once a day.'

'And I'm too old to be a boy.'

'You're not that old.'

'I'm seven years older than you.'

'So? Do you think that makes you wise? Pyre's arse, I hate being locked up.'

'Yeah? Well, now you know how it feels.'

'What? I was imprisoned for thirds, I mean months. Chained up and hidden away in basement cellars and isolated farmhouses in the middle of the desert; for months.'

He glanced at her in the shadows. 'You were? Why?'

'Why do you think? For the same reason I'm locked up now, you numpty; because of my powers. Sable wanted to hide from the gods, and...'

'Wait; it was Sable who imprisoned you? Your aunt?'

'Eh, aye. It was. She's a bit messed up. I hated her for a very long time, but in the end she released me and the guy who was chained up with me, and she handed herself in.'

'You were chained up next to a guy for months?'

'I was.'

'I see.'

'You see what?'

'Nothing.'

'Van Logos, are you jealous?'

'Of course not.'

'I wouldn't worry; he was in love with Sable. She has that effect on guys; they go all wobbly and weak at the knees.'

Van thought about making a comment saying that it was a pity he had Kelsey there instead of Sable, but felt it might cut a little too close to the bone. He was happy to annoy her, but she genuinely believed that they were destined to be together, and would be unlikely to forgive or forget a comment like that. He couldn't even remember what Sable looked like, as if she had removed her image from his mind when she had messed with his memories.

The door scraped open, the hinges creaking. Van shielded his eyes from the lamplight, but noticed that the sky was dark outside. Three soldiers pointed crossbows into the room, then Leksandr walked in, a guard hurrying behind him with a lantern and a chair. The soldier placed the chair down, then bowed. Leksandr ignored him, and sat.

'Holdfast girl,' he said; 'you will answer my questions.'

Kelsey narrowed her eyes. Across her face, Van could see a bruise from where she had been hit when protesting his beating, and he felt anger boil inside him.

'First,' said Leksandr, 'I want a list of every one of your relatives, followed by their respective powers and current locations.'

Kelsey said nothing.

'Mortal girl, respond.'

She glanced away, and started to whistle out of tune.

Leksandr raised a hand to strike her.

'Hey,' said Van. 'Didn't you tell Belinda you wouldn't hurt her?'

Leksandr smiled. 'Of course.' He turned to the soldier. 'Strike them both.'

The soldier placed the lantern on the ground.

'The Undying Flame, eh?' said Van. 'The gods scraped the bottom of the barrel enlisting you lot. Where did they find you; the gutter or a prison cell?'

The soldier clenched his fists and smiled. 'The Golden Fist has been disbanded; just thought you should know. Their defeat was so complete, they could barely put a company together. Every one of the survivors is out of a job; what a shame. And all those widows and orphans; tragic.'

Van swung his fist, catching the soldier in the eye. He raised his hands to his face, and Van punched him in the guts, doubling him over. He wheezed, and fell to his knees. Van raised his fist a third time.

'Cease this,' said Leksandr. He glared at the soldier. 'Get out, you fool.'

The soldier staggered upwards, swayed, then stumbled out of the room.

The Ascendant turned back to Kelsey. 'Answer my question.'

'Alright. Let's see,' she said, lighting a cigarette. 'Now, where to begin? There's my mother, we could start with her. Her power is to irritate me to within an inch of my life; she's a natural at it. My brother Keir must have inherited that ability, because, believe me, he is an irritating arsehole at times. Corthie, you already know about; he killed his first god when he was thirteen or fourteen, I can't remember. He smashed his skull in with an ashtray. Does my sister-in-law count?'

Leksandr stared at her. 'Arete warned me that this would be a waste of time, but as she wanted to spend a moment alone with Belinda, I thought it was worth a try. Do you have any idea how fascinating you are to me? Are you fertile?'

'What?'

'It was a simple question. Are you able to conceive and give birth?'

'Why?'

'Because I would be interested in examining any progeny resulting from our union. Imagine, they could have the powers of an Ascendant, combined with your blocking abilities. Any such god would be close to invincible. I shall petition the Blessed Second Ascendant to have you placed within my harem once we arrive on Implacatus, as a reward for having captured you. He may wish to inspect you first, of course, but I am very patient.'

Van punched him in the face. Even as his fist was flying, he knew it was the most stupid thing he had ever done. Leksandr's head tilted back from the impact, then he turned to glance at Van, a look of wry bemusement on his features.

'You are the first mortal to have struck me in over ten thousand years. I had actually forgotten what it felt like.' He reached out a hand and gripped Van's arm, his strength almost snapping it. 'You, however, will be unlikely to forget this.'

Pain ripped through Van's body, sending him into convulsions. He writhed on the ground, his teeth slamming down onto his tongue, and foam gathering at his lips. He lost his sight amid the agony, but he remained conscious as his flesh rotted. Leksandr released him, and Van shuddered, his limbs twitching. Leksandr placed a finger onto his forehead, and he felt himself being partly healed, his skin and organs revived, but the pain continued.

'That is good to know,' Leksandr said. 'Even with the Holdfast girl sitting here, my powers can still work through touch. Hmm, very interesting.' He stood, and glanced down at Kelsey. 'You will answer every question I ask you, sooner or later. It is up to you, mortal girl, how much pain those answers cost you and your friend.'

He opened the door and strode through, leaving the lantern on the floor. Kelsey went to Van's side, and crouched by him.

'Oh, Van, why did you do that?'

'You blew smoke in his face,' Van said, as the pain started to recede; 'I needed to do something to match that.'

'He could have killed you.'

Van struggled back into a sitting position. 'You don't believe that.'

'No, but you do. I know you think my visions are crazy; who wouldn't?'

He leaned forward and kissed her.

Her eyes went wide and she backed away. 'What in Pyre's unholy name do you think you're doing?'

'Wasn't it obvious?'

'Woah, steady. Uh-huh. No kissing. No.'

'But you're the one that thinks we...'

'Shut up.' She raised her palms and backed away further. 'You don't even like me. You were just a bit delirious from having your brains fried by an Ascendant, and you didn't know what you were doing.'

'What? No, I...'

'Stop talking. That's what happened, and I don't want to speak about it again.' She leaned back against a wall, her eyes narrow.

'Fine,' he said. 'Give me a cigarette.'

She tossed him the packet and the matches, her eyes never leaving him. He took one and lit it, then brought his knees up to his chest and leaned his arms on them. Maybe she was right. Why had he tried to kiss her? He didn't like her, and she didn't like him. The pain in his head had faded away, but his nerves were still ragged, and the old, familiar ache in his chest had returned.

'What are you thinking?' he said.

'Never ask me that; it's the most annoying question ever invented. If I wanted to tell you what I was thinking, I would do it.'

'You're a pain in the ass.'

'That's better. Aye, that makes me feel better. Trading insults with you gives me a sense of normality.'

'Amalia was wrong about you; you're not a *little* bitch; you're a complete bitch.'

She frowned. 'Are you saying that because I wouldn't let you kiss me? If so, then you're a bigger arsehole than I thought.'

'No, I was just trying to do more of the insulting thing. Was it a bit much?'

'A bit.'

'Oh, alright. I'm not sure of the boundaries.'

'They're fluid. Basically, whatever I say is fine, but you're not allowed to call me a bitch.'

He half-smiled. 'Sorry about before. You were right; I was clearly out of my mind.' He looked at her as he said the words, and couldn't shake the feeling that he was lying. He glanced away. Had she bewitched him somehow? No, he told himself; it was just the situation they were in. The shared threat of torture and a painful death messed with the heads of people flung into close proximity; that's all it was.

He glanced back at her, determined to change the subject. 'Does Belinda have a plan?'

'I don't know; she seemed just as surprised as the rest of us. I understand why she surrendered; for her it was the rational response to the circumstances, and Belinda is usually pretty rational, sometimes ruthlessly so. But now?'

'And they've found the Sextant. This hasn't been a great day.'

'Just concentrate on how we're going to escape.'

He glanced at the lantern. 'We could set fire to the building?'

'How about a way to escape that doesn't involve us burning to death?'

'Then I'm out of ideas.' He lifted his left arm and flexed his fingers a little. 'I think that asshole inadvertently healed my hand.'

The door swung open again, and a soldier pointed his crossbow inside the room.

'Get up,' he said to Kelsey.

She looked up. 'Where am I going?'

'Toilet ditch.'

She glanced at Van, then stood and went to the door. Another two soldiers arrived and led her away, then the door was closed again. Van sat and listened to the footsteps as they left the building. He had wondered if they would be given an opportunity to relieve themselves and had hoped they might be led outside at the same time, but Banner soldiers weren't usually that stupid, even ones from the Undying Flame. He pulled the lantern towards him and turned it to its lowest setting to preserve the fuel, then leaned back against the wall.

They would kill him in the morning, of that he was sure. Kelsey would be taken away with Belinda and the two other Ascendants, but they had no need of Van; he was just an extra prisoner to guard, a prisoner who had no value. He realised that he wanted Kelsey's vision to be true. He didn't believe it, but he wanted to. If she had really seen the future, then he would survive another day, maybe even survive long enough to father a child with Kelsey. At that moment, locked in a small room, and in more pain than he had admitted to her, he would have taken that path if it were offered to him. He smiled to himself, trying to picture what life with Kelsey would be like. Maybe they would buy a house, and live a peaceful, quiet life, but then he remembered her powers, and what she had said about being chained up before. Her ability to block vision made her a target for anyone wishing to hide from the gods; she would never live a peaceful, quiet life.

The bottom of the door scraped off the ground as it opened. Kelsey walked back into the room and sat, and the soldiers gestured to Van.

He struggled to his feet and went to the door. Two soldiers lowered their crossbows at him, and he was shoved down the hallway and out into the darkness of night. A few lamps were illuminating the valley, but they were dim enough for Van to have a clear view of the stars. The two soldiers took him to a path by a row of outbuildings.

'Is it true that you're Captain Van Logos?' whispered one as they walked.

'I am.'

'We've heard of you,' said the other.

'Good things, I hope?'

'We're all Banner, if you catch my drift, Captain.'

'I suppose we are.'

'You're going to be executed in the morning.'

'Oh. Thanks for letting me know, I guess.'

The two soldiers glanced at each other, frowns creasing their expressions. They came to a halt and one pointed to a wooden hut.

'The toilet pit is in there, Captain,' he said.

'We're going to stand here,' said the other one. 'Give you a little... privacy.'

'Yeah,' said the first. 'There are no other soldiers in this part of the valley; just thought you should know, Captain. Take your time.'

They turned their backs to him, and gazed off in the other direction.

Van blinked. Had he understood them correctly? Were they letting him escape? He thought about what the soldiers under his command would have done in the same situation. Despite fierce rivalries, there was still a solidarity among those who signed up to one of the Banners, a solidarity that could sometimes outweigh the strict application of the law.

He slipped into the shadows of the outbuildings, and took his bearings. To his right, he could make out the opening to the cavern that led back into the forest. If the soldiers had been telling the truth, it wasn't guarded. He had no pack, no supplies, and no weapon, but all he had to do was keep walking south, and eventually he would come to the plains of the Southern Cape. He could dig up the gold he had buried, redeem his horse from the farmstead, and be on a boat within a few days. Freedom awaited him, and all he had to do was run. He imagined sitting in a dingy bar in Alea Tanton, spending Corthie's gold on wine, women and weed. The city was huge, and he would be able to lose himself in it with ease. He had done what he could, but he was no match for two Ascendants, and there was no disgrace in running, especially from a deal sealed with a handshake.

He almost screamed in frustration. He couldn't do it; he couldn't walk out on Kelsey; he couldn't leave her locked up and alone in that cramped room all night, not after what Leksandr had told her about her future. The future. What if she was right? No, that was nonsense, a distraction. If he went back, he would die. He closed his eyes. So be it. At least he would die with his honour intact.

He walked back round to where the two soldiers were standing. They glanced at him, and one raised an eyebrow.

'You're good lads,' he said quietly as they began to walk back to the cottage, 'but I made a promise to that girl in there, and the Banner don't break their word.'

'Understood, sir,' whispered one.

'If you bump into any Golden Fist boys in Serene, you'll tell them what happened to me, yeah?'

'Will do, Captain.'

They reached the cottage, and Van was placed back into the cell. Kelsey glanced up at him as the door was locked, but he said nothing, and slumped down into a sitting position, his head in his hands.

Perhaps an hour of silence had gone by before the door opened again and Silva walked in with a tray of food. The soldiers closed the door once she had entered, and she set the tray down onto the bare ground next to the lantern.

'What's happening up there?' said Kelsey.

'Her Majesty is deep in discussions with the two Ascendants,' the demigod said, keeping her gaze averted from the prisoners.

'Is she on their side now?' said Van.

She glanced at him with narrow eyes. 'Do you expect me to answer that question, mortal? What her Majesty does is her Majesty's business.'

'I have a different question,' said Kelsey. 'Why were you sent here with our food? Any servant could have done the job.'

'Her Majesty wanted me to ensure that you are both alive and well. She cares about you, as she cares about all of her subjects.'

'How did it feel,' said Van, 'to watch her kneel before Arete and Leksandr?'

Silva said nothing for a moment, her arms crossed over her chest. 'Like a knife to the heart.'

'She didn't have a choice,' said Kelsey.

'Her Majesty had a choice, and she chose to save the lives of everyone in Shawe Myre. Perhaps it is wrong of me, but I would have rather died than watch her submit to those... those...'

'Arseholes?' said Kelsey.

'Ascendants,' said Silva.

'Pretty much the same thing,' said Van.

'Her Majesty is an Ascendant,' said Silva, 'and I will not have you speak about her in that manner.'

Van shrugged. 'Excluding Belinda, then. I hear I'm due to be executed in the morning.'

'Her Majesty will not permit that to happen, but you will not be coming with the rest of us when we depart,' Silva said. 'Her Majesty has struck a deal – the lives of everyone here for her cooperation. In the morning, you will be freed.'

Van nodded, though he remained sceptical. 'Tell her thank you, from me.'

'I shall.' She turned to Kelsey. 'The same cannot be said about you. The Ascendants are insistent that you accompany us to Yoneath.'

'Where?' said Kelsey.

'Yoneath. It is a hidden city of Fordians in the mountains between the wastelands and Kinell, a few miles from the coast. It is where the Sextant was taken, and where your brother is being held. The Ascendants intend to open a portal to take us and the Banner soldiers through. If they keep their word, then Shawe Myre will be left untouched.'

Kelsey nodded. 'Any sign of Amalia?'

'None whatsoever. She must have fled; as a rebel, she was no doubt afraid that the Ascendants would take her into custody. As far as I know, Arete and Leksandr are unaware that she was here, which would be due to your powers blocking them from sensing her.' She glanced back at the door. 'I'd better go; I shall see you in the morning.'

She knocked on the door, and the soldiers let her pass, then locked it behind her.

Kelsey glanced at him. 'You're not going to die in the morning.'

'But we're going to be separated.'

She smirked. 'Does that make you sad?'

'Yes. How can I claim my pay if you're not here to protect? Corthie will probably demand a refund.'

'I'll insist you pay him back in full.'

'I'm keeping the horse.'

'Those farmers have probably eaten it by now.'

He glanced at the tray of food. 'You hungry? You should eat something.'

'Are you my mother now?'

'According to you, I'm your soulmate.'

She fell silent for a moment, her eyes lowered. 'What will you do when we leave tomorrow?'

'You know what I'll do.'

'I haven't had a vision about it, so, no; I don't know.'

'You don't need a vision to know.'

'You could go anywhere.'

'I know.'

'Stop playing games with me, Van. Tell me.'

'As soon as you leave,' he said, 'I'll be coming after you, and I won't stop until I find you, even it if means going all the way to Implacatus.'

She turned off the lantern and moved closer to him until their sides were touching.

'What are you doing?' he said. 'What about the no kissing rule?'

'We aren't kissing, you numpty,' she said. 'Just hold me.'

He moved his arm round her shoulder and held her close. He shut his eyes, and listened to the sound of her breathing.

CHAPTER 24

THE TANNERY

Catacombs, Torduan Mountains, Khatanax – 12th Lexinch 5252

Maddie clambered up the last steps and entered the tomb, the heavy basket clutched in her hands. She grimaced from the smell, and began walking through the high cavern towards where Millen was working. Stretched out before him on the ground were over a dozen hides. Millen had skinned the animals while they were still warm, and was scraping off the fur with a stone. To his right was a shallow basin, in which more hides were soaking.

'This is just about the most disgusting thing I've ever seen,' she said, as she approached. 'And the smell; Malik's ass, it's revolting.'

Millen glanced up. 'Do you want another harness or not?'

'If it means I have to live next to all this horribleness, then I'm not sure. Those poor goats.'

'And deer; there are a few deer skins as well. Did you get the salt?'

She glanced down at the basket. 'What do you think I'm holding? Of course I got the salt; I had to walk for miles to find it.'

She put the basket down and he frowned at it. 'It's a funny colour.'

'I found the pool exactly where Blackrose said she had seen it; it's not my fault if it looks a bit weird.'

'If it has impurities, it might not work.'

'I'm not going back to get more, if that's what you're trying to say. Not today, at any rate; it's getting dark, and I'm exhausted.'

Millen rolled his eyes. 'Stop complaining. I'll let you know when I need my next ingredient.'

'Which is?'

He smiled. 'Dragon urine.'

'What?'

'I think you heard me.'

'And how am I supposed to... No, never mind; I don't want to know.'

'If you think it smells bad in here now, wait another ten days or so; your eyes will be watering.'

'Can't wait. Is Sable making dinner?'

'She was supposed to, but I haven't seen any sign of her actually doing it.'

'I liked it better when you made dinner.'

'Yeah? Well, I have this job to do now; I'm not your skivvy.'

'Pity. I'd like a personal skivvy. Maybe you could start waking me in the morning with breakfast.'

She walked away before he could respond, and strode towards Sanguino's cavern. The dark red dragon was inside, along with Blackrose, Frostback and Sable. With three dragons, there was very little space for Maddie to walk, and she weaved her way round their tails and limbs.

'And then,' Sable was saying, as the dragons watched her, 'Sanguino's vision flows through mine, and he can see what I see. And remember, I have battle-vision, so I can pick out as much detail from a distance as a dragon can.'

'Won't this effort exhaust you quickly?' said Blackrose.

'It is tiring, yes,' Sable said. 'Some keenweed would be handy. Still, I reckon I could do an hour without a break, maybe longer with practice.'

'Good,' said the black dragon; 'it pleases me that you are making progress. Perhaps you and Sanguino are made for each other.'

Frostback snorted.

'Do you have something to say?' said Blackrose.

'A dragon should never have to depend on an insect,' she said; 'it's degrading. I think I'd rather be blind.'

'I could arrange that,' growled Sanguino.

'How?' said Frostback. 'You're fat and slow; you'd never catch me, even if this witch was riding on your back.'

'That's enough,' said Blackrose. 'Frostback, you must learn to withhold your judgement about matters of which you are ignorant. In a civilised society, humans and dragons are interdependent; each relies upon the other. The hands of humans are small and crafty, and they can fashion things that improve our lives, while we can offer them protection and leadership.'

'Ahem,' said Maddie.

The dragons turned their necks towards her.

'Rider,' said Blackrose; 'did you locate the mineral pool?'

'Yeah, and I lugged a huge basket of salt all the way back from it. It was Sable I was looking for.'

'Yes?' said the Holdfast woman.

'Where's dinner? I'm starving.'

'Oh. I was just explaining to Blackrose and Frostback about how Sanguino and I intend to fly.'

'Yes, I heard. Where's my dinner?'

'Come on, Maddie. How difficult can it be to boil weeds? You could always do it yourself.'

'That's not the point; I was out getting salt, Millen's scraping fur off a dead goat, and you were supposed to make dinner.'

Sable sighed. 'Very well.' She turned to the dragons. 'If you'll excuse me.'

Sable and Maddie walked out of the cavern, and the Holdfast woman lifted a hand to her nose.

'What a vile odour. I'm not preparing dinner out here; the smell will make me vomit.'

Millen glanced up as they approached.

'Hi, Sable,' he said.

'Let me guess; you want your dinner too?'

'Well, you know,' he said, his cheeks flushing, 'I suppose I am a bit hungry.'

'But I'm a terrible cook. I don't know the first thing about it, whereas you, Millen, have a real talent for it. I always enjoy eating what you've made.'

Maddie gritted her teeth. 'Weren't you pretending to be a servant in Alea Tanton? You told me you worked in the kitchens of some palace or something.'

'It was the Governor's residence, Maddie, and I made the coffee.' She smiled at Millen. 'I'm damn good at making coffee.'

'Stop smiling at him,' Maddie muttered; 'am I the only person here who sees through you?'

'Don't be so bad-tempered,' Sable said. 'Fine, I'll make dinner. Millen, where did you put Maddie's weeds?'

'They, um, they're over by the tomb entrance.'

'Thanks.'

She walked off, and Maddie saw Millen's eyes follow her. She snapped her fingers in front of his face, and he jumped.

'You'd be doing me a real favour,' she said, 'if you stopped staring at Sable's bum every time she walks past.'

He flushed. 'What? No, I... Oh, alright, I'll try.'

'Thanks.' She frowned. 'I suppose I'd better supervise her, otherwise she'll burn my dinner just to prove she doesn't know how to cook.'

She set off towards the entrance to the tomb, skirting the skins spread out over the ground. Sable was kneeling by a sack, and was removing bundles of vegetation.

Maddie, it's Naxor; I need you to listen to me.

She halted, blinking.

Did you speak to Blackrose? Did you ask her to help us?

Yeah, I did.

Good, because we need your help now more than ever. We've been locked up – me, Aila, Vana and Corthie. The vision shield that was hiding the city has been deactivated, and Banner forces are marching into Yoneath. The soldiers are going to take the Sextant, and there's nothing we can do to stop them.

Please come, and as soon as you can. Right now, there are no gods or Ascendants here in Yoneath, but they could arrive at any time.

Maddie noticed Sable stand and glance into her eyes, a strange expression on her face.

Hold on a moment, Naxor. She raised an eyebrow at Sable. 'Yes?'

'What are you doing? Is someone in your head?'

She nodded. 'Naxor.'

Sable laughed. 'I think I'll join this conversation.'

Naxor! Sable said within Maddie's mind. *How's tricks? Is Belinda alright?*

I... I don't know.

Why not? Is she there?

Belinda and I are... no longer in a relationship, Sable.

So she finally realised you were a rat?

I don't have time for this foolishness, he said; *matters have become very serious.*

I know, said Sable; *I've already read what you told Maddie; I'm in her head, remember? Are you begging us to rescue you?*

I suppose so.

Place your location into Maddie's head; I can pass it on to Blackrose.

Maddie felt an image of a place appear in her mind. The view moved up and away from a cavern, showing a city nestled within the gentle slopes of a valley, and then moved further away, until its location could be seen relative to the ocean.

Got it, said Sable.

Does this mean you're coming? said Naxor.

Not sure; we'll need to run it by the big black dragon; she's in charge. But I'll say this, if we do come, we're taking the Sextant; no arguments.

You may have to speak to your nephew regarding that; just like you, I am not in charge.

Goodbye, Naxor.

Sable severed the link between Naxor and Maddie, then she withdrew from her mind.

Maddie staggered, feeling dizzy. 'I didn't like that.'

'Excuse me?'

'That was wrong; you were both in my head at the same time, having a conversation. I didn't like it; my head's not your personal meeting room.'

'Sorry, Maddie, but I needed to speed things along. I know how you like to chatter. Come on, let's tell Blackrose.'

Sable strode away, leaving Maddie standing with her fists clenched. It was so like Sable to barge in and take over the conversation, and Maddie felt anger surge through her. And she still hadn't had any dinner. She took a breath and started to follow the Holdfast woman, passing Millen again as he was soaking a hide in water, a bowl of ground-up rock salt by his side. She went into Sanguino's cavern, where the three dragons were sitting.

Sable and the dragons turned to her as she walked in, and Maddie was a little surprised that Sable had resisted the temptation to start without her.

'Tell them, Maddie,' said the Holdfast mage.

'Corthie's been imprisoned in Yoneath,' she said, 'along with Naxor, Aila and Vana. They want us to help them.'

'Do they now?' said Blackrose.

'There are soldiers, but no gods, and the Sextant's there.'

'That was our price,' said Sable. 'That's what we told them. If we help, we get the Sextant.'

'And what use is this... Sextant to me?'

'You can use it as a Quadrant. It can take us all to Dragon Eyre.'

'Another empty promise.'

'Naxor promised nothing,' said Maddie. 'Corthie's in charge; he's the one we'd need to negotiate with.'

'Then nothing has been agreed?' Blackrose exhaled. 'My answer is no.'

'It's not far from here,' said Sable; 'a few hours of flying, and there are no Ascendants, just squishy mortals. We free my nephew, take the Sextant, and we're gone.'

'I said no, Holdfast witch.'

Frostback raised her head. 'Why not?'

Blackrose turned to her. 'I would not have expected you to be in favour of rescuing humans.'

'It's not the rescuing part I'm interested in,' she said. 'If there are no gods, only insects, then it could be fun. Could we burn and kill as we please? Do they have nets or catapults?'

Sable smiled. 'I didn't see any kind of anti-dragon defences, but you must only kill the soldiers, not the ordinary people.'

Frostback tilted her head. 'And how would I be expected to tell the difference?'

'The civilians are all Fordian – they have green-coloured skin. Don't kill them.'

'Just the others?'

'Exactly.'

'Stop this,' said Blackrose; 'we are not going.'

'Please,' said Frostback; 'we would get to fly together. I've been stuck in this tomb for nearly three days; it's not natural. I want to spread my wings and soar, and I want to burn insects; watch them as they scatter and run about screaming. I could show you what I can do; I'm fast, and agile, and I can turn in the air quicker than anyone. I can also fly really low; they'll never see me coming.'

Blackrose groaned. 'You're giving me a headache.'

Frostback lifted her chin. 'Then say yes.'

'This Sextant,' Blackrose said to Sable and Maddie; 'where is it, exactly?'

'Hold on,' said Sable. Her eyes glazed over for a second.

'I see,' said Blackrose. 'I have flown over that area in the past, and yet I saw no city.'

'Naxor said something about a vision shield that was hiding it,' said Maddie.

Blackrose gazed down at her. 'And what is your advice, rider?'

'I don't trust Naxor,' she said, 'and there are no guarantees that we'll get the Sextant, but, I guess, rescuing them would be the right thing to do. We're on the same side; we all oppose the gods of Implacatus, yet we're divided and each doing our own thing in isolation. Maybe we could help each other.'

'And Corthie is my nephew; he's family,' said Sable. 'I feel a duty to help.'

Blackrose glared at her. 'I don't recall asking you, witch.'

'I know,' she said, putting her hands on her hips, 'but my opinion counts too. Everyone gets consulted; you set that rule yourself.'

'Very well,' said Blackrose, her eyes glowing red; 'fetch Millen.'

Sable curtseyed, then strode from the cavern.

'Sanguino,' Blackrose went on, 'what is your view on this?'

'I cannot go,' he said, 'as Sable and I are not yet ready for such a flight, and we would only hinder you. It pains me to be left behind, but I think you should go to the aid of the humans. If I understand correctly, they used to be your allies, and the one who betrayed you is no longer in their company.'

'That is true. Karalyn Holdfast has departed this world.'

'What will you do,' Sanguino said, 'if the Ascendants arrive while you are there?'

'Turn and flee,' Blackrose said; 'there is no alternative. One Ascendant, I could face, but two? No, I would prefer to retreat in the face of such odds.'

Sable returned with Millen, who was hobbling along on his crutch.

'Do you really want my opinion?' he said.

'I do,' said Blackrose.

'Sable has explained about the Sextant, and what it can do. I guess it's worth the risk if we could get our hands on it.'

Blackrose lowered her head. 'I see that everyone's opinion goes against my own. I could over-rule you but, in this case, I will accede to your wishes. Corthie Holdfast was once a friend, and this may reconcile us. Maddie and Frostback will accompany me, and the others will remain here. A dawn attack is my preference, therefore we shall leave three hours before sunrise, and approach Yoneath from the south, over the Fordian Wastes. Now, I must go to inform Deathfang; and you should eat, then rest.'

She turned from the cavern and disappeared into the main section of the tomb.

Maddie glanced at Sable. 'Did you hear that? She said "eat". Now, whose turn was it to make dinner?'

The air was warm as Maddie walked to the entrance of the tomb. The sky outside was dark, and the stars were shining above the glow from the lava pools. Mists and vapours were rising in thick tendrils across the valley, obscuring the land beyond. Frostback was standing next to her, her neck extending out of the opening, and she was flexing her silver-grey wings.

Maddie shivered, and wrapped the blanket round her.

'You should really have a harness for this,' said Millen to her left.

She frowned. 'Why? Is there one ready?'

'Of course not; the first one won't be ready for ages; there's still tons of work to do.'

'Then why did you say it? Do you think it helps? You're supposed to be coming up with constructive comments, not making me more nervous than I already am.'

'If you fall off,' said Frostback, 'I will laugh.'

'It's time,' came Blackrose's voice from further inside the tomb, and Frostback beat her wings, sending a pulse of air down into the cavern. Maddie shielded her eyes from the dust, as Frostback ascended and began to circle above the valley.

Blackrose strode up to the entrance. 'Climb on, rider.'

The dragon angled her forelimb, and Maddie clambered up. She reached the broad shoulders, and grasped onto the folds in the black scales, wedging her feet in to either side. She stuffed the blanket under her so it was a little more comfortable, then glanced down and waved at Millen. She took a look over her shoulder, but Sable was out of sight inside Sanguino's cavern, consoling him for being left behind.

'Are you ready, rider?' said Blackrose.

'No sudden turns, please,' Maddie said, 'and no flying upside down.'

'I'll bear that in mind,' said the dragon, as she launched herself from the tomb.

Within seconds, they were wheeling above the valley with Frostback, and Maddie was wishing she had brought another blanket. Below them, the rivers of lava were bubbling and glowing amid the dark shadows of the Catacombs, and a few dragons were watching them from the cavern entrances. Deathfang had been happy to allow Frostback to go along on the journey; what he wanted, Blackrose had explained, was to keep her from mixing with the other dragons under his control, rather than forbid her from flying altogether.

'This feels good,' cried the silver-grey dragon as she banked in tight circles; 'I missed it.'

'Then imagine how Sanguino feels,' Blackrose responded; 'you have only been confined for a few days. When we return, I want you to encourage him, not mock him.'

Frostback wheeled away as if she hadn't heard.

'But for now,' Blackrose went on, 'we shall fly south-east; show me your speed, Frostback.'

The silver dragon straightened, then surged away with a burst of pace. Blackrose waited a moment, then followed, and the two dragons sped off into the dark night sky. They left the lava pits of the valley behind them and, in a few short minutes, began to cross the empty, flat Fordian wastes, the air warming as it flowed over them. Blackrose pulled up alongside Frostback and they changed course, veering a little more to the east, keeping the dark line of mountains to their left. They passed the region where Grimsleep and the other outlawed dragons lived, and Frostback glanced in that direction a few times, examining the sky for movement. Most of her wounds had healed in the three days since Blackrose had taken her in, but several scars still stood out along her flanks and neck.

'His time will come,' said Blackrose; 'concentrate on the task before us.'

Maddie kept her head down as they flew. She had become so used to the safety of the harness that she felt she might topple from Blackrose's shoulders at any moment. Her fingers began to ache as they gripped onto the black scales, and she resisted the temptation to look down.

An hour passed, and the dragons changed course again, steering back to the south-east in a wide arc, until the mountains passed from sight, and there was nothing around them but the barren wastes. A dim glow appeared on the eastern horizon, which grew and spread as they continued over the featureless desert, and Maddie picked out a few ruined settlements and dried-up riverbeds beneath them. How could the gods have done this, she thought; the devastation was on a scale which bewildered her – mile after mile of nothingness, where once there had been green pasture, fertile fields and flowing water. If they could do that to Shinstra and Fordia, then what could they do to the City of Pella if given the chance? Her thoughts turned to Dragon Eyre, and she wondered how bad things were there. Blackrose's rage would be beyond anything she had witnessed if her beloved homeland had been destroyed in the same way as Fordia.

The stars began to twinkle out as the light in the east blossomed, and the sky brightened into a deep blue, with not a cloud in sight. The dragons turned again at a signal from Blackrose, and they began to head due north, racing back towards the mountains. They descended until they were barely thirty feet above the flat landscape, Blackrose leading, with Frostback a little behind. The ocean appeared on their right in the distance, and the mountains crept closer with every passing minute.

'There is movement ahead of us,' Frostback said, 'at the base on the mountains.'

'I see it,' said Blackrose. 'A human convoy, travelling along a road leading into the foothills.'

Maddie squinted at the brown range of hills rushing towards them, but saw nothing.

'I see the glimmer of steel,' said Frostback. 'If they are soldiers, can we attack?'

Blackrose waited a moment. Maddie strained her eyes in the gathering light, and eventually began to make out a dark line on the ground ahead, snaking its way into the hills through a valley.

'They have armour,' Blackrose said, 'and I see catapults, but they are secured to the back of wagons, and are no danger to us.'

Frostback's eyes glowed with anticipation. 'Are they enemies? Can we attack, please?'

'Wait a minute,' said Maddie; 'how do we know they're enemies? They could be any bunch of random soldiers.'

'I recognise their standard,' said Blackrose. 'They are the Banner of the Black Crown; mercenaries in the pay of Implacatus. I fought them on Dragon Eyre more than once, and I also saw them in the vision placed into my mind by Sable. They are indeed our enemy.'

'Then we'll attack?' said Frostback.

'Yes, but await my command. Stay in formation, and we will sweep over them; with you on the right, and myself on the left. Devour them with flames, then wheel round for a second pass. They will have bows, but nothing that should pierce our armour. This will be a good test of your skills, Frostback; I will be watching you closely.'

'I won't let you down,' the silver dragon said. Her jaws opened slightly, and sparks fizzed and leapt across her teeth.

Ahead of them, the convoy was still moving, oblivious to the dragons' approach. Maddie could see a long line of wagons, flanked by companies of soldiers marching on either side. Upon the lead wagon, the Banner's tall standard was flying, depicting a black crown on a white background. Soldiers at the rear of the convoy were marching with their backs to the dragons, their packs loaded onto their shoulders, and Maddie was reminded of the Banner soldiers she had seen in Alea Tanton.

The dragons sped over the last of the desert, and scrubby bushes appeared, dotting the low hillsides. A few cries rose up from the soldiers as the dragons were seen at last, but it was too late.

'Now,' growled Blackrose.

Side by side, the two dragons opened their jaws.

Twin streams of gushing flame poured down from Blackrose and

Frostback, and the rear wagons were engulfed in seconds. They raced up the line of the convoy, incinerating the flanking soldiers, their screams echoing off the hillside. The dragons passed over them, then split, Blackrose wheeling to the left, and Frostback to the right, and Maddie clung on with all her strength as the black dragon banked and turned. Crossbow bolts flew up at them, but the soldiers were in disarray, shooting blindly as the burning wagons belched smoke into the sky. The two dragons then attacked from either side, sending more bursts of flame down at the survivors. Blackrose was methodical, working her way down the line, picking off any soldiers that tried to flee, while Frostback seemed to lose herself in the moment, swooping down and circling round and back. She cried out in joy as she chased a cluster of soldiers attempting to escape into the valley. Flames enveloped them, reducing them to smouldering corpses that littered the barren valley floor. Blackrose returned for a final pass, and the last of the wagons were consumed in the inferno.

Maddie glanced down at the carnage. Nothing had been left alive on the road beneath them, and bodies were piled in smoking heaps along the valley. The crown standard was burning, and the lumbering gaien that had been pulling the wagons lay dead amid the flames. The air was thick with dark, acrid smoke that caught in the back of Maddie's throat as she looked at the bodies. She tried to count them, but there were too many – a hundred?

'We got them!' cried Frostback as she wheeled closer to Blackrose.

'We did,' said the black dragon as they circled over the scene of devastation. 'Well done, Frostback; you were fast, and you were agile; just as you said. Are you ready for the real test?'

'I am.'

'The city of Yoneath is a mere ten miles from here,' she said. 'It will require more patience, and more discrimination. Remember, the green-skinned humans are innocent civilians; target only the soldiers.'

'What if I kill civilians by accident?'

'There are always accidental casualties in battle; that cannot be avoided, but you must do your best. There is also the chance that soldiers will have set up ballistae or catapults that could be turned against us. If that happens, burn them if you can, but do not risk your life. There is no shame in temporarily retreating from machines made by human hands. Our target is a vast cavern in the side of a mountain; I shall enter, free Corthie, and retrieve the Sextant. You will remain outside and guard my position.'

'I understand; shall we go?'

'Not yet; there is one more thing to tell you, one more command that you must obey.'

'What?'

'If the Ascendants arrive, flee at once.'

'But...'

'Do not question my authority on this. There are two Ascendants in Khatanax; if they appear in Yoneath, then we cannot oppose them; to do so would be suicide. If one comes, then between us we can make the attempt, but not if both arrive. You must promise me this.'

Frostback's eyes glowed a deep red. 'I promise.'

'Very well,' said Blackrose. 'To Yoneath; follow me.'

CHAPTER 25
BATTLE OF FORDAMERE

Yoneath, Eastern Khatanax – 13th Lexinch 5252

Corthie stood by the slit window of his cell, gazing down into the cavern at the soldiers swarming over and around the temple. They had arrived the previous evening in their hundreds; civilians had been cleared from the vast space, and work had begun on removing the Sextant. The noise from the hammering and sawing had kept Corthie awake all night, and still the task had not been completed. The soldiers had erected wooden scaffolding around the ancient structure between the two pools, and had assembled cranes and slipways leading down from the roof, but the Sextant itself remained in the same position as it had when Corthie had first seen it.

Lord Gellith was down among the soldiers, pleading with them to be careful, and the mercenaries appeared to be complying with his wishes, taking their time to plan every step of the operation. A huge, six-wheeled wagon had been pulled into position alongside the temple, and four gaien were harnessed to it, ready to haul the Sextant away once it had been brought down from the roof.

There had been no sign of the Ascendants, or any other gods. Perhaps they were present in another part of Yoneath, but Corthie doubted it. If they had arrived, they would be with the Sextant. An officer yelled at a work crew to begin lowering ropes from a crane, and Corthie watched as the ends were looped around the base of the Sextant. Soldiers began to heave on the ropes, and the huge device wobbled an inch or two. The top of the crane started to bend under the weight, and the officer yelled again, bringing the attempt to a halt. A cluster of officers and army engineers stood arguing and gesturing up at the roof, and Corthie turned back to his bed and sat down.

Something would happen; it had to. It couldn't be his fate to sit in a cell as the Sextant was taken away; he had a destiny, and that wasn't it. But he also had Aila to think about, and it was to her that his thoughts had continually turned throughout the long night of waiting.

He heard movement in the hall outside and glanced towards the door. The clank of armour could only mean Banner soldiers, as the Fordian militia didn't wear anything as sophisticated. Were they taking custody of the prisoners? Muffled voices echoed through to him, and he stood as the door was unlocked and opened.

A Banner officer was in the doorway, flanked by armoured soldiers.

'Corthie Holdfast?'

'Aye.'

The officer nodded. 'So you're the man who destroyed the Golden Fist? The stories of what you did at the Falls of Iron have made their way round the barracks and alehouses of every Banner on Implacatus. And yet, here you are, captured without a fight. Is this a trick of some kind?'

Corthie gave a wry smile. 'I wish it were. What Banner are you?'

The officer eyed him warily. 'I am a captain in the Banner of the Black Crown. I have orders to shackle you, and take you down to where the Sextant will soon be loaded onto a wagon. Will you cooperate?'

'Am I going to be executed?'

'Not that I'm aware of, but you never know with the Ascendants. However, if you decide not to cooperate, then I will command the soldiers standing next to me to loose their crossbows. Two bolts in the guts should slow you down.'

'I want to speak to my friends.'

'Who, the three demigods? Very well. I'll have to shackle your wrists first, but then I will take you to their location so you can talk for a minute.'

'Where's Sohul?'

'The lieutenant has been released from custody. We debriefed him last night. According to his testimony, while he was your prisoner, he was treated with dignity, which is why I'm doing the same with you. Hold your arms out.'

Corthie took a breath, then lifted his arms up in front of him. Two more soldiers appeared and entered the cell, one carrying a length of chain, the other with pins and a hammer. They attached the shackles to Corthie's wrists while the officer watched, then they retreated from the room.

The officer stepped back, and gestured towards the doorway. Corthie walked forwards, and saw that the hallway was packed with soldiers, each training a crossbow on him.

'All this for me?'

'Indeed,' said the officer. 'As I mentioned before, we heard what you did to the Golden Fist. Now, this way.'

The soldiers escorted him to a set of stairs, and they descended to the floor below. He was led to a door, where more soldiers were waiting.

'Are my friends in here?'

'There are,' said the officer; 'they were moved to more comfortable accommodation last night, as they are still under the authority of Lord Gellith. Only you have been transferred into our custody.' He turned to the soldiers outside the door. 'Open up, but let no one enter or leave. We shall allow Holdfast a minute to two to say his goodbyes.'

'Yes, sir,' said one of the soldiers. He unlocked the door and pushed it open.

Inside, sitting on low beds, were the three demigods. Aila got to her feet and hurried to the door, but one of the soldiers raised his arm.

'That's far enough, ma'am,' he said.

'Where are they taking you?' cried Aila.

'I don't know,' said Corthie. 'I think I'm leaving with the Sextant. Listen, whatever you decide, know that I love you.'

She glanced at the shackles on his wrists, and her eyes widened.

'Do you know what's going to happen to you?' he said.

'Lord Gellith said we would be released once the soldiers have evacuated.'

'And then he's going to expel us from his lands,' Naxor said from his chair.

Aila stared through the doorway at Corthie. 'We should never have come here; I should have let you go home with your sister.'

'Forget your sister for a moment,' said Naxor. 'Imagine what your aunt would do if she knew what had happened. Think on that.'

Corthie nodded.

'Time's up,' said the officer.

'I will see you all again,' said Corthie. 'I have a couple of Ascendants to kill first.'

'Don't do anything stupid,' Aila said as the door started to close; 'I love you.'

The soldier pulled the door shut and relocked it. The officer gestured to another stairwell, and they set off, Corthie in the midst of two dozen armoured soldiers. They went down the steps and through a hallway, then emerged into the vast cavern. The lava pool was filling the space with red light, and a multitude of small lanterns were illuminating the outside of the temple. Banner soldiers were busy at work on the roof and scaffolding, and many more were stationed in the cavern, guarding the side tunnels and the bridges. The only Fordians in sight were Lord Gellith and a few of his courtiers. The ruler of Yoneath was talking to a high-ranking Banner officer next to a large white standard depicting a black crown.

Corthie was led over to Gellith and the officer, and the captain saluted as they arrived in front of them.

'I have brought the prisoner as instructed,' the captain said.

The high-ranking officer glanced at Corthie, his eyes tightening. 'I see. Thank you, Captain. So, we have captured the infamous Corthie

Holdfast, Killer of Lady Joaz, Lord Baldwin, and several hundred men of the Golden Fist? I am the commanding officer of the Banner of the Black Crown, and you shall be accompanying us to Alea Tanton once we have removed the Sextant. There, the Blessed Ascendants will decide your fate. Personally, I hope they gut you in front of the survivors of the Golden Fist.' He glanced back at the captain. 'Secure him to a wagon, and ensure he is adequately guarded. The Blessed Ascendants have a strong desire to meet him.'

'Yes, sir,' the captain said, then he turned and strode down the cavern, heading towards the lava pool. The soldiers followed, keeping Corthie in their centre, until they reached a row of wagons.

The captain pointed at the first in line. 'Up there. Shackle an ankle to the chassis, and we'll wait for the others to get that damn Sextant down from the roof.'

Soldiers shoved Corthie towards the wagon, and he climbed up onto its open back. Two got up with him, and attached a length of chain to his right ankle, then secured the other end to an iron hoop protruding from the base of the wagon. When they had finished, they jumped back down and the soldiers settled into formation, forming a circle around the wagon. The officer remained close to Corthie, and offered him a cigarette.

'No, thanks.'

The officer nodded, then lit one for himself. 'You have battle-vision.'

'Was that a question?'

'No. From what I have been told, it was a statement of fact. One that I find hard to believe, but I've spoken to the survivors of the Golden Fist in Alea Tanton, and they were adamant.'

'Why do you serve the Ascendants? You know they care nothing for mortals; to them, we're less than insects.'

The captain shrugged. 'Life's a lot simpler if you stay out of politics.'

'Then you're complicit in their evil.'

'Evil?' the captain laughed. 'Now you sound like a fanatic.'

'Is it fanatical to want to save your world from being destroyed? If the Ascendants get the Sextant, that's what will happen. You may not like me, but surely you can understand why I'd rather fight.'

The captain smirked. 'Then why did you give yourself up to the Fordians? You could have run; you could have fought, but instead, you surrendered. And now you'll be heading back to Alea Tanton in chains; merely another captured rebel.'

Corthie lowered his head. He wasn't despondent, but he was tired of listening to the officer. The lava pool was bubbling and sending up wisps of vapour and smoke, while behind him, the sounds of the soldiers labouring to remove the Sextant continued. The captain finished his cigarette and walked away. Corthie glanced at the hoop in the floor of the wagon. There was no way to remove his shackles, but it might be possible to rip the hoop up through the wooden boards. He channelled his battle-vision and pulled on the chain, not enough to make a sound, but more to gauge the hoop's strength. It would move; he could feel it. If he used all of his power, he could rip it out of the wood, but then what? Twenty soldiers were surrounding him, and he could remember what being shot in the gut by crossbow bolts felt like.

The minutes dragged by. From the shouts and grunts coming from the temple, he guessed that the soldiers were still struggling to move the Sextant. Around him, the soldiers were mostly gazing away from him, though a few were keeping their eyes firmly on the wagon. He was quick, but he wasn't quick enough to evade twenty crossbows.

A cry of agony rang out, followed by shouts of alarm and the thud of boots running. At once, the attention of every soldier surrounding the wagon was drawn towards the temple. Another loud cry rose up.

'Archers!' someone shouted. 'Up on the balconies.'

Corthie shifted position and turned to look. Three Banner soldiers were down, and others were running for cover or hiding behind their shields as a hail of arrows spat down from the side of the cavern. He glanced up, looking for their source, and saw several dozen Fordians. Some were standing on high balconies, while others were loosing from open windows. The soldiers on the temple roof were working without their armour on, and most were hit, falling to their knees, or toppling from the scaffolding.

'Get a company up there!' cried an officer.

Soldiers rushed to get into formation as more fell. A few had loosed their crossbows, but the Fordians were out of range of the Banner weapons, while their own arrows were pinning down half of the cavern.

As the Banner company started to charge, their shields and armour were peppered with slingshots, and their momentum faltered. A new force of Fordians emerged from a tunnel entrance, young men and women, armed with slings. They rushed forwards, sending small, round stones flying into the Banner soldiers.

'After them!' screamed the officer.

The company turned to face the new threat, and charged, while arrows continued to strike their right flank. The slingers darted back into the shadows of the tunnel, the Banner company in pursuit.

'Third Company,' said the officer from behind the protection of a shield. 'Those archers still need taken care of. Take over Second Company's role, and clear them out.'

A further company extricated itself from the mass of soldiers, and ran towards the cavern wall, passing directly into the Fordian archers' range. As they reached the entrances to the buildings on that side of the cavern, the slingers reappeared, coming out of a different tunnel, and loosing their stones into the Banner soldiers.

Lord Gellith was brought out in front of the temple, a group of Banner soldiers pushing him ahead of them, and the Fordian leader was hit in the throat by an arrow and went down.

'First squad,' said the captain guarding Corthie, 'go and help; Second squad, stay and watch our prisoner.'

Half of the soldiers surrounding the wagon peeled off, and the captain led them in a charge towards the slingers. As soon as they were gone, Corthie heaved, and ripped the hoop out of the floor of the wagon. He glanced around, ready to run, but none of those guarding him had even noticed, their full attention on the chaos erupting throughout the cavern. Corthie turned to glance at the bridge over the river of lava, judging the distance. As he was about to spring up, arrows whistled through the air towards the wagon, and three of those guarding him were hit.

Corthie leaped from the wagon, landing onto a soldier and knocking him to the ground. To his left, another band of Fordians were approaching, their bows loosing into his guards. Corthie swung his fists into the face of a soldier, then ripped the crossbow from his grasp and loosed it into the neck of another one. The Fordians rushed over the stone bridge, and swarmed round the wagon. Hand to hand, the Banner soldiers were the superior fighters, but the numbers of Fordians pushed them back, and they broke. Green-skinned youths surrounded Corthie, cheering. A man barged his way through.

'Get those shackles removed,' he cried, 'and bring his armour up.'

'Sohul?'

'Yes, sir,' said the lieutenant. 'Now, if you wouldn't mind, place your wrists on the ground.'

Corthie crouched down as Fordians approached. They removed the pins and the shackles fell, then others came forward carrying pieces of his armour.

'Pick up the shields of the fallen,' yelled Sohul, as Fordians began strapping armour onto Corthie. 'Use them to protect Commander Holdfast.'

The Fordians did as they were ordered, and formed a wall of shields between Corthie and the temple, where the bulk of Banner soldiers were gathered.

'Why are you doing this?' Corthie asked the lieutenant.

'You are my employer, sir, and the Banner don't break their word.'

Corthie smiled. 'I thought I was paying you for military advice.'

'That's right, sir, and I advise you to start fighting as soon as your armour is on.'

'You don't happen to have...'

'Of course, sir.' He snapped his fingers, and a Fordian approached with the Clawhammer.

'That's it, Sohul; I'm doubling your pay.'

Cries came from the Fordians in the shield wall, as the Banner sent soldiers against them. Crossbow bolts ripped through the air, and several of the unarmoured youths went down. As they fell, others ran forward to take their place, lifting the shields high. With the last piece of his armour attached, Corthie squeezed the helmet over his head and pulled the visor down. He gripped the Clawhammer in both hands.

'Pull your force back, Lieutenant, and ensure the demigods are safe. Oh, and thank you.'

Sohul nodded, then turned to the Fordians. 'Everyone but the shield wall, get back over the bridge; follow me.'

He raced off, taking most of the Fordians with him, and leaving half a dozen green-skinned bodies on the ground. Corthie glanced down at the dead for a moment. They had given their lives to save him, because they believed in him; they believed that he could stop the Banner and the Ascendants from taking the Sextant and occupying their home. He took a breath, and flooded himself with battle-vision, feeling it ripple through his body. He glanced at the enemy. This was his destiny, and no one could stop him. He walked out in front of the shield wall, and the first bolt hit him within seconds, glancing harmlessly off his steel breastplate.

He laughed, and charged.

He reached the Banner lines before they understood what was happening, and waded into them, swinging the Clawhammer with both hands. The greenhide talons ripped through their armour, cleaving bodies in two. At close range, no one could get near him, his movements faster than they could keep up with, and he lost himself, just as he had done at the Falls of Iron. This is me, he thought, as he slaughtered the soldiers round him; this is the real me.

'I am Corthie Holdfast,' he cried; 'know my name.'

The Banner soldiers were disciplined, but against his onslaught, none could stand. The high-ranking officer who had spoken to him tried to flee, and the Clawhammer ripped him from shoulder to groin. As the commander of the Banner fell, his men broke in panic. Arrows were continuing to fly down from the balconies and windows at the side of the cavern, and the soldiers raced through the hailstorm towards the main cavern entrance. The Fordian slingers appeared from the tunnels by their flank, adding to the carnage as Corthie hacked through the backs of those fleeing. He passed the temple, now deserted and littered with the bodies of the fallen, and pressed on, as over a hundred Banner soldiers ran through the main tunnel.

A flash of light erupted at the other end of the tunnel, and the Banner soldiers screamed.

'Dragons!' one cried, as flames swept through the front ranks of those fleeing.

Some turned, preferring to face the slingshots, arrows and Corthie's Clawhammer rather than be incinerated within the confines of the tunnel. Corthie charged them, and they threw down their weapons and fell to their knees. Corthie ignored the terror in their eyes and raised his arms to strike down at them.

'Corthie!' cried a voice, possibly the only voice that could have broken the spell.

He halted, the Clawhammer in mid-swing, then stepped back. All around him, Banner soldiers were surrendering, and the hail of arrows ceased. To his left, Aila ran out from a tunnel entrance, and rushed towards him.

He raised his visor and took her into his steel-clad arms. She looked into his eyes, then glanced around at the bodies. Fordian fighters were cheering from the balconies, and the slingers were disarming the Banner soldiers, taking their shields, swords and crossbows.

'You did it,' she said.

'Did you doubt me?'

'Not when it comes to... this, no.'

'The cavern is ours, sir,' said Sohul as he approached. He was flanked by Fordians wearing pieces of Banner armour, and clutching crossbows in their hands instead of slings. 'But now,' Sohul went on, 'it appears we have a dragon or two to deal with.'

Corthie took a breath, letting his battle-vision cool. The Banner soldiers were being herded into a large group, while Fordians were taking possession of the temple. Ahead of them, smoke was still rising from the smouldering corpses in the main tunnel, and the head of a black dragon appeared, her eyes scanning the interior of the cavern. Several Fordians stopped what they were doing to stare, while others gripped their weapons.

Corthie strode forwards, Aila and Sohul by his side.

'You did… all this?' Blackrose said.

'Not on my own,' said Corthie. 'Every Fordian who didn't like the idea of letting the Ascendants get the Sextant helped.'

'I see you haven't changed, Corthie Holdfast,' Blackrose said; 'you kill like a god.'

'Sir,' said Sohul, his eyes wide as he gazed at Blackrose; 'do you know this dragon?'

'I certainly do,' he said. 'Everyone,' he cried, his voice carrying across the cavern; 'welcome the mighty Blackrose to Fordamere. This dragon is a friend, an old friend, and she has come in our hour of need.' He lowered his voice. 'Well, I hope so.'

'I received a call for help,' the dragon said, 'and I did not come alone. Beyond this cavern, my young ally Frostback is pursing the last of the Banner soldiers that were stationed outside in the city, and, naturally, Maddie is upon my back.'

'Hi,' said Maddie from up on the dragon's shoulders, waving.

Corthie grinned up at her, then took his helmet off, shaking the sweat from his hair.

'Before we go any further,' he said, 'I want you to know how sorry I am for what my sister did to you. It was wrong, and I should have tried to stop her.'

'I seem to recall that you were drunk at the time.'

'Aye, I was.' He took a breath. 'And for that, I also apologise. I lost my way for a while, but now I know my true purpose.'

Blackrose tilted her head. 'You have a purpose?'

'I'm going to kill the Ascendants.'

Blackrose stared at him for a long, silent moment, then she turned her head to face Maddie. 'Climb down, rider. The cavern is secure, and I suspect I may have to spend some time trying to bring Corthie to his senses.'

Maddie clambered down the dragon's side and dropped to the ground. She glanced around at the bodies of the Banner soldiers, then approached the others.

'Good to see you, Maddie,' said Aila. 'How's Sable?'

'Annoying,' said Maddie. 'But she's well, if that's what you meant. Malik's squidgy bits, what a mess in here. You still have the Clawhammer, I see?'

Corthie shouldered it, and nodded. 'It's never let me down.'

Maddie half-smiled. 'Blackrose wants the Sextant.'

'Rider,' said the dragon, 'let's get the pleasantries out of the way before we start negotiating.'

'Why do you want it?' said Corthie.

'I am told,' she said, 'that it can function as a Quadrant, and as your sister stole mine, I think it would be a fair price for coming to your assistance today.'

'So you would use it to travel to Dragon Eyre?'

'Yes.'

'And would you then destroy it?'

'Why would I do that?'

'Because it's how the Ascendants will find my world, and the world of Yendra and Pella. If it's destroyed, then our worlds will be safe.'

Blackrose approached, until her head was a yard away from Corthie. 'And if I agree to destroy it, you will give it to me without any further objection?'

'I will.'

'Agreed. I swear by those I hold dear, that once I have used it to reach my home world, I will incinerate it, and break it into a hundred pieces. Maddie, you are my witness. Now, regarding your words about the Ascendants – you have won, Corthie. As soon as I remove the Sextant, the gods of Implacatus will not be able to locate your world. Leave now, with your life, and the lives of your companions. Do not stray into believing in your own invincibility.'

'Thank you, Blackrose,' said Aila. 'This is what I've been trying to tell him. He's got it into his head that he's been chosen to destroy the Ascendants.'

Corthie bit his tongue. Why couldn't they understand?

'I fought an Ascendant once,' said Blackrose; 'his powers overcame me in seconds.'

'I'm immune to those powers,' he said; 'that's why it has to be me. But today, here, I'll concede. Take the Sextant, and we'll leave, all of us.'

Aila flung her arms around him. 'You mean that?'

'Aye,' he said; 'I'll not risk harm coming to you. There will be another time, another opportunity.'

'Thank you,' she said, her head against his breastplate.

'A wise decision,' said Blackrose. 'You have grown, Corthie. When we first met in Arrowhead, you were still a boy, but I can see that you have become a man.' She glanced at Maddie. 'Come, rider; let us see about removing this device, and then we can go home.'

CHAPTER 26
POWERLESS

S hawe Myre, Southern Khatanax – 13th Lexinch 5252

Belinda opened her eyes. Her bedroom was filled with light coming through an open window, and she stretched her arms. Dawn, she thought. She pulled back the covers and walked to the window, yawned, then gazed down onto the valley of Shawe Myre. Everything seemed normal – workers were out tending the vines and vegetable gardens, and a row of charcoal kilns were being loaded with fresh wood, and for a moment she pretended that the Ascendants hadn't arrived the previous day. Then she remembered kneeling in front of them, and the illusion fragmented.

Telling herself that it wasn't her fault didn't help. She knew she had acted in the only way possible to save the lives of the civilians living in the valley, but that knowledge didn't make her feel any better. She was a prisoner in her own home, and soon, she would be leaving. She walked over to where her new servants had arranged her clothes. She had been wearing loose and flowing dresses since she had arrived in Shawe Myre, and they had felt like a sign that her life had changed for the better, but she pushed them to the side and pulled on her old fighting clothes; her tough, worn boots, and her hardened leather armour. She tied her hair back and glanced in the mirror, once again seeing the woman that looked like a stranger staring back at her. Who was she?

She picked up the Weathervane from a table, strapped the scabbard to her belt, and drew the blade. Its dark metal glistened in the dawn light, and she wondered how many lives it had ended. It had a history, a history as dark as hers.

She pictured herself sneaking downstairs, finding the two Ascendants sleeping, and killing them before they could awaken. With two strokes, she could free Lostwell, but, more likely, they would overpower and kill her before she could strike, and more of them would come from Implacatus even if she were successful. She slid the blade back into the scabbard and left her bedroom, wondering if it was the last time she would ever see it. She descended a set of spiral stairs and came out onto the floor of the house where the two Ascendants were staying. Rooms were arranged around a central, open space, and Leksandr was sitting on the floor cross-legged, his eyes closed. Behind him, Arete was pacing up and down, a deep frown on her face.

'Good morning,' said Belinda.

Arete glanced at her. 'Is it?' she snapped. 'And how would you know that?'

'I suppose that I was wishing you a good morning,' Belinda said, confusion clouding her mind, 'not stating a fact. I don't know if the morning is good or not.'

Arete looked at her as if she was stupid. 'I was being sarcastic, Belinda. What's wrong with you? And why are you dressed like that? You look like a common soldier – how are the mortals supposed to worship us if we dress in the same manner as they do?'

Belinda frowned, unsure which question she was supposed to answer first.

'Your anger is disturbing my tranquillity,' said Leksandr from the reed mat. 'I haven't seen you this agitated in a hundred years, Arete.'

'Can you blame me?' Arete yelled. 'This is the longest time I've gone without using my powers in... in... oh, I don't know; a long time. I need my vision; I need to see what's going on. I feel... naked without it. Perhaps we should cut off the Holdfast girl's head and take that back to Implacatus; do we really need the rest of her?'

Leksandr opened his eyes and sighed. 'This is exactly why you should take a breath and calm yourself, Arete.'

'Don't tell me to calm myself, you arrogant oaf.'

'Your temper is affecting your judgement. Kelsey Holdfast is an asset, an extremely valuable asset, and for the moment we need her head attached to the rest of her body. If you long to sense your powers, then feel your self-healing, feel your battle-vision, or, if you must, place your hand onto a servant and drain their life force.'

'You don't get it,' said Arete; 'I have never once, not in millennia, gone somewhere without first checking what's there. We're due to travel to Yoneath this morning, and I can't see what's happening. I feel blind. Powerless.'

Leksandr got to his feet and walked to a large window. He gazed down at the valley, nodded, then sat.

'Have you nothing to say?' said Arete.

'I have already said what I intend to. Let us eat, and then we shall depart.'

Arete stormed over to him. 'That's not good enough.'

'Perhaps we should go for a walk,' said Belinda.

They turned to her as if they had forgotten she was there.

'A walk?' said Arete, her voice dripping with condescension.

'Yes. The valley is a quarter of a mile in length; we could walk until we are out of Kelsey's range, and then you could vision.'

'Oh,' said Arete, her expression lifting. 'That's actually a good idea. Leksandr, are you coming?'

'No,' he said, his eyes turning back to the valley. 'From here I can see the cottage where the Holdfast girl is being kept. One of us should remain to keep watch, in case she tries to escape.'

'Very well. Belinda, you shall accompany me.'

'Alright,' she said.

Arete went over to a couch and laced up her sandals. She stood, paused, then picked up her sword and attached it to her belt.

'I can't believe I have to carry around a piece of sharpened metal,' she said, frowning. 'I loathe the Holdfast girl for making me feel this way.'

She and Belinda descended the stairs to the lowest level of the house, and passed a cluster of soldiers, Arete waving their attentions away.

'We are going for a walk,' she said; 'alone.'

Belinda followed her in silence as they crossed the rope bridge and went down to the valley floor. The sun was rising over the hills to the east, and the air was warming.

Belinda took a deep breath. 'What is Implacatus like?'

Arete eyed her as they walked along the path. 'We live high in the mountains,' she said, 'so that we don't have to look at too many mortals. We use demigods as servants, and Ancients as advisors and assistants. The city of Serene is the closest mortal settlement, and everyone that lives there serves some purpose; the Banners for instance. They act as a buffer, separating us from the mass of unwashed mortals who live at ground level. It's a neat system.'

'And where would I fit in?'

Arete smiled. 'I suppose that depends on whether or not the Blessed Second Ascendant believes you. His Majesty will no doubt be a little frustrated that he cannot read your innermost thoughts if, indeed, that is the case. I know you've said that your mind is impenetrable, but the Second Ascendant's powers are the greatest in existence. Personally, I think he will be able to break through any blocks put in place by a mere mortal, and then all of your secrets will come out.'

'Say he does believe me, and I am accepted by the other Ascendants – what would I do?'

'I don't understand the question.'

'What would be my role? Would I work, or would I lounge all day, being waited on by demigods, while Ancients carried out my commands?'

'His Majesty King Edmond would find something for you to do, if you were worried about being bored. Perhaps a governorship of one of the colonies, or you could spend time working on a project; it took Leksandr a thousand years to create the greenhides.'

Belinda blinked. 'He what?'

'He's very proud of his achievement, though it's open knowledge that he stole the idea of green skin from Nathaniel's Fordians. Your former partner was a great innovator. You know, the Blessed Second Ascendant has never quite got over your betrayal. You and Nathaniel were his most loyal supporters and allies for millennia, and I still remember the moment his Majesty was told that you had both joined the rebellion. His rage lasted a century.'

'But why would anyone deliberately create a being such as a greenhide?'

'They're perfect soldiers, if you want to utterly devastate an enemy's territory; and they're much cheaper to maintain than the mercenary Banners. Decidedly more efficient, too. Of course, they lack subtlety, but who needs subtlety when overwhelming brute force is required?'

'I fought them on the world of Pella,' Belinda said; 'they're mindless beasts; monsters.'

'Presumably, they had been allowed to run wild; they get that way without strict controls. Leksandr made their minds particularly susceptible to manipulation by the Ascendants; with one thought, we can command them – lay siege here, attack there; we can even order them to destroy their own queens, if we need to reduce their population. Each warrior only lives for about ten years, so if you get rid of the queens, the rest will die out in a decade or so.'

Arete halted on the path, her eyes wide. 'That feels good, oh.'

Belinda felt for her powers, and found them. She glanced back along her path. They were a hundred and twenty yards or so from the cottage where Kelsey was imprisoned. She glanced back at Arete, and felt a buzzing around her temples.

The Seventh Ascendant pursed her lips. 'So, you weren't lying; I am unable to read your thoughts, despite us being out of range of the Holdfast girl. I'm glad you were being honest, but this is disappointing nevertheless.' She narrowed her eyes a little. 'What the Holdfasts did to you, my old friend, I pray that King Edmond will be able to undo. Now, I shall take a look at what is occurring at Yoneath, and then we can make our preparations to depart.'

Ten minutes later, they were back in the hanging house. Arete was shaking with rage, while Leksandr was trying to remain calm.

'Two dragons,' she cried, 'and the Holdfast boy is loose; he's already slaughtered half of the Black Crown. We must leave now. Kelsey can remain here under guard, and we'll annihilate everything that lives in Yoneath; they have betrayed us.'

'Relax,' said Leksandr. 'They will not be able to use the Sextant; its workings will be beyond their puny comprehension. Furthermore, its sheer weight and size will make it impossible for even a dragon to lift. We have a little time; we should act, but we don't need to go to Yoneath yet. As for the Holdfast girl, we cannot leave her here; she is too important. In fact, we cannot let her out of our sight, not even for a moment.'

'But if we take her with us, we won't be able to use our powers.'

'Then we ensure that we bring a force large enough for the job. Several Banners, and their artillery, are sitting waiting for us in Alea Tanton. We could be there in five minutes, and then in Yoneath in under an hour. If we open a portal, we could move dozens of ballistae and net-throwing machines into position; they will take care of the dragons, and we, my dear, will take care of Corthie Holdfast.'

He stood. 'Shall we?'

Arete glared at him, then turned to Belinda. 'Are you ready to leave?'

'I am,' she said.

'You're too quiet,' said Arete; 'it makes me suspicious.' She turned to Leksandr. 'Her mind is indeed shielded; she could be thinking anything.'

'We must trust her for now; what is the alternative? If we removed her head, then the Blessed Second Ascendant would probably do the same to us. Besides, if she steps out of line, we can place her in a restraining mask.'

'Maybe we should do so now.'

'No. We must give her a chance to prove her loyalty first. Belinda, are you ready to do your duty?'

'Yes.'

'Then let us go.'

They strode through the house, and the soldiers there began to follow them.

'We are withdrawing to Alea Tanton,' Leksandr said to an officer. 'Summon the Banner.'

Belinda glanced at the backs of the two Ascendants as they descended to the valley floor. What was her duty? She had sworn allegiance to the Second Ascendant, but did she have to keep her word? She knew one thing for certain; if they tried to put her into a god-restrainer mask, then she would fight, vow or no vow. Her duty was to her people, she decided. If the Ascendants honoured their word, and left those living in Shawe Myre unharmed, then she would not resist going to Alea Tanton or Yoneath.

They emerged into the open air of the valley, and strode to the cottage. All around, soldiers of the Undying Flame were gathering on the grass, and she saw Silva bow as they approached.

'Your Majesty,' she said. 'Are we leaving?'

'You're not going anywhere,' said Arete. 'We have enough demigods on our staff; you are not required.'

'Stay here,' said Belinda; 'guard my people after I am gone.'

'But, your Majesty, I...'

'That's an order, Silva. This is something I must do alone.'

Silva's eyes closed for a moment, and a tear rolled down her cheek. 'As you wish, your Majesty.'

'Bring out the Holdfast girl,' said Leksandr.

'And the other prisoner, my lord?' said the Banner officer.

'Who? Oh, him. Leave him; he is of no interest to us.'

Soldiers entered the cottage, then returned a few moments later, Kelsey in their midst. The Holdfast girl glanced around, her eyes blinking in the sunlight, until her gaze landed on Belinda.

'Bind her hands,' said Arete, 'then place a hood over her head.'

'She is not to be harmed,' said Belinda.

Kelsey frowned. 'Where are we going?'

'Gag her too,' said Arete. 'I have no desire to listen to her voice.'

The soldiers tied a gag round Kelsey's mouth, and pulled a hood down over her head and bound her wrists with cord. They pushed her towards where the Banner had assembled, a soldier on each side gripping her arms. Leksandr produced a Quadrant from his robes.

'I will see you in a few moments,' he said.

'The same spot we left from?' said Arete.

Leksandr nodded, glided a finger over the Quadrant, and vanished. Arete rolled her shoulders, checked her sword, then took out her own Quadrant.

She glanced at the officer. 'Is the entire Banner here?'

'Yes, ma'am,' he bowed.

'Good; I don't want any stragglers.' She turned to Belinda. 'See? Not a single one of your precious mortals was harmed during our stay; are you satisfied?'

Belinda nodded.

'I preferred it when you actually spoke. Believe it or not, you were quite talkative in the olden days.'

'I'll try.'

Arete raised an eyebrow, then shook her head and glanced down at the Quadrant. She moved her fingers across the metal surface, and the air behind her shimmered, then settled into a large black void. It seemed to swirl with nothingness, then cleared, showing a large court-yard next to a palatial building.

'The Governor's residence in Old Alea,' said Arete. 'Have you been there before?'

'No.'

'Well, we shan't be staying long.' She gestured to the Banner officer, and he raised an arm.

The soldiers began marching, and walked into the portal, their boots switching from the grass of the valley to the gravel of the courtyard in a single stride as they passed through. Kelsey was bundled along, followed by the cart that was carrying the Ascendants' private possessions and supplies. Arete waited until the entire Banner had passed through, then she touched the Quadrant and the portal dissolved and disappeared.

For a split second, Belinda realised she had an opportunity to strike, but before her hand could move to the hilt of the Weathervane, Arete touched the Quadrant again, and they were both transported to the same courtyard as the others.

Leksandr approached, a female god by his side.

'I have informed Governor Felice of our requirements,' he said.

The woman bowed low. 'Every Banner in Old Alea has been summoned, your Graces,' she said, her voice subdued, 'along with the entire collection of artillery; over sixty mobile ballistae, and a dozen net-throwers.'

'Good,' said Arete. She gestured to Belinda. 'This is the Blessed Third Ascendant; she has returned to us. Rejoice.'

'I am honoured to meet you again, your Grace,' Felice said, bowing.

'Again?' said Arete.

'Yes, your Grace. I was in the Falls of Iron when Corthie Holdfast and the Blessed Third Ascendant destroyed our forces there. If Lord Renko hadn't triggered his Quadrant, I would have been slain next to Lord Baldwin.'

Arete laughed.

'My Grace,' Felice went on, frowning. 'Something is blocking my vision, just as it did in the Falls of Iron. I need to contact certain regiments and companies based in the city garrison, but it seems that I am unable to.'

'Walk to the edge of the courtyard,' said Arete, 'and do it from there.'

Felice bowed and hurried away.

Arete shook her head. 'The calibre of gods around here seems rather low. How did she become governor of Lostwell?'

'The old governor is still locked up in the dungeons, and I think Corthie Holdfast killed the rest. We can see about appointing someone more suitable when we return to Implacatus.'

Arete folded her arms. 'Now we wait, while the dragons and the Holdfast boy run riot in Yoneath.'

'Relax,' said Leksandr; 'they will still be there when we arrive. The Sextant cannot be moved by muscle alone.'

'They could destroy it.'

'They could try, but they wouldn't succeed. In a little over an hour, we shall be wading in blood. I'm ready to issue the order that no quarter is to be given; are you in agreement?'

'Yes. Someone in Yoneath betrayed us, and I don't have the patience to find out who it was. Kill them all.'

'All?' said Belinda. 'What about the civilians; the children?'

'That is what "all" means, Belinda. They are a nest of rebels. We made an agreement to spare them, but they broke that by inviting two dragons along and by freeing the Holdfast boy. The mortals have to learn; if they cross us, then they will receive no mercy, otherwise we'd be putting down rebellions on every world we control. A firm hand is required to rule; you used to understand that.'

Belinda stared at Arete for a moment, then turned and strode away. She noticed Kelsey within the mass of soldiers, and walked up to her.

'Remove her hood and gag,' she said.

'Ma'am?'

'I am the Third Ascendant. Are you questioning my authority?'

'No, ma'am,' the soldier said. He and one other untied and pulled the hood off, then did the same with Kelsey's gag.

'I wish to speak to the prisoner alone for a moment,' Belinda said.

The soldiers bowed, and moved back a few paces.

'How are you?' Belinda said.

'How do you think, Belinda? You and your insane friends are going to kill me. Maybe not today, but at some point, when the Ascendants are tired of trying to find out how my powers work. You've betrayed us, again.'

'If I'd fought them in Shawe Myre, I'd be dead, and you would still be a prisoner. Submitting was the only thing I could do to save the lives of the people there.'

'These are just words, Belinda. I should never have trusted you.'

'Listen. Corthie is free, and he is being assisted by two dragons.'

'What?'

'That's why all of these soldiers are being gathered. Please try to be patient.'

'Why? What are you going to do?'

Belinda leaned in, her voice a whisper. 'I can't say, not until we get to Yoneath and I understand the situation. Try to stay close to me. If I see an opportunity, we'll take it.'

She noticed Leksandr glance over, and she gestured to a soldier. 'Place the gag and hood back onto the prisoner. My interrogation has finished.'

'Yes, ma'am.'

Belinda turned away, and walked to the edge of the courtyard to gaze over the city of Alea Tanton. A strong tang of foul ocean air drifted around her as she looked down from the high promontory onto the vast miles of slums. Sable had lived down there, she thought. She glanced back at the residence. Somewhere inside that building was where Naxor had tried to seduce the Holdfast woman with promises, after she had taken the Quadrant from Governor Felice. If that one event hadn't occurred, then Belinda would probably be fighting alongside Corthie at that moment, instead of being part of the forces being sent against him.

'What were you discussing with the prisoner?'

She turned to face Leksandr. 'I told her that her brother had been freed.'

'Why?'

'To use as leverage. If she realises that his life is in danger, then she might be more cooperative.'

'I see.'

'What are our plans for Corthie Holdfast?'

'Well, ideally, I'd prefer to take him back in chains to Implacatus along with his sister; he would be a rare novelty to display to the Ancients and other Ascendants, a curiosity. We could make him fight all manner of beasts, you know, to test the limits of his battle-vision. Of course, we don't live in an ideal world, and it might very well become essential to slay him. The Sextant remains the priority.'

'You said that the dragon would be unable to lift it. Surely it can't be that heavy?'

'It depends if one knows how to operate it. If inert, it exhibits a mass far greater than its size would suggest, and it would take several dragons to haul it even a few feet. However, once activated, it can be moved or lifted with one hand. When you hid it seven years ago, Belinda, you must have activated it, otherwise it would still be in Shawe Myre.'

'And how does one activate it?'

He laughed. 'You are not yet in a position for me to trust you with that information.'

'How would I gain that trust?'

'Killing Corthie Holdfast would be a good place to start. That would prove your allegiance, even to Arete, who is a little more suspicious than I.'

'I understand.'

'Good. Both Arete and I will be watching you very closely in Yoneath; I pray that you do not let us down.'

It took under an hour for the Banners to assemble in the large courtyard. Each stood by their standard, and alongside was a long double line of wagons mounted with ballistae and net-throwing machines. Belinda walked over to Arete and Leksandr once the preparations seemed complete.

'No quarter is to be given from the moment we arrive,' Leksandr said to a group of Banner officers. 'Start the killing immediately; house to house – none are to be spared. The Banner of the Undying Flame shall remain responsible for watching the prisoner at all times; her security is paramount. Every artillery piece will be deployed against the dragons, but leave Corthie Holdfast to us. Once the Sextant is secure, we shall destroy the Fordian shrine in its entirety. An example is to be made of Yoneath, an example that will signal our determination to the rest of Khatanax. Dismissed.'

The officers bowed low before the three Ascendants, then returned to their individual Banners.

'Five thousand soldiers,' said Arete; 'we could have managed this with none if we didn't have to bring the Holdfast girl along.'

'True, but they're only mercenaries; does it matter if we lose a few?' Leksandr withdrew his Quadrant. 'I shall travel to the eastern edge of the city, where the old vision shield was in place.'

Arete nodded. 'I know it.'

Leksandr touched the Quadrant and vanished. Without a pause, Arete took her own Quadrant and opened up a portal. It shimmered black, then showed a dusty road, beyond which spread fields, terraced vineyards and olive groves. Arete gestured to the Banner officers, and the soldiers began charging through, their weapons at the ready. Belinda watched as company after company rushed through the portal, fanning out as soon as they reached the dusty ground. When half were through, it was the turn of the ballista wagons, each pulled by a team of horses, and flanked with armed soldiers; and after them, the remainder of the Banners passed through at a march. Smoke was already rising from farmsteads in the distance, and Belinda started to feel sick. Last to go through was the Banner of the Black Crown, escorting Kelsey, and then Arete dissolved the portal, leaving only her and Belinda standing in the courtyard.

Arete glanced at her, then activated the Quadrant, and they appeared on the road to Yoneath. Screams were coming from the streets and houses of the city, and Belinda caught her first glimpse of Fordians; a pile of green-skinned bodies lying headless by a farmhouse. Soldiers were surging in a wide line along the flanks of the valley, slaughtering everyone in their path. Crossbow bolts were raining down on the civilians as they ran away from the advance of the Banners, and, in the distance, Belinda made out a large opening in the side of a cliff face. Above it, a dragon was circling.

'No mercy!' cried Leksandr, as the Ascendants strode after the soldiers in the direction of the cliff. 'Kill them all.'

CHAPTER 27
THE RELUCTANT HERO

Shawe Myre, Southern Khatanax – 13th Lexinch 5252

Van leaned against the wall of the dark cell, his injuries still aching despite Leksandr's partial healing the night before. He listened, but could hear nothing. A few minutes had elapsed since he had last heard the heavy footsteps of the Banner soldiers, and fifteen since Kelsey had been taken. He put his fingers onto the handle of the door, pushed and, to his surprise, it opened. He staggered out, limping and stiff from a night spent on the hard stone floor of the cell. He reached the back door of the cottage and swung it open, raising a hand to shield his eyes from the bright sunlight.

In front of him, Silva was standing, weeping.

'Have they gone?'

She turned to him, her hand wiping the tears from her face. He walked forwards, but without a wall to support him, he stumbled and fell to his knees. Silva crouched down by him, and helped him stand.

'They left a few minutes ago,' she said.

'All of them?'

'Yes. They took the Queen and Kelsey with them. I tried to go along, but the Seventh Ascendant forbade it.' A tear rolled down her cheek. 'It was just like the last time I lost her; except then it was Agatha who told me I had to stay behind. I failed.'

'I've failed too; I was supposed to protect Kelsey, and they took her.'

'You are a mere mortal, Van. There is nothing you could have done against two Ascendants. Even her Majesty would be unlikely to survive a fight against Arete and Leksandr combined. Come, I will take you to a place where someone can look at your wounds.'

They started to walk along the grass. Around them, the valley was deserted, but a few civilians were peering out of their windows or doors.

'Do you have a demigod who can heal?'

'No,' she said; 'unfortunately not.'

'Then where are we going?'

'We have a mortal who is good with broken bones and the like.'

'There's no point,' he said, halting on the path. 'I'm sick from Leksandr's death powers. He healed me afterward, but not fully. There's nothing any mortal can do about it, unless, well, unless they have any salve.'

'We don't have any salve here, I'm afraid.'

He nodded, part of him relieved that he wouldn't have to take some. All the same, he would take it if it was the only way to be fit enough to go after Kelsey. Silva led him to a bench, and he frowned as he sat. Go after Kelsey? It was impossible. By land or sea, they had a ten day start on him, maybe more, and he wasn't sure where Yoneath was.

'Did they leave the same way they arrived?'

'Yes,' said Silva, sitting next to him. 'They opened a portal and went to Alea Tanton.'

'Alea Tanton? I thought they were going to some place near Kinell called Yoneath.'

'They are, once they've collected reinforcements from the Torduan capital.'

'I wonder why they need reinforcements; I thought Corthie was locked up?'

'I don't know, Van; they didn't tell me anything.'

He leaned his elbows on his knees and rested his aching head in his hands. He had promised Kelsey he would go wherever she was taken, and he would, but first he needed to heal. The morning sun was heating up the valley, and he wanted to hide from its rays, curl up somewhere dark, and sleep. He felt himself drift off, and tried to focus on what the Ascendants were doing. If they needed reinforcements, then something unplanned had occurred in Yoneath; perhaps the locals had risen up against the Banner stationed there. Whatever it was, did it matter? By the time Van reached Yoneath it would be a smouldering ruin, and the Ascendants would have moved on. A wave of despair overcame him, and he slumped, then toppled off the bench and on the gravel path, unconscious.

When he awoke, he was flat on his back on a mattress, and voices were whispering close by. He opened his eyes, and was relieved to be inside a dimly-lit room, as the sunlight had been making his headache worse. He frowned. The last thing he remembered was sitting on a bench; how had he got inside?

'He's awake,' said Silva.

Van turned his head, and saw Belinda's loyal demigod standing by the bed. Amalia was next to her, her expression one of suppressed fury.

'Am I dreaming?' he muttered.

'No,' said Silva; 'Lady Amalia has returned; perhaps her conscience got the better of her.'

'How dare you?' said Amalia. 'Remember your place, demigod. I merely made a tactical withdrawal. Had I not, I would be dead; it's as simple as that. As it is, I am not dead.'

'Where did you go?' said Van.

'Dun Khatar.'

He narrowed his eyes. 'How?'

'How do you think? I used my brains, and went by Quadrant.'

He tried to sit up. 'You have a Quadrant?'

'Clearly.'

'You lied to us,' said Silva; 'you told her Majesty that you'd left the Quadrant in Dun Khatar, and you had it all the time.'

'Yes, I lied. I was scared and vulnerable when I first arrived, and so I told you that I'd hidden the Quadrant, in order to keep its location a secret. I had no idea what you were going to do to me; I needed a way to escape, just in case. And, luckily for me, when the Ascendants arrived, my way was clear.'

'We know where they've gone,' Van said, slumping back down onto the bed. 'You can take us there.'

Amalia smiled. 'I don't think so. Having just escaped the clutches of the Ascendants, what makes you think that I'd be willing to rush back into their fatal embrace?'

'Because deep down, you want to rescue Belinda.'

Amalia laughed. 'Oh my. You really don't know me at all, do you?'

'He's right,' said Silva; 'her Majesty trusted you, and you told me a hundred times that you wanted to be her friend again. What about your plan? You and the Queen, ruling the salve world together? Was that all lies too?'

'No, a lot of that was true. I did indeed desire to have Belinda by my side, but fate, in the guise of two Ascendants, has intervened.'

Van gasped in pain. 'You could be the hero,' he said; 'you could save Belinda and Kelsey, and help stop the Ascendants.'

'I have no wish to be a martyr, thank you very much. Now, let's go over the new arrangements, shall we? Silva, I'm now in charge of Shawe Myre, pending Belinda's return. Van, you are permitted to stay, at least until you are fit enough to leave. I think I will select one of the hanging houses; the view from up there is much better than from my old house in the valley.'

'You could get rid of me sooner,' said Van.

'How?'

'You have death powers, don't you?'

'Oh, you want me to kill you? I'm sure I could manage that.'

'I want you to heal me. You could do it in seconds.'

'I could, but I'm preserving my powers in order to heal my arm. I have none to spare on mere mortals.'

'Do it,' said Silva. She crossed her arms. 'Do it, or I'll refuse to assist you in any way. You are behaving disgracefully, Amalia. To think of how meek you were when we took you in and cared for you. Was it all an act? Is this what you're really like?'

'I don't know what you're talking about.'

'I will tell everyone in Shawe Myre; I will tell them how you lied to the Queen, and hid the Quadrant from her, and that you're refusing to help. No one will support you, do you understand? Everyone here owes their life to the Queen; you will never rule over them.'

Amalia lowered her gaze.

'The Sextant,' said Van; 'the Ascendants will use it to conquer and oppress your world. Your world, Amalia.'

'I admit,' she said; 'the thought of an Ascendant living in Maeladh Palace does irk me a little.'

'We could be in and out in minutes. I've trained with Quadrant snatch squads. If we time it well, we could take Kelsey and Belinda from right under their noses, and there would be nothing they could do about it.'

'They could come back here.'

'Then we wouldn't. You could prepare the Quadrant to go to some-place else, then Kelsey's powers would keep us hidden. We tell no one here what the plan is, so that when the Ascendants come looking for us, they'll realise right away that we've abandoned Shawe Myre.'

'They might still kill everyone,' said Silva.

'Then we tell them to evacuate before we leave.'

Amalia gazed into the distance. 'Kelsey's powers. You may be right; that girl could shield us indefinitely, well, at least until she dies of old age. Hmm. Very well, I'll consider it.'

She pressed a finger against his cheek, and he felt a burst of blissful healing saturate his body. He twisted on the bed, then relaxed, panting.

'There,' she said. 'Better?'

'Yes. Thank you.'

He sat up, and rubbed his head.

Amalia glanced at Silva. 'See? I'm helping.'

'What about the next step?' said the demigod. 'Will you take us to Yoneath?'

'I'd need to know where it is, first.'

'I know the rough location,' said Van.

'Silva,' she said, 'fetch that demigod girl, the one that used to get the news from Capston for us. She has vision powers that might reach as far as Kinell.'

'And then?' said Silva.

'You have convinced me; it's time to be a hero.'

Van climbed up to Belinda's hanging house while Silva and Amalia worked with the demigod who possessed range vision. The house seemed deserted, though the signs of its occupation by soldiers and the Ascendants were everywhere. He spotted Kelsey's bag lying on a reed mat by the rear railing, picked it up, then sat on a couch. He rummaged through it for a moment, then pulled out several packets of cigarettes.

He glanced at them, shaking his head. 'You were holding out on me, Kelsey,' he said. 'Well, they're mine now.'

He took one out of a packet and lit it, then sat back and watched as the smoke rose and was taken away by the breeze. Amalia's arrival had changed everything, and his feelings were oscillating between an anxiousness to be underway, and fear about what would happen once they reached Yoneath. He had no weapon or armour, but that didn't matter; what they needed was speed and surprise. In, grab, out. He remembered undergoing a training course on how to abduct people with Quadrants. He had never done it on a real operation, but what he had learned had stuck in his mind. All he needed was Amalia's cooperation, but that was the problem. He didn't trust her, and had been surprised by her abrupt change-of-mind.

He stuffed the cigarette packets into his pockets, then stood and shouldered the bag. He glanced around at the house for a moment, then returned the way he had come. At the bottom of the stairs, Silva and Amalia were waiting for him.

'Did you find what you were looking for?' said Silva.

'Yeah; I've brought Kelsey's stuff. Are we ready?'

'Yes,' said Amalia. 'I have prepared the Quadrant to take us close to Yoneath, and we will arrive in the hills to the south of the city. However, there is something you should be aware of before we go.'

'Yes?'

'The city of Yoneath is in chaos,' said Silva. 'Thousands of Banner soldiers are slaughtering the Fordians, while at least one dragon is opposing them from the sky. Also, there is a large cavern, where the Sextant is located. In there, Corthie is free, and in control of the area.'

'Corthie's free?'

'We think so,' said Amalia; 'the description certainly fits.'

'Then the interior of this cavern should be our second stop. We go the hills, then we observe. Once we've found Kelsey, we swoop in and snatch her, then we jump to the cavern. Agreed?'

'And Belinda?' said Silva. 'We're going to Yoneath for her as well as the Holdfast girl.'

'We're going to have to make a judgement on that at the time. We have to face it; she may be siding with the Ascendants.'

'Impossible,' said Silva.

'I hope so. What about the civilians here?'

'Most are packing up their possessions, although I suspect that many will return in a few days, despite my warnings.'

'You did what you could. Let's go.'

Amalia hesitated for a moment, then reached into her robes and took out a Quadrant. She gazed at it, her eyes troubled.

'Let us move into the shadows,' said Silva.

Amalia frowned, then slid her finger over the surface of the device, and a moment later they found themselves on a scrubby hillside, the sun beating down from the eastern sky. Van glanced at its position, then turned towards the north. Ahead was a ridge, beyond which the faint sounds of screams and fighting were coming. A dragon darted into view, silver-winged, and unleashed a burst of fire into the valley on the far side of the ridge, before banking away to avoid a volley of ballista bolts that tore through the sky.

'Come on,' he said.

They scrambled up the slope until they reached the top of the ridge, then Van lay down on the ground and crawled the last few feet. He peered over the edge. The ridge ended in a sharp cliffside, dropping fifty feet to the valley floor. The streets of the city were laid out along the bottom of the valley, with terraced fields further to the east. Directly below, formations of Banner soldiers were rampaging through the town, efficiently slaughtering the inhabitants. Doors were being kicked down, and soldiers would enter, then screams would rise up into the cloudless, unforgiving sky. The silver dragon was fighting back, soaring down to deliver fire onto the soldiers, before spinning and twisting to get away from the barrage of bolts and nets coming from a long convoy of wagons arranged on the central road through the city. To the left was a large, dark opening in the cliffside; the location of the cavern, Van guessed. He glanced to his right, and saw Silva and Amalia crouching beside him.

'I'm covered in dust and grime,' muttered Amalia.

Van narrowed his eyes. 'That's your reaction to the massacre going on below us?'

She gave him a look of contempt. 'This isn't the first massacre I've witnessed.'

'Nor I,' he said, his eyes glimpsing a stream of blood flowing down a steep alleyway. 'There have been a few times, when it was me down there, doing what those soldiers are doing. Not on Lostwell, but in other places.'

'Why are they doing it?' said Silva.

'Because they were ordered to,' he said. 'They're Banner soldiers; they do what they're told.'

'There,' said Amalia, pointing. 'I see the Ascendants; close to the front of the column of ballistae.'

'The standard of the Undying Flame is right behind them. That's where Kelsey will be.'

'Unless they left her in Alea Tanton,' said Silva.

'They didn't,' said Amalia. 'My powers are being blocked; the girl is down there.'

'Here we go,' said Van. 'We'll want to appear right in the middle of the Undying Flame. As soon as I've got Kelsey, we'll jump into the cavern.'

'This is insane,' said Amalia, taking the Quadrant out of her robes.

'Not yet,' he said, 'otherwise we'll still be lying down when we get there.'

Amalia laughed. 'That would be unfortunate.'

They scrambled back down the slope, until the ridge was high enough for them to stand without being seen from the valley. Amalia brushed her good hand down the front of her robes, sending dust everywhere.

'What do I do?' said Silva.

'Stay close to Amalia,' Van said, 'and keep a look out for Belinda. If she's in range, then we get her too; otherwise, she's the target for our second attempt.'

'Perhaps we should get the Queen first.'

'No,' said Amalia. 'Van's right; Kelsey first.'

'Why?'

'Because the Ascendants are less likely to kill Belinda,' Van said, feeling as though he were making up an excuse. He didn't want to admit it in front of the two women, but Kelsey was his sole target; everything else was secondary. He closed his eyes for a moment, telling himself not to allow his feelings to get in the way. He was a professional.

Silva looked unconvinced, but said nothing.

Amalia clutched the Quadrant, her fingers poised over it. 'Stand close. Three, two, one.'

The air shimmered, then they appeared in the midst of a squad of Banner soldiers. Van reacted at once, barging past a sergeant and knocking him over, as angry cries erupted around them. He saw Kelsey, hooded, and being held by two soldiers. He barrelled his way towards her, then dived, pulling her to the ground and out of the grasp of the soldiers.

'Now, Amalia!'

His location shifted again, and he appeared in the air two feet off the ground in a vast cavern lit by a red glow. They dropped, and Van landed next to Kelsey on the hard ground. She grunted and struggled, and he pulled the hood from over her head. She stared at him, her eyes wide.

He smiled. 'Fancy meeting you here.'

They turned, and saw a bristling wall of spears and bows pointed at them. Amalia and Silva were standing a few paces to their left, also surrounded by green-skinned Fordian warriors. Van lifted his palms to show he was unarmed, then crouched by Kelsey and untied the cords binding her wrists.

There was a noise behind him, and he glanced over his shoulder to see the head of an enormous black dragon a yard away, her eyes glowing red.

'Captain Van Logos,' the dragon said. 'This is a surprise.'

'Van!' yelled a young woman. She ran through the crowd of Fordians, and threw her arms around him.

'Do I know you?' he said.

'I'm Maddie; you helped me escape from prison. Well, Sable was controlling you at the time, but, you know, you did your bit. Oh, I've got your silver cigarette case; well, I don't actually have it on me; I left it back at the Catacombs; we're staying in a tomb.'

Next to him, Kelsey got to her feet and pulled the gag from her face. She glanced at Van and Maddie for a moment, then looked away, staring at a large pool of bubbling lava a few yards away.

'Where are we?' she said.

'Fordamere,' said Maddie. 'Who are you?'

A tall figure in armour strode through the crowd of Fordians, his helmet under his arm.

'Corthie,' said Van. 'I have your sister.'

'Why did you bring her here?' said Corthie. 'We're in the middle of a battle. Word has reached us that thousands of Banner soldiers have entered the city; it's not safe.'

'Good morning, brother,' said Kelsey. 'Van has just rescued me from the Ascendants. Three of them are outside; one of whom you know pretty well.'

'The Ascendants are here?'

Aila appeared with Naxor and Vana at the edge of the crowd. None of them were looking at Van or Kelsey; instead, the three demigods were staring open-mouthed at Amalia.

'What in Malik's name is she doing here?' cried Aila.

Corthie turned, and his eyes narrowed at the sight of the former God-Queen. He pulled the Clawhammer from his back and strode towards her.

'No,' said Van, shoving his way past the Fordian warriors to stand in front of Amalia with his hands raised. 'She brought us here; she helped save Kelsey.'

'We can't trust her,' said Corthie.

'I didn't say trust her,' said Van, 'but she doesn't deserve to die; she risked her life to get Kelsey away.'

'I can speak for myself,' said Amalia, gently pushing Van to the side, 'though you might not like what I have to say. The Ascendants Arete and Leksandr are approaching, and Belinda is with them. They are here for the Sextant, and for you, Corthie Holdfast.'

'Let them come,' he said.

'Where is the Sextant?' said Kelsey.

Corthie pointed to the sole building in the middle of the cavern, close to the pool of lava.

'It's still on the roof,' he said.

'It has defeated my strength,' said the black dragon. 'I cannot move it, and none of us know how to operate it.'

'The Sextant can only be moved if it is activated first,' said Silva.

Corthie frowned, his frustration evident on his face. 'And how exactly do we do that?'

'I don't know,' said the demigod, 'but her Majesty Queen Belinda knows, or knew, and she's outside this cavern with the other Ascendants. We need to rescue her, the same way we rescued Kelsey.'

'Belinda won't remember how to activate it,' said Kelsey.

'We still need to rescue her.'

'Wait a minute,' said Aila. 'Why is the God-Queen here? What's her part in this? Has everyone forgotten what she's done?'

'We don't have time to explain,' said Van; 'we need to act. The Ascendants are slaughtering everyone in Yoneath, and they're on their way here, to this cavern. Amalia has a Quadrant; I suggest we use it.'

'To do what?' said Corthie.

'We should flee, now,' said Blackrose. 'We cannot face two Ascendants, Corthie, and if we cannot move the Sextant, then there is nothing else to be done here.'

'No,' cried Silva. 'We came to get Queen Belinda; we can't leave her.'

'You can all go,' said Corthie, 'but I'm staying. I'm not afraid of the Ascendants.'

'Don't be a fool, Corthie,' said the dragon; 'we should use the Quadrant to retreat.'

'What about Frostback?' said Maddie. 'She's still out there, fighting.' She turned to Van. 'Did you see her?'

'Do you mean the silver dragon?' he said.

'Yes.'

'She was doing a fine job of holding back the Banner soldiers from the cavern entrance, but they've brought dozens of ballistae, and Kelsey might be far enough away from the Ascendants to allow them to use their death powers on her.'

'We're wasting precious time,' said Silva, her voice tinged with fear. 'We must get Queen Belinda. She saved the people of Shawe Myre; we cannot leave her behind.'

'I agree,' said Kelsey. 'If we leave her, she'll think we abandoned her.'

'Alright,' said Corthie; 'it's worth a try. Amalia, are you prepared to help us again?'

The former God-Queen frowned. 'Very well. I'll need Van; he seems quite efficient for a mortal. And then, we'll leave Yoneath as soon as we return, yes?'

Corthie nodded, then glanced at Van.

The mercenary hesitated for a moment, his eyes on Kelsey, then took a breath. 'I'm ready.'

'Do we have time for this?' said Vana. 'No offence, but Belinda appears to have made her choice; if she wanted to help us, she'd be here, not out there standing shoulder to shoulder with the Ascendants. I say we cut her loose.'

'How dare you?' said Silva, turning to confront the demigod.

'Don't touch me,' said Vana.

'Stop,' yelled Maddie. 'What about Frostback? She's the reason we're still in here talking; she's out there, doing her best to stop all those soldiers from getting in. We need to help her.'

Naxor, who had been standing in silence by the edge of the crowd, walked forward as if he was going to say something, then he lunged at Amalia, his fingers grasping at the Quadrant clutched in her hand. They fell to the ground, Aila and Maddie tumbling down with them. Van, Kelsey and Corthie piled into the chaos, each trying to grab Naxor's shoulders to haul him away, but he was entangled with the former God-Queen.

'Get him off me,' cried Amalia, as Naxor's fingers stretched towards the Quadrant.

Corthie took hold of Naxor's arms and hauled him back.

'Is this what I get for trying to help?' cried Amalia from the ground. 'You fools are doomed; the Ascendants are coming to kill us, and all you can do is squabble like children?' She glanced down at the Quadrant in her hand.

'Stop her!' cried Aila, her arms reaching for her grandmother.

There was a shimmer in the air as Aila collided with her, then she, Kelsey and Amalia vanished.

CHAPTER 28
RESCUE

Yoneath, Eastern Khatanax – 13th Lexinch 5252

The cavern fell into silence as everyone stared at the space on the ground where the former God-Queen had been.

'What do we do now?' said Maddie.

'This was her plan all along!' cried Silva. 'Amalia only helped us because she wanted Kelsey; she had no intention of rescuing Queen Belinda.'

'Once again,' said Blackrose, 'I am let down by the bickering and betrayal of humans. Mortal or immortal, it makes no difference; all cheat and lie for their selfish aims.'

'Not all of us,' said Corthie, his arms still grasping Naxor. 'We'll deal with Amalia, and get Aila and my sister back, but first we have to face the Ascendants. We cannot let them take the Sextant.' He threw Naxor to the ground, and placed a boot onto his back.

'I was trying to save us,' the demigod yelled. 'The Ascendants would have captured Amalia and Van, and taken the Quadrant.'

'He's right,' said Vana, pulling at Corthie's arm. 'The plan was insane. How are we going to get out of here now?'

'There are other ways out, cousin,' said Naxor from the ground; 'tunnels that lead to the other side of the valley.' He glanced at the dragon

'None that will fit Blackrose, unfortunately, but we can't have everything.'

Corthie glanced into the crowd. 'Sohul?'

The lieutenant ran forward, then stopped as he saw Van. The two men smiled and shook hands.

'Take the demigods out of here,' Corthie said, lifting his boot from Naxor's back. 'Escort them to safety, and then you are released from our agreement. Van, you too.'

Van frowned. 'But, Corthie...'

'Do it,' he said. 'This is my final order to you – take Naxor, Vana and Silva and run. There's nothing you can do here.'

'This isn't over,' said Van. 'I made a promise to Kelsey.'

'Then keep it,' Corthie said. 'Find her.'

Van frowned, then nodded.

Corthie raised his arms and turned to the mass of Fordians clustered round the temple. 'Evacuate!' he cried. 'Save yourselves. The dragon and I will face the Ascendants.'

Sohul began urging them on and, slowly at first, the Fordians started to make their way to the low tunnels at the rear of the cavern. Naxor got to his feet, assisted by Vana, but Silva remained defiant, her arms folded across her chest.

'I'm not leaving,' she said. 'You can issue commands all you like, but my place is with the Queen.'

Corthie nodded his agreement, and the others departed, crossing the stone bridge over the flow of lava without looking back. Within moments, the interior of the cavern stilled, as only Corthie, Silva, Blackrose and Maddie remained among the scattered bodies of Fordians and Banner soldiers.

'You are mistaken,' said the dragon. 'I will not face two Ascendants.'

'We have to,' said Corthie. 'What other choice is there?'

'You should flee with the others, and I should go to Frostback's assistance and guide her from Yoneath.'

'No,' said Corthie. 'We can't allow the Ascendants to take the Sextant. You will always have my gratitude for helping us today, but it will mean nothing if the Sextant is taken. I've lost Aila, and my sister...' He stopped, his voice breaking, and took a breath. 'All of it will have been for nothing if we lose the Sextant as well.'

'Then stand back,' said the dragon; 'move away from the temple.'

Maddie, Corthie and Silva stepped back as Blackrose turned towards the ancient structure. Outside the cavern, the sounds of violence were getting louder as the dragon opened her jaws. Sparks ignited, leaping across the rows of fearsome teeth, then she emitted a great blast of fire. The centuries-old temple burst into flames as the fire enveloped it. Smoke belched from the doors and windows, then the roof collapsed as the structure was consumed in the inferno. The Sextant fell into the centre of the conflagration and disappeared from sight amid the raging fire.

Blackrose closed her jaws and watched the flames burn through the temple for a moment, the light reflecting from her black scales.

She turned to Corthie. 'If we can't have it, then no one shall. Now, run, my young friend, you have done more than anyone could possibly expect; do not throw your life away in a vain show of resistance.'

Corthie stared into the flames, then nodded. 'Farewell, Blackrose. Good luck.'

'Rider,' said the dragon, 'let us be gone from this place of death.'

Maddie pulled her gaze from the burning temple and ran to the dragon's flank. So much had happened in such a short space of time that her thoughts were a confused jumble. She had been happy to see Van, then terrified at the appearance of the hated God-Queen, then angry at the fact that no one else seemed to care about poor Frostback, fighting all alone against thousands of soldiers. Then Amalia had taken Kelsey, who seemed to be another Holdfast; and Aila, just because she had been the closest to the God-Queen at the moment she had triggered the Quadrant. It could have been her, Maddie realised, as she climbed up onto Blackrose's shoulder. If Aila and her positions had been reversed, then she would have been whisked away by the evil God-Queen.

'Are you ready?' said Blackrose.

'I don't know,' she said; 'my mind is spinning. Did all that really happen?'

'We can talk about it later, once we return to the Catacombs. For now, just hold on tightly.'

The dragon beat her great wings and took off. She soared through the cavern, avoiding the smoke and flames rising from the shattered temple, and aimed for the high entrance tunnel. Beneath them lay the bodies of hundreds of Banner soldiers, hacked to pieces, or burnt by the dragon when she had first entered. At the far end of the tunnel, over a hundred disarmed soldiers of the Black Crown were struggling to get out, having escaped in the confusion after the earlier battle, and they were blocking those from other Banners who were trying to get in. Beyond, smoke was drifting upwards over the city, along with the screams of the trapped civilians.

Blackrose raked fire across those at the entrance to the tunnel, and burst out into the open air. A ballista bolt whistled past her left flank, and she banked in a tight circle and ascended, Maddie barely clinging onto her shoulders. Above, out of range of the ballista wagons, Frostback was circling, and Blackrose surged up to join her.

'Is it over?' the silver-grey dragon said. 'I'm exhausted; I cannot do any more.'

Maddie noticed several fresh wounds on her flanks, and a rip in her left wing.

'I couldn't be prouder of you, Frostback,' Blackrose said, 'even though you disobeyed my command. I told you to flee if the Ascendants arrived, and yet you continued to fight.'

'I stayed for you; I could not leave.'

'If you had been slain, I would never have forgiven myself.'

Maddie glanced down. Ballista bolts were still being loosed at them, but the dragons were too high for them to reach. On either side of the long row of wagons, the streets of Yoneath were covered in bodies, and soldiers were still moving through neighbourhoods, killing from house to house. Among the dead Fordians were piles of smouldering Banner soldiers, their armour glinting among the ashes.

Maddie felt a jarring intrusion into her mind.

Why are you still here? You must flee, Maddie. The Ascendants have seen you.

Who are you?

It's Belinda. Please, Maddie, do not think that you are safe because of your altitude. If I can reach you with vision, then Arete and Leksandr can reach you with death powers.

'Blackrose,' Maddie yelled; 'we have to go. The Ascendants, they've seen us.'

'We are too high for them to reach us.'

'We're not; Belinda just warned me; we...'

Blackrose cried out as a wave of power rose from the city below them. She clenched her jaws closed, then moved to shield Frostback, placing herself between the silver dragon and the ground.

'Frostback, go!'

The silver dragon's wings shuddered, and she dropped, hitting Blackrose beneath her. Their wings entangled for a moment, then the black dragon powered forward, freeing herself and pushing Frostback away in the direction of the cliffside. Maddie clung on, feeling nothing from the death powers below, the black dragon's body protecting her from the attack of the Ascendants. Frostback surged ahead in a desperate burst of speed, passing over the side of the high cliff, and out of range of the assault into safety. She tried to circle back to help Blackrose, but it was clear to Maddie that the silver dragon was badly hurt, and she descended erratically, disappearing from sight over a ridge.

Blackrose beat her wings, but her great strength was fading, and she started to lose altitude.

'You can do it!' cried Maddie.

The black dragon arched her neck and let out a cry of agony and despair. Her wings faltered, and she started to drop from the sky. Below was a scrubby hillside to the north of the city, a few hundred yards from the edge of the settlement, and the ground rushed up towards them in a blur. Maddie closed her eyes as she tried to cling onto the dragon's scales, the wind rushing past her. Blackrose ploughed into the ground at an angle, her limbs collapsing under her weight as her momentum carried her along the dusty brown slope. Maddie was flung from her back; she twisted through the air and landed upside down in a thick, thorny bush, her clothes ripping. For a moment she lay still, too stunned and dazed to move, then she struggled against the branches of the bush, pulling her arms free from the thorns. She slid to the ground and rolled away. She glanced around. A cloud of dust was hanging in the air, and all she could see of Blackrose was the end of her long tail. It was twitching, but Maddie wasn't sure if that was a good sign. She pulled herself up. Blood was trickling from a dozen cuts from the thorns, and she felt winded, as if her breath had been sucked out of her. She stumbled along, following the line of Blackrose's tail as it thickened. Ahead, her body was lying across the hillside. Her rear forelimbs were jerking, their claws digging and scraping into the soft brown earth.

'Blackrose; Mela,' Maddie gasped. She fell to one knee, then got up again. 'Blackrose.'

The dragon's neck moved, and her head turned towards Maddie. Blood was coming from her jaws, and the light in her eyes was dim.

'You need to run, rider,' she said, her voice rasping and full of pain.

Maddie staggered up to her. 'No; you know I won't leave you.'

'Soldiers will be coming soon to take my head as a trophy. The Ascendants have finished me; I cannot fly, I cannot even walk.'

'If you die, then I die with you; that's the deal I made.'

'Did Frostback get away safely?'

'I'm not sure. I saw her fly past the ridge, but then she dropped.'

'She is young; her hide is barely thick enough to withstand even a small amount of death powers. We were lucky...'

'Lucky?'

'If we had been lower, all three of us would be dead. This way, two might survive. You must find Frostback; tell her that my last command is that she bear you back to the Catacombs.'

'We can't go to the Catacombs without you.'

'But you can't stay here, Maddie.'

'Blackrose, tell me honestly,' she said, as tears rolled down her cheeks; 'Are you dying; have they killed you?'

'Not yet. If left in peace, I would recover, but I cannot defend myself, or you, which is why you must go before the soldiers get here.'

Maddie sat, her limbs aching. 'No. They might not come. They might be too busy to come. Even if they did come, we're on the other side of a hill from Yoneath; they might not find us. I'm not leaving you if there's even the smallest chance; do you understand?'

The dragon laid her head down on the ground. 'Your words grieve me, girl.'

'Well, I'm sorry about that, but it's not going to change my mind. I'm glad you burned the Sextant; that might be only good thing to come out of this.'

'At least it wasn't the Holdfasts who betrayed me this time,' said Blackrose, 'and I'm glad I had the opportunity to be reconciled with Corthie.'

Maddie shifted position and leaned against the dragon's head, her hand stroking the scales beneath her closed right eye. The sun was halfway up the eastern sky, and the temperature was rising. Maddie hated the sun of Lostwell; it was too bright and hot, and had no right to climb the sky so high each day; in fact, she hated everything about Lostwell.

'This is an awful place to die,' she said.

'Don't say that, rider. When the soldiers come, surrender to them at once. Van has taught me that not all Banner soldiers are evil; they may find enough pity in their hearts to let you live.'

Maddie said nothing, her spirits crushed. They sat in silence for a few minutes, Maddie's mind numb. All she could think of was how she had lied to the dragon, and conspired with Sable to keep her Quadrant a secret. What had happened was Maddie's fault; how had she let the Holdfast woman persuade her?

She heard footsteps, then a voice shouted, 'Over here!'

She glanced up, and saw three soldiers at the top of the hillside.

'Blackrose,' she said, but the dragon didn't respond. Maddie pushed her head. 'Blackrose.'

Nothing.

She turned to her right, and saw the rise and fall of the dragon's breath. More soldiers appeared, coming round the base of the hill and climbing up the slope towards them. Maddie waited until the dragon was surrounded, then got to her feet.

The soldiers were grinning and pointing at the body of the unconscious dragon. One drew his sword and strode towards her neck.

'I'm going to take her head,' he cried, 'and then mount it on the wall of the barracks back home.'

'Hold up there, Private,' muttered a sergeant, his crossbow aimed at the dragon. 'Let's wait until the officer gets here.'

'Hey,' said one; 'there's a woman by the dragon's head.'

'A Fordian?'

'No, Sergeant.'

The soldier who had seen Maddie approached her, his crossbow level with her chest. 'Who are you?'

She raised her hands. 'I'm Maddie Jackdaw.' She remembered how the Banner soldiers outside Alea Tanton had treated her a little better when they had discovered she had been in the army. 'I'm a sergeant in the Auxiliary Work Company and, before that, I was a corporal in the Fourteenth Support Battalion, Auxiliary Detachment Number Three, based at Arrowhead fortress.'

The soldier frowned at her. 'Which Banner?'

'The Banner of the... Black Dragon. Isn't it obvious?'

'You just made that up.'

The sergeant and a few other soldiers approached.

'What will we do with her, Sergeant?' said the one who had found her. 'She says she's military.'

'Our orders were to eliminate the Fordian population of Yoneath,' the sergeant said. 'She's not Fordian, so she couldn't have been living here. We'll take her into custody and let the officers decide what to do with her.' He glanced at Maddie. 'How did you come to be here, miss?'

Maddie thought for a moment, wondering if she could get away
with saying that she had been wandering through the hills, and had
happened upon the fallen dragon by accident; but it would a worse
betrayal than not telling her about the Quadrant. Her bond with Blackrose was the most important thing in her life.

'I am a dragon rider,' she said, 'and this is my dragon.'

The soldiers' eyes widened.

'What about that stuff you told me about being a sergeant?' said the
one who had found her.

'All true.'

The sergeant shook his head. 'No dragons on Lostwell have riders.'

'Did I say we were from Lostwell? No, I don't recall that I did.'

'Where's the silver dragon?' said the sergeant. 'We didn't see this
black dragon attack us; it was a smaller, silver one.'

'She flew away west, I think.'

A line of wagons appeared round the base of the hill, piled with nets
and chains. Around fifty soldiers dismounted and began walking up the
slope, while others remained behind to unload the wagons.

'Here comes the major,' said the sergeant.

The officer approached, flanked by soldiers. 'Just the one?' he said. 'I
saw two dragons in the sky.'

'The girl here says that the other one flew off west, sir,' said the
sergeant.

The officer regarded Maddie. 'And she is?'

'She says she's the black dragon's rider, sir.'

The officer frowned and turned to examine Blackrose. 'There's no
harness; she's lying.'

'That's what we thought, sir.'

'We'll take her to the Ascendants; they might want to read her mind.'

'Yes, sir. And the dragon, sir?'

'We'll net her up and chain her.'

'Some of the lads were hoping they could take her head for the
barracks, sir.'

388

The officer smiled. 'While I applaud the sentiment, the Banner is in line to fetch an excellent price for the beast. The pits of Alea Tanton are offering very high amounts for a captured, live dragon; enough to provide every soldier in the Banner with a bonus.'

'Excellent news, sir, but how will we move her?'

'We'll have to wait until one of the Ascendants is free to use a Quadrant, and then transport her directly to Alea Tanton, preferably straight into one of the arenas.'

Maddie's heart sank as she listened. Of all the fates that Blackrose would wish to avoid, returning to the pits of Alea Tanton would be among the worst. It was better than death, but not by much.

'Have the prisoner escorted back to the city,' said the officer, 'and we'll see about getting the nets and chains onto the beast.'

'Yes, sir.' The sergeant gestured to a pair of soldiers, and they walked up to Maddie.

'Turn around,' said one.

She did so, and her arms were pulled behind her back, and her wrists bound. They led her down the slope, one gripping her arm, the other following a pace behind with his crossbow aimed at her back. Maddie turned at the base of the hill to glance up at Blackrose, then the soldiers shoved her along a track towards the settlement. Smoke was still rising from Yoneath, discolouring the deep blue sky with a light grey pallor. As they walked, the soldiers chatted about what they were going to spend their dragon bonuses on, and Maddie remained silent. They reached the edge of the city, and the soldiers quietened as they entered the blood-soaked streets. The slaughter was still going on, but clusters of Banner soldiers were by the side of the road, taking a few moments to rest from the carnage. Their armour was streaked in blood, and many were staring into space with faraway looks in their eyes, their features drawn. The bodies of Fordian civilians lay everywhere, men, women, old folk, children, most killed with a single blow, or with two crossbow bolts in their chests.

'You did this,' said Maddie, her voice low.

One of the soldiers frowned. 'No one said war was a pleasant business.'

'This isn't war,' she said. 'Armies fight each other in wars; there's no enemy army here.'

'Orders,' he said; 'we're following orders.'

Her lips formed to issue a rebuke, but she stopped herself, knowing it was futile. They reached a square at the end of the street, where a standard was flying, depicting a winged heart. At the base of the standard a group of officers was standing, and more soldiers were gathered round them.

One of Maddie's escorts gestured to the other soldiers. 'We got the dragon, lads, and the major said there would a bonus for the entire Banner.'

The soldiers' expressions lifted, and a few cheered. Maddie was led up the group of officers.

'We have a prisoner, sir. The major said we were to escort her back here. He said that the Ascendants might want to read her mind.'

'Why?' said an officer. 'Is she important?'

'Don't know, sir.'

'Well, we're a little busy right now, Private, and we have nowhere to keep prisoners, as I was under the impression that we weren't taking any.' He frowned. 'Stick her in a house, and guard her until the major gets back.'

The two escorts saluted. 'Yes, sir.'

'Captain's in a foul mood,' muttered one of the soldiers as they led Maddie to a house on the other side of the square.

'At least we're out of the slaughtering,' said the other; 'there's only so much of that I can take.'

They entered a house, and the soldiers checked the rooms on the ground floor, settling for the only one with no bodies in it. They pushed Maddie against a wall, and made her sit on the floor, while they took seats, and watched her with their crossbows ready.

'We could be here a while, miss,' said one, as he lit a cigarette. 'It'l probably be hours before the Ascendants are ready to move the dragon.'

'Yeah,' said the other, 'they've got that armoured maniac in the cavern to deal with first.'

'You know, I'll be glad when...' His voiced tailed away as Sable appeared in the middle of the room, the Quadrant in one hand, a drawn sword in the other. She lunged forward, and with two clean strokes the soldiers were dead, their heads rolling on the wooden floor.

'Sable?' Maddie croaked.

'What? Did you think I wasn't watching you? I've been visioning since dawn.' She walked over to Maddie, pulled her to her feet, and cut the cords round her wrists. 'Did they hurt you?'

Maddie shook her head. 'You came here to rescue me?'

'Your lack of faith in me is a little upsetting,' Sable said. 'However, I forgive you.'

'Blackrose is in trouble; we need to help her.'

'I know what's happened to her; I watched the whole thing. That hillside is now covered with soldiers, and her limbs and wings have already been shackled. What I'm trying to say is that, if we go, there's a good chance we'll die.'

'But we still have to try, Sable.' Maddie's eyes tightened. 'You'd better not be thinking of leaving her.'

'Where is this mistrust coming from? Of course we're not going to leave her; I just wanted you to know the risks first. What kind of person do you think I am, Maddie?'

'Sorry. It's just that, earlier, the God-Queen... never mind.' She pointed down at the dead soldiers. 'Should I take one of their crossbows?'

'I don't think that's a good idea. Carrying one will make you a target, and it's not like you know how to use it.'

Maddie scowled at her.

'I'm going to scout the route before we go,' Sable said. 'Wait one moment.'

Her eyes glazed over for a second or two, then she frowned.

'What is it?' said Maddie.

'Belinda's on her way.'

'What, here?'

'No. She's on the road towards the hillside where Blackrose is accompanied by a few soldiers.'

'Maybe she's going to help?'

Sable laughed, but there was no warmth in it. 'No, Maddie. Belinda stood by and watched as hundreds, maybe thousands of innocent Fordians civilians were slaughtered. Children, Maddie. And now, Arete and Leksandr are heading towards the cavern to kill my nephew, and again, she's doing nothing to stop them.' She shook her head, and a tear rolled down her cheek. 'This is the hardest choice I've ever had to make – help Corthie, or help Blackrose; I can't do both, and it's Belinda's fault. I always suspected that she would return to her own kind, and today she's proved me right. Karalyn should have killed her, but I'll do what needs to be done.' She glanced at the Quadrant and placed her fingers over it. 'Stay close to me, but not so close that you'll get in my way.'

Maddie stared at her, then the room shimmered and they appeared on the dusty track. Ahead, four soldiers and Belinda were walking towards the hills where Blackrose was lying, their backs to them. Sable moved like lightning, charging forward without a sound, her sword out. Maddie stood back, her eyes wide as Sable tore through the soldiers, her blade flashing in the sunlight as she cut them down. They were armoured, but her sword found the gaps. Belinda turned, whipping her own sword out as the last soldier fell.

'You?' said the Third Ascendant.

'Yes,' said Sable, her sword extended. 'You've betrayed us for the last time.'

'Don't lecture me about betrayal,' Belinda said, her eyes never leaving Sable as they circled each other on the track.

Sable lunged forward, her sword swinging. Belinda parried; once, twice, then Sable spun and slashed Belinda across the waist, spraying blood across the dusty earth. Sable attacked again, battering her sword down as Belinda blocked and backed away. The Ascendant's wound was healing, and she was defending herself with the same speed as Sable was attacking, their swords a blur as Maddie watched. Sable aimed a blow at Belinda's neck, and the god ducked, and plunged her dark blade into Sable's stomach.

Sable looked down at the wound as blood spread across her clothes, then fell to her knees, her eyes wide in shock.

'I didn't want this,' said Belinda as she raised her sword. 'You gave me no choice, Sable.'

The Ascendant swung her sword, and Sable vanished just as the blade was racing towards her neck. Belinda stared at the empty space on the ground.

'Maddie,' she said, glancing up. 'You must believe me, I...'

She got no further. The air behind her shimmered and Sable reappeared. She rammed her sword through Belinda's back, the tip appearing through her leather breastplate, and the Ascendant collapsed to the ground. Sable let go of the hilt and staggered. She pulled the Quadrant from her bloody clothes. The copper-coloured surface was smeared with blood, and she wiped it, her fingers shaking.

The air shimmered again, and Maddie and Sable appeared within a dark cavern in the Catacombs. Sable fell to the ground and Maddie rushed to her side.

'Sable!' she cried, lifting the woman's head and cradling it in her arms.

'I'm sorry, Maddie,' she gasped, then her eyes closed.

Tears rolled down Maddie's cheeks, not just for Sable, but for Blackrose, and the Fordians, and Corthie, and even for Belinda.

Millen appeared next to them, his eyes distraught.

'What happened?' he cried.

Maddie tried to speak, but she couldn't stop the tears, and her voice seemed lost.

Millen lowered his head to Sable. 'Praise the gods; she's still breathing,' he said. His glance went to the wound by her waist, and he ripped off a strip of his tunic and pressed it against her. 'Help me, Maddie. Where are Blackrose and Frostback?'

Maddie stared at Sable, at the blood, and at Millen, then slumped onto the ground and let the tears overwhelm her.

CHAPTER 29

IN VAIN

Yoneath, Eastern Khatanax – 13th Lexinch 5252

Long rows of armoured Banner soldiers were lining up in front of the wide entrance to the vast cavern of Fordamere, their shields arranged in a solid, unbroken wall. Behind them, half a dozen large ballistae were pointing into the cavern from the backs of wagons, and several standards were flying, one depicting a winged heart, another a red flame.

Corthie sat by the banks of the pool of water, watching the soldiers organise themselves. He had pulled down and broken the wooden bridge that crossed the stream, but the Banner troops had given no sign that they were going to advance, and he guessed that their presence was to prevent him from leaving Fordamere that way.

'You can still escape,' said Silva, from behind him. 'The tunnels that Van and the others used are unguarded, and lead through the mountain to a valley on the other side.'

'Not yet,' he said.

'Do you wish to die?'

'Not particularly, but I'm not leaving until I know the Sextant has been destroyed.'

'We watched as it fell into the flames of the temple.'

'That means nothing. If a dragon the size of Blackrose couldn't budge it, then it could be protected somehow; I need to make sure.' He glanced at her. 'Why are you still here? Aren't you worried the Ascendants will kill you?'

'They may; it matters not to me, not any more. If Queen Belinda has truly joined forces with Arete and Leksandr, then I have no desire to live on. I have spent my entire life serving her Majesty, advising her, and supporting her through her times of need. If she has become like the other Ascendants, then my life has been a waste.'

Corthie frowned. 'Did she really kneel before them?'

'I have already told you what occurred at Shawe Myre; do you doubt my word?'

'No, it's just... hard to fathom. Belinda is like a sister to me; I loved her, I still do. I know what you think of me for killing Gregor, and for fighting against Agatha, but Belinda was a friend. I remember when she first awoke after Karalyn had emptied her mind. She couldn't speak; she didn't even know how to feed herself. I helped care for her, and watched as she started to relearn everything. My old tutor Laodoc used to give her lessons on history and politics, while I read stories to her from picture books about rescuing princesses from towers. I wish I could go back to those days.'

Silva put a hand on his shoulder. 'Let me tell you a secret. I hated Agatha. As soon as her Majesty appointed her to rule Khatanax in her stead, she grew obsessed with power, and treated the Queen as if she were unimportant; just someone else to order about. I used to plead with her Majesty to revoke Agatha's authority, but she was too upset about King Nathaniel to listen. I too wish I could return to the olden days, Corthie, but we can't.'

Corthie turned to the smoking ruins of the temple. The flames had died down amid the blackened stumps of rubble and debris.

He stood. 'It's time to go poking around the ashes.'

They walked across the cavern towards the temple, avoiding the dozens of bodies strewn across the ground. The remains of a huge wagon was sitting beside the ruined structure, its gaien lying dead in front of it, their harnesses still attached.

Corthie noticed movement from among the piled bodies, and gripped the Clawhammer. Between the gaien and the temple, a figure was crawling over the ground. Corthie and Silva hurried over.

'Lord Gellith?' Corthie said, taking his helmet off and placing it on the ground.

The Fordian leader groaned and lifted his head. 'You?'

'You survived.'

'I took an arrow to the throat,' he said, sitting up. 'I have only just managed to heal myself.' He glanced around, his features distraught. 'What happened here? What did you do to the temple?' He started to cry. 'You have brought about the very events that I was trying to avoid, you have defiled Fordamere, turned it into a charnel house.'

'Lord Gellith,' Silva said, as she and Corthie crouched by the Fordian leader, 'there is something else we must tell you. The Sixth and Seventh Ascendants are outside, in Yoneath, and their Banner forces are slaughtering the inhabitants, down to the last child.'

Gellith hung his head. 'My life's struggle has been in vain. All I ever wanted to do was protect the families that sheltered here; help them lead normal lives, away from the chaos and violence that plague Khatanax.'

'The Third Ascendant is also outside,' said Silva.

'What?' said Gellith. 'Has the Queen come to Yoneath? Is she opposing the Sixth and Seventh?'

Silva bowed her head. 'No. She submitted to them in Shawe Myre.'

'She may still return to our side,' said Corthie; 'I have faith in her.'

'Our faith in the Third Ascendant is what has brought us to this pass,' said Gellith, 'as the city was doomed the day I bowed to her Majesty's desire to hide the Sextant here. At least it has gone; perhaps Arete and Leksandr will depart and leave the survivors in peace.'

'It hasn't gone,' said Corthie. 'It fell into the temple when the roof collapsed. We're hoping it's been destroyed.'